'Visceral
and acute'
Emily Edwards

'Totally savage
and wickedly
funny'
Heather Darwent

'A hilarious, dark,
raw and honest
exposé of early
motherhood
and friendship'
Jo Callaghan

'Does beautiful justice
to life on all sides of
the baby divide, and
treats every character
with such tenderness –
but there's a blazing
political fire at its heart'
Lauren Bravo

'The best book I've
ever read. Raw, relatable,
riveting. Holly Bourne
is the best contemporary
novelist out there, bar none'
Laura Jane Williams

'Wonderful,
wonderful, wonderful'
Caroline Corcoran

CW00402834

Early praise for *So Thrilled For You*

'I raced through *So Thrilled For You*. I think
it's brilliant: so funny, so sad, so scary. (And oh, dear
God, it brought back so many memories!)'
Jacqueline Wilson

'I loved it. Part whodunnit, part dark take-down of
motherhood, and the vast love and limits it imposes on
women. It will be huge'
Gillian McAllister

'This dark and intoxicating portrayal of female
friendship cleverly captures how the choices we make
as women threaten to divide us. Compelling, thought-
provoking and unputdownable – I absolutely loved it'
Sarah Turner (@TheUnmumsyMum)

'Bourne's propulsive plot pulls her readers through an
emotionally charged day whilst exploring the tenderest,
most shameful and funny aspects of the divisive
experiences of motherhood, almost motherhood and
being child-free by choice, culminating in an explosive,
but ultimately universally empowering, denouement'
Kate Sawyer

'Reading *So Thrilled For You* I found myself pulled
into an all too familiar landscape where the pressures
on women – mothers and non-mothers like – were so
visceral and acute I had to close the book to gasp at
times. A hearty congratulations and a high five to Holly!'
Emily Edwards

'I enjoyed it so, SO MUCH. I was utterly GRIPPED. So
many unexpected but wholly believable twists and turns. I
think it will resonate for all women. Yet it's so much fun'
Marian Keyes

So Thrilled For You

Holly Bourne is a bestselling author. Alongside her writing, Holly is passionate about gender equality and is an advocate for reducing the stigma of mental health problems. She is also an ambassador for Women's Aid, working with the charity to spread awareness of abusive relationships.

Also by Holly Bourne

How Do You Like Me Now?
Pretending
Girl Friends

So Thrilled For You

HOLLY BOURNE

HODDER &
STOUGHTON

First published in Great Britain in 2025 by Hodder & Stoughton Limited
An Hachette UK company

1

Copyright © Holly Bourne 2025

The right of Holly Bourne to be identified as the Author of the Work has been
asserted by her in accordance with the Copyright, Designs and Patents Act 1988.

All rights reserved. No part of this publication may be reproduced,
stored in a retrieval system, or transmitted, in any form or by any means
without the prior written permission of the publisher, nor be otherwise
circulated in any form of binding or cover other than that in which it is published
and without a similar condition being imposed on the subsequent purchaser.

All characters in this publication are fictitious and any resemblance to real persons,
living or dead, is purely coincidental.

A CIP catalogue record for this title is available from the British Library

Hardback ISBN 978 1 529 30163 2
Trade Paperback ISBN 978 1 529 30165 6
ebook ISBN 978 1 529 30164 9

Typeset in Plantin Light by Manipal Technologies Limited

Printed and bound in Great Britain by Clays Ltd, Elcograf S.p.A.

Hodder & Stoughton policy is to use papers that are natural, renewable
and recyclable products and made from wood grown in sustainable forests.
The logging and manufacturing processes are expected to conform to
the environmental regulations of the country of origin.

Hodder & Stoughton Limited
Carmelite House
50 Victoria Embankment
London EC4Y 0DZ

The authorised representative in the EEA is Hachette Ireland, 8 Castlecourt Centre,
Castleknock Road, Castleknock, Dublin 15, D15 YF6A, Ireland

www.hodder.co.uk

To Becky and Rachel – we DID go to the spa!

Prologue

The flames take the vulva piñata immediately. The crepe paper ripples in the magenta smoke, the sweets inside popping like corn kernels as they explode inside their wiry cage. The piñata falls onto the decking, and there's a moment of stillness in me. The first time I've felt calm in so long, as I take in the view, thinking, *Wow, I've never seen pink smoke before.*

Soon the flames will claim the pile of duck-patterned wrapping paper, gorge on the coarse wool of the hand-knitted blankets and turn the fallen wall of peonies into a sweet, toxic, perfume.

I can tell already that everything is lost.

My life has already burned down metaphorically, so it makes sense I've now burned it down literally too. All I wanted to do was torch it all until there was nothing left but sooty soil, rich with nutrients to grow something new. But I never thought I'd actually do it . . .

I watch the smoke plume out of the canon, dancing as it eclipses the vista and spirals around in the heat, juxtaposed against the bluest sky. The fire around it ignites instantly, the smoke doubling, trebling, as flames catch and dance in the kindling.

The heat slaps my face and wakes me up.

I hear myself screaming at what I've done.

And I run towards the heat.

BABY SHOWER STUNT IGNITES WILDFIRE INFERNO

A wildfire started by a gender reveal firework has torn through 35 acres of land in Surrey, destroying local wildlife, and causing millions of pounds worth of damage.

The 'smoke-generating pyrotechnic device' was set off during a baby shower celebration during the hottest summer on record and quickly started the inferno. The blaze burned down the rural residence then raged across the parched countryside, incinerating a further two properties. Firefighters battled the flames for seven hours before it was extinguished.

The police have taken in key witnesses for questioning to determine who is responsible for setting off the smoke grenade. [*click to read more*]

Story has been shared 45,872 times

GodAsMyWitness1974 has shared this story
The 'smoke-generating pyrotechnic device' reveals the parents to be narcissistic, idiotic, cunts

BoomerAndProud3543024 has shared this story
Millennial parents: 'My baby can only wear organic bamboo and second-hand clothes because of climate change'
Also millennial parents: 'BURN DOWN THE WORLD FOR CONTENT'

ArthurJJdd has shared this story
This is why some people shouldn't be allowed to breed. Castrate everyone who has ever posted a pic of AvoOnToast

FinnJK32d5rd has shared this story
I know this isn't the point, but, aren't gender reveal parties and baby showers supposed to be separate events? Why did they combine the two?

GodAsMyWitness1974 replied to this comment:
LOL. They could've got DOUBLE the content for socials. Amateurs.

AVoiceOfReason has shared this story
Everyone is ripping the piss about this, but can I point out three families have lost their homes and everything in them? Not also forgetting the huge destruction of local wildlife.

DontKnwAbtUImFeeling22 replied to this comment:
BORING!

IHateWomenAndSoDoYou has shared this story
WOMEN SHOULDN'T BE ALLOWED TO HAVE BABIES

TheRightSideOfHistory replied to this comment:
How are we supposed to address the dwindling birth rate then?

FemSocForLife replied to this comment:
I bet you're anti-abortion too.

IHateWomenAndSoDoYou replied:
SHUT UP AND DIE YOU FUCKING FEMINIST WHORES

DAY OF THE FIRE

Transcript: Inspector Simmons interviewing Nicole Davies

Simmons:	Can you talk us through your movements on the day of July 14th please?
Nicole:	[shuffles] Before we start, can I go to the bathroom, please?
Simmons:	You just went.
Nicole:	I'm aware of that. But I'm also eight months pregnant. Is it true what they say? That I can pee in your helmet if I need to?
Simmons:	There's no need to pee in my helmet. We'll get someone to escort you to the bathroom.

NICKI

I can't believe today is my baby shower. *My* baby shower. It's surreal but it's finally happening.

I'm going to be a mother. I'm going to have a baby.

Honestly, I feel like the last decade of my life has been low-key obsessed with the question of *am I going to have a baby? Can I have a baby? When should I try to have a baby?* One of the best things about having a baby seems to be finally knowing, *yeah, you did,* and being able to let go of all that questioning shit. Letting go of all the anxious energy is way more relaxing than this lukewarm bath at dawn, but my baby will poach in here if I don't cool down.

I stayed at my parents' house last night, and I was looking forward to the peace of the countryside and having a double bed all to myself. But the birds' morning chorus here is louder than our dub-step loving neighbours. I've been up for an hour already, since 4am, alongside the ferocious sun. I yawn as I attempt to lower myself further into the water in a fruitless attempt to cool down. Comedic squeaks join the birdsong as my puffy flesh chafes against the bath. My bump icebergs out of the thin layer of unscented soap, and I pour water over it – finding relief for three whole minutes, which is good going for eight months pregnant. I close my eyes, cradle my stomach, and practise my hypno-birthing breathing. I feel my baby rustle under my stretched skin. I watched a TikTok video that says our fingerprints are created in the womb by the mother's amniotic fluid moving around our hands. Every twist and turn of a pregnancy is etched onto a baby's skin – a nine month house-share between mother and child turned into a glorious art on your baby's palms. I cried watching it, and though I'm sure it's not scientific fact, I need some magical thinking to get me through my third trimester in a hellish heatwave. And today I need to get through my baby shower, in a hellish heatwave, in my parents' house made entirely of glass. A baby shower I didn't even particularly *want,* or ask for, but has nevertheless been bestowed on me by Charlotte.

'It's going to be a perfect day,' she keeps telling me over the phone, over messages, over carrier pigeon if she gets the chance. '*Perfect.*'

'Honestly, I don't need any gifts, yeah?' I've tried pleading with her. 'Will you tell everyone that? This isn't a *baby shower,* just an opportunity to see everyone.'

'You should still have a registry. People are going to buy you gifts, no matter what you say.'

'No registry, Charlotte.'

'I've set up a John Lewis one with a few standard pieces.'

'Charlotte!'

'It's going to be perfect. Perfect.'

'You really don't need to do this. I know things have been hard for you . . .'

'PERFECT.'

I'm not sure I know what a perfect baby shower entails. A really short one? That's what I thought before I got pregnant myself. I used to begrudge baby showers lasting longer than two hours, but now that today's is *mine,* I'm worried people will flake or won't stay til the end.

I bet Steffi stays for ten minutes, max, if that.

It doesn't help that Charlotte insisted my parents' new home is the 'perfect' location despite being in the middle of nowhere. They've retired to this converted luxury barn, miles from a train station. Their countryside vista views are less impressive than normal since this heatwave turned every surrounding field into a post-apocalyptic wasteland. I'm worried people won't be bothered to make the journey. Regardless, Charlotte's coming over at the crack of dawn to 'set up'.

'8am isn't too early is it?' she asked.

'It starts at eleven. What are you setting up, Charlotte? A petting zoo? This baby shower, it's low-key, right?'

Charlotte lives her whole life in Soprano but I don't want anyone to think I'm going to become one of *those* mothers. You know. The ones who refer to themselves as 'mama'. I've warned Matt the following words are banned from our baby journey – 'mama', 'baby bubble', 'newborn bliss', and writing Instagram posts TO the baby, even though they're pre-verbal and can't legally get a social media account to read it until they're twelve. Yet, Charlotte, bless her, is determined to turn my baby shower into my worst nightmare. 'Don't you worry, mama,' she'd said. 'It's all in hand. Relax.'

My phone buzzes from where I left it on the bathmat but I ignore it. It can't be anyone but Charlotte this early. I'm so tired after a sweaty night in this Grand Designs clusterfuck. It was already 25 degrees when I woke up this morning. I'm so huge and uncomfortable and permanently thirsty, and it's been too goddamn hot for too goddamn long. I can only sleep in two- to four-hour bursts, waking to down pints of cold milk, run my wrists under the cold taps, and, of course, pee. It's on my banned phrase list, but I'm now desperate to 'meet my baby' just so I can cease being a pregnant narwhale.

My baby. I still can't believe it. I got here. Matt and I got here.

The baby wakes up and my stomach twists. I meet their movements with my hand.

'Good morning,' I coo. 'Are you up too? Yes, I know, it's much too hot.'

Sweat droplets glisten on my bump and slide down to merge with the bathwater. The back side of this barn conversion is solid glass, and everyone's going to spend today sodden with sweat. But I push that worry from my mind and focus on connecting with this baby. *My* baby. On the day of *my* baby shower. It's happening. Somehow, Matt and I overcame everything and did it – committed to each other in this huge way. Created life. Entwined our genes and blood and hereditary diseases and squashed them together into a living, breathing, human that we're going to 'meet' in a month. It's crazy. It's beautiful. Thank God we made it through the dark times. Thank God we could have a baby, especially with everything Charlotte's going through. I'm lucky. So lucky.

I sing gently to my bump and feel nothing but profound bliss – mixed with a pelvic girdle pain – until the heat of my body warms the water and makes it too uncomfortable.

I struggle out of the roll-top bath, swearing, and unable to comprehend my ginormous alien bodysuit. I wrap myself in a towel and pad back to the guest bedroom, hearing my dad's snores muffled through my parents' bedroom door. I let the air dry my skin, humming to myself, feeling my stomach still as the baby sleeps again, wondering if I can squeeze a nap in now before Mum wakes up and activates.

Then I remember my phone buzzing earlier. I heave myself off the bed and waddle back to the bathroom to retrieve it. It must be Charlotte. And yet, I feel a novel chill as I deep squat to get it off the floor, one that dances instinctively down my arm, leaving me to pause before unlocking it.

Then I see the message and my phone clatters back to the floor, the screen cracking open on the geometric tiling.

Transcript: Inspector Simmons interviewing Lauren Powell

Simmons: Can you talk us through the day of July 14th, please?

Lauren: When was that?

Simmons: The day of the fire

Lauren: Oh, of course. Sorry. All the days blur into one when you have a baby.

Simmons: In your own time, Lauren.

Lauren: Umm, do you know how long this will take? Because my baby's currently on a wake window of 2.45 hours, and you were late letting me in, so he's got to go down in only 1.37 hours, and he needs my boob to get to sleep . . .

LAUREN

It feels like an act of violence when the baby wakes me up again.

'No,' I whisper, as I hear Woody start to howl. 'Please, no.'

Tristan stirs next to me in the bed. He's heard it too, but we remain silent, like Woody's the T-Rex from *Jurassic Park,* and, if we stay still, he'll go back to sleep and not eat us whole on a toilet. Does that make sense? I'm not sure. I'm so, so, fucking sleep deprived. Honestly, I could weep. Hang on, my pillow's wet. I *am* weeping. Great. We'll have to start the tally again. Tristan thought it would be 'funny' to keep a daily tally of how often I cry. Because, you know, PND is much easier when it's gamified.

Another howl from Woody's cot. I reach for my phone to check the time and it's just as bad as it feels. It's been precisely *one hour and fifteen minutes* since Woody fell asleep . . . Since Woody fell asleep after us spending one hour and *fifty* minutes trying to get him back to sleep. And, after he finally went down, I was so full of adrenaline and that crippling feeling that I'm trapped forever in this total nightmare, that I couldn't get back to sleep for ages. In fact, I only dropped off twenty minutes ago.

A more urgent howl. Tristan inches closer to me.

'Shall we leave him?' he whispers, but not quietly enough. Woody lets out a desperate screech. One so shrill that I want to lurch up and tell him to shut up because I'm such a good mother. Make me a mumfluencer. What's my USP? I tell my baby to shut up. To its face. Regularly. And I'm still really fat. And I hate every minute. What do you mean I don't have any followers? No brand deals for *#AuthenticMamaBabiesFuck-UpYourLife?* I really am delirious, aren't I? Oh my God, why won't Woody stop crying? Why is he awake again?

'The sleep lady said we need to leave him for fifteen minutes to see if he self-settles,' I whisper back, just as Woody screams so loud the neighbours will complain again.

'He isn't settling,' Tristan says, not bothering to whisper now.

'I don't know what you mean, he sounds delighted.'

A blood curdling scream.

'We have to get him up,' Tristan says.

'No, the sleep lady says . . .'

'Lauren, he's distraught.'

'Well, he shouldn't be. He should be asleep.'

'I'm getting him up.'

'Don't you dare.'

But his screams are so desperate that I give in. Take a deep breath. Push my aching body out of bed, rub my eyes that feel like they've been sandpapered.

Fuck this. Fuck this.

Fuck fucking this.

'Are you OK my darling?' I say, plucking Woody from the cot, with his angry old man face neon red from the whole thirty seconds of me not responding to his every fucking relentless need. 'I know, I know. Mummy's here, it's alright. I'm here. I love you.' I shove my nipple into his mouth, and he sucks greedily, even though he shouldn't be hungry. He can't possibly be hungry. He sat on my nipple for an hour and fifty minutes only an hour and fifteen minutes ago. Tristan sighs and turns over in bed, relaxed in the knowledge he can't do anything to help. I sit in the rising dawn, seething with jealousy as Tristan's breath steadies, while Woody sucks himself back into sleep too. Once he stills, I wait an extra ten minutes to ensure he's in deep sleep before I attempt to pop my little finger into his mouth to unlatch him. Slowly, with anxiety rising in my stomach, I peel his suckered lips off my body. Then I hold Woody's face against my breast for an additional ten minutes to ensure he's in the deepest part of his sleep cycle, before lowering him back into the cot with more precision than Tom Cruise dangling from a ceiling in *Mission Impossible*.

It works.

He's asleep.

Finally, again. For now.

But, of course, it's taken so long, and I'm now so pumped with stress, I won't be able to get back to sleep myself.

5:30am, but the sun's raging behind the curtains like it's midday and Woody's body heat is cooking me through my skin. I can smell my pungent armpits without even leaning into them. I'll need to wash before the baby shower today. Try to not look how I feel – knowing everyone will be subconsciously analysing me to see if I've lost the baby weight yet. Of course I've not lost it. I hardly have time to wash, let alone exercise, or cook food that isn't Nutella spooned directly into my mouth. I'm so exhausted there needs to be a different word for it. Something German to describe the tier of exhaustion you feel if you've been duped by society into having a baby. I can't believe I used to *complain* about tiredness before Woody. I was such an utter twat – declaring 'I'm exhausted' after I'd gone out dancing til 4am, actually HAVING FUN and ENJOYING MY LIFE, and CHOOSING NOT TO SLEEP – knowing I could catch up the next night, and the next. These days, I'm tired in my *bone marrow*. I feel parts of my brain shrivel and whisper to each other, 'Shall we develop some Alzheimer's?' And I'm this broken without having fun. Just the daily, relentless, grind of keeping Woody alive. Oh, I wish I could go back to sleep, but it's not going to happen. Not with today looming.

Oh God, Nicki's baby shower.

I head downstairs. My eyes hurt each time I blink, but I tell myself at least this is alone time. Time to just be me – broken, rotting, shell of Lauren. The kitchen's full of chores that urgently need doing. Last night's dinner still needs washing up. We didn't get a chance to do it as Woody woke, screaming, only 45 minutes after we put him to sleep. Baby paraphernalia scatters most of the floor space – jarringly cheerful hunks of plastic coated with dried baby drool. I collapse onto the sofa and my arse lets out a novelty shriek as I pull out Sophie the Giraffe.

My house used to look quite nice.

My body used to look quite nice.

My face.

My life.

It didn't even just look quite nice. It *felt* nice.

I was happy. On reflection, really quite deliciously happy.

And I've ruined it. Bulldozed it. Fucked it up forever.

Nicki's baby shower today . . .

Nicki and Matt are happy. So happy. They've been together since university and known each other almost as long as the Little Women. Practically childhood sweethearts. And *happy*. With their nice house, and good jobs, and thriving social circles, and their eight hours a night. Now I have to go to her party, see her swollen bump, and pretend I'm excited for her rather than terrified.

I bet she thinks she's going to have a nice water birth like I thought . . .

Memories of screaming.

My body making noises I didn't know it was capable of.

A dying animal.

Breathe, Lauren. Breathe.

Just my luck. I get a precious half hour to myself and I waste it with another panic attack.

I breathe. I push the memories aside. Push the endless worries into the crammed cupboard in my mind. The worries that the sleep training clearly isn't working and Woody will therefore never sleep and therefore I'll never feel sane again. The worries about how to fucking drive Woody to fucking Nicki's parents' house in the middle of fucking nowhere, and having to pick up fucking Steffi on the way, on this little sleep, when Woody hates his fucking car seat. The jarring infantilising games, pretending Nicki is about to embark on a good thing, rather than treading on the same snare trap that clamped down on me. Will I crash the car trying to drive on this little sleep? Kill Woody? Kill us both? Horrific visuals play across my mind in high resolution, turning my stomach to acid, and . . . No. Distract yourself,

Lauren. I get my phone out and hold it up in front of my psychological abyss.

I attempt to keep up with current news and flick through various news stories about the heat wave and how global warming is going to kill us all. There's an opinion piece about the carbon footprint of children – apparently having Woody is the equivalent of twenty flights to Australia a year in terms of his carbon emissions, and they've not smelt his nappies. On a different site, another columnist laments the plummeting birth rates and how women are too selfish to have babies. I sigh and tap into Instagram instead. I scroll mindlessly past the frozen grins of people showing off their best lives. It hurts seeing anyone doing anything nice – looking free and fulfilled and glamourous. I see Steffi was out again last night, at some elaborate-looking dinner with loads of editors, with cocktails afterwards in a hotel bar. The jealousy tastes literally sour on my tongue. No doubt she'll be hungover later when I pick her up and complain about being tired – and I'll try not to stab her in the eyeball. *It must be something important to do with her new agency,* I remind myself, in an effort to be kind rather than jealous.

All of this is a delay tactic. I know what I'm really doing online. I'm about to do what I always do when I have a spare second. If I send them enough messages, maybe they'll say sorry. Maybe they'll stop playing this dangerous game. The one that almost killed me. I feel myself float away as I log out of my regular account and into my newest burner one. I know their account name by heart and I type it into the search bar. Up comes their smug face – the one I used to love and trust.

I open a new DM to them and tap out my message.

'You've got to stop the lies. Seriously. Stop. Fucking. Lying.'

Transcript: Inspector Simmons interviewing Steffani Fox

Steffani: Did you know editors are already asking me for the rights to this fire?

Simmons: You've mentioned before, how busy you were that day with work.

Steffani: Busy? It was crazy. Literally the last thing on earth I needed was to be at that baby shower, let alone a baby shower that turned into . . . that.

STEFFI

Out of all the weekends in the history of my life, of course *Nicki's* baby shower lands on this one. This weekend should be about me and in celebration of *my* amazing life-changing news. So, of course, it's *Nicki's* baby shower, of all people's, meaning I definitely can't miss it. No matter how much both of us want me to. I'd argue it's much harder and braver launching your own business than having a baby with your perfectly OK husband, but Nicki's the one getting all the presents and support so I've had to celebrate myself, by myself.

In fact, I've been up since 5am, buzzing my tits off, after I was woken by a message from Liv, the editor at ShutterDoor. We only said goodbye in the hotel bar a few hours previously, so it's a cosmic sign of utter brilliance she's messaging already, especially on the weekend.

Liv:
I haven't slept, Steffi. I can't stop reading. This book, Steffi. THIS BOOK. Expect a significant pre-empt on Monday first thing. Don't you DARE let another publisher buy this book.

I squeal and run around my flat in my silk pyjamas before the heat catches up with me. I wipe my palms off on my tiny shorts and type back.

Steffi:

I KNOW, RIGHT?

It's out with ten other editors. Sorry, but not sorry. I really think you and Rosa Williams are perfect for each other though. Let's talk Monday.

Liv:

Still got a third left. How is this so good? Where did you find this woman? This book is everything. EVERYTHING. If anyone else gets it, I will DIE, and then I'll haunt you forever.

Obviously I will be much more professional on email on Monday. But holy shitballs, Steffi. This book is The One. You must be so thrilled. What a perfect way to launch your agency. I'm so happy for you. Everything is about to explode!!!!!

Publishing is an industry that expresses itself solely through the use of multiple exclamation marks and five translates to 'super lead title, NYT bestseller, multiple foreign auctions, and a giant marketing budget'. Sleep was never going to happen after five exclamation marks. Especially when it's ten bazillion degrees outside, at dawn, and living in London adds an extra two degrees to Dante's inferno. Also, I live in a loft conversion so I'm essentially a baked bean right now. It's not even six, but I may as well shower and get ready for this baby-shower vibe ruiner. Google maps predicts it will take me *eight hours and twenty-four* minutes to get to the venue. Well . . . technically only two hours, but when that includes a bus journey, two tube changes, a train AND then Lauren picking me up from the nearest station, I may as well be Mary on her way to Bethlehem on some donkey. You know who didn't have a baby shower? *Mary*. That's my girl. Nobody ever celebrates that about her when they do all the deifying.

My power shower roars into action and the water's actually warm out of my cold tap, even with it turned to the lowest. I throw myself under the jets anyway, lather up my hair, and sing a little tune to myself.

This is it, this is it, this is fucking IT.

I was right to trust this. Trust setting up my own agency, trust the *Blood Moon* manuscript, trust that this huge risk will pay off. It's been beyond terrifying, especially as I have literally no safety net, other than Charlotte's promise I can squat in her granny annexe if everything goes tits up. But I know I'm making Mum so proud and it's not a risk really. Not when *Blood Moon* is so ridiculously good. Another, delicious, message arrives on my phone while I'm wrapped in a towel and lathering myself in moisturiser. This one's from Jane at Eagle Press. She's slightly more professional as we've never worked closely together, but I know she's been desperate to get something like *Blood Moon* on her list.

Jane:
Hi Steffi. It was lovely to see you last night. Thank you for putting together such a great evening. I'm not usually one to message on the weekends, but I started reading Blood Moon on the tube home, and I've not stopped reading. It's exquisite. It's everything I've been searching for. Congratulations. Expect to hear from me first thing Monday. Have a wonderful weekend. Sincerely, Jane.

I let out another whoop and re-sweat myself doing a victory dance around my sauna of a flat. However, exceedingly quickly, the magnitude stops me, cold, in my bedroom. I realise my entire life now depends on how I play this over the next three days. I've been given a great starting position, but this vital race is far from won and I really don't want to live in Charlotte's granny annexe. She'll make me dust the inside of the microwave like when we were students. I pull out my desk chair and sit down, wiping my forehead with the back of my hand.

Right. *Strategise.* I must let these two editors know about the super early excitement. Make them spend the weekend worrying they're not going to get it. Plus, I need to let the other eight know there's this much interest already so they read it in time for Monday. This must be delicately done. I can't wind them up too much, or make them think, initially, the final offer will be too high, or they'll get spooked about budget and maybe not bother offering at all. I need to send exactly the right messages, in exactly the right tone, at exactly the right time, and play everyone off with precision. It's going to be a carefully choreographed dance and I must execute every step perfectly. Oh, seriously, why do I need to be schlepping to Nicki's baby shower today? *Nicki's.* She'll spend today watching me like a hawk doing an eye test so I have to be *super* present and *super* enthusiastic to show her how *super* happy I am for her. Which is why I've spent over fifty quid on a box of hand-embroidered babygrows, alongside forty quid on a vat of Neal's Yard Bump Juice. Oh, I know how to play the game, even if I can't afford the gifts because I've put everything into my agency. A ridiculous risk for a single woman with no living relatives, but

Blood Moon is going to change the world, and Rosa's world, and my world. The firework is lit and it's spectacular and everything is about to take off and yet I've got to hoick some hand-embroidered babygrows to the middle of nowhere, in 32 degrees, so I can pretend to be happy for someone who has decided they hate me. I put my face on the cool of my wooden desk and sigh into my shoulders. I could fake a dodgy tummy then go to the loo regularly to send emails?

I wish I could just not go and it not mean anything. Or, I wish I could go and at least say, 'Hey, Nicki. I'm really happy for you, honestly. But, this weekend, my business is about to take off, which is very useful since otherwise I'll go bankrupt and homeless. Today is actually super important for me too. No, I've not timed this deliberately to spite you. Do you mind if I just send some work emails while I'm at your baby shower? As this is literally my life, my career, my everything? Can we just let me do that and it not mean anything to do with your weird twelve-year grudge? Please? Because we're not twenty anymore? PLEASE?'

But I can't say that. I pride myself on being an honest person. A no-nonsense, cut-the-shit, dare I say *authentic* person. Apart from in this particular friendship group – *The Little Women*. Lauren and Charlotte are essentially family, and, sadly, Nicki's dysfunction comes with this package – making it a more realistic family I guess. I have to swallow some inauthenticity to keep my siblings.

So, yeah, the most important day of my life and I'm going to have to fake diarrhoea . . . Great.

My phone bleeps again.

Transcript: Inspector Simmons interviewing Charlotte Roth

Charlotte: I'm telling you, Inspector. It was the perfect day.

Simmons: Up until a wildfire caused 35 acres of damage and incinerated three residential properties.

Charlotte: Well, if you *insist* on focusing on the negative . . .

CHARLOTTE

On reflection, it's a good thing I didn't go for the stork ice sculpture.

I mean, it would've set off the peony wall beautifully, and the balloon arch, but it definitely would've melted, and that's not a good sign, is it? A stork perishing slowly at a baby shower? So, no stork. Good call. It's still going to be perfect. *Perfect.*

I've been up since dawn, counting everything to go into the pastel goody bags. The article I bookmarked – 'How to Throw the Perfect Baby Shower' – was very clear the host should give something back. Nicki shouldn't have to worry about that, so I've ordered lip balms and luxury popcorn online, as well as some cute personalised bottles of shower gel that say *Thank you for showering with us.* How funny is that? I saw them on a 'Quirky Baby Shower Favours' listicle. Once everything's counted, I head to the kitchen and check through the catering. I open the fridge, sighing as cool air hits my skin, and reach in to stir the three jugs of pink lemonade I brewed last night. They're perfect, ready to pour into the mini glass milk bottles I've tied with pastel bows. On the top shelf, the cupcakes are holding up nicely that I baked after school yesterday. Hopefully they won't taste of fridge. I took everything out and bleached the fridge beforehand, just in case, and now I'm worried the cupcakes will taste of bleach. They look stunning, with their whirls of piped icing and delicate sugar paper hearts. In the bottom fridge drawer, I've got the chopped strawberries and blueberries, ready to assemble closer to start time as I don't want them to get soggy. Then there's the pink wafer biscuit towers to build. I'll wait till I get to Nicki's parents' house to assemble those. They'll sit alongside the jars of blue liquorice I ordered online from a speciality US store. I'm so relieved the liquorice arrived in time. Honestly, I've been having *palpitations*. Right. Fab. Now I need to check everything for the games. I head to my organised piles in the living room and start re-counting. Have I printed enough copies of the Famous Babies quiz sheet? Check. Do I have the baby food ready to spread into nappies for Guess the Flavour? Check. I've got 30 dummies. Check. They cost more than I thought they would, but they're going to be great for Hook a Dummy. I check the homemade fishing rods are sturdy enough. Was it wrong to get my Year 5s to make them as our crafts project this week? Probably. But I was running out of time. I can't wait for that game. The roll-top bath is going to make the best pics. Then there's the dyed hard-boiled eggs, ready for the spoon race – waiting in the cooler. That's going to make great pictures too. It's a shame the hosepipe ban has probably turned their garden to dust, but, still, it will be fun and—

'Oh, babe,' Seth's voice makes my ears tingle. 'Please tell me you slept some?'

I put down the papier-mâché vulva I made for the piñata and smile.

'Maybe between twelve and four,' I tell my husband.

'You need to rest.' He hugs me from behind, his body almost uncomfortably warm, resting his chin on my head. I seep back into him.

'Organising is restful to me.'

He laughs. 'So you keep claiming.'

I stretch my neck up and we share a kiss. Seth tastes of morning, but I'm minty fresh as I always brush first thing. That's how you're supposed to brush your teeth, you know? You're supposed to brush first thing to scrub off the plaque that's formed overnight. Plus, it coats your teeth with toothpaste and protects them through breakfast. If you eat breakfast and THEN brush your teeth, you're actually brushing off the enamel as the bacteria is feeding off your food. I read about it when I googled 'How to Brush Your Teeth Properly' after reading 'Can Gum Disease Cause Infertility?'

'Are you still OK to pick up the doughnut wall this morning?' I ask him.

He smooths my hair down lovingly. 'Yes. I'll collect Matt and head over to the bakery. I'll keep the air con on so the glazing doesn't melt.'

I love this man.

'Make sure they have exactly 29 of blue and 30 of pink.'

'I know, babe. I'll count myself if I have to.'

'I hope people are hungry enough to eat them when you arrive. There's a two-hour gap between lunch and the surprise.'

'It's doughnuts, Charlotte. People always eat doughnuts when presented with doughnuts.'

I'm picturing Nicki's face when she realises just how many clues I've left for her today, in plain sight, before the big finale. I could almost combust I'm so excited about her surprise. I've dug into the very deepest trenches of myself to organise today. I got out my own baby shower mood board – the one I've been curating for years – and, one by one, I donated all my ideas to Nicki.

I release this into the world with peace and acceptance, I said, as I ordered the wall of peonies from the florist, my heart literally aching from the effort of truly meaning it.

I release this into the world with peace and acceptance, I said, as I planned which pouches of food to wipe in the nappies to make them look like poo.

I let go of my broken hopes, I said, as I organised the craft corner, where guests can draw pictures of what they think Nicki's baby will look like. *I gift this out into the universe.*

I accept *this isn't my baby shower,* I said, as I ordered a box of teddy bears off eBay to use in the nappy-changing race. *It's alright to feel grief but it's time to release it into the universe and be free.*

I've sacrificed my own dream baby shower on the altar of personal growth. It's Nicki's now. Not mine. One of my oldest friends. A worthy recipient. I might have cried a dozen times, but I've done it. I'm free of it. And today's going to be perfect. *Perfect.*

Seth tugs me towards the kitchen, a big dopey smile on his face. 'Can I tempt you away from your chores and at least make you have some breakfast?' he asks.

'I'm not hungry. I still feel off.'

'At least have something. Dry toast is supposed to help?'

He sits me at our breakfast bar, slices some sourdough, and makes me a decaf coffee. He sits opposite me as we eat, stretching his leg out to play footsie.

'I still have so much to do,' I say, taking a tentative nibble of my toast, worrying I've not left enough time to stuff the goody bags.

'We've been married three years now, Charlotte. I can say, without a shadow of any doubt, that you had it all sorted a month ago.'

'Are you sure I shouldn't have ordered the ice sculpture?'

He laughs. 'It would be a puddle.'

'I know, but . . .'

'Nobody knows you'd planned to have a stork ice sculpture. Nobody will miss it.'

'But *I* know.'

'Please, try and relax. You've planned the most wonderful day for her.'

'And you'll arrive at two on the dot? With Matt?'

He takes another sip of his espresso and nuzzles my foot further. 'We're going to watch the final on the outside screen at The Wellington first because we have to do Real Men things before coming to a baby shower.'

'It's not technically a baby shower, it's a gender reveal disguised as a baby shower.'

'Even more macho then. I better not tell everyone on the trading floor.'

'You can't get drunk.'

'Babe, I know. I'm driving.'

'I just want it all to be—'

'Perfect, I know.'

We smile at one another in the pinky glow of our kitchen. His dark hair perfectly offsets the dusty tiles I picked. They suit both our colouring perfectly, in all different lights.

'I'm so excited to have everyone together,' I say. 'I've hardly seen Lauren since she had Woody. Only that one time after he was born. And Steffi's so busy launching this agency.'

'The Little Women.' Seth smiles. He finds it hilarious our group is called that when I'm the only one who actually read it at uni.

'We're never together anymore. It's literally like the novel.'

'Not that the other three would know that.'

'Steffi read some of the book, I think. And, seriously, I miss us. As a group. It's not been the same for ages.'

Seth drains his tiny cup and reaches out to rub my stomach gently. Profound bliss blooms through me and I allow myself another ten seconds.

'Well didn't they have a falling out?' he asks, taking our cups straight to the sink and washing them right away, feeling my eyes on him. He uses the special sponge to ensure there's no coffee residue at the bottom. He knows I'll creep back and do it myself otherwise.

'That's not true,' I say. 'We're still all best friends, we've just all got our own stuff going on. You know what it's like at this age when everyone starts having kids.'

He raises his eyebrows at me. '*Everyone*, eh? Typical.'

I raise my eyebrows back, and we giggle at one another, and I can't believe we're able to joke about this. I allow myself a further ten seconds to be mindful of this feeling of gratitude and then return to planning today.

'I'm going for a shower,' Seth says, calling over his shoulder. 'And don't worry, I won't forget to count the doughnuts.'

'I just want it to be perfect,' I call after him, and then mutter it one last time to myself.

Evidence item no.7

Consider this your . . .

<u>BOOTIES CALL</u>

Nicki Davies has a baby on the way

Hope you can join us for her baby shower

When: July 17th 11am-3pm

Where: Vista Cottage, Honeysuckle Lane, Surrey

RSVP: CharlotteRoth1990@gmail.com

NICKI

I lay naked on my bed staring at my cracked phone screen in horror. It's been over a year since Phoebe last messaged me, and the relics of our last conversation hang awkwardly above this morning's new one.

Phoebe:
I can't believe this
You're betraying yourself
Fine then. Be like this. Have a great life.

The messages weren't replied to, but two ticks reveal they'd been read. Oh, how I'd read those final words until they were branded onto the back of my eyelids – crying whenever I re-read them. But, gradually, month by month, the scar of them softened as Matt and I healed and rebuilt and tried to forget about Phoebe. Now, here sits a fresh message to reignite the chaos she brought into our lives.

Phoebe:
Happy baby shower!! Looking forward to seeing you today. It's been agggeeeeesss xxxx

It seems innocent but it's a stark juxtaposition to the poison lying in the text boxes above. Surely she can see them too? Are we just going to jump the shark here? I sit up and lean forward and sweat drips off my forehead onto my phone screen. I wipe it with my thumb and then wipe under my sagging breasts too. They're already double their pre-pregnancy size and don't get me started on what the hell's happened to my nipples which now resemble mauve dinner plates. They droop inelegantly, resting on my bulging stomach, harvesting little ponds of sweat underneath them. Honestly, the never-ending grotesqueness of pregnancy and I haven't even dislodged my 'mucus plug' yet. Is it the heat making me sweat, or this message? I never thought I'd hear from her again. I'd got used to that. I've mourned our friendship. WHY is Phoebe coming today? Who the hell invited her? She MUST know I'm pregnant for fuck's sake, she's used the words 'Happy Baby Shower'. Why would she do this to me?

Baby kicks beneath my skin as the cortisol pumps into their placenta. 'Shh, it's alright. Sorry. It's alright.' I rub their foot through my stomach, trying to calm myself down as much as my baby.

I'm initially in shock but the rage arrives shortly after and I push myself off the bed, pacing to get it out. *How dare she?* What's *WRONG* with her? I'm pregnant. Doesn't she care how pregnant I am? It's been a pretty jarring experience, getting pregnant and realising just how little the world gives a shit. I've been stunned by the daily battle to get someone to give me their seat on the train to work, even in this heat when I'm so visibly huge. I guess it's naive to expect strangers to care about my delicate condition, but Phoebe—

'Nicki?' Mum calls from the kitchen, her voice bouncing through the glass of the house, jolting me from my phone. 'Are you awake, darling?'

If I wasn't, I would be now.

'I'm up,' I call back. 'Is everything alright?'

'Everything's fine. Just wondering if you want a cup of tea?'

'OK then.'

I sigh and glance down at my phone again, trying to arrange this into my projection of how the day was going to go. Phoebe is coming to my baby shower. Phoebe the albatross. I'm finally going to see her again. I should tell her not to come . . . Surely it's for revenge or something? At least Matt's not going to be here. Maybe she's decided to not totally nuke my new life and only contaminate a small part of it. I step into some really giant pregnancy knickers and tell myself she'll know Matt won't be coming today. Maybe this is a peace offering rather than an unpinned grenade. Maybe we can move on from what happened and let go of all the animosity?

Maybe it will be nice to see her?

I allow myself that thought as I stuff myself into my stretched silk kimono. The shock's settling down now and I recalibrate the day, inserting Phoebe into the celebrations. It could actually be quite lovely? A great way of finding peace before the baby arrives? Plus, it's a guilt-free way of seeing Phoebe again. I didn't invite her. I'm innocent and yet I get to see her and smooth things over. Create a different ending to our doomed friendship. That would be nice. By the time I meet Mum in the kitchen, I'm actively looking forward to her coming, and finally, therefore, to the day itself.

'Morning darling, how did you sleep?' Mum's elbow deep in their new fancy sink, Marigolds on, scrubbing a non-existent stain on the deep, stainless steel bowl.

'Hardly at all. I think I peed seven times.'

She laughs. 'I remember it well. Still, honestly, try and enjoy this last month of your body keeping your baby alive.

It's much easier with them on the inside than the outside.' She unsheathes her hands and zooms straight to turn on the kettle, plopping a teabag into a mug for me. She pecks the top of my head then re-gloves and gets out a bottle of spray bleach and starts attacking the gleaming countertops.

I struggle to get myself up onto the stool at the breakfast bar. 'I'm not sure about that,' I tell her. 'Being pregnant is really hard.'

'Hmm.'

Her hand blurs over the countertop, raking up non-existent dirt, just as the kettle sings. Without blinking, she's handing me a steaming cup of herbal tea.

'It really is,' I repeat, wanting a bit more sympathy. 'Honestly, the list of things that's wrong with me right now . . . Insomnia, pelvic girdle pain, the heartburn. Counting the kicks each day and worrying the baby's dead and deciding whether to go to maternity triage for a scan . . .'

'We never had scans in my day,' Mum interrupts, already on her knees with a dustpan and brush. 'Your generation knows too much. We didn't even know if it was a boy or a girl, let alone if they had Down's syndrome or whatever. You just got pregnant and nine months later, you got a baby and it was what it was.'

I cradle my mug with both hands and inhale the steam to ground myself.

'Did you not worry there'd be something wrong with me?'

'No, why would there be?'

'Did you not count the kicks each day?'

'I didn't have time, Nicki. I was too busy working.'

'I work too.'

'Yes, well, God knows when you fit in all this fretting. We just got on with it.' I feel my temper flaring, and, sensing it, she jumps up and dumps the dust into the bin, and starts attacking the skirting boards.

'Mum, the house is already spotless.'

'We've got babies crawling around today, we must be super careful. Now, are you sure there'll be enough food?'

'Charlotte said she's organised catering. Just relax. You've done enough by letting us host it here.'

'You say she's sorting travel cots for the babies. I'm doing what I can about the heat but there's so much glass . . .'

I smile and glance around at the vast see-throughness of their outer walls. 'There is, indeed, a lot of glass.'

'Your dad said it would be lovely to have all this light in the winter, but we forgot about summer. It's so hot.'

'I mean, you did decide to move into a greenhouse.'

I can't manufacture much sympathy as I still haven't quite forgiven my parents for selling my childhood home, especially without consultation. Dad just casually dropped it into con- versation, 'Oh, we got an offer accepted on the house today,' like it was an old sofa they'd put on eBay and not the container of all my childhood memories. I'd burst into tears and Mum had called me 'selfish'.

'You know your father has always dreamed of living in the countryside. Honestly, it's not like you visit much anyway.'

It's worse she defended him when I knew she didn't want to sell either. Mum had carefully curated the perfect retired life. Every day of the week, she'd have a 'Biddy Walk' or 'Silver Swim' with a local friend, before getting coffee and talking about their grown-up children or physical ailments. Now, to make Dad happy, she was a 30-minute drive away from that life. Not even an easy 30-minute drive, but one on winding countryside lanes which made her anxious. But she toed the party line, and said how excited she was to embrace village life, for views over the downs, and have a vegetable patch – which seemed like an additional chore to be honest. I wept packing up our old house, my foetus only the size of a cherry tomato back then. The baby would never see my childhood bedroom, would never take their clumsy first steps in the same garden I did. And, if it wasn't all symbolic enough, Mum dumped five giant boxes of crap onto my lap and said, 'this is all yours'. And, through morning sickness, I'd had to spend two weeks figuring out what leftovers from my formative years I could fit into our tiny two-bed flat.

'Clutter just doesn't work in the glass house,' she'd said. 'Sorry, Nicki. You have to find room at yours.'

I rub my stomach through my kimono and promise my baby that I'll cherish every piece of GCSE artwork, every outfit that might come back into fashion, and every book they've ever loved. Cherished memories aren't 'clutter'. The list of the things I plan to do differently from my own parents is longer than the terse silences between them. I will be less stressed, more present, I will validate my child's emotions, I will showcase a positive experience of an equal partnership—

'Did Charlotte say she's bringing ice? I worry we don't have enough ice.' Mum's eyes widen as she decides on her latest catastrophe, j-cloth still in hand.

'She'll bring ice. It's Charlotte.'

'Maybe I should drive into town, just in case?'

'There'll be ice.'

'I'm going to go.'

'Mum.'

'You'll thank me later.'

Mum vanishes before I can even message Charlotte to ask, and I hear the car start in the driveway, roaring over gravel. I sigh, trying to erase the contamination of her anxiety. I told Mum providing the venue was more than enough. No need to worry about anything else. But she insists on malfunctioning anyway. I pick up my phone and read Phoebe's message again. I should reply. It will be awkward if I don't. It already is awkward. At least, if I reply, it pushes those horrible messages up and off the screen. My pudgy hands hover over my phone, awaiting instruction for the response, but it feels like every button is a landmine. I stroke the crack in the screen and punch something out.

> You're coming? Who invited you?

That sounds confrontational. It must've been Charlotte who invited her anyway. Obliviously.

> Wow OK. It will be lovely to see you.

I wince and delete that too. Imagining reading it through Matt's eyes.

> I can't pretend this isn't a huge shock, Phoebe. I wish you'd warned me.

No, too aggressive again. Despite everything, I want Phoebe to like me. I delete for a third time and drum my pudgy fingers against the marble countertop. A giant hacking cough comes from the bathroom. Dad's up. What is it with men over a certain age and their supersonic morning coughs? Matt's developed one too, during his first piss of the day, and I swear we're only a hop, skip and a jump from skid marks in baggy y-fronts, and him growing giant grey nose hairs. Dad shuffles out of the bathroom, scratching himself.

'Morning Poppet,' he greets me, ruffling my hair on his way to the coffee machine. 'How did you sleep?'

'What's sleep?'

He laughs. 'Your mother was the same when she was pregnant with you. Up every hour with her bladder . . .' He swings open a cupboard door and retrieves a mug, pours coffee, and misses a bit, spilling over Mum's freshly cleaned counter tops. Oblivious, he takes a deep slurp, and then bashes the mug down again, creating a fresh brown circle. '. . . I remember it so well. I can't believe it was 32 years ago.'

He perches on the stool next to me, slurping and grinning at my bump, decorating the table with coffee circles like it's a potato press. 'Where is your mother anyway?' he asks. 'I can't hear her worrying about anything.'

We laugh conspiratorially. 'She's convinced herself we don't have enough ice, even though Charlotte has probably couriered in our own personal iceberg. She insisted on going to town anyway.'

'Sounds like your mother. If there's a stress to be had.'

'She's been up since five, cleaning . . .' I look at the decorated kitchen top.

'I told her not to. I wish she'd relax more.'

I switch from co-conspirator to mum-defender. I know she's A Lot, most of the time, but Dad doesn't seem to realise his behaviour causes so much of her stress. If he'd only help more, he'd magically get the chilled wife he's spent his whole life pining for. They live in this ridiculous mausoleum because they BOTH made good money before retiring. It's not like he was the sole breadwinner. I remember meeting Lauren a year or two ago for wine, and we'd drunk too much and complained about our mothers. She'd said Boomer women were the real losers of '70s feminism. '*They were told they could go out and have a career, but they also married these man-children, brought up by '50s Stepford wives, who don't know how to clean the bog,*' I remember her slurring. '*Feminism backfired on them. They had to go work and feel liberated about that, but ALSO did the childcare and housework. It's no coincidence that every woman in this country over the age of 60 has some kind of clinical anxiety disorder.*'

I really do miss Lauren. I didn't think she'd go all Baby Cult on me. But, since having Woody, whenever I've tried to call her, she rarely picks up the phone, claiming Woody's about to feed, or about to nap, or about to 'kick off'. It felt so magical, to both get pregnant in the same year, but I hardly hear from her. It's so weird. She always used to check in but she's basically vanished. She didn't even reply to my last message about my pelvic girdle pain.

'Maybe if you cleaned more, Mum would be less stressed?' I tell dad, rubbing my stomach again.

'We have a cleaner and she still gets stressed.' He grins and finishes off his coffee with a dramatic *ahh*. 'Don't worry Poppet. Your mum will calm down once everyone arrives.'

'And once she's collected all the ice in a twelve-mile radius.

'That too.'

He stands up and smells his own armpit before wincing at what his nostrils have found. 'Enjoy today, Nicki. It's very special.'

It hits me again. Today is my baby shower. *My baby shower.* It's still so surreal. 30-odd people are coming over to officiate this overwhelming life choice I've made, and now Phoebe, apparently, is going to be one of them.

The doorbell chimes, making the house feel like a church, and Dad jumps up to get it – unashamedly answering it in his saggy old man pants. I hear him chat to someone, laughing, as I pull out my phone once more. I decide not to overthink it, there's no way Phoebe would've. She's no doubt decided to come today on a whim, because she's got a spare gap between art exhibition openings and other hipster parties.

'Well, this is a surprise.' I type out to Phoebe. Then I add a winky face.

There. Sent. Done. I sigh and lean back on the hard stool, shaking my head. I hold my bump in both hands to remind myself why I'm here. It's what I wanted.

It's here. Today. My baby shower. A shadow of my past attending. I may as well just surrender to the surreal of it all. It's already so weird, it can't possibly get any weirder.

'Umm, Nicki?' Dad calls, sounding like he's behind something. He staggers into the hot box of the kitchen, under the weight of what seems to be an entire field of flowers. 'Did you order a *peony wall?*'

Lauren

I hate Past Me who didn't try and go back to sleep at five.

I'm crashing so hard right now. It hurts to blink, like I've accidentally used a sandpit as eyedrops. Woody shrieks across the living room and ripples of fury unfurl through my body.

Stupid Past Me, thinking weeping in the kitchen was a better idea than sleeping.

Stupid Past Me for thinking it was a good idea to have a baby.

Stupid Past Me for thinking I'd be a good mother.

Stupid Past Me for marrying my stupid fucking husband.

Woody shrieks again, this time in pain. In the time I dared take a long blink, he's toppled over from where he'd been cruising along the coffee table.

'Shit.' I rush over and his little hands reach for me as I scoop him up. I feel this deep, nourishing thrill at being so needed, and then instantly suffocated by it too. 'You're OK, buddy,' I tell him. 'Did you go ouch? Poor thing.' He wipes snot onto my shoulder as his cries subside. 'You know?' I say, switching out of Motherese into an adult voice. 'If you were having your morning nap right now, you wouldn't have hurt yourself, would you? Have you considered that, Woody? Napping when you're supposed to?'

Recovered, he grunts and twists out of my arms. I release him and watch as he heads straight back to cruising along the coffee table again. I lower my tired body to the carpet so I can catch him when he inevitably topples. 'You know what else?' I ask him in my adult voice as he grabs for my mug of tea. I swipe it out of reach even though it's cold by now. Tea is always cold these days. 'Daddy's supposed to be taking you this morning, isn't he? I'm supposed to be having *a little break*. But where is Daddy? He needed a poo, didn't he. He needed another epic shit.'

Woody turns back and cackles like I've told a joke and I check the time on my phone. 8.05am. Tristan 'quickly needed the bathroom' over half an hour ago. Every morning, I'm surprised he's got any shit left to shit out when he so thoroughly empties himself when he's supposed to be helping with Woody. It's also surprising how these indulgently long shits aren't necessary on the days he's in the office, as I can't imagine his boss allowing him to leave an important meeting for a 30-minute dump. It's also weird how BBC Sport and Reddit have such a laxative effect on Tristan and therefore need to be read while on the toilet, you know, for medical reasons. A familiar pulse of rage speeds up in my heart. I'm supposed to get some time to myself this morning as I'm taking Woody all day while he gets to watch the tennis. They talk so much about weaponised incompetence in men, but I swear weaponised *incontinence* is the bigger feminist issue.

'I can't believe you're making me feel guilty for having an actual shit,' Tristan said, aghast, when I tried bringing this up before. 'What do you want me to do, Lauren? Crap my pants in the name of equality? A literal dirty protest for feminism?'

He made it seem so unreasonable that I apologised. I even wondered, briefly, if I was abusive? I mean, who doesn't let their husband go to the toilet when they need it? It's just . . . well . . . I have to shit too. And, when I'm alone with Woody all day, I can't look at memes as I do so. In fact, I have to restrain Woody in the BabyBjörn chair and sing 'Blink Blink Little

Green Frog' manically to him, all while defecating. Or I give myself stomach cramps holding it in until Woody naps, which only lasts twenty minutes anyway. Those are my options. A private poo while the baby sleeps, or crying into a cup of tea on the sofa. Pick your luxury, *Mama*. Choice feminism rules!

Oh God, I'm being unhappy again, aren't I?

Why am I so determinedly unhappy, all the time? When I'm supposed to be enjoying *every precious moment, that goes so quickly, they grow up so fast, you'll miss it when it's over.*

Tristan finally emerges from the bathroom, phone in his hand, and, bless him, he looks shattered. Even after a half-hour break. Eyes red raw, his shirt not tucked in properly. He hovers on the threshold of our living room and visibly steels himself, before inhaling energy and bursting into a grin.

'Woody mate?' he says, his accent still so twangy Australian after all these years. 'Are you cruisin' buddy?'

Woody chuckles in delight at his newfound skill and gives Tristan a giant one-toothed grin. Tristan opens his arms wide. 'Come here bubba. Show me those chubby frog-legs.'

I watch Woody hurl himself towards my husband, giggling like his open arms are Disney Land, and my heart warms as they hug.

This is what having a family is about, I remind myself. For this feeling. Right now. It's worth it. It is. It has to be . . .

Tristan yawns and holds Woody out to me. 'Wanna hug Mummy, now, do you, squirt?'

I'm an even more tantalising option, and Woody cackles as he approaches. My back hurts and I'm so exhausted but I can't really say, '*No, I don't want him.*' So, I push through and smile as my baby thwacks himself into my chest.

Tristan and I end up sitting with our legs out, the bare soles of our feet touching, as Woody stumbles clumsily between us, naked apart from his nappy. I feel my husband's skin against mine and realise this is the most we've touched in weeks. I take in his red raw eyes again, the purple bruises of bags under them, the skin that sags around what used to be a good jawline. He's fucked too. Not as fucked as me, but still beyond capacity.

You do not fully know your partner until you've had a baby with them.

I remember a faceless older woman saying this to me at a publishing Christmas party. She'd commented on my new engagement ring, and I droned on about how happy I was to have found Tristan and what a good father he'd be when the time comes.

'Hmm,' was her reply. And I remember thinking that was rude. 'You think you'll know what they'll be like as parents, but kids break people. You don't know what you're both like under torture conditions.'

'Torture conditions?'

I laughed it off at the time and made an excuse to go refill my glass, my nose wrinkling as I walked away. Now I see this lady for the seer she was.

Woody falls on his bottom between us. And, though his nappy cushions the impact, he starts wailing. Tristan scoops him up for a cuddle and nods at me.

'Right, Mummy. This is all under control. Go shower and get ready. We're all good here, aren't we, sport?'

'Thank you,' I say, standing up to get dressed.

Thank you for letting me fulfil a basic life function.

But my gratitude wanes when I hear the *Bluey* theme tune before I even reach our bedroom. I clench the door frame. We've agreed Woody's only allowed ten minutes of screen time a day until he's two. That equates to two episodes of *Bluey*. And Tristan's using one up to make his life easier when I didn't use up any *Bluey* during his 30-minute shit. I only get one episode of Bluey today and . . . Breathe, Lauren . . . Stop seeing it as a competition. Tristan is your husband, not your enemy. I turn on the shower and check my phone while I wait for the water to warm up. The DM lays there, still unread. They'll block me the moment they see it. They always do. Then I'll have to set up another burner account.

The hot water is a sanctuary, even though it's sweltering outside. I turn it up as much as I can stand and watch the glass door turn to steam, before I slide down and sit with my knees up, back against the tiles. I hold out my palms and make tiny ponds that I release and re-fill, release and re-fill. I still remember my first shower after the birth. I wept as I staggered into the shitty cubicle in the shitty maternity ward of the shitty hospital, washing the dried gore from my skin, watching my deflated stomach hang down, no longer carrying a baby with me. I had only five minutes before Woody howled from his plastic container – me able to discern his cries from the other babies already. But it was the first five minutes I'd been alone in nine months. We were separate now. Untethered. I'd held my stomach and grieved and celebrated this tiny piece of aloneness in the hot water. And, still, now, today, I relish in this slice of me-ness. I stand, lather up, give my hair a long overdue wash. Try to look forward to today rather than dread how much it's going to mess up Woody's non-existent schedule. The girls back together again. Women who have known and loved me for so long. It may jumpstart me out of this swamp – remind me who I am a bit.

My optimism, however, gets strangled when I emerge dripping and stand naked in front of my wardrobe. The former clothes from my former life hang there taunting me. It's been nine months and none of them fit yet – both literally and emotionally. They're so bright and cheerful and jarring and go in at the waist, because, in the Before Times, I used to have one of those. I remember, on my first date with Tristan, telling him I worked in Children's Publishing, and he'd laughed and said, 'Of course you do. I assumed it was that or kids TV.' It wasn't a requirement of the job, of course, to dress as brightly as the picture books I commissioned, but I loved wearing a rainbow wardrobe of novelty prints. Dresses covered with hot air balloons, neon jeans, '50s skirts splattered with giant banana prints – all counter-balanced with grown-up makeup. A perfect red lip, a perfect winged eyeliner, a perfect ponytail high on my head. Every day was A Look. My fashion choices used to bring me such joy, and now they hang, lifeless, in front of me. The metaphor is so obvious it's written somewhere in someone's GCSE English coursework.

These clothes don't fit anymore because I am not this person anymore.

I will never fit back into these clothes again because I can never be that woman again.

When could I ever have a perfect red lip again? Woody would be a raspberry of kisses by 5am. Me too, as his favourite thing to do is jam his chubby fingers into my mouth, yanking the side of my lip like he's fishing for me with a hook. And all my old outfits look strange and unfinished without heavy makeup – like a person who's taken their glasses off.

Cool Mum taunts me in the reflection, twirling to showcase her returned figure, clad in her pre-baby clothes. Like everyone who worked in publishing, I'd read the Cool Girl rant in *Gone Girl* and had an epiphany. But I'd outgrown comparing myself to a Cool Girl, and, since having Woody, now ruin my self-esteem with this fictional 'Cool Mum'. Well, I say 'fictional' – every fucking mumfluencer online seems to fit the part, literally.

Cool Mum bounces back after having a baby. Wow, where did this six pack come from? It's just from perfectly breastfeeding easily, with no issues, and pushing my designer pram up the hill. Sometimes I use the baby as arm weights, lol. I exercise because it's time for myself. I get up at 5am to work out before the baby's up. Why lie sobbing on the carpet as your me-time when you could be doing burpees?

I sigh and hoick out my slightly stained navy maternity dress. Everything maternity is navy. When you become a mother, your life becomes navy. Practical. Invisible. Inoffensive.

I shrug it on, catching sight of the angry scar spliced across my stomach and the way my skin hangs over it like a dilapidated shelf. A scar that still feels numb to touch. My tummy still looks at least three months pregnant. I wonder what the other Little Women will wear today. Nicki – some funky pregnancy dungarees, rather than the standard floaty, 70 quid dress from Seraphine, because Nicki will want to prove she's not a 'typical mum'.

Yeah, Nicki, I used to think that too, but I've worn my hair in a gross topknot for over 200 days straight.

Steffi will showcase her amazing Peloton body in some understated sleek something-or-other from a shop I've never heard of in East London, where they only sell twelve items of clothing.

And Charlotte will be wearing one of her typical Anne Boleyn headbands paired with some great dress you can never buy as she's so tiny she can shop in the kids' section.

I twist in the mirror and groan at every part of me that droops. What are they going to think when they see me? You know what, fuck it. I'm going to put some lipstick on.

Tristan wolf-whistles when I re-enter the living room. I've managed to shower, wash my hair, dry it, get dressed and apply lipstick in a shorter amount of time than his morning dump. Woody's lying on his stomach, sucking our old TV remote that we gave him to stop him sucking our current one, while Tristan sits next to him on the floor, re-reading the 'bespoke sleep schedule' we received yesterday from the expensive consultant.

'Have you seen this?' he says, flicking at the print out. 'This bit here, about the morning nap?' He adopts the dulcet tone of Sammy – the lady we hired out of desperation last week. She spoke like The Talking Clock. 'If your baby wakes from this nap before nine thirty, ask him to re-settle.' He raises both eyebrows. 'What the fuck does that mean? How do I ask a nine month old to settle? "Hey, Woody, mate. Do you kindly mind resettling now and going back to sleep please?" Is that what we're doing wrong, we're not asking?'

I laugh but the joke is too expensive to be funny. That piece of paper he's holding cost £200 and was basically the last of my maternity leave fund. 'I think, by "asking" she means, leaving him to cry a bit,' I say, settling myself down next to them. My dress crumples but nobody will notice. It's navy. That's the point of navy. I chew on my lip. 'You know? Like you wouldn't let us do last night.'

'And you're happy letting our baby scream himself to sleep, are you?'

I shrug. 'At least then he'll be asleep.'

Tristan gives me one of the looks he's given me many times since we reproduced. The *I-never-knew-this-side-of-you* horrified look.

Cool Mum gets a look from her partner, but a I-cant-believe-you're-such-a-natural-mother look.

'Honestly, Lauren. No. I'd rather be knackered than let him cry.'

I'm more knackered than you, I snap silently. I do all the feeding back to sleep. I didn't sleep the first four months of pregnancy due to my nausea, and I didn't sleep the last three months due to being such a giant blimp. And I breastfccd, so I do all the night wakes. I am so much more knackered than you will ever know, and now you're not letting me mend the thing that will stop me being such a weeping, disgusting, exhausted husk of a person. Why won't you let me fix this?

'It's not going to work unless we're both willing to do what's required,' I tell him, my voice so much calmer than my inner monologue.

'And you're OK with letting Woody cry, are you?'

I watch our baby cram half the dummy TV remote down his gullet. 'No,' I say. 'But I also know things can't go on like this.'

'He'll grow out of it.'

'We've paid for her and everything. It's worth a try.'

Tristan stands, leaving the schedule on the floor. 'Are you looking forward to later?' he asks, super breezy. If we're ever on the verge of arguing, Tristan always stands and changes the topic. Sometimes I'm grateful – other times, like now, I feel like he may as well slap his hand over my mouth.

'Yeah, I guess,' I swallow. 'I'm nervous about Woody's naps. He's only slept twenty minutes today. He must be knackered.'

'He doesn't look knackered.' Tristan heads over to the kitchen area and grabs the loaf of bread to make himself a sandwich. The man, I swear, eats about twelve sandwiches a day. He tells me one of the best things about England is how readily available sandwiches are – apparently they're not a thing in Australia. 'People think Aussies come to London for the culture, or because it's so close to the rest of Europe, but, no, it's really for Pret,' Tristan tells anyone as his party joke. How he's still so skinny I'll never know. I wish he could've been the pregnant one, like a seahorse. Tristan would've lost his baby weight within an hour postpartum.

'I'm hoping he'll sleep on the way there. He hates the car seat though.'

Tristan slaps cheese onto buttered bread .

'It will be nice though, won't it? Seeing the girls?' He says, ignoring my anxiety.

I roll my eyes and absentmindedly stroke Woody's back. 'I'm looking forward to catching up with Steffi on the drive. It will be so nice to talk about work. Work! Not, freakin' baby weaning recipes on the NCT WhatsApp. *Organic courgette muffins made from coconut flour I ground myself Anna.*'

'You're always so mean about Anna.'

'She said the hardest part of pregnancy was the maternity bras not being sexy enough.'

'I thought you were angry at Steffi anyway?' Tristan ignores my dig. He always defends NCT Anna. Anna 'seems great'.

48

Anna is definitely a Cool Mum. Her baby slept through at *four months* – 'I didn't even do anything. It just happened, sorry.'

I sigh. 'I'm not angry at Steffi. I just found that article she posted a bit insensitive.'

'The child free one . . . I know.' Tristan doesn't roll his eyes, but I sense him yawn inwardly. I've complained non-stop since Steffi posted it alongside the caption, *'Finally someone is saying it – whoop'*. I read the linked article at 4am and felt so wounded by it I'm surprised there wasn't blood on my phone.

'I just still can't believe that's what she thinks of me.' He sighs and takes a bite of his bread, speaking through his mouth. 'We've gone through this. It's not about you. It's about Steffi. How *she* feels, about *her* life choices.'

My blood starts itching as I think about it again. 'Yeah, but that doesn't mean she has to judge mine.'

'She's not . . .' he sighs again and swallows with his eyes to the ceiling. 'We've been through this.' He puts his snack down and comes over and squeezes my shoulders. That's the most affection I get from him these days – shoulder squeezes, like it's the closest he can get to physically shaking me until his old wife reappears. 'She's a good friend,' he says. 'You love these women and they love you. You've not seen them in ages. It will be good for you. You're going to have an amazing time today. *And* you look gorgeous.' He plants a kiss on my lips then, sticks his tongue in, turning it into a jokey snog.

'Tristan,' I squeal, delighted. A joke snog is still a snog. I'll take it. He mock hits my arse too, before retrieving his sandwich and demolishing half of it with one giant chomp. I look from him over to Woody on the floor who's essentially swallowing the dummy remote like a cobra, and get another glow at the magic of genetics. I wish these moments of it feeling 'worth it' were longer, less tiny and less fleeting, but they're here sometimes. Bursts to get me through. And he's right about Steffi. Her posting that article is about her, not me. What did it say again? I've hate-read it so many times I can basically recite it.

'*How come it's OK that my friends are always late now? When did having children make their time more important than mine?*'

And . . .

'*One of my mum friends posts links about the climate crisis, and then, the next day, posts a smug scan announcing the birth of her THIRD baby. Can she not do the math? And I'M the selfish one, for being child-free, am I?*'

Does Steffi really believe that I think she's selfish? Have I been that shit since having Woody? I don't have *time* to think she's selfish.

There's a *doink* as Woody chucks the remote to the floor. He twists up onto his arms, spots me, his face arranging into the biggest smile of delight. It's like having a super fan with you at all times, having a baby. One that literally regularly shits themselves they're so excited to see you. He crawls towards me, panting with excitement about meeting my arms. He collides with my legs, uses me to pull himself up.

'Hey darling. Oh Woody, no . . . not my hair . . . ouch . . . that hurts Mummy. No, not my mouth . . . no . . . no . . . Tristan? . . . no Woody . . . oh . . .'

And, just like that, Woody pokes his fingers in and out of my mouth, smearing my perfect red lip right across my cheek.

STEFFI

There's nothing like the London Underground to remind you that the world doesn't care about you, even on your most dramatic days. It's never ceased to amaze me, how eyes-down, *disinterested*, this city has been whenever I've publicly fallen apart in it. Weeping at Liverpool Street station after Mike dumped me, tube after tube swooshing to a stop, people spilling out, clocking the sobbing woman on a bench and then pretending it's not happened as they rush past. No, London doesn't care when your heart is breaking, and it apparently doesn't care if your life is soaring either. This morning I feel like, surely, there should be some kind of parade in my honour. With elephants wearing tiaras. But when I skip off the sweaty bus, and descend the manky steps of Mile End station, there's just fuggy air that tastes of lung cancer, and no elephants. Thankfully, it's pretty empty this early, as I wilt onto a bench and pointlessly fan my face. It's uncomfortably hot and I feel my makeup sweat off, but my good mood can't be sidelined. I tap dance as I wait for the squeak and roar of the tube pulling in. I get out my phone and re-read the emails. Nothing more has come in yet, but I know it will. This book is going to be huge. These deals are going to be huge. Rosa is going to be huge. And, most importantly – as I've remortgaged my flat to make this all happen – my agency is now going to be huge. *How* huge is up to how I play the next two weeks, and I groan out loud at the thought of today's shower.

The tube hisses in and I stride on board, pulling my skirt around me as I sit down so I don't get flea bites. I tap my foot as we jolt through the hot black air. It's good not to have phone signal for a while. It gives me a chance to calm the fuck down. I won't check my phone until I'm on the train, I decide. I need to reset my nervous system so I don't send my life-changing emails in BLOCK CAPS. We screech into Bank and I hop off, mosey along the tunnels towards the northern line, grin inanely at a busker and toss two quid into his guitar case. He nods and smiles back and I want to gambol like a lamb, I'm so excited. Another tube down to London Bridge and I check my watch. I've honed it to perfection. I have precisely enough time to have a wee, get a good coffee, and browse the station bookshop to put all my clients' books on the front table. I allow myself to get nostalgic as I amble around the concourse, collecting my goods and waiting for my platform to get called. When the Little Women moved to London, scattered around the city like dropped coins, we'd always meet at London Bridge for our catch ups. In fact, Charlotte and I sat on that very bench, off our faces drunk, eating Leon with our fingers and singing the Pocahontas soundtrack all the way through until many people joined in. We were all dementedly living a Bridget Jones fantasy and were excited by tourist traps like Borough Market. The four of us would clip-clop towards South Bank, past the money shots of the Tate Modern, the bouncing bridge, and St Paul's twinkling on the water. We'd occasionally meet at the National Theatre to watch plays Nicki and Charlotte pretended to understand while Lauren and I sniggered through drunk. We'd pour into Wagamama, dressed like we were in *Sex and the City*, making a tiny bowl of noodles last ages, cutting one bao bun into four tiny mouthfuls because we knew they were the cool things to eat, but we were too broke to order one each. Lauren, Charlotte and I would bemoan our dating hardships over the cheapest bottle of red wine while Nicki nodded sympathetically (smugly, in my opinion). Then we'd be too pissed to remember how broke we were and end up getting cocktails at the top of the OXO tower, asking strangers to take our pictures. *Look at us,* young, and in the best city in the world, making it somehow, even though we're English graduates, spat out into the worst job market in twenty years. It was so much easier to be friends back then. Maybe I'm misremembering it, but I swear even Nicki and I got on back then. The Matt thing wasn't such a big deal (*to her, anyway*) until they got engaged. I think that's when she realised we'd both permanently be in her life, as a permanent reminder of how they met. I went from dear former uni housemate to unwanted albatross that she needed rid of. Thankfully Charlotte and Lauren were having none of it. 'It's just a phase,' Lauren promised me, clasping my hand. 'She'll get over whatever it is. We will always be here for each other, I promise.' I held on tight to the Little Women, and they held on tight to me. Although it's not been a phase, and Nicki has been a bitch to me for years now. I really have felt like Amy since. I bet, in Nicki's warped brain, she thinks Matt is Laurie or something. Do what you must do to keep things fresh when you've been shagging the same man since university. But leave me and my best friends out of it.

My platform's announced, and I'm so desperate to check my phone, I practically run up the escalator, almost spilling my iced coffee. The train's blissfully air-conditioned and blissfully empty. I fall, relieved, onto a seat, spreading my legs out to let my sweaty knee-pits dry, and close my eyes as London slips away behind me. I last about 30 seconds before I snap my eyes back open, grasping for my phone. No news. Agh. I'm frustrated my zen-like patience hasn't been rewarded.

I pull up Lauren's number.

Steffi:
I'm on the train and it's running on time. Miracle of miracles.

Thanks again for driving me to the arse end of nowhere. There better be gin, that's what I say!!!

I see she's online and she replies right away.

Lauren:
K

I pull a face. That's a bit weird. Just K? Did she read too much into my gin jokes and think I'm being bitchy about Nicki? No. She knows I like to keep the peace *(unlike Nicki)*. She's probably just got the baby in one arm, I reassure myself. They are demanding little creatures, as everyone likes to constantly tell me, like I cannot possibly understand unless I have one myself because I'm selfish, no doubt. That's what people think. I can't understand caring for people, and the burden of it, even after looking after Mum right until her dire last days. Nope. Unless it's your own child, caring for someone doesn't make you caring.

I shake my head, surprised by myself. That 'K' has really wound me up it appears. This is Lauren. She loves me. It's been so damn long since I've seen her that I've forgotten

Lauren always means well. She's as sunny as the outfits she wears. We're just misfiring because we've not seen each other in ages. Today will be a reminder of how tight we are – even if we're all in such different places right now.

My phone pins, alerting me to an incoming email and blood rushes into my fingertips.

Breathe, Steffi. Breathe. The train hurtles through a tunnel and I can't tell if that's making my ears ring, or the anticipation of seeing what's come in next. And, when I see the name on the email, I swear an eardrum explodes.

'No way,' I say to myself. 'No way. No. Oh my God. Oh my God.'

It's from Nina Baldwin. *The* Nina Baldwin. A Hollywood darling, who, after turning 25, got fed up of there being no roles for older women or minorities so set up her own production company. Since then, everything she's touched has turned to rose gold. She's become her own conveyor belt of success. She options great books, turns them into great shows, then, as an added bonus, usually makes these books her monthly choice in her book club that has over 30 million followers . . . so, of course, when the show airs – the book and the show do supremely well.

And there's her name. In my inbox.

> Hi Steffi
>
> I know it's totally unorthodox to email on a Saturday – though it's technically the middle of Friday night over here in La La Land. Anyway, when a book like BLOOD MOON comes along, I know you have to act fast. Steffi, I am blown away by it. I want to option it immediately and BLOOD MOON is exactly

the project a streaming platform I work with is looking for. I can just see myself playing Cassandra – it's the part of dreams! Do you need a formal offer over the weekend, or can this wait until Monday? I swear *She Believed She Could Productions* is the perfect home for this. I swear we will do it proud. I've CC'd in my lawyers to pretend this is vaguely official, but, truly, from a personal place, I NEED this book. I will do anything. It's perfect. Perfect. It's been an honor to read it, and I cannot wait to hear back from you.

Happiest of days and hope the sun is shining over there

Nina Baldwin xxx

My ears pop as we roar out of the tunnel and my sweaty palms smudge my phone screen. It's weird what you focus on when your entire life changes. I find myself muttering, *Wow, Nina Baldwin uses kisses in work emails. Who knew?*

Then I drop my phone to the ground. I stand up.

Fuck.

OK.

This has never happened. Even with my biggest books at Slick Agency. I've never had *Nina Baldwin* bite. I never thought she even saw my submissions. Nina Baldwin rarely-to-never bites – she's so sharp, she only picks the super bestsellers. She's like the Willy Wonka of Hollywood and has minimal golden tickets to hand out a year. Giddy euphoria fills me up, and, it's just as well the air con is on max and the carriage is empty, because I erupt into an adrenaline sweat. I air punch. I pick up my phone and kiss it. I squeal, I thump my chest in delight, I . . .

. . . I miss Mum so much I think I'm about to be sick.

Because I'm already about to call her to share this, to glory in it with her. My success is hers after all. But she won't pick up. I wilt back on my seat and hold my heart through my dress, like she did when I was younger.

There, there, you're going to be alright, I'm here.

Except she's not here. Not now. Not ever.

I sigh again, clench and release my palms. The grief starts to drain away, back to where it dwells. The wave has crashed, the waters are calming down. It's been four years now. I smile and hear her voice whisper.

You did it, Steffi. All by yourself, you did it. Just like I knew you could.

I let happiness return, with its now tender edge of bitter-sweet. Lauren will be thrilled. I can tell her the second I get off the train. That's something. She'll definitely have a lot more to say than 'K' about this. And she'll get the bittersweet nature of the good news. One of the few memories I have of Mum's funeral is the grasp of her hand in mine, whispering to me, 'She was so proud of you, Steffi, so proud.' And now this . . .

Oh Christ. Nina Baldwin!

I laugh and bite my fist. Oh, Nina. If only you knew my agency is run entirely from my one-bedroom flat overlooking a graveyard where a man with mental health problems climbs into my bins at least once a week, and just stands there, quite happily, sucking his thumb. If only you knew that my assistant Grace Shadowfax is fictional. She's just an email address I made up because I can't afford a real assistant yet. Grace is so efficient she's already been headhunted by Eagle fucking Publishing. I know, at some point, I'm going to have to let everyone know Grace Shadowfax isn't real. People will soon expect Grace to come to parties and pitches and meetings. But I can't out Grace as non-existent until I'm a huge success and she's just a funny side story of my giant success.

Grace, you're being outed.

This is it. I'm going to be huge.

HI NINA BALDWIN.

OK, how to play this? I put a finger to my temple to calm myself down. Legally, I have to present every deal to Rosa and let her decide. But, she'd be mad to turn down Nina. However, if Nina FUCKING Baldwin, is biting, this means other major studios will too. So, *Christ,* I'm going to have to play major Hollywood studios off one another, and also let the publishers know about Nina's interest. This will cause international ripples. The UK market will go mad, now the US will too. This will bounce into the German market, the French, Spanish . . . I can see it all now. Multiple auctions in multiple countries. I'm not going to sleep for a week, but, by the end of it, if I've done my job properly, she'll be a multi-millionaire. She's going to lose her mind! She's on twenty something grand at a tiny literacy charity. She's living in a flat share in Brixton with six other housemates. She was late to our first breakfast meeting, apologising as she'd had to wait 40 minutes for the shower to be free. Oh, Rosa, babe. Such startling good things are coming for her. She really will lose her mind. News this big cripples authors. They get overwhelmed. Can never write a second book. She's going to need a lot of my emotional support. Yikes – who's going to emotionally support *me* through all this? I soothe another pang for Mum as we hurtle into another tunnel. I'm glad I'm about to see Lauren. I can happy-dump all on her – get it out of my system before the baby shower. Honestly, how the hell do I have to attend a baby shower today? I have so, so, so, much to do.

We shoot out of the tunnel and my phone pings again. I grasp it up, already grinning. Maybe it's another studio? Or another editor? Nothing in my phone can bring bad news today.

Or . . . so I think.

A message from Jeremy. Initially, I get a flutter of excitement. It must be his plans for date five. I get a small pulse between my legs as I remember date four. Our bodies slick with sweat, the taste of salt on his skin, the windows of his flat wide open for everyone in London to hear us.

Jeremy:
Morning Steff. How's it going? That big submission coming off? I hope so. You're a really good person and I really want good things to happen for you.

He's sent it but I see he's still typing. 'What the fuck?' I mutter. My heart's twitching. This isn't a normal message, or a flirty message. It's weird. *I'm a 'good person'?* What's that got to do with date five? I rub my heart again as I wait for the second message to arrive.

Jeremy:
I know you're flat out with work this week, but, to be honest, it's been useful for me to have some time to think. This really sucks, Steff, I'm sorry but I don't think this has a future. You're amazing. You know I think you're amazing. But the whole kids thing . . . I've

realised this week it is a dealbreaker for me. Sorry. I
would call but I know how swamped you are. Sorry
again x

I shake my head and let out an exasperated noise as date five
with Jeremy turns to vapour. It hurts instantly, and more than
it should, considering how many times I've been here before. I
know the Little Women think I'm this hardened, wisened dater,
out having exciting dates with exciting men, with the sort of
good sex that can only come from the smell of a stranger's
fresh pheromones . . . But, holy hell, it's also quite painful and
lonely and soul-destroying at times too. *Of course,* Jeremy's
sent this message now. Today. The best day of my career to
date. *Of course,* I have to be reminded of my malfunction right
now – keep my ego in check.

*The whole kids thing . . . I've realised it's a dealbreaker for
me . . .*

Weird how it's always *after* I've had sex with a man that
they decide it's a dealbreaker. No matter how much I delay
sleeping with them, they're always like, '*Wow, it's so refreshing
to date a women in her thirties who's not desperate to have kids,*'
right up until the moment they ejaculate inside of me. Then,
suddenly, it's like, '*Actually, the child-free thing is weird. I want
children after all.*' Like, I dunno, they're fucking resentful that
the spunk in the condom they're still wearing has been rejected
by me.

I lay my head against the grainy train window and keep
rubbing my heart.

Maybe I'm just bad at sex . . .

Then why do men always tell me the opposite?

I was there with Jeremy. I didn't imagine it. The noises he made. I'm not bad at sex.

Oh my God, for actual fuck's sake. How dare he send this message right now? How dare he ruin this?

No. I refuse. I will not let him ruin this.

What a coward too . . . sending a message. This man thinks he can be a father when he can't even dump a woman face to face? The actual cheek of it – this dysfunctional selfish cretin thinking he has any right reproducing.

I am so sick of this happening.

How many times am I going to have to relive this before I meet a man who wants what I want?

Last week, I read this great article about being child-free that summed it up so much. That, initially, you're called a 'unicorn' because it's so rare and brilliant to be a woman in your early thirties but not desperate to get knocked up. When the situation inevitably comes up around date three, (*I now know not to sleep with anyone until at least date three unless I'm very very horny*) as it sort of has to when you're dating in your thirties, I can visibly see men's faces relax when I tell them I'm not looking to start a family. One literally, theatrically, mopped his brow (didn't shag him, obviously). But the relief is short-lived. Once they realise they're out of the frying pan of *quick-quick hurry up, say you love me, move in with me, propose please, you cannot fucking waste my time, I'm 32 don't you know, it's actually basically against my human rights to not be sure about committing when every egg I ovulate each month basically crumbles to dust, GET ME PREGNANT YOU FUCKING MAN CHILD or go date a 23-year-old who wasn't alive when the Spice Girls were*

Number One . . . Yeah, anyway, once the heat is off them, they have a few weeks of feeling free and thinking I'm the best thing since fucking . . . *kimchi* . . . and then it switches. It turns to suspicion.

Oh, this article put it so well. **'Childfree and free to be pissed off.'** What was that paragraph? The reason I re-shared it, I felt so seen. I sort of wanted all my exes to see it and realise what shits they are.

'My friends keep telling me to be patient. That soon all the divorcees will be joining the dating pool. Men who've had their children, and it's broken the marriage apart, and how exciting to meet a sexy unicorn woman who doesn't want her own kids. Perfect. And I'm like . . . "Excuse me. The whole point of being child-free is just that . . . I don't want children. Let alone to look after someone else's fucking children every other week." Also, I'm not particularly attracted to men who leave the mothers of their children. Unless they've been chased out of the house at knifepoint (and, to be honest, with weaponised incompetence being as bad as it is, even then I can hardly blame a knife-wielding wife), then I simply cannot get a lady-boner for someone who left the person who grew an actual human for them, almost died pushing it out, and then sacrificed their career, identity, tits and pension raising it . . . But, oh yay, come into my dating pool. Let me count my spoils. Mmm mother-leavers. Lucky selfish child-free me!'

God, I loved that bit. I mean, there were other bits of the article I didn't agree with, and the author didn't seem particularly nice. But the stuff about the dating was spot on. And here we are. Dumped.

I sigh and return my head to the window, watching the growing suburbs flash by. It hurts. This message really hurts. I can't believe someone called Jeremy has made me hurt this much. Nobody gets their heart broken by a *Jeremy*. Not that it's broken. My heart is so toughened these days it's like a slab of overcooked beef. Jeremy will be forgotten this time next year, just like all the other losers before him who came, saw, lied to me about not wanting kids, conquered, then fucked off and then implied I was the selfish one. But it stings it's happened today. On the cusp of everything taking off – always there to remind me only one thing is allowed to go right in my life at the same time. Well, if it was a choice between Jeremy or launching the best boutique agency in the UK, Jeremy, you can fuck off quite frankly. I'm going to make a million pounds in the next 72 hours, just you wait.

Steffi:
Aaaand, weirdly enough, grown men who can't handle having an adult conversation with a woman they've slept with are *my* dealbreaker, so I guess we're even. You're a child to do this by text. Speaking of the child issue, let's hope, if you ever have a daughter, they sleep with men who have more respect for women then you've just shown me.

I send it and then block him just as we head into another tunnel. I promise myself to be over it by the second we emerge, and, for about seven seconds, as the train roars in my ears, I close my eyes and let myself feel the pain. Then the world turns brighter behind my eyelids. I open them and he's in the past, alongside all the others. Now, Rosa. *Blood Moon.*

Nina Baldwin.

What. A. Day.

I need to call her right away. That will cheer me up. Honestly, telling clients they're going to become published authors is literally the best part of my job. What other careers mean you get to make people's dreams come true, other than, I dunno, TV game-show hosts? And this won't be any phone call. Rosa's going to be richer than she knows what to do with. She can write for a living forever – not that she'll even need the money after this book. I bring up her number, an authentic smile truly on my face now, and I bash 'call'. An even better surprise as it's a Saturday. I told her we wouldn't hear anything until Monday at the earliest.

My phone beeps instead of connecting. I frown and see I've got no reception in this particular blip of suburban hell. The reception bar loads up and I try again, but, nope, we go through a fourth tunnel. I sigh with frustration. I don't want this phone call to be ruined by bad coverage. I also won't be able to do it at Nicki's. I'll have to wait til I get to the train station and call Rosa then, before meeting Lauren. It won't take more than ten minutes, and I'll treat her to an iced coffee from Starbucks to say sorry.

Lauren won't mind a ten-minute delay, will she? Ten minutes is nothing.

CHARLOTTE

Wow. This house is just perfect for today. Perfect.

Nicki didn't do it justice when she was describing it to me. In fact, she was practically lacklustre about her parents' new place, but wow, it's like Grand Designs-*tastic*. A glass cathedral in the sprawling downs countryside. I whip out my phone and take some pictures, because that's surely what the house was built for – content. I put my tray onto the gravel and carefully pluck out one of the cupcakes. I hold it in front of the house and take a picture, uploading it with 'Here for the baby shower for the luckiest baby in the universe!!!!!!!!! Little Women reunited!!!!'. I tag Nicki in, even though she rarely uses social media, then Lauren and Steffi. I return the cupcake to its slot in the tray and bend down to pick them up. OK. I have been too ambitious in how much I can carry from the car in one go. I wish I didn't have such tiny child arms. I hop up the wooden steps to the front door, knocking on the glass with my elbow. As I wait for someone to answer, I notice that the cupcake icing is melting just from two minutes of being out in this heat. No no no. Don't ruin the perfect swirl of the butter-cream. I watched so many videos on how to get the right flick of my wrist for those. People think you angle the piping bag at a 45-degree angle, but you actually want to ice cupcakes dead on. I made two batches of practice cupcakes to get it right . . . Oh, it's a shame about the heat. The surroundings would've been glorious but everywhere looks like straw. I hope there's enough fridge space for all the food. I brought three coolers but maybe I should've got five, I— Oh, there's Nicki. Wow, she is so pregnant!

Through the glass door, I see her slightly warped shape waddle into view.

'Happy baby shower,' I squeal when she opens the door, putting the cupcakes down again so I can hug her.

'Charlotte. Wow, you're early. I'm not dressed yet . . . sorry.'

'You're huge,' I squeal again. 'So huge.' Hugging her is proving to be quite difficult. Nicki is almost six feet tall and the most pregnant I've ever seen anyone. My head essentially lines up to the top of her bump.

'Cheers, Charlotte,' she raises both eyebrows as I pull away.

'You look gorgeous, of course,' I add. 'Glowing. Perfect. Your hair! Your skin!'

She genuinely grins then. 'Thank you. I feel like a gross fat sweaty whale, but I'll try and see myself through Charlotte eyes. Wow, those cupcakes look amazing. Did you make them?'

I nod and wave her away as she tries to lower herself to pick them up. 'No no. I'll get them. Wow. Air con. Amazing. I was so worried.'

I pick up the tray and follow Nicki into the main living space. She moves slowly, her hand on her lower back. Does she have pelvic girdle pain? She should go to an osteopath. I know a great one in Richmond. The cool air feels amazing and the cupcakes practically sigh in relief.

'Yeah, the air con is essential. My parents bought a portable unit. It's only on in this room, and means we can't have the big windows open, but it will hopefully stop everything melting. I've been standing in front of it the last ten minutes,' she smiles again. 'It's why I'm not dressed.'

'Perfect. This is just perfect.' My eyes dart around the room, making calculations about what to put where. Wow, this view. The whole back wall is solid glass and there's sprawling fields wherever you look. They're mostly dull and brown but the sight still makes me want to burst into a rendition of 'Jerusalem'. The air con unit hums aggressively in the corner, a giant tube running out of it into the glass doors. It ruins the aesthetic slightly – maybe I can cover that with some bunting? I spot the peony wall. 'Oh, fab! The flowers are here,' I say. Why have they put it there? In the corridor, so there's no space to take photos? 'Do you love them? Aren't they the best?'

'They're . . . there's a lot of them.'

'Your baby is *so* lucky to be born in peony season. Did you plan it?'

'Oddly enough, no.'

'You'll be able to give them peonies for their birthday every year.'

'I guess. Not sure a baby is going to be that bothered by flowers though. Er . . . what are they for?'

I put the cakes down on the charcoal countertop and bounce over to check it out in more detail. 'For photos, Nicki! It's going to be such a lovely backdrop. I've got some props too. In my car, along with some other stuff.'

'Props?'

Why does she sound suspicious?

'You know, just silly things. Some cardboard storks, nappies, dolls, etc. It's going to be hilarious.' People always think photo booths are cheesy until they're actually in one – then you have to basically yank them out. You can't go wrong with a photo booth, that's what I say. Flower walls too. Scorn all you like but they have a siren call.

Did Nicki just shudder? Surely not? She went wild at the photo booth in my wedding. We got given a copy of the pictures and I think Nicki was in at least 75 per cent of them. She waddles over to the air con and stands in front of it again, putting her hands out like she's warming them in front of a fire. She lifts her top up, closes her eyes, and lets the air attack her bump. I can't help but look at her stretched stomach with the popped bellybutton.

'Sorry, give me a moment,' she says, eyes still closed in bliss. 'I swear I have to do this every ten minutes to stop my foetus boiling inside of me. The baby's going to come out fucking . . . poached if this weather continues.'

'I'm going to get stuff from the car before it all melts.'

'Do you want some help? My dad's around here somewhere being useless. But he knows how to carry stuff.'

'That would be great, thanks. I don't think I've seen your dad since your wedding.'

'He's the same. I'll go find him. Give me another second.'

I gasp quietly as I see the baby move beneath her skin. I expect tears to sting, but none arrive. In fact, I get a thrill. In eight months' time, if everything goes OK, my stomach will look like that. My body will be stretched, my face doughy, my ankles double their size. I will be at my own baby shower, which will be very difficult to organise as I've used up all my manifestation ideas on today.

It's too hot to wait for Nicki's dad, so I run back outside, the heat feeling even heavier compared to the air con of the glass house. Just as I'm trying to fit as many baked goods onto my tiny arms as possible, a car pulls up, and out comes Nicki's mum carrying four giant bags of ice.

'Oh my, Charlotte. How are you?' She greets me with a wide smile. 'Wow, those all look amazing. Do you need any help?'

'Hello Mrs Davies. Yes, that would be great.'

She swings all the ice into one hand and loads two cupcake trays onto her other arm. I don't know why Nicki whinges about her mum and how 'stressful' she is. She unpacks my car in five minutes flat, and, even during that time, devises a 'system' for what goes where. We'd just finishing floating the dummies when Nicki's dad comes downstairs wearing the most ridiculous pair of shorts. 'I'm here to unpack the car,' he announces, like he's bringing actual cavalry.

'Too late Mr Davies,' I say, plopping the last dummies in. 'But let's get a photo of the three of you in front of the peony wall.' I beckon Nicki over. 'Come on, closer closer.' Nicki's dad stares at the flower wall like it's made out of triffids. 'That's what this is for then?' He asks.

'For photos, Dad,' Nicki replies, turning sideways and cradling her bump while I grin. Nicki acts reluctant, but she also knows her angles. 'Literally just for photos.'

'I . . . I'm not sure I get it.'

'Just smile,' I tell him. 'Stand behind Nicki. Yes, that's it. Well done. Cheese on the count of three. Ready? One, two, three, cheese!'

I take about twelve snaps so there's hopefully one they all like. What did people do before smartphones? I have vague memories of getting film developed in Boots when I was a child. If you gurned at a key historical moment, you were stuck with that gurn. How did we all cope?

'You all look wonderful. Right.' I check the time on my phone. 'Lauren and Steffi will be here in an hour. Let me just check my spreadsheet.'

'Spreadsheet?' Nicki asks, peering over my shoulder.

'When have I not had a spreadsheet?' I ask her, and we grin at each other.

'True. Umm, can I quickly look at the photos you just took?' I smile again, this time to myself. Told you! Nicki's secretly as basic as all of us. I hand her my phone and she swipes through.

'Oh, I look horrific. My face is double the size! Can you take them again?'

'Of course.'

'Dad!' Nicki herds him back like he's a dog on the loose. To be fair, he was about to stick his finger in the icing of one of the cupcakes. 'Back here. We're taking the photo again. I look horrific.'

It takes thirty attempts before there's one everyone's happy with. 'At least the peony wall looks amazing in every photo,' Nicki grumbles, as she reluctantly pings herself the one photo they all like.

'That's the point,' I say, keen to get my phone back. I hadn't scheduled this photoshoot to last over ten minutes and I'm keen to return to the spreadsheet and see where I can make up time. Also, I worry Matt will message while she's holding it and ruin the surprise for later.

'OK. So, what's next on the list?' Nicki asks. 'I've got a burst of energy, give me a job.'

'No jobs for you. Well, hang on.' I skip over to my wheelie suitcase and come back with a package.

'What's this?' Nicki holds it up, squinting. 'A bump mask?'

I nod. 'I thought you'd need some downtime before everyone arrives. This is a sheet mask for your bump.'

'A *what?*'

'I got one that's supposed to be cooling and hydrating. I've given you 45 minutes of self-care in the spreadsheet. I'm afraid we're down to 33 minutes because things have run over a bit. But look here, the instructions say you leave it on for twenty, so there's still plenty of time.'

'I never knew such things existed.' She holds it gingerly between two fingers. 'I can't just laze about while you set everything up though.'

'Nicki, it's your baby shower. You're supposed to just relax and enjoy.'

'Let me help for a few minutes, so I don't feel like a giant useless blimp, then I promise I'll have a nap.' She claps and her mum stands to attention like a hyper dog, awaiting instruction. 'What needs doing?'

I feel a ripple of stress. How long is she going to help for, exactly? And will her nap then clash with the tea and catch-up time I've scheduled in with the other Little Women? She's supposed to rest *now,* not later. No, no, no, Charlotte. Stop it. Come on. Things don't go to plan. That's OK. And you've built the spreadsheet to include 20 per cent flexibility.

'We don't want to set up the food yet because it's too hot,' I tell her. 'But balloons need blowing up for the arch, while I set up the rest of the games.'

Nicki grins. 'Perfect. Show me balloons. I can blow balloons.'

'And, Mrs Davies? I was hoping you'd be able to baby proof? And then set up the cots upstairs? I've got two travel cots. They should be easy enough to assemble.'

Her mum gives me a huge hug. 'Oh, Charlotte. You think of everything, don't you? I can't wait until it's your turn, you're going to make such a good mother someday.'

'Mum!' Nicki grabs her arm. 'Sorry Charlotte. She . . . er . . . she . . .' It's too awkward a sentence to finish and we all blush against the slate of the kitchen tiles.

'It's OK,' I tell Nicki.

'What is it?' her mum asks. 'Sorry love. I was just saying—'

'So, what's on the spreadsheet?' Nicki cuts her off. 'Is there anything for Dad to do other than eat the food before anyone arrives? I CAN SEE YOU DAD,' she calls, and we all whip around to see him finger-deep in a cupcake in the kitchen.

'I'm just taste-testing them,' he replies with no guilt whatsoever. Nicki will no doubt put this all down to male entitlement or something, but I'm actually quite pleased the cupcakes are that irresistible.

'Are they OK?' I ask him. 'Not too much rose water?'

He makes a perfection sign back, and takes that as a free pass to pick it up and stuff it into his mouth.

'Please give him a job so I don't kill him,' Nicki whispers.

'When you're done taste-testing, do you mind setting up some black-out blinds for us?' I ask him. 'To go in the napping rooms?'

He gives a thumbs up with his mouth full of pink icing and Nicki rolls her eyes.

We all set to work, and it's nice it being just Nicki and I while her parents create the napping stations.

'Sorry I didn't stuff the goody bags until now,' I tell her, as we set up a mini factory line on the table.

72

Nicki's holding up the personalised shower gel bottles and tilting her head. 'No, it's fine. I just . . . this is so much Charlotte. I'm sure nobody minds about goody bags . . . but, they're lovely. Thank you.'

I hand her a party bag decorated with storks that's ready to be finished off with the bottles. 'It's nothing. I love you. You're having a baby. That's wonderful. I told you, today is going to be perfect.'

She takes the bag, plops in the bottle and adds in an iced biscuit and a flourish of scented confetti. She won't meet my eye. 'Sorry about my mum just now.'

'Honestly, it's fine.' I hand her another bag, wanting to keep up momentum so I don't blab out my news. It's way too early to tell anyone and it's her day. I can't overshadow it like that. Lauren once came back from her sister's wedding and said a bloke had proposed during the reception. Can you imagine? I almost had to lie down when she told me.

'Are you OK? With today? Everything . . .' Nicki trails off.

I hand her two more bags. 'I'm more than OK. I can't wait.'

'But with . . .'

Oh, Nicki. I'm fine. I'm so fine I've hand-baked sixty cupcakes. What does she want? Me to wear a flashing *I'm fine* badge at all times?

'I'm honestly so, so, happy for you.'

And it's true, mostly. I've not let my own fertility journey make me sour and unable to share in my friend's happiness. I've been determined to have grace. When I tried manifesting a baby, part of The Secret is acting like your dream has already come true. So, I imagined I was as fertile as Queen bloody Victoria was, so, of course, I'd be *delighted* when my friends fell pregnant one by one, almost without trying. For the whole first year of us trying. '*Congratulations, congratulations. Oh, well done, what magical news. Congratulations.*' I even managed to grit my teeth and grin through the accidentals. '*Wow, unplanned, eh? Gosh, yes, it must be hard that you weren't prepared to get pregnant right now. But happy accident, yes?*' I liked every photo scan that arrived on my feed – commenting '*CONGRATULATIONS WHAT AMAZING NEWS. OMG WHAT A LUCKY BABY TO HAVE YOU AS PARENTS.*' One day it would be my turn. One day I'd get to post the scan. One day I'd complain about morning sickness or ask for advice online about the best maternity pillows.

One day, one day, one day.

Then, after two years of me trying and two failed IVF attempts, Lauren fell pregnant.

'A bit of a shock,' she confided, followed with, 'Sorry Charlotte.'

I finally got jealous when an old school friend posted on Instagram about her miscarriage. Not even a post about her baby, but her traumatic miscarriage.

'*At least you know you can get pregnant,*' a dark voice whispered.

The Secret wasn't working. Good karma wasn't being returned. My ravaged body couldn't keep up the pretence anymore.

I didn't react to the post. I pretended it hadn't happened. She won't have noticed. She was being deluged with support, and people telling her how brave and inspirational she was. That's when I realised I might be getting a little bit broken.

And, the next week, when Nicki told the Little Women group chat that she and Matt were pregnant.

'A little bit unexpected, as we'd only just started trying, but here we go . . .'

. . . something really broke.

Nicki had sent me a private message first.

> Hey lovely. How are things? It's been too long as always. I thought about calling you, but I figured you'd perhaps want some time to react to this news and be allowed to feel whatever you feel without pressure, so I'm messaging you instead. I'm 13 weeks pregnant. I'm about to tell the other LWs but wanted to give you a heads up. I can imagine this news will bring up mixed emotions for you, and I love you and I really hope and believe this will happen for you one day soon. Lots of love xxx

I read it and reread it.

It was so thoughtful. So well considered. And yet I still found myself saying, 'Oh fuck you,' out loud.

It's so easy to be magnanimous when you can get pregnant through fucking . . . osmosis, just by holding a Clear Blue test in Boots or something.

How did she know I wasn't delighted for her? How dare she make that assumption? She has no idea what it's like. *Fuck you, Nicki, and your bulging uterus. Fuck you.*

Then I started crying.

And I was still crying when Seth came home from work drinks five hours later. I showed him the message and all he had to say was 'I see,' and I knew he truly did as he was the only one who'd gone through this hell with me. He cried a bit too, and we sat with our backs to the wall until past midnight, just steeping in our sadness like forgotten teabags. When we finally scraped ourselves into bed, we both lay awake, staring at the ceiling, unable to sleep in our pain. It had hurt too much for too long now and it needed to stop hurting. Seth and I had become miserable and exhausted from years of false, expensive hope, prearranged lovemaking, invasive tests, and horrible success statistics where you slowly realise you're the rule, not the exception. I had to let go.

'I'm going to organise Nicki's baby shower,' I told him in the dark. 'I'm going to make it the best baby shower the world has ever known.'

'What? Charlotte, no . . .' He turned over and kissed my shoulder. 'It will hurt too much.'

'I'm going to give her everything I ever wanted. I have to let go, Seth. We both need to.'

'There's still hope. Another round of . . .'

'No.' I shook my head, beyond resolute. 'I'm organising her baby shower. I may as well put time and energy into a baby that's actually going to exist rather than the false hope of one existing.'

He hugged me close to him and kissed the top of my head. 'If that's what you need to do then that's what you need to do.'

We'd both cried until morning.

And now, here I am. Stuffing party bags for Nicki, with Nicki. Free of the jealousy. Free of the pain – apart from mild cramping in my stomach that Google reassures me is from implantation. It wasn't my plan but the universe has rewarded me for my emotional maturity and graciousness under immense pain. And, wow, the relief. The relief that my body *can* get pregnant. It can produce a urine stream that turns two lines blue on an expensive stick of plastic. We didn't even conceive through IVF! I literally manifested this baby through positive energy. And, if this party goes perfectly, if everything goes to plan, then I know that my baby will make it to full-term. Today has to be perfect, everything depends on it.

'Well you're amazing, Charlotte,' Nicki tells me, reaching over and squeezing my hand. 'I don't know how you do all this, and teach, and also look so well-groomed all of the time. You've been so strong in the face of . . . everything.'

The white elephant loitering between us isn't an elephant but Nicki's straining stomach. She takes a few more bags off me and adds the finishing touches. Her voice shifts and she glances at me sideways as she adds confetti. 'Did you . . . err . . . see that article Steffi posted last week?'

She asks innocently enough but I can hear edge. I put down the bag I'm holding. 'The one about being child-free?' I ensure my voice is totally neutral.

'Yeah, that one.'

'I saw it.'

I start working again. I put a lollypop in the bag and hand it to her.

'And?' she presses.

'And what?'

Nicki holds the bag and adds nothing to it, looking at me full-on now. 'You don't think it was a bit . . . insensitive?'

I refuse to nibble. Only good energy today, please, Nicki. 'If it's how she feels, I guess that's how she feels.'

'*Really?* After everything you've been through with . . . you know . . . you didn't feel . . .?'

She's surveying my face closely, looking for an entry point. I know I would make her day if I lay into Steffi right now, but I'm not going to. When all that Steffi stuff kicked off, Lauren and I made a solemn promise to never be drawn into it, knowing the Little Women would disintegrate if we did. I even made Lauren write the solemn promise out on paper and put it in my safe, that's how important this group is to me. I'd really hoped everyone would be over it by now, but those two are determined to piss each other off. OK, yes, privately I admit, Steffi posting that article really messed with my frequency. I still wouldn't have told that to Nicki.

'It wasn't tactful, no,' I say breezily.

'I just don't see the fuss about the whole child-free thing,' Nicki begins. 'Like, nobody is thinking about her that much. It's just not A Thing.'

I raise both eyebrows and determinedly pick up another goody bag. 'She told me she's got you a super nice present today,' I say. 'She's really chuffed with herself.'

'Oh . . .'

'And I think she has a hard time dating and not wanting kids. I don't think men are very kind to her about it.'

In fact, I know they're not. Steffi may game face around Nicki, but not me. She has rung me crying many times, asking to come stay for the weekend. I always quite like it when Steffi gets dumped. Obviously, I want her to find her penguin, but I also really enjoy sleeping in my granny annexe with her, watching Disney films, and giving each other manicures.

'Oh . . . that's shit.'

It's certainly time to change the subject and I break into a smile. 'I'm so excited for us all to be together again. It's been too long. I can't wait to see Woody! Isn't it crazy he's going to be in the same year at school as your baby? What if they fall in love?

I visibly watch Nicki take the hint. She smiles and follows my lead. 'It's mad isn't it? Oh my God, a Little Women wedding. Can you imagine? I wish I knew what it was going to be.'

I push her playfully on the shoulder. 'I thought you wanted a surprise?'

Nicki rubs her stomach. 'I know. I'm an idiot. I made such a big thing of it but now I'm too proud to tell Matt I've changed my mind.'

We laugh, then stop as it makes us too hot. Only two bags left. I sprinkle them with goodies and pass them on. My armpits are starting to smell already. I've been too scared to wear any deodorant in case it causes miscarriage. There's no evidence from anywhere that's even a thing, but I'm getting this *vibe* from my Dove stick, and won't apply it. 'Not long to wait now at least.' I poke Nicki's tummy, feigning ignorance about today's masterplan.

'I guess. Only a month more to wait.' She sprinkles the last of the confetti. 'Voila! Oh, I can't wait to see Woody and Lauren and everyone. It's been so long. Thanks so much, Charlotte.'

'I told you, today's going to be SO GREAT.'

If I say it enough, it will manifest. If I believe it enough, it will come true. 'Right, these are all done,' I say, collecting the bags up. 'You should take some Me Time before the others get here. Your mum and I can set everything else up.'

Nicki stretches and yawns, her top riding up so I get another peek of weird alien skin. 'You know what? I will nap. The baby woke me at five. Thanks again Charlotte, for everything.'

'It's going to be perfect.'

'So you keep saying.'

She staggers out holding her lower back. I watch as she pauses in front of the air con unit, blasting her stomach with it, then she picks up a handful of crisps from a bowl on the main table and waddles up towards the bedrooms.

'Nicki! Wait!' I hold up her baby bump mask. 'You forgot this!'

When the door closes behind her to keep the cool air in, I check the spreadsheet. I'd scheduled five minutes downtime after Nicki went for her rest, so I could rest myself. Seth's obsessed with me resting since we found out. But, ticking off my to-do list is more restful than sitting down and now is my only chance to set up the surprise. I get my handbag from where I tucked it next to the front door, and I carefully lift out the smoke grenade. I twist the device around in my palm, smiling as I imagine the joy it's going to cause. Right. Let me read the instructions again.

'*Take off cap, pull ring pull, point away from body and face . . .*'

Right, safety first. Especially with this tinderbox of conditions outside. I rummage in a cupboard til I find a mop bucket, then I fill it with water and drag it towards the sliding doors. The heat has intensified in the short time I've been inside. I've already cancelled the egg and spoon race sadly, which happily buys me twenty extra minutes. It's peaceful to be away from the roar of the air con, and I stand and appreciate all the nature sounds for a moment. The chorus of birdsong and rustle of leaves in the soft breeze. In the distance, the low drone of a neighbouring lawnmower drifts over. Maybe, once the baby comes, we should move to the countryside? If the baby comes . . .

I scan the decking to figure out where best to plant the smoke grenade. I rang Matt yesterday to finalise the plan and he's going to hide under the decking until he hears me call attention to the vagina piñata outside the window. Then Matt will tug the grenade, release the coloured smoke, and then step through it, holding his sign saying 'It's A Girl!' I worried that Nicki will be so surprised her waters will break, but I googled it and that's apparently an urban myth.

'I'm so excited it's a girl,' Matt said. 'A really little woman to join your club.'

I actually cannot wait for today. The stars are aligned. Mercury isn't in retrograde. Good karma is sprinkling itself onto us like confetti.

Right, if I wedge the firework here, between the decking, with only the top out – people won't notice it, will they? I carefully take the top off – it's like peeling back a cylinder can of sardines. All Matt has to do is tug the ring pull. There. Done. I scan around and drag over a plant pot of summer pansies, arranging it slightly in front so the cylinder doesn't show. I take a quick photo and ping it off to Matt, with ten firework emojis and ten heart-eyes emojis.

And finally, *safety first.* I put the mop bucket at the bottom of the steps in case anything goes wrong. But it won't. It can't. The universe and I forbid it.

Evidence item no. 9

Attached photograph shows four of the suspects, posing under a balloon arch outside Vista Cottage. Data from the smartphone indicates it was taken at precisely 9:37am, almost four hours before the fire broke out. All suspects are smiling.

NICKI

I love Charlotte but she's too much sometimes, she really is. I don't even want to know what's happening on the other side of the bedroom wall. I can hear doors sliding, chairs squeaking as they're moved. I wouldn't be surprised if I come out in 30 minutes and she's turned the whole room into a giant womb, and we all have to climb through a crepe paper birth canal to get to the cupcakes.

With that all being said, this bump sheet mask is actually amazing.

I wasn't going to use it, but then I knew I'd feel bad about lying when she inevitably grills me. *Did you love it? Was it moisturising enough? Has it cooled you down? Can I see if your skin is any different?* So, I clambered back on top of the guest bed and slid it out of its foil packaging. I bunged it goo-side down on my stomach and let out a moan of actual joy.

'Jesus Christ that feels good.'

The baby twisted with shock at the temperature change, and I watched as their foot poked through the mask, making itself a little tent. Then they relaxed, and so did I, closing my eyes and drifting off until I was just woken now, maybe ten minutes later, by my parents arguing through the wall.

'I thought you were putting up the black-out blinds,' my mum hiss-shouts.

'I am.'

'But you've not done them.'

'I will.'

'You're literally just lying on the bed in your shorts.'

The argument diminishes to mutters and instructions and the aggressive ripping noise of double-sided Velcro being applied to window frames. How did Charlotte find black-out blinds big enough for these wall windows? Did she pay for them herself? I start adding up the things I've seen already – the flower wall that looks like it's been shoplifted from the Kardashian household, all those pastel dummies floating in the roll-top bath, the food . . . the endless food. Charlottes's always been wealthy and, without meaning to, married Seth, the nicest hedge fund manager you'll ever meet, and became even richer. It's not like today is expensive for her . . . but still . . . I should stop being such an ungrateful cow.

My phone beeps again. Initially, I kept leaping at it, thinking it was Phoebe, but over the past hour it's gone off nonstop – my inbox cluttered with people telling me they're excited, or on their way, or they're sorry but they might be a bit late as they didn't realise it was so out in the sticks, or the inevitable '*I'm so sorry hon but I can't make it, present in the post.*' I keep expecting Steffi to cancel and sort of wish she would. I'm annoyed Charlotte wouldn't admit that ridiculous child-free article was awful and so obviously posted as a dig at me. I can't believe Steffi can't just be happy for me, after all this time. She always has to make out that her single life is so glamorous, and exciting, and invigorating, compared to the security that I have with Matt. Well, you know what I find invigorating, Steffi? Being in a healthy relationship, rather than being pressured into choking and anal by some 27-year-old porn addict you met on Hinge. I read the news, I know what it's like out there.

I'm not jealous at all, in fact I feel sorry for her. It must all be so empty.

Maybe that beep is actually Steffi cancelling. I go to check it, anticipating my gleeful annoyance at being let down. But typically, because I thought it wouldn't be from Phoebe, it is.

'Oh wow.' I struggle to push myself up so I'm sitting with my back against the headboard.

Phoebe:
You're surprised? Have you SEEN your invite? Nicki, I thought I knew you. X

She sends through a photo of an invitation on a desk. One dutifully picked out and sent by Charlotte.

'Oh hell no,' I say again, zooming in to see it properly. The thing is so pastel, I'm surprised it's not made of Parma Violets so you could eat it afterwards. An illustrated pair of baby booties spell out the name 'Phoebe' with entwined laces. Underneath, some impressive cursive reads, '*Consider this your booties call . . .*'

I take a slow blink and cringe as I imagine my guests receiving this and thinking I picked it. Why did I give Charlotte such free rein.? *Bootie call?* Where did she even think that up? How is she real sometimes?

Phoebe:
And that's not all . . .

Another photo arrives, of pink and blue pastel glitter all over Phoebe's carpet.

Phoebe:
This fell out of the bloody envelope. You never told me you were a fucking terrorist?

Oh shit. No. No no no. She put *glitter* in the envelopes? Doesn't she know there's a company that sends glitter to your enemies as an act of revenge? How many friends had to get their hoover out, sighing and cursing me?

Phoebe:
It came with a note that said the glitter is plastic-free. Cos that's the biggest concern I have, considering it's going to live in my carpet FOREVER. It's like two Smurf were atrociously murdered in my flat, but, don't worry, as long as the fish aren't eating it.

I rush to reply, desperate for Phoebe to know this isn't me.

Nicki:
Mate, I'm so so sorry. A friend organised today. She's really into Pinterest. I had no idea.
Phoebe:
No worries. See you later.
Mate x

I wince, just as my alarm goes, informing me it's time to peel off my stomach mask. It leaves a layer of goo across my bump and I try and rub it in, resorting to wiping my hands and the backs of them too in order to soak up the excess. Their little foot pokes out at my touch and I smile. 'I'm scared to leave this room,' I tell my bump. 'What has Charlotte done out there? What if she's installed an actual shower?'

When I emerge, I see everything through Phoebe's eyes and turn neon with embarrassment.

'Oh, wow, Charlotte. You've . . . er . . . been so busy.'

'Nicki! How was the sheet mask? Did it work? Was it lovely? I hope you rested.'

Phoebe's scornful eyes take in the transformed space. She's not recreated a womb out of crepe paper, but she's come close. Blue and pink balloons decorate every corner. There's a giant poster of what looks like a vagina, with a stack of sticky sperms to one side. Lined up against a wall is a queue of teddies, with their legs up in the air, nappies to one side of them. Baby photos of me litter every available surface that isn't covered in food. There's the cupcakes, but also fruit platters, tiny sandwiches covered in cling film, biscuits, bowls of crisps – all of them somehow baby blue or baby pink – even the sandwiches. The pink ones must be ham, but *blue* sandwiches? What the fuck are in those? I cross my arms, imagining Phoebe taking in all these details.

'It was great. Umm . . . this place looks . . . How did you do all this by yourself?'

'I wasn't by myself. Your mum helped.'

Just then, Mum comes through carrying a giant piece of laminated cardboard adorned with what looks like a picture round of celebrity babies. 'We've got a system,' Mum says, staring adoringly at Charlotte, like she's her rightful daughter. 'It's been great.'

'Charlotte. This is so much. I can't even . . .'

She comes over and tries to hug me again, even though it was a total fail earlier – like a Smurf trying to hold an egg.

'It's OK. You're welcome. I wanted to do it.'

And I know I sound like a totally ungrateful bitch, especially with everything Charlotte's been through, but I can't help but think this cornucopia of basic is nothing to do with me. Or for me. It's about Charlotte.

But would I be thinking this way if I didn't have my Phoebe goggles on? The lens I've not worn over my eyes in over a year. Which is the last time I saw her.

Until today.

I'm seeing her today.

LAUREN

Woody refused to feed before we left, so is now, predictably, screaming like a banshee on acid in the back of the car.

'Shh, darling. It's OK. It's OK. We're almost there. Almost there.'

I'm not sure why I'm lying to my pre-verbal infant about our journey time, which is still fifty minutes away, with Google predicting traffic on the A23, but I lie on nevertheless.

'Almost there, my baby. Almost there. Can you not play with Sophie the Giraffe? No? Oh, you've dropped her down the side. Ouch. You're hurting Mummy's ears, darling.'

A car honks me as I indicate into the right lane, and Woody startles and screams. Ear-piercing, can't concentrate, feel like your whole spine is being ripped out, screams. A scream that I know won't be satisfied by anything other than my breast.

'OK, OK. Don't cry darling. I'll find somewhere. Shh shh. Oh babe. *Babe!*'

The shrieks are so loud I'm half expecting a whale to come beach itself here in South Croydon. I indicate off the main road and start frantically scouring the residential streets for somewhere to pull over. It's all permit-only parking and speed bumps to enforce the 20mph limit. Woody screams like each speed bump is a personal violation as I thud over them, swearing under my breath, sweat pouring from my armpits, my cortisol levels turning half my body into pre-cancerous cells.

No parking spots. My boobs start leaking with each cry. I wish breast milk could just stop being so fucking sentient.

'I'M TRYING TO FIND A PARKING SPACE, BE PATIENT,' I find myself screaming at my own breasts, who ignore me, and bloom milk through both my ugly, sagging feeding bra and lacklustre navy dress of shattered dreams. Finally, eventually, there's a space. One that requires a reverse park, which I somehow manage despite the tirade of abuse ringing in my ears. I consider risking not buying a ticket, but this is Croydon, and I'll definitely get clamped and towed with Woody still attached to my breast in the backseat, so I make him wait for ten minutes longer as I have to download a fucking parking app and pay five pound seventy for my twenty-second stay. I open the back seat, yank him out, and he buries himself into my neck, inconsolable and red and hands grabbing, and here it comes again. The maternal guilt. Wave after wave of it, crashing over me as I yank down my front and let Woody rummage for what he needs. There's calm silence as I get the weird tug of my let-down and he guzzles, his pudgy hand reaching for my finger, then squeezing it and releasing it, his eyes fluttering shut.

'No, no. You can't sleep. Not yet. Not until I've got you back in the car seat.'

I check my phone. I am, madly, somehow, still on time. I left a 45-minute buffer for Woody to ruin timings, and it seems like my 'paranoia' – according to Tristan – is once again, paying off. According to our new sleep schedule, Woody was supposed to be asleep 20 minutes ago, and stay asleep for the length of the car journey. If he can drop off now (in the car seat, not attached to my breast), he'll still not quite get long enough, but it's not the end of the world. I switch him to the other side and he essentially dream-feeds until he empties that breast, while I see Steffi's message saying she's got the train on time. That's one of the many things I love about Steffi – she's always punctual. The goldilocks of the Little Women. Charlotte always arrives way too early. I've seen her loitering outside my house a full hour before she's due around, checking her phone for when it's not 'too' early to knock. And Nicki's always late with an air of slight grandioseness.

I unlatch Woody and burp him to wake him. He starts wailing as I put him back in the car seat, but I can't stay in this side street forever, so I take a deep breath, get into the front and start driving again. He cries for another ten minutes while I ride an adrenaline rollercoaster, twisting around as much as I dare without crashing, to offer assurances and to half chuck toys at him, hoping they'll land on his lap. Usually, Tristan drives and I sit in the back to placate him with songs and Melty Sticks. It's still so hellish we stay roughly within a mile radius of our home thinking it's not worth the stress.

Woody finally sleeps as Google tells me we have fifteen minutes to go. As I watch his eyes droop in the mirror we installed on the back seat, my shoulders loosen, and my grip gets lighter on the wheel. I'm alone again. For fifteen blissful minutes. I am just me, and this car and this traffic jam. A gasp of freedom and myselfness.

So, of course, I use this precious time to run through the horrid fight I had with Tristan just before I left.

'Where's his lunch?' I'd asked, returning from the bathroom where I'd spent ten minutes cleaning up my ruined lipstick mouth. 'You'd said you'd pack it?'

Tristan was throwing Woody in the air and catching him while he gurgled in delight.

'I wasn't sure what he was having,' Tristan said, rolling Woody down for a raspberry blow on his stomach. 'I didn't want to pack the wrong thing.'

'So you decided not to bother at all?'

'I just knew you'd get angry if I packed the wrong thing.'

I stormed over to the cupboard, flung the door open, and wrenched out a spaghetti bolognese pouch, a prune pouch, and a half-open packet of the maize Melty Sticks that are so expensive they must be made of saffron or something. I tossed them into the nappy bag with two spoons – one to feed Woody with, one for him to hold to gaslight him into thinking he's feeding himself as that's the only way he'll eat.

'What makes me angry,' I said. 'Is you're his actual DAD and you don't know how to feed him.'

Tristan, sensing trouble, put Woody down, who crawled off to probably stick his finger in a plug socket while necking a small battery. He got up off the floor, holding his hands up like the Melty Sticks in my palm were a loaded pistol. 'I know how to feed my own son, thank you very much, Lauren. Just not to your very precise standards.'

'Oh, so it's my fault? For being too controlling? How convenient.'

'You know I always get it wrong when I pack the food.'

'And you'd have thought you'd get it right by now!'

He'd sighed and pinched the top of his nose. 'The rules change every day. *Your* rules change every day.'

'They're not my fucking rules, Tristan. They're the fucking NHS weaning guidelines. And, you feeding him actual human food, full of salt, and not cut small enough so he might choke to death, like last time, isn't me being controlling. It's literally just trying to ensure our child doesn't die of heart disease before he's two.'

'A tiny bit of salt wasn't going to give him heart disease.'

'Oh thank you, Doctor and Qualified Nutritionist. I didn't know marketing managers were so multi-disciplined.'

We never used to be sarcastic with each other. Never used to get caught in the loop-the-loop of *'you're controlling'*, *'no, you're useless'* cliche of The Married. I sometimes hear how I talk to Tristan and words float into my head. *Henpecked. Nagging.* Before I got my break in kids publishing, I was an admin assistant in some start-up full of macho-geek IT workers, who every Friday would tease each other if they were allowed out that night from their wives. *'Have you a pass?'* they'd yell over the desks, all red and jeering, and applauding when the men gave a thumbs-up. Oh, those awful marriages, where men have to *ask permission* before they could go out and have fun and get drunk and live their life to the fullest. Oh, those awful, controlling wives, watching the clock, and asking *'when are you getting home'* and *'I can't believe you're too pissed to look after the kids now and too hungover to look after them tomorrow.'* Such killjoys, these women. I used to shudder at the thought of becoming like them.

No, scrap that.

I used to shudder at the thought of anyone *perceiving* me to be like that.

Now, I don't give a fuck. I'm too desperate.

Since Woody, now, yes, I do expect Tristan to have the common courtesy of asking if it's OK for him to stay out and have fun, leaving me alone to put his own child to bed, leaving me alone in the house all evening, not having fun. We've had so many fights about him staying out late without asking, leaving me to wrestle Woody's bedtime by myself, then stumbling in and waking me up at midnight, pissed and stinking, wanting to fuck me roughly in my prolapsed vagina, and then acting wounded when I push him off because I'm so angry and bitter about him waking me up, when sleep is so precious and I know I'll have to take Woody all tomorrow morning too, while he groans and complains about his hangover like it's not totally self-inflicted *AND* selfish because it means I can't get a break on a Saturday morning, when the weekend is the only escape from this relentless motherhood grind.

Anger pulses through me like a heartbeat while I sit in the traffic jam, having a thousand arguments with Tristan in my head – saying all I want to say. Then, before I've even finished my imaginary dramatic closing speech, the shame arrives, beating me around the face for not being a nicer and more self-sacrificing wife and mother.

Cool Mum doesn't mind when her husband goes out and leaves her alone all night. She's just glad he's having a good time.

Cool Mum doesn't need to instruct her husband on how to wean the baby. She's already got a weekly meal plan of organic baby-led weaning recipes that she batch-cooked on a Saturday morning, while her baby played quietly on the floor, and her happy husband slept off his hangover and morning blowie. She's put them into cute little pots and labelled them for each day.

Cool Mum doesn't argue with her husband all the time. They are a perfect family unit, romping around a beach somewhere, throwing their child into the air to the backdrop of a sunset, sneaking in great fucks during their baby's four-hour nap.

I can feel suburbia arriving as I drive closer to the station. The dense housing either side of the A road is now being punctuated by fields, further punctuated by little puddles of new-build complexes that I remember from GCSE Geography being called 'urban sprawl'. Once I pass two Land Rovers, I know we're almost there. I visited Nicki's hometown a few times when we were students and stayed at each other's during the long holidays. It was always so strange seeing my uni friends out of that context, and Nicki would give me an autobiographical tour of every passing pub or school or streetlight. *'That's where I got drunk for the first time and pissed myself in the carpark. That's where my friend, Mary, went to primary school but I couldn't go because it's catholic. That's the streetlight where I kissed this guy called Harry who played bass in this terrible punk band called We're Not Criminals.'*

I check my rearview mirror. Woody is still a sleeping cherub. I never love him more than when he's unconscious. It hits me then, the love – rushing in like the world's most powerful drug. Reminding me this darling baby is half Tristan's – how both our blood pumps through his veins. I shouldn't have shouted at Tristan. I should've just packed the nappy bag myself. He's exhausted too. He's stressed too. He doesn't go out as much as the other NCT blokes. I should count myself lucky really. One of them left their girlfriend with their six-week-old baby to go on a cycling holiday.

I remember the last time I was dumb enough to confide in Mum about how much Tristan and I are fighting.

'It's not good for the baby, Lauren. Hearing you row like that.'

'I know, I know. It's just . . . if Tristan could just be a tiny bit less useless.'

She sighed down the phone. 'Honestly, your generation expect too much of men. *Of course,* he's not as good with the baby stuff. You're the mother.'

'Mum, that's outdated and . . .'

'No, sorry. I know your generation just LOVE to ignore the basic facts of biology but I wouldn't let your father *near* you when you were a baby. Why would I want to? He was inept.'

I sighed and tried to explain. 'But that's weaponised incompetence. It's . . .'

Mum's scorn almost melted my phone. 'Weaponised what now? Crikey. No wonder you're always arguing. Just accept things how they are. Enjoy the baby! Men like *copers*, Lauren, so start coping better. Stop attacking your husband too. What good is that going to do any of you? You don't want him to leave you.'

I'd shaken my head and wiped under my eyes, wondering why I'd used up Woody's precious twenty-seven-minute nap thinking this would help. 'So, you're saying, I've got to suck it up to stay happily married,' I said, 'because wanting basic equality in parenting will result in divorce?'

'Probably . . .'

I could hear her shrug over the phone.

Cope better. Cope better. Cope better.

Not even *better.* Just fucking cope.

This is my mantra when I get to the train station two minutes before the train is due and panic ripples through my body for what this means for Woody's nap.

Cope better. Cope better. Cope better.

He'll wake up if the car's stationary for more than ten seconds. I'm already anxious Steffi's going to take too long getting into the car and that she won't do it quietly enough and that she'll also mind the craziness of sitting in total silence for the whole drive. I'm hoping years of friendship will mean she understands, but I don't know how to handle this unfamiliar station carpark. There's nowhere to circle it seems, so I do what any reasonable person would do, and I head straight out of it and decide to come back when the train gets here. Woody stirs as I wait to turn out of the carpark and my heart rate surges up a notch.

'No, shh, shh, we'll be moving soon.'

I get back on the ring road and just keep turning left and left and left again until my phone tells me the train got in two minutes ago. That should be enough time for Steffi to get through the gates. I 360 around a roundabout and turn into the carpark again, just in time to see a surge of people streaming from the doors. Everyone's in sundresses and shorts, flip-flops, sunglasses, smiling and fanning themselves. There's a slow queue of cars waiting to pick passengers up and I join, craning my neck to find Steffi's face in the crowd. She'll be wearing something understated and slinky, no doubt, to show off all the Peloton and such. It will probably be cream or white, to show off her gorgeous darker colouring and the fact she doesn't have a child with grubby hands to ruin it instantly. Cars fill up in front of me. Woody stirs and I flinch whenever a door slams. Where's Steffi? Where is she? I'm driving as slow as I humanly can so we're still in motion, rather than stop-starting. The car behind me – typically a red-faced potato of a bloke in a BMW, is getting visibly angry that I'm not up the arsehole of the cars in front, like it makes any difference at all.

'Calm down, calm down,' I whisper – to him, to myself. *Where's Steffi?* There's only three cars in front now and I can't see her. The stream of people has slowed to a tiny trickle. Everyone must be off the train now, so where is she? I crawl forward, hoping I'll see her emerge, but no. Now two cars ahead. No Steffi. One car ahead . . . then nothing. Blank space and no Steffi. If I drive super slowly maybe she'll appear? I inch and inch but I can see the guy behind me get redder.

He honks his horn. Woody stirs.

'There's no need for that.'

Then he honks three times – long and loud – and hangs his rotten face out the window. 'GET A MOVE ON, YOU SLOW BITCH.'

Woody wakes and howls. Past Me, without a baby, would never accept being spoken to like this. I'd have given him the finger. I would've gotten out and had a go back. But this arse-wipe is forgotten because all that matters is getting Woody back to sleep because he's not had a long enough nap yet. Waking up now will throw the whole day, the whole night, my whole *SHIT RELENTLESS LIFE*. I roar out of the carpark and get back onto the ring road, hoping the movement will lull him back.

'Shh, Shh-shhhhhhh. Go back to sleep, baby. Back to sleep. Please.'

But it's not going to happen. His face is contorted into a scream. His little hands clenched in pudgy fists. He's furious at being woken but not willing to go the fuck back to sleep. I know he needs me. That he won't calm without me. So, I rev up and speed through the ring road for the fourth time, clunking to a hard stop in a parking space about ten metres from the station entrance. I run out the car, muttering, *'fuck fuck fuck, fuck this, fuck you Steffi, fuck my life, fuck my endless fucking life,'* and hoist Woody from his car seat – the scream he releases so loud that several people turn to look. He's exhausted, red-eyed, inconsolable. I bounce him, I rock him. I fold myself into the backseat and try to shove a nipple in his mouth but he spits it out like it's a poisoned entree. I hoick him back out of the car and bounce him, narrating as I go to try and calm him down.

'Look babe. There's a billboard. There's a traffic light. There's a queue of taxis. Isn't life great? Please stop crying. Are you OK? Do you have a fever? Are you teething? What's wrong? Why won't you sleep? Why are you never asleep?'

Cope better. Cope better. Cope better.

And yet all I feel is disaster at the ruined nap. How this is going to play out all day. An overtired Woody at this baby shower. An overtired baby on the car journey home. An even worse night's sleep than last night's which maybe isn't scientifically possible. I feel tears threatening to spill. A panic attack deciding whether to turn up or if, like me, it's too tired and will send an IOU instead – probably at 2am tomorrow, when Woody no doubt wakes up.

'Shh, shh. Don't cry. It's OK. Shh, shh.'

He starts to calm, and then, like the click of someone's fingers, he's fine. He gurgles. Smiles. Reaches out and grabs a piece of my hair in total delight. I stand down from the ledge. I blink back the tears. I cope. Sort of. Then I jump as someone taps me on the shoulder.

I whip around and there's Steffi. Tanned and toned, slinky and perfect – the late fucking bitch who has ruined my life. She grins. Takes in Woody and squeals. Then she holds up two bits of giant plastic, and smiles, incredibly proud of herself.

'I got us iced coffees! Whoop! What a treat!'

STEFFI

Woah.

That's the word that almost escapes my mouth when Lauren turns around.

Wo and ah.

Also.

Fuck.

'Wow! You look amazing!' The lies pour from my mouth as I try to hand her the coffee before realising she has no spare hands. 'Oh hi, Woody! Lauren he's adorable!'

'Steffi. You're here. I didn't know if you were on the train or not.' Lauren jiggles her baby on one hip and reaches out awkwardly to take the coffee. Her voice is as strained as mine, and I know her well enough to know she's pissed at me. I scan her face, Woody's face, the fact she's parked over two spaces, and curse myself.

'I had to make a work call when I got off the platform because the coverage was so bad on the train,' I explain. 'Sorry,' I say, with total sincerity.

She softens as my apology lands and smiles. 'A work call? On a Saturday? How's the agency going then? Is it . . .'

Woody lets out a screech and lurches in her arms, making a swing for the coffee, almost spilling it over her. 'No Woody. Not for babies. No. That straw will stab you in the eye babe. Here! Look! It's Aunty Steffi!' She dangles him in front of me, like I'm a toy, and I put my coffee on the roof of her car and take him from her, feeling that anxiety that the baby will reject me and cry, and it's embarrassing for all involved. But Woody accepts me, lunges for my necklace and puts one of the giant beads in his mouth. I wince but let my jewellery take the hit.

'Sorry. We've had a bit of a journey,' Lauren leans against the hot metal of her car and gratefully gulps the coffee like she used to throw back shots at Vodka Revs. 'We've been doing this sleep training thing. He was supposed to go down in the car, but there was this man. He's only had 40 minutes this morning which isn't enough but . . .' She stops, shakes her head. 'Sorry. Boring fucking baby stuff, pouring out of my mouth the moment you arrive. When I promised myself I wouldn't.'

I pat her arm, still adjusting to this strange, manic, Lauren. 'Dude, it's fine. I'm sorry he's not sleeping. Nightmare. I don't know how parents do it.'

She drains the coffee, swishes the straw around to dislodge the last dregs from the ice, and necks the last slurp. I watch her, taking her in, still acclimatising to this woman in front of me who appears to be my old friend Lauren. She's almost unrecognisable. She's wearing *navy* for one. A colour I thought she was actually allergic to. I don't think I've seen her in any outfit that doesn't involve at least one primary colour and one neon. Her face has some makeup on, but not the usual bold statement lip I'm so used to. And the makeup's already flaking on dry patches around her nose, purple bruises showing through under her eyes, a wonky eyeliner. Her hair's scraped up in one of those '*mum buns*' – I'm guessing to stop Woody yanking it. He's already tugging at mine as he coats every necklace bead in slurpy drool. And, I feel like a bitch for noticing it, but Lauren's weight is hugely different. She's always had that enviable hourglass thing going on – lovely boobs, tiny waist

– though her sex appeal was always dented by her dressing like an exploded paintbox. Now, in her navy sack, there's no ins or outs, just plumpness and sagging both at the same time, if that's possible? I hate myself for thinking it, but I think it nonetheless.

Wow, she's really not lost the baby weight.

Which shocks me as Woody is, what, almost a year old? And Lauren's figure has always been so effortlessly amazing.

'Shall we get in the car?' she asks. 'God knows how long it will take to get there. Google maps is just shoving a pin in the middle of a grey nothingness.'

'Yes. Fab. Please tell me your car has air con.'

'It does!'

'Amazing. Oh, it's so good to see you.' I try and hug her again, but, as I lean over, Woody smells his mother and starts straining out for her crying. I can't be sure, but there's a roll of her eyes almost as she takes him.

'Yeah, you too,' she says, distracted. 'Right, baby, are we going to be good in the car? Yes? No crying please in front of Aunty Steffi. It's open,' she calls over, and I hop in the front while she buckles Woody up, stifling a gasp at the state of the car. It's *filthy,* with crumbs everywhere, toys covered with lint, empty biscuit packets and cans of coke rattling by the feet. I quietly put my jacket down on the seat before I clamber in, to protect my dress. Woody's clipped in and assigned a toy in each hand which he flaps about in apparent good temper. Lauren ducks in, starts the engine, and chucks her phone over to me.

'Do you mind Google mapping? I have no clue where we're going, but I officially hate Nicki's parents for moving somewhere so photogenic yet so fucking far away.'

I laugh and dutifully load up the route. 'It's quite an ask, isn't it? Come to the official middle of nowhere. Bring a nappy tree for good measure.'

'Did I even have a baby shower?' Lauren asks, indicating out. 'I can't remember.'

'We went to a spa, the four of us instead.'

'Oh God, yes. Fucking *Mummy-To-Be Pamper Day* my arse. Pay 200 quid and you're not allowed in the hot tub, or the steam or sauna. And I couldn't even eat the afternoon tea cos I had gestational diabetes. No wonder I've wiped it.'

I hold my hands out in front of the blasting air con. 'I, however, had a great time eating all your cakes and watching Charlotte spend the day picking up discarded towels and folding them.'

She laughs and I feel the tension between us drop its arms. We steer out of town, around some tricky roundabouts, Lauren concentrating too hard to talk much. Then her phone chants '*Follow this road for ten miles,*' and I prop it up in an empty cup holder and turn to smile at Woody.

'He's so cute, Lauren.'

She smiles and lets go of the steering wheel to fluff her hair. 'He is. Nine months is proper nappy-advert age. What you imagine a baby to look like, right? Rather than a deformed alien frog twitching on the floor uselessly.'

'I can't believe how big he's gotten since I last saw him. I've missed you, Lauren, it's been ages.'

She nods. 'I know. I'm sorry. I've been a useless pathetic waste of a human since Woody was born.'

I wince at how she's just described herself and reach over to pat her arm. 'You're a new parent, Lauren. Be kind to yourself.'

She lets out a bark of a laugh. 'I think that's an excuse for about six weeks max. One of the NCT lot has taken their baby on four long-haul holidays already.'

'Well, it's different for everyone.'

I'm not sure what else to say. I always feel like any advice I give my parent friends is unlikely to be listened to since I don't have the experiential element to back it. I've seen enough of my friends go from happy to mess to know they're not alone (and to remind myself being childfree is such a valid choice) but you can't really say, '*if it helps any, everyone I know who's had a baby seems to have ruined their lives?*' That's my judgement anyway. They always game face and tell me determinedly how 'worth it' it is.

This car journey's quite the fall to earth after such a surreal morning. I can't keep my hands still, they twirl like a combine harvester in my lap, and coffee wasn't a good plan. I'm DYING to tell Lauren about what's happening – especially as she works in publishing so gets what it all means. But I want her to bring it up in case I seem self-obsessed.

Theres a thunk behind us as Woody drops one toy down the gap. Another thunk as the other toy joins it. I twist around to see him beaming, like gravity is the best thing ever. And, when I turn back, Lauren's face is more hers again. She glances over.

'I've just realised, you're submitting that book this week, aren't you? To start your agency with. Oh my God, how's it going? Sorry I've not asked sooner.'

'Oh, no worries.' My hands start pat-a-caking with joy as speaking it out loud makes it even more real. 'It's going really well actually. I had two offers come in from UK publishers overnight.'

Woody lets out a shriek, and I twist, unable to tell from his face if it's a happy one or not.

'Ignore him. Oh my God, Steffi. That's brilliant. Offers on a Saturday! That's huge. Wow. So, you're thinking auction on Monday, right? Or do you think a pre-empt is going to come in. How do you . . .' Woody starts bawling. Zero to 70. 'Oh Woody, what's wrong? What's wrong baby? Have you lost your toy?' He screams and starts banging the window, his whole face red. 'Steffi, do you mind trying to get his toy? Can you reach?'

'Err. Sure.' I contort myself to try and grab a plastic giraffe ear I can see poking out from behind the seat but can't reach it. Woody smacks my hands away as I try, screaming louder. 'Hang on. I'll unbuckle.'

'So, you must be delighted?' Lauren attempts, as I risk death by leaning through the middle partition. I sigh in relief as I clasp the giraffe, pass it to Woody, and expect some respite, but he just grabs it and throws it to one side, screaming louder at the audacity that I thought it would help. 'Ohh.'

'Ignore him, honestly. He'll calm down in a sec.'

'Umm OK.' I buckle up again, trying not to pull a face at how jarringly horrible the sound of his screaming is.

'So, auction, yes?' Lauren yells to be heard as we hurtle past rolling fields, sheep lying uncomfortably in their wool coats under the trees.

'Yes, unless I get a seven-figure pre-empt. Which I might, because . . .' I really wanted to share this news without my eardrums being violated but saying it out loud will still feel amazing. Just like ringing Rosa on the platform felt amazing. She dropped the phone and started crying and couldn't get the words out to tell her housemate what was going on. It took a while to convince her that *Blood Moon* isn't only getting published, it's going to be a global phenomenon.

Those calls are the reason I do the job. When I feel like a Fairy Godmother. Everything I do is so I can make calls like that. People say publishing is a fixed game, and *it's not what you know but who you know*, etc. And, to some degree that's true. Everyone went to similar boarding schools before alighting the English Lit train at Oxbridge station. Loads of novels get published because they're written by *so and so's* granddaughter, or because they've got a podcast, or a certain number of Instagram followers. God knows I represent some of those authors myself, because I know where the bread is buttered, and it's nepotism side up. But there are moments of true meritocracy. Where a regular civilian quietly writes an incredible, game-changing novel, not realising how good it is, or they are, and is only dreaming of maybe a tiny publishing deal, and the chance to have a launch party, and to see their book in the shop. Making that dream come true but multiplying it by a million and getting to be the one who tells them . . . Well you can't beat that feeling. People think I'm unmaternal because I never want to have kids but if they knew how I feel about my clients. How *they're* my children in that their joy is my joy, their hardships my hardships. I will do anything in my power to make life better and easier for them and want the world to know just how special they are . . . If people understood that maybe I'd be dumped less by men who think I'm uncaring . . . fucking *Jeremy*.

'Seven figures?' Lauren asks, though she's distracted by the back mirror, watching Woody squirm about in his car seat. 'Wow, that would set your agency up so well.'

'I hope so. It would be such a relief.'

'Oh, Steffi. If only your mum was here. She'd be so proud. *I'm* so proud.'

'Stop it or I'll cry.' This was what I needed. Lauren getting it. Being able to tell her in person. I really have missed her.

'So, what next? Have you . . . Woody? *Woody!* It's OK. It's just the car. It's OK.'

Her baby throws his whole body back, face red.

I try and carry on as usual. 'Yeah, well, you'll never believe it, but Nina Baldwin herself literally just emailed this morning. She wants to option, with Nina playing the main part.'

'Fuck!'

'I know, I'm still in shock.'

'Woody! What the hell is wrong now?' She takes a hand off the steering wheel and wraps it around the back of the chair, clicking her fingers to get him to calm down. It doesn't work. 'Nina? Wow, Steffi. That's . . . Sorry. I want to give this my proper attention but don't know what's got into Woody. Woody please. Stop crying. Go to sleep.' She suddenly shouts out of nowhere, 'You're tired because you won't ever go to *fucking sleep.*'

I cover my mouth to catch my shock. Woody is stunned silent for a second, before erupting into more screams. She darts a horrified look at me.

'Sorry Steffi. I just . . . He woke from his nap just before we picked you up. He's knackered. I'm knackered. I . . . sorry. I . . . Oh Woody, baby, Mummy didn't mean it. Hey, hey, it's OK.'

He's beyond inconsolable. Screaming so loud he's probably opened a portal to another reality. 'Don't worry,' I say, unsure what else to add, 'Umm, are you OK?'

She takes a deep breath and plasters on this weird face I've never seen before – vacant, gone. 'Sorry Steffi. I'm going to have to pull over. Do you mind getting into the back with him?'

'No, of course.'

'Nowhere to pull over on these country roads, are there? Shh Woody. Shh. It's alright. Hang on, this will do.'

She jerks the car into a turn off for a private farm and we all whiplash to a halt. 'OK, get in the back. Thank you. Hang on, you'll need this.' She brings up her phone, opens YouTube and types in 'baby sensory' before hitting play and handing it over. I was expecting her to get out and comfort Woody herself but the blankness is still on her face. I scramble next to him and hold the screen up to his face.

'OK, wow,' I say, as the car pulls away again, and Woody literally breaks into a smile, tears suspended on his cheeks. He stares intently at the dancing strawberries on the phone.

'It's like baby crack,' Lauren shouts back. 'Sorry for all the drama. I should've just put you in the back with him from the off. Serves me right for trying to be a grown-up.'

'It's fine. It's just, funny.' I wave my hand in front of Woody's face, but he doesn't even blink. He's too ensconced by the kiwi fruit with giant eyeballs raining from the sky on top of the bouncing strawberries.

An awkward calm descends as we continue into the middle of nowhere. I can't deny it's gorgeous out here and is probably even lusher when we're not mid-drought. There's so much sky, and hedgerows and space, and London already feels like a squished-up polluted nightmare to return to later. Woody's silent, his eyes drying out from not blinking. Lauren is navigating the twisting roads calmly and slowly, and you wouldn't think she'd screamed her head off only a minute ago.

'So,' she calls back. 'Nina Baldwin. Honestly, Steffi. You must be losing your mind!'

I smile. My dear friend has returned, if only temporarily. I can hear it in her voice. 'I just rang the author now. She's made up. I told her there'll be other offers but she's going to say yes to Nina, no matter what the other studios throw at her. I won't tell them that, obviously, until I negotiate a sweet deal.'

'I'm not surprised at all, Steffi. I always knew you'd soar like a firework the moment you went solo.'

'Thank you. This is beyond my wildest dreams though.'

'I'm so proud, babe.' Lauren glances down at my phone, guiding her way. 'Hang on, I think we're almost there. It says it's along here in a mile or two . . . Woody OK back there?'

Woody still hasn't blinked. Some crazed pineapples are spinning upside down, while Woody's little fingers twitch with joy.

'He's suitably comatose.'

'Brilliant. Oh my God. Hang on. How the hell are you going to broker all these deals at Nicki's baby shower?'

I laugh, loving Lauren even more for totally getting it. 'It will involve diplomacy,' I say.

'Diplomacy? It will involve bare-faced lying! What are you going with? Stomach upset? Shall I help fluff Nicki for you? Say you looked green when I picked you up?'

The car slows as a calm voice tells us our destination should soon be on the left. I don't understand how a house could be here. This isn't a road, it's a track. There are no streetlights, or pavement – only hedgerows and dried up fields.

'That would be useful, thank you. You know I would never miss today but it's not ideal timing. Oh, look, there it is. Wow.'

The house appears like a mirage, shimmering in the heat at the end of a dirt track Lauren just about turns onto on time. It's basically a greenhouse on stilts. Modern, gleaming, expensive . . . Definitely designed by some architect who doesn't mind if passersby can see you naked. A giant balloon archway looms over the front steps, removing any taste from our initial impression.

'We are going to melt in that thing,' Lauren says as we crunch along the gravel. 'And how the hell is Woody supposed to sleep when the whole house is a giant window?'

Even Woody's wowed enough to twist his little head away from the phone. He starts flapping his hands, cackling, sensing an upcoming change in environment. Lauren parks up and lets out a low whistle before twisting around with a grin.

'Steffi, I am so, so excited for you. Truly. Well done. This is only the beginning.'

Right at that moment, my phone dings, and she passes it over, seeing the urgent bulge of my eyes. 'Who is it? Is it another offer?'

I scan the email and squeal. 'Oh my God. It's Mountain Scape Studios! Another movie deal. What is actually going on?!'

'Steffi! This is . . . oh my! I'm so thrilled for you! So thrilled! Do you want us to stay in the car a sec, so you can read the email and reply? Woody's on his baby sensory crack so he's fine.'

'That would be amazing, do you mind?' I'm already scanning the email. They've gone in big and sent through a figure. There are zeros. Lots of zeros. I'm going to have to take it to

Rosa right away. This may be worth turning down Nina for. Wow. Yikes. Even *I* don't know what to do! I'm supposed to know what to do. This is my business. I'm the expert. I'm in charge. Oh help. Help.

'I don't mind at all. I might just sit here and close my eyes if that's not weird? Take a second to . . . Oh.'

We all jump as someone bangs on the car window. Charlotte's giant pupils beam through the windscreen, her teeth glinting in the sun.

'You're here,' she screams so shrilly, that Woody, predictably, I've learned, starts crying.

CHARLOTTE

It's all happening. Perfect. Perfect. Exactly how I pictured it. Exactly what the four of us need. I'd scheduled in 45 minutes for us to have a cup of tea and a catch-up and we're right on time.

'Woah,' Lauren says, craning her neck around as she sips from her cup of tea. 'I don't know whether to be blown away by this house's architecture, or the fact Charlotte's managed to craft an actual piñata into a vulva. Or both.'

They all burst into hysterics while I pretend to be annoyed.

'Personally,' Steffi says, her iced coffee in one hand, her phone glued to the other. 'I feel the paper-maché vulva really sets off the modern minimalism.'

'Thank you.'

'Did you get your class to help?'

'Not with the vulva, no.'

'Why not?' Nicki asks. She's seated lower down than us, bobbing on a yoga ball. 'Surely we should be teaching kids the right terms for body parts?'

'What's inside the vulva?' Lauren stands up to catch Woody who's crawling into what I've already warned her is the 'danger zone'. I've put red tape up, to let mothers know which parts of the house have been baby proofed, but, sadly, Woody isn't obeying the tape.

'Sweets . . .' I say slowly, waiting for the joke.

'Well, maybe you should stuff it with blood and tampons and clots so we can be educated.' I make a giant eww face and Lauren and the others laugh warmly at me.

'And penises!' Steffi adds. We all giggle childishly, apart from Nicki who rolls her eyes and says, 'Trust you to make it about penises, Steffi.'

There's a beat as her comment lands sourly. If either Lauren or I had said it, we all would've laughed, but from Nicki's tongue, it's as loaded as the vulva piñata. Nicki, realising this, rushes to make amends. 'I mean, I still remember the props you brought to my hen do, that's all,' she adds, and Lauren and I share a look of relief.

Steffi nods and accepts the olive branch. 'Nicki, you were all against the neon blow-up cock at first,' she says, 'and then, if I remember correctly, you wouldn't let go of it all night. Didn't you end up sleeping with it in your hotel bed like it was a teddy bear?' We laugh harder, to overshadow the awkward.

'It was comfier than those shit Premier Inn pillows,' Nicki protests. 'I only slept with it for ergonomic reasons.'

Lauren splutters at the term 'ergonomic reasons' and dribbles tea down her dress. Woody's delighted at this and starts belly laughing so hard I want to film it for a viral video. His joy is so contagious and we all piss ourselves for at least five minutes, until Steffi uses the opportunity to refresh her phone and Nicki notices and rolls her eyes. Why can't they stay in this present moment? It's so lovely. And it's on time! People think I can't relax but I totally can as long as it's in my schedule. Which it is now, so I'm not even thinking about what times the various foods need to come out of the fridge, or to check on Seth and ensure they're running to schedule too, or worry about people arriving early . . . no. I'm allowed to go with the flow for another twelve minutes and live in this precious moment, laughing with my best friends. Scheduled fun is still fun. It took a while to convince Seth that scheduled sex was still sex, and actually *better* sex, because I wasn't all tense and tight because the sex was getting in the way of whatever's on my schedule. Until it got heartbreakingly painful, scheduling sex on ovulation days was, like, my most favourite foreplay ever. The timetabling! The body temperature checks! The mucus testing! There were graphs! There were best positions to try! Best times of day! God, it was great until none of it worked.

Woody crawls around, mouth wide open in genuine joy at his new playground. He stops at Nicki's ball and tries to stand up against it. She hauls him up for a cuddle and he buries into her and her giant bump, while we all aww.

'He's so adorable,' Nicki says, stroking his back. 'I hope my baby's as objectively cute as Woody.'

I examine myself watching my pregnant friend hold my other friend's child, feeling only joy and serenity for them. Woody's cute little laugh does not demolish my heart. Nicki's bulbous figure doesn't make me feel empty and pointless. In fact, I'm excited.

Steffi jumps up, pushing her phone into the pocket of her dress. 'I just need to go to the loo,' she says. 'Umm, where is it? Is the wall made of glass there too? Will birds be able to see me wee?'

Nicki flinches a bit, defensive of her parents maybe. 'It's all glass, but it's one-way in the bathrooms, I promise. It's just through that door there.'

'Where are your parents?' Lauren asks, as Steffi climbs over us, taking her phone out before she reaches the door. Luckily

Nicki's facing the other way and doesn't notice. When they arrived, Lauren whispered that something big's going on at Steffi's new agency but she doesn't want it to eclipse today which I hugely appreciate. I'm super happy for Steffi but I do worry about her pinning her livelihood on an industry as mad as publishing, where nobody really understands how to make money. Honestly, whenever she and Lauren talk about it, I basically get hives.

Nicki carefully unclamps Woody's hand, who's decided to yank out tufts of her hair. 'My Dad thought it would be *useful* to spend the day out on his new gravel bike,' she sighs. 'He left about 30 minutes ago, wearing such tight spandex I think there's going to be several car crashes along the downs.' She places Woody on the floor and rubs the part of her head he'd removed hair from. 'And Mum panicked that we didn't have a reed diffuser for the bathroom and thought this would ruin the day. She's rushed into town to get one.'

'I'm obsessed with your mum,' I tell her.

'Well, that's good, because she's obsessed with you.'

A part of me glows at that. I know I can be a lot sometimes and it feels wonderful when people not only get me, but appreciate me. I refuse to dial down my frequency for anyone, but my efficiency definitely triggers a lot of people, which is *their* problem, quite frankly.

'Are they excited to be grandparents?' I ask. 'Do you think they'll be helpful?'

Nicki contemplates this. 'Dad? No way. Not until they're old enough to cycle, anyway. We're so lucky to be having babies now rather than when men were all useless, smoking cigars in the hospital waiting room, and giving the baby the occasional piggyback or whatever.'

Lauren waves her finger and gets down on her knees to stop Woody straying into the danger zone again. 'Don't be so sure about that. I've got horror stories from my NCT about their husbands. Absolute horrors.'

We all turn to her, keen for details. 'Really?'

'There's one husband who hasn't done *one* night wake, because he's *"not good on no sleep"* and *"needs to be well rested for work"*. He literally works in an office, in IT. He just sits there and types. It's not like he's a brain surgeon or pilot. Woody no . . . not over there . . . See this squeaky toy?' She picks up a ball that squawks like a chicken. 'And another went to the World Cup for ten days, even though his baby was in hospital with bronchiolitis.'

Nicki pulls a disgusted face. 'But Tristan's good, right? He's always been such a star.'

Lauren tilts her head, and, if I didn't know her so well, I wouldn't have noticed the change in her face. The way it falls slightly, like a scaffold has collapsed behind it. 'Yeah, he's better than most. But it's mad how you do find yourself falling into these gendered roles, no matter how hard you try not to.' She tickles Woody's cheek and he giggles while Nicki looks so horrified that she almost bounces off her ball. 'Sorry,' Lauren says, sensing she's panicked her. 'I just wish I'd known how pointless it is to fight it. Nobody told me. And I'm very tired. As if you can't tell by the state of me.'

We're quiet for a second. It's the first time Lauren's addressed the jarring change in her appearance. I leap from my chair in my earnestness to reassure her we haven't noticed. 'You look gorgeous, hon. Being a mum really suits you.'

'Yes, Lauren. You're stunning,' Nicki adds. 'You always have been.'

Lauren ignores us and rummages in her nappy bag to find something to placate Woody, who has started trying to breast-feed through her dress.

'Yeah, yeah. Anyway . . . plenty of motherhood talk to come today . . .' Her eyes glance briefly in my direction, and I know she's trying to direct Nicki to be careful around me. I want to shake my head and jump up and down – desperate to tell them. But today is Nicki's day and I can't snatch her thunder and risk the wrath of fate.

Steffi wafts back in, phone still in her hand, looking sleek and svelte as always. She pats my head before arranging her-self back on the sofa. 'Umm, Nicki?' she asks. 'Why is there a sign in your bathroom in all caps that says *"NOBODY LIKES POO FINGERS"*?'

'What? There isn't.'

I put my hand up. 'Umm, that was me.'

'What?'

The other two start cracking up. 'You don't want to get sick when you're this pregnant,' I protest, 'and today is a super spreader event. I read this study about how to nudge people to be more hygienic. Apparently signs simply reminding them to wash their hands don't work? You've got to shame people. They tested loads and apparently *"Nobody likes poo fingers"* was the most effective.'

Their laughter cranks up.

'Remember when we sponsored Charlotte to not google anything for Lent?' Steffi asks, wiping her eyes.

Nicki bounces on her ball, holding her stomach. 'And then she tried to convince us that, searching for "*are Pop-Tarts carcinogenic?*" was needed for her Dickens essay? The essay we were all also writing?'

'They ARE carcinogenic!' I point out.

'Better not eat them with poo fingers,' Lauren butts in. 'Otherwise you'd be dead within the year.'

I don't mind that they're all laughing at me. I'm just so pleased everyone's getting along. I can visibly see the signs of effort on both Nicki and Steffi's faces. We need each other. We've always needed each other. I'll always treasure that seminar in the first week at Sheffield when we were put together. I'd been delirious with homesickness – missing Mum terribly, my whole family, and my bedroom that wasn't directly next to a communal fire door that banged every two minutes. But, alongside that, there was this dawning horror that no-one on my corridor was going to be my *friend for life* when all the literature I'd read about the university experience said I'd meet my 'Friends for Life'. Instead, I was on a floor with a bunch of girls really into Class A drugs, and music that only apparently makes sense when on them. They declared me A Martian for never having even tried a 'spliff', and pissed themselves laughing when I'd said 'I don't want to die' after being offered 'Molly'. In fact, they dragged in the lads from upstairs and made me repeat what I'd said to them about fearing a prison sentence, all laughing with gurning jaws.

'More than a quarter of women in prison are in for drug-related crimes,' I meekly chirped, while they all fell about like

I was the new Michael McIntyre. (That was another thing they found hilarious, that I liked Michael McIntyre.) I spent my Freshers' Week with clenched fists, at packed club nights I didn't understand, too short to be able to see over the mass of sweaty, drugged-up bodies before getting a taxi home, alone, usually by midnight and crying down the phone to Mum. *I was there to get a degree*, she reminded me. And she'd rent me a nice flat if things really couldn't improve. Anyway, it was all pretty terrible but I was glad for lectures to start so I could actually *get my degree*, which was *why I was there*, to *excel in my studies*. Plus, I had *friends for life* back home, anyway, in Hampstead. I was just about coping, though I did spend a lot of time crying in my pyjamas. But, luckily, in my first seminar for my American Literature module, I got put in a group with Lauren, Steffi and Nicki, and even more fortunately, they also hated their allocated *friends for life*. Nicki suggested we get a drink together to toast the fact we'd all only flicked through one book on the summer reading list, and that was *Little Women*, and that was only because of the Winona Ryder movie. I was so excited these girls hadn't yet used the words 'doobie', or 'racking up' that I concealed the fact I'd read the entire list over the summer – and put all my notes on each novel into colour-coordinated folders based on their historical context. My mum was still hoping I'd stop *wasting my clear talents* on becoming a primary school teacher. But that's the one job I wanted to do because it works with a parenting schedule.

Anyway, we went to a nearby Vodka Rev, and Nicki ensured we all got righteously drunk on these powder pink cocktails, while we talked about our favourite episodes of *Sex and The City*. Finally, a conversation I understood and could enjoy!

Finally, girls I liked. Were *these* my friends for life? After our fifth cocktail, as night drew in but conversation hadn't once run dry, Nicki slammed her glass down and said, 'God I wish you girls were on my corridor.'

'You do?' I asked, sipping my dusty pink martini with hopeful intrigue.

'Hell yes. I came here through clearing. Long story short, I was meant to go to York with my boyfriend, but then I panicked about going to uni as a couple and how that would probably make me a social leper. So, I veered last minute and the only accommodation available was in the building for the overseas students. I'm now still a social leper because I don't speak Chinese and they've all been here three weeks more than me to settle in to this country.' Nicki finished her drink. 'Please can we all hang out more?'

I was about to nod my head furiously but was beaten to it by Lauren. 'Hell yes. I'm on a corridor with goths. Me!' She gestured down to her outfit made entirely out of primary colours. 'They're very friendly goths, but, as you can imagine, we don't have a huge amount in common. They wouldn't go to any Freshers' Week stuff and instead spent the whole time dragging me to these music venues where people scream down the microphone.'

Steffi started laughing. 'How did *you* end up in a corridor with goths?'

Lauren took a sip of her drink, leaving a red lip print on the rim of the glass. Even after five rounds, she was dutifully and perfectly reapplying her statement lip. 'We've all asked ourselves the same question. We think it's because of the 'activities and interests' questionnaire they got us to fill in for housing. We all wrote our favourite book was *Alice in Wonderland.*'

'Uh oh,' Steffi said. 'Well, that explains it.'

'What's wrong with *Alice In Wonderland?*'

'Nothing, but it's, like, the goth bible. They time-share between Alice and *The Nightmare Before Christmas.*'

Lauren nodded. 'That explains many of their tattoos.'

We all laughed again. Nicki, noticing we were running dry, pointed to each of us. 'Another round?'

I'd nodded, squiffy. I would stay until all these women were my best friends for life, I'd decided. It was fate. And, if I had to do a tactical vomit to keep up with their drinking with my tiny body, then that's what the universe demands.

'What about you?' Lauren asked, as Nicki went to get another round in. I watched as she got served easily. Nicki was very pretty in a very girl-next-door way, and all the boys seemed to look at her.

'What about me?' I parroted, aware my voice was sludgy and too loud, even with the music blaring from the speakers.

'All OK on your corridor?'

'Oh no, not at all.' I tried to slurp up non-existent cocktail from the bottom of my empty glass. 'My flatmates call me The Martian because I don't want to take MDMA. I do worry about their teeth, you know? They're really going to wear down their enamel if they keep gurning like that and enamel can't be regrown. Once it's gone, it's gone. But they think that's hilarious.' I sighed. 'They think everything I say and do is hilarious but I'm not trying to be funny.'

Lauren patted me on the shoulder with a hefty whack of someone equally intoxicated. 'They don't understand your energy,' she explained to me, while my heart went *ding ding ding*. *Energy* was in my top ten favourite words and she'd just used it.

Nicki returned with another tray and we all applauded.

'And what about you?' Nicki asked Steffi. 'Are you in corridor hell?'

Steffi shook her dark hair. 'No, they're all great,' she admitted, almost sheepishly. Steffi, I'd soon learn, was able to get along with pretty much anyone. It's what made her such a great agent. 'But I like you girls a lot better.'

We'd smiled at one another, all of us acknowledging The Moment occurring. I really love *Moments*. The word is also in my top ten. And, that was it. University experience rescued. The Little Women formed. Uni became enjoyable as well as survivable, especially as Lauren let me share her bed most nights. By the time we all got a house together in second year, I really was having *The Time Of My Life*, like the world promised me I would.

Now, here we are, over ten years later, and still the best of friends.

'We must get a photo,' I stand up, overcome by the urge. 'Before everybody else arrives.'

The others groan.

'You are always thankful for my photos when enough history has passed,' I remind them. '*Charlotte, do you mind sending those pics through that you took today? Charlotte, do you have those snaps of us from when we did fancy dress as Bananas in Pyjamas?*'

'OK, OK,' Nicki stands slowly and carefully removes the yoga ball from beneath her. 'Let us at least pretend we're not clinically vain.'

'Come on,' I pull Steffi up off the sofa, only to reveal the phone she's carefully concealed, screen on, in her lap. It clatters to the bleached-wood floor and she dives down, darting a look at Nicki. Luckily, Nicki's too busy helping wrestle Woody out of Lauren's arms to notice.

'Shall we use the flower wall as the background?' Nicki asks, carrying the baby over.

I shake my head. 'No, we used that for the family portraits earlier. You want variety. How about under the balloon arch?'

I lead them out into the sweltering heat. Nicki starts fanning herself. 'Oh God, I'm too pregnant for this. Why is God doing this to me in my third trimester?'

'Let's make it a quick photo. Hang on . . . I'll just set my phone up.'

'Umm, Charlotte?' Lauren asks, taking Woody off Nicki so she can fan herself with both hands. 'Is that a *selfie stick* you're using?'

'Yes.' I screw my phone onto the end of it.

'Wow.'

Steffi starts laughing. 'Shouldn't that be in a museum?'

'Stop it! They're a really useful invention. The only reason people stopped using them was because they felt shamed. I refuse to feel shame at using something that solves a practical problem.'

'*Wands of narcissism?* Wasn't that what they were called?' Lauren asks.

My phone locks in and I lengthen the stick and poke her with it. 'Oh shut it. You're all going to ask me to send you a copy of this picture. Why does everyone pretend this is all beneath them? It isn't! Yeah, yeah, yeah, social media is curated perfection wa wa wa. But, like, also maybe it's *nice* to post pictures of your life, and *nice* to see other people lives, and maybe it's just *nice* for things to look *nice*. Maybe that's not shallow, just *nice*.'

Nicki claps her hands. 'OK, Little Women. She's right. It's nice. The balloon arch is lovely. Today is perfect. Charlotte is amazing. In fact, I think it's time for a Charlotte sandwich!'

They all smush me into a hug, to let me know they're only ever teasing – like they used to at uni when I felt I'd over-Charlotted and was being judged. I haven't had a Charlotte sandwich in forever and we all laugh into each other's hair.

'You're all too sweaty,' I complain, when, really, I'm the happiest I've been in two years. 'Now, let's take this photo.'

I arrange them into the right height order and position them so the balloon arch is framing us perfectly. 'Say *Little Women*,' I instruct, taking at least two dozen options. Woody isn't facing the right way in any of them because he's spotted the balloons and strains to reach them. Lauren lets him squeak one, while the other two scroll through my phone, telling me which ones I can use.

'Aww this one is perfect,' Nicki says. She holds it up and we all crowd around to see.

'I agree your selfie stick is most brilliant,' Steffi says. 'I'm going to find my old one buried in my flat somewhere and resurrect it.' Her phone buzzes twice in her dress but she dutifully ignores it.

'Thanks, Charlotte,' Nicki says. 'As always. You've pulled a blinder.'

And, with all of us huddled together like this, getting on so well, the news fizzes on my tongue. You're supposed to wait twelve weeks but . . .

'Guys,' I start . . . But we're interrupted by a car crunching into the driveway. As we turn to look, Steffi grabs the opportunity to check her phone and strides back inside. Woody makes the balloon squeak so hard he starts crying. The car door opens to reveal Nicki's mother, waving something over her head like she's in *The Railway Children* and she's trying to stop a train with her red bloomers.

'It's going to be OK,' she shouts to Nicki. 'I've got three reed diffusers!'

'Thank God,' Nicki calls back. 'I was going to cancel the whole thing otherwise.'

I'm the only one who waits for her before retreating into the air-conditioning. 'Thanks, Jane,' I call back. She's right – an event really isn't an event without a signature scent. As I wait to greet her, I look at the picture of us still up on my phone screen and smile again.

Perfect.

Crime Stoppers
Speak up. Stay safe.

Thank you for deciding to tell us about a crime. We know it can be a really difficult decision to speak out so it's great that you've taken the first step. Crimestoppers takes information about crime 100% anonymously.

What is the crime or incident you would like to tell us about? ⇟

Arson

Where did the crime take place?

Honeysuckle Lane, Surrey

Tell us more about the crime. What you saw, heard, or know about.

I don't think it was an accident. The big fire. I was at the baby shower, and it was carnage. People were full on screaming at each other, multiple people were crying, and then we all got shoved out, half way through, and told to leave. I'm sorry, but we're supposed to believe it's coincidence that, moments later, a fire just accidentally broke out??? Those women may claim they're the best of friends, but they seemed to hate each other.

BABY SHOWER BLAZE BECOMES SHOCK ARSON ENQUIRY

A wildfire allegedly started by a malfunctioning smoke grenade at a baby shower is now being treated as an arson enquiry.

Police say emerging evidence suggests the fire wasn't started by accident and have brought suspects in again for further questioning.

Inspector George Simmons, of Surrey Police, said: 'The community has, rightly, been horrified that the careless actions of these women have caused such devastation. But after interviewing eyewitnesses at this baby shower, we're increasingly convinced the circumstances of the fire could, legally, be considered arson.'

Last week, the story of the fire went viral and made international headlines, sparking conversations about the progressively grotesque nature of baby showers. This shocking development is likely to renew media interest in this incident, nicknamed the 'Blaze-ic B*tch BBQ'

Inspector Simmons added: 'Even if the fire wasn't started deliberately, an arson charge may still be considered appropriate if we believe it was started recklessly. We encourage anyone who might have any information to come forward, no matter how seemingly insignificant.'

Feminist101 has shared this story:

Alright. Who did it? Reveal yourself so I can buy you a drink.

ThirtyFlirtyAndThriving has shared this story:

We've all WANTED to start a fire at a baby shower, now some legend has actually done it

TakeTheRedPill has shared this story:

Bet it was started by some ugly bitter bitch who can't get anyone to knock her up

Transcript: Inspector Simmons interviewing Nicole Davies

Nicole:	OK, so explain to me, please, why I'd set fire to my own parents' house?
Simmons:	You tell us.
Nicole:	I'm full term, you know? My waters could break at any moment, but you want me to explain all the reasons why I wouldn't burn down my own parents' house, while heavily pregnant, ruining our lives, and risking my unborn baby?
Simmons:	It would be useful to have them on record, yes.
Nicole:	OK, reasons I'm not an arsonist. One, me and my unborn baby almost died. Two, it has destroyed my parents' lives.
Simmons:	Didn't they get a big insurance payment?
Nicole:	<deadpan> Yes. That makes everything they've lost worth it.
Simmons:	Were you enjoying your baby shower, Nicki? Witnesses say you looked uncomfortable.
Nicole:	It was 38 degrees and I'm heavily pregnant.

NICKI

Oh my God, my mother. Why? She's so overstimulated she's like a bottle of coke someone's chucked a pack of refreshers into and then shaken up for extra measure.

'Girls! Girls! Oh, it's so marvellous to have you all here. Do you like this smell?' She shoves the diffuser under Steffi's nostrils. 'Isn't it lovely? Oh Lauren! He's gorgeous. Hello, little guy. What's his name again? Woody? Like the woodpecker?'

'Mum!'

'Is it Australian or something? Like your husband? So handsome, isn't he? Nicki showed me pictures from the wedding. Are you girls hungry? Thirsty? Tea? Coffee? Pink lemonade? Juice? Herbal tea? Are you breastfeeding darling? God, I remember gagging for more than a coffee a day. I fed Nicki til she was eighteen months, didn't I?'

'I can't say I remember,' I reply.

'Well I did. Eighteen months. Right. Drinks. Drinks. What can I get you all? Oh, everyone's coming soon. Isn't it exciting? Hasn't Charlotte done an amazing job?'

She explodes around the kitchen like a pong ball, with Charlotte scuttling after her as she's taking glasses off their display trays in her haste to get us the drinks we didn't say yes to. My body ripples with irritation that's laced with guilt, which is pretty much how I always feel around my mother. Annoyed, and then angry at myself for being annoyed. We've had moments of such closeness since I got pregnant. We've compared food cravings and levels of morning sickness. I've had so many questions for her about her pregnancy with me. Every answer feels like a precious pearl I want to clutch onto and remember. As I rub my kicking bump each morning, it dawns on me how I was carried in my mother's stomach, just like this. I must've kicked her and woken her, and told her through weird placenta telepathy, that it was imperative to eat raw strawberry jelly for two weeks straight. My fingerprints are relics from everything she did for the nine months we shared a body. I've never felt closer to her. But, as she insists on taking Woody, without even letting Lauren object (*'No. Sit down. Drink up. I've got him. Enjoy a cup of tea for five minutes just for yourself'*) I find her just as annoying as always. Why can't she just relax with us? Why does she act like every chair is a bed of nails?

Charlotte downs her glass of water and scutters about, doing her 'final touches'. Steffi has gone to the toilet again. 'Shouldn't have had that giant iced coffee on the train.' That's three times she's been since she got here. She's either sick, or something else is going on and she's trying to hide it from me. Honestly, why do I bother with her when she insists on being so secretive? She's probably sending bitchy messages to her other cool London 'child-free friends' who liked that horrible opinion article she posted. She'll have plenty of ammo, with all of Charlotte's sugar sweet decorations. I wish I could stand up on a chair, at some point today, and say, *'None of this was my choice or taste, please everyone realise that,'* without upsetting Charlotte. I'm already worried today's hugely triggering for her and want to hide my bulging stomach with my hands in case it's upsetting her.

When I found out I was pregnant, I even turned into Charlotte when figuring out how to tell her. I googled '*how to tell a friend who has fertility issues you're pregnant*'. The general consensus was to do it a) privately, b) via message, not by phone or in person so they have time to privately digest their own pain before replying, and c) to do all of this, obviously, before you post the '*We're pregnant*' announcement online. I didn't need to worry about C, as I'd rather die than post a black and white scan of my uterus on socials. But I followed the other advice, worried sick it would affect her, especially as it was only a few months after Lauren got pregnant. And yet, after all that, Charlotte replied within two minutes with seven lines of heart eyes and fireworks emojis. I check the clock. Almost start time. I stand in front of the air-con for a moment, watching Lauren lean against the counter and sip her tea as Mum starts a manic game of Peek-A-Boo with Woody on the kitchen floor. Maybe I can squeeze in a micro-nap before everyone arrives? I lower myself onto the sofa and I close my eyes, hearing Lauren and Mum's voices drift over my head.

'So, how are you finding it all?' Mum asks. 'Motherhood?' followed by, 'Where's Woody? Where is he? Oh, there he is! Peekaboo!'

'It's . . . it's a lot sometimes. Isn't it?' Lauren replies. 'Oh, he loves you, Jane.'

'Peek. A. Boo! Where's Woody? . . . Oh, my love. Welcome to the best kept secret in the world . . . just how hard parenting is . . . Peek a boo.' There's a delighted belly chuckle from Woody.

'It *is* quite hard, isn't it?'

'The thing is, everyone tries to tell you beforehand, but nobody listens because nobody listens to mothers, do they? Then, when it happens to you, you're all like *'why did nobody tell me how hard it is?'* Then you realise, you *were* told, over and over, but you weren't listening. You were too busy tutting at some poor woman who's struggling to get her buggy off the bus. Woody? Where's he gone? Oh! There he is!'

There's a quiet gulp of Lauren drinking her tea. I've not heard Mum talk like this. Not even heard this tone of voice from her before. Lauren's never told me it's hard apart from the odd funny message, but I've hardly seen her properly since Woody was born, to be fair.

'I don't want to become one of those women who vanishes when they become a mother,' I remember her telling me when she was pregnant. And yet, Lauren has turned down every invite since Woody came along. *'Sorry I'm too exhausted. Sorry he won't sleep. Sorry he won't wean. Sorry I don't have enough time to get into and out of town within his wake window.'*

I keep my eyes closed but this nap won't come. I'm worried. Will this happen to me too? I've already got quite a boring, traditional life . . . will this make it worse? Motherhood can't be that hard, can it? I honestly don't think having a baby can be as hard as pregnancy. At least when the baby is here, I'll get my body back. I'll get more sleep once I'm not hunched around an animated fleshy beachball that kicks me in the ribs all night. When the baby is here, I won't have gurgling heartburn anymore. I'll be able to have a hot bath, drink more than one coffee, do a shot of tequila, not worry they're stillborn every time they don't kick for an hour. I won't be like Lauren, I forbid it. And I'm sure Lauren's doing better than she looks anyway. I mean, Woody seems gorgeous.

I close my eyes and tune out my mother's voice, allowing my body to rest before everyone comes.

Before Phoebe comes.

Phoebe.

As I doze off, her face comes into focus. Cat-eyes, a smile that's almost a smirk, a nose that looks hand-painted with freckles.

Meeting Phoebe was like when I tried salted caramel for the first time, activating taste buds I didn't know existed.

'Come on. Do a shot,' her voice says in my head, dragging the past back. The two of us were in a speakeasy in Shoreditch, perched on stools at the packed bar. Everyone around me looked like they'd only completed puberty the week before.

'It's Tuesday,' I'd protested.

'I'm aware it's Tuesday. And so?' She winked as she slurped up the last of her cocktail through an unnecessarily thin straw, whereas I still had half my drink left.

'So . . . it's a work night and I'm not a student anymore. Hangovers morphed from amusingly uncomfortable to downright *I-question-everything-in-my-life* overnight when I turned 25.' I pushed my drink away. 'Not that anyone in here knows the meaning of the words *twenty-five*. Do they all have a young person's railcard? I bet they fucking do.' Phoebe cackled and pushed my drink back. 'Plus,' I sighed, knowing it was useless. 'I don't want to be sweating tequila during our pitch to Femme tomorrow morning.'

Phoebe just gestured to the bartender and a tray of shots arrived. Not just two shots. A whole tray. Where had everyone else gone? How had we got here from the old man's pub around the corner of the office? I didn't remember the journey. What was the time? I blearily checked my phone and groaned. How was it half eleven? Two missed calls from Matt.

Matt:
Umm, where are you wifey? You said you were leaving work drinks two hours ago?

'Phoebe, it's half eleven.' I tried reasoning with her. I'd explained it was Tuesday. I'd reminded her it was almost midnight. Surely that was all she needed to know.

But she plucked a shot off the tray and handed it over with such authority that I took it. 'I'm aware of the time, Nicki.'

'It's a Tuesday.'

'We've already established that too.' She clinked her shot glasses and threw the aniseed liquid down her delicate throat. The muscle memory of peer pressure kicked in and I found myself copying and wincing. I coughed as she laughed and offered me a sip of her water.

'Where did everyone go?' I asked, wiping my mouth.

'Home. Losers. Not us. Come on. Down the hatch.'

'Phoebe, I can't.'

Yet down the hatch it went. And there was laughter, and more gossip, and telling Matt, *sorry I'm leaving now*, and then, *whoops*, how is it half midnight already, shit I've missed the last tube. Then there was *oh wells, we may as well go dancing*. Phoebe was, of course, one of those people who *knew a great place*, not very far away, which had great music and friendly people and killer cocktails, not that I could taste anything by that point anyway. We danced, the music thudding through my white work plimsols, paired with a midi skirt and pressed white silk blouse. Compared to what everyone else was wearing in that club, I may've well been wearing a toe-length petticoat and a fucking . . . ruff. I wondered if we'd bump into Steffi. This was her sort of place, her sort of life. I'd always thought it was mildly pathetic but it was undeniably enjoyable. My face hurt from laughing. My body ached from dancing. Matt's message on my phone, saying he was going to sleep now, have a good night, are you sure you're OK to stay at this Phoebe's house? *Yes, yes, sorry for keeping you up.*

I'd only known Phoebe for a month. I was marketing manager for this ethical gemstones company and she'd joined as 'young blood' to help get our brand to appeal to Generation *WhateverTheHellTheyAre*. The ones on TikTok who only eat viral salads while diagnosing themselves with ADHD. I'd initially been intimidated by her, as you only can be when you used to be the young cool one in the office, but now, somehow, you look at the generation below with judgemental bafflement and panic your career's over. Phoebe and I were paired to 'learn from each other', and, despite my fear she'd make me feel ancient, we'd really clicked. I was amazed to learn she was 29, not 24. 'I have three younger sisters from when my dad remarried,' she confided in me when I marvelled at her ability to understand Gen Z. 'Once they grow up, my career is ruined. But I'm happy to milk them until then.'

'Do they want to post an Instagram of themselves wearing our new Rose Quartz charm bracelet on their grid?'

She laughed so hard her freckles scrunched together to form one giant freckle. 'They're not even on there, Nicki. Oh bless you.'

I'd taken her out to lunch on the first day, to show her the nearby street food market and explain which stalls were the best. We'd sat with salads perched on our laps, cross-legged on a tiny stretch of grass, knees scrunched up to make room for the other London office workers. She apparently had no first-day nerves, or first-day levels of appropriateness. By the end of lunch, she'd already mentioned taking weed gummies, how much money she had currently in her bank account ('less than two hundred pounds and you guys are paying me in arrears, fuck') and given me entry-level information on the sexual politics involved in being a femme lesbian . . . a term I'd had to google afterwards. By the end of her first week, we'd had lunch every day and our company had launched its own TikTok channel. A month later, I was staggering from the night bus back into her house share in Dalston, my white trainers now grey, laughing as she shhed me in case I woke her housemates.

'Be quiet. I don't want to piss them off, it's a Tuesday.'

'OH, ONLY NOW YOU ADMIT GOING OUT ON TUESDAY IS FAR FROM THE NORM.'

'Shh! Nicki! Hey. You don't need to drink direct from the tap like that. I'll get you a glass. Hang on.'

It was like walking through a portal to my youth, wandering around her house, borrowing her pyjamas, brushing my teeth with my finger in her filthy shared bathroom. I ached with nostalgia for how much this house, this night, reminded me of my Little Women days at university. The four toothbrushes in a cup on the side of the basin, the novelty posters lining the staircase, an assigned shelf in the fridge and freezer, and a pot on the kitchen counter for milk and loo roll money. Phoebe and I passed out, head to toe, on a rickety rental bed, on a Tuesday night, with not a care for what that meant for the reality of Wednesday morning.

'I'm not like this,' I told Phoebe as we tried to get some sleep in the rising dawn. My life felt very far away down this portal. My husband, my sensible two-bed flat in a sensibly priced area of the city, the pitch I had to deliver at work in seven hours' time, the practicalities of what the hell I was going to wear tomorrow. Instead, I just had aching feet from dancing, aching face from laughing, aching heart from how much life I might've been missing out on.

'Not like what?' Phoebe's voice was heavy with almost-sleep.

'A clubbing-on-Tuesday person.'

'You talk like you're so old,' she said. I could feel her smile, even though her head was by my feet. 'But you're not. It's funny.'

'I am old.'

'You're only two years older than me.'

'Yeah but you're youthful. I'm . . . I've only ever seen two penises in my whole life. Two.'

She giggled and my toes shook on her pillow. 'That's two more than me.'

'So you never?'

'I always knew I was gay,' she replied. 'Didn't see the point of experimenting with something as aesthetically displeasing as a cock, just to check.'

'They are very strange, aren't they? Like little cartoon characters.'

'I'll have to take your word for it.'

'Still though. You must've slept with more than two people.'

'This month? Yeah. But that doesn't make me young. Youthfulness is a feeling. A lightness. An openness. An optimism.'

Was I not those things? I asked myself, as heavy weights tugged my eyelids shut. I had every reason to be grateful, to be *optimistic*. I knew that. I'd sat there smugly coupled up with Matt throughout my twenties as the Little Women had cried on my sofa about their dating woes, the stakes getting higher as the years passed. *Why won't he call me his girl-friend? Why won't he say I love you? Why has he decided to go travelling? Why won't he move in with me? Why won't he marry me? Why won't he have children with me?* The hunt, and the chase, and the insecurities, and the *is this ever going to happen*, and *what's wrong with me*, or *is it what's wrong with men*, and *am I going to die alone* . . . and there I have sat, passing tissues to Lauren and saying *'you don't deserve this'*, going to see a psychic with Charlotte, taking hot photos of Steffi for her dating profiles . . . smugly, smugly with lovely Matt. Matt who has loved me, unwaveringly, since he was 20 years old. I've never been dumped. I've never been ghosted. Never had to deal with commitment-phobia or covert narcissism or feminist fuck bois. I should feel light, and open, and youthful. And yet, as my eyes fluttered shut on an unfamiliar pillow, with an unfamiliar body in bed with me, even if it was just a colleague who'd let me crash . . . I felt stale, closed, cynical.

Old.

The more time I spent with Phoebe, the more I started viewing my twenties with a different prescription. The chats over our desks, our lunches in the park, the afterwork drinks that started regularly turning into shots and dancing and crashing at hers . . . the more I felt I'd *missed* something rather than dodged something.

'Doesn't it depress you, knowing you'll never fall in love again?' Phoebe asked, half a burrito hanging out of her mouth as we sat on a park bench. 'Never have a first kiss again?'

And, 'I can't believe you've never been dumped!' she'd exclaimed, thudding her empty shot glass down on the bar. 'How do you know your heart if it's never been broken? It's capable of such pain, Nicki. Such glorious, exquisite, pain. You need to know who you are when you're heartbroken. You learn so much about yourself.'

'Well, er, Matt and I did take a break for a week after graduating to see if we missed each other,' I offered blearily. 'But we both missed each other after two days, so we got back together.'

She'd blown a raspberry with her delicate mouth. 'Doesn't count. If you're not hyperventilating on the ground, clutching your heart through your top to try and stop the sheer physical, actual, agony of it breaking . . . nope.'

'I was quite gloomy for those two days.'

'Christ. You've never had a break-up song, have you?' Phoebe would've looked less shocked if I'd said I hadn't had the MMR vaccine.

'A what?'

'A song that you play repeatedly when you're heartbroken that's then forever tainted and triggering.'

'Umm, I get sad when I listen to that one about Eric Clapton singing to his dead son.'

'So, you're not a psychopath, congratulations.'

I tried leaning my chin in my hand but missed and almost fell off my stool. 'Aren't I just lucky?' I argued. 'To have met The One, dodged all that?'

'But how do you know he's The One if you haven't had a chance to see what you're like when you're with other people? What they bring out of you?' She had that glint in her eye again, pushing another shot glass my direction. *Tuesdays are the new Fridays,* was our motto. I hadn't shared a bed with Matt on a Tuesday for weeks now.

'Matt brings out general happiness.'

'Are you sure you're not confusing happiness with just comfort? Safety?'

'What's wrong with being safe?'

She raised both eyebrows at me and downed her shot.

'You tell me.'

It's hard to know if Phoebe was the blight that had started to spread through Matt and I's marriage, or if she'd just merely pointed it out. But, by the end of that summer, I was no longer happy. I was definitely no longer comfortable.

'Don't you mind, me going out so much?' I'd asked Matt. When, yet again, I'd come home on a Wednesday night, with red eyes and hardly any sleep.

He'd shrugged and carried on playing Football Manager on his iPad. 'I quite enjoy having the big telly to myself to be honest,' he'd replied. 'And I get Chinese, which you don't like.'

One night, when we'd gone for a drink around the corner at our local, like we always did, I asked him if he ever thought about doing role-play.

He'd pulled a face into his pint. 'Not really, no. You?'

'No. Do you think we should want to do role-play?'

'What would we even play?'

God it was so sad. The only sexy roles I could imagine was us not knowing one another for the past twelve years.

My 'lucky' life started to feel like a choker. I, quite quickly, began to feel resentful I'd met Matt so young. Resentful that he was so loveable, and dependable, and into me, and never made me doubt or question anything. The only drama we had was the Steffi stuff, and to be honest, sometimes, when I wanted to fancy him enough to have sex with him, I'd have to remember the Steffi drama to get turned on.

Had I settled, marrying the guy I met at uni? Had I missed out on the best sex of my life? The worst sex of my life, but funny enough it would make a hilarious story? Steffi always had the funniest stories – us snorting into cocktails while she'd wail, 'Stop it, it's my life,' but laughing too. I never had any stories to tell. Would I have been happier with another person? Had I met Matt later, would I appreciate him more because I'd been dicked around (literally) through my twenties? Or was I taking him for granted?

'You're making me question everything,' I complained to Phoebe, over drinks, celebrating the client pitch we'd somehow pulled off despite this morning's hangover. So much was possible since I'd met her. You can be hungover at work and still deliver. You could make new friends in your thirties. It's not too late to change. To question what you've been doing up until now and ask yourself if it's for the best.

'That's not true,' she replied. 'You were questioning it all anyway. I've just made you admit it to yourself.'

I'd sighed heavily and looked at the large glass of red wine in front of me. Already it didn't seem large enough and I'd not had a sip yet.

'For a lesbian, you've got an extraordinary amount of patience for me droning on about my husband,' I said, aware this was a conversation she'd endured many times over.

'Hey,' she held up her glass to cheers me. 'Maybe I've got a vested interest.' Her freckles scrunched together again as she smiled, and I found myself smiling back . . .

. . . The doorbell.

A flustered Charlotte squealing, 'They're here. People are arriving.'

My mum's hands on my shoulder. 'Wake up, honey. Your guests are arriving. You dropped off.'

The baby stirs inside me. My life falls back into focus. It's my baby shower. The baby I'm having with Matt. It's today. It's 35 degrees outside. All my friends are coming. I'm in my parents' new greenhouse home. It's two years later. Everything has happened the way it should.

Woody's crying on the wooden floor. Apparently the doorbell has upset him. Lauren bends over to pick him up. Steffi is ensconced on her phone in a squashy chair in the corner, trying to get away with as much scrolling as possible while I napped.

Charlotte's greeting people at the door like this is her house. Multiple voices saying hello, gasps at the balloon arch. I feel the hot air drift in from the open door. My ears prickle as they listen out to who is saying hi and asking where to put their gifts.

There's only one voice I want to hear.

Transcript: Inspector Simmons interviewing Lauren Powell

Simmons: Notes from your GP say you've recently been suffering from symptoms of Post-Natal Depression?

Lauren: Have you ever googled the symptoms for Post-Natal Depression?

Simmons: Er—

Lauren: —Because if you then google the symptoms of severe sleep deprivation, they're basically the same thing.

Simmons: Are you saying you're not ill?

Lauren: No. Yes. I don't know. I guess, what I'm saying is, I'm too sleepy for arson. I don't have the energy to wash my hair more than once a week – let alone start a fire.

Simmons: But you've been struggling, haven't you? With having a baby? The GP said you were requesting counselling.

Lauren: How is that even relevant?

Simmons: The baby shower might've been quite hard for you . . . all these images of motherhood, when you've been finding motherhood so tough.

Lauren: I was happy for my friend.

LAUREN

I can't stop staring at Nicki's stomach.

It's like one of those portraits where the eyes follow you around the art gallery, except, wherever I am in this ridiculous greenhouse party, there's her swollen tummy, in my eye-line, churning my stomach as it strains out of its dungarees.

Every time I see it I want to cry. Or scream. Or run away. Or run towards her, hugging her, crying for everything that's coming her way that's too late to stop. My poor poor friend. And poor poor me. And poor poor all of us. I can see it now I'm on the other side – how motherhood is a banana skin we all trip up on. Everyone warns you it's slippery, and the fall really hurts, but we distrust and dislike the whinging mothers that come before us – shut up, it's your choice, woman – until it's our turn to tread on the same banana skin, and over we go, ouch, flailing on the floor, our bodies piling high, warning the others behind us about the danger, but none of them listen and, ouch, here they are in the pile too, saying, 'Why didn't you warn me how hard it is?'

Or, I don't know, maybe it's just me? Maybe other mothers are fine, and happy, and don't have a prolapsed mess where their vagina used to be, and I'm a selfish cunt who shouldn't have had a baby and holy hell is it too late now.

That's the biggest headfuck about motherhood – there's no going back. There's no trial period or refund with a receipt. You can't possibly imagine how ridiculously hard it is, and when you do, it's too late. You can't go back to before, and, because of the ludicrous love you feel for your life-ruining baby, you wouldn't want to anyway. Even though you would. But you'd like to keep the baby, too. Maybe suspended in some special fluid somehow, that keeps it warm and safe and fed and loved and alive while you can still be you . . . a womb, I guess. Nicki's complained a dozen times since I arrived about how uncomfortable she is, and I've been feigning smiles and concerns and empathy, but, in my head, all I can think is, *just you wait, my poor babe. Just you fucking wait. Pregnancy will feel like a dream.*

Basically, I'm in the perfect mood for this baby shower on steroids. Can't you tell?

There's something about baby showers that makes everyone arrive punctually, and the twenty or so guests arrive in a frenzied fifteen-minute clump which almost breaks Charlotte.

'Hello. Greetings. Welcome. Thanks for coming. Here's your welcome cupcake. Be careful biting into it. There's a prize if you get a pregnant one.'

One in five of the cupcakes has apparently been 'fertilised' with a 'gooey centre' so nobody really wants to eat them after hearing that. But everyone coos as they take their red velvet womb sponges and glittery prosecco cocktails, and coo appropriately when they see Nicki. Luckily for me, the next thing to coo over is Woody, and the older women especially have basically taken him off my hands. Mrs Davies is currently squidging his cheeks and throwing him up and down, allowing me to down this prosecco which leaves edible glitter all over my lips. The air-con unit is almost combusting with the effort of keeping the packed room cool. I'm already sweating, as is my uneaten cake to one side of me. For some reason, the prospect of a fertilised cupcake isn't giving me an appetite. This is surprising as the only joy I've found during my maternity leave has been sitting in coffee shops and stuffing myself with butter icing while Woody cries in my arms. One day, during the 'four-month sleep regression', *(can you regress from waking every two hours? It appears, yes, you can)* I ate an entire cake. A whole one. Like Bruce fucking Bogtrotter in *Matilda*. If only that cake was 'fertilised' with 'a gooey centre' then maybe I'd be put off baked goods and then I'd fit into at least one item of my pre-pregnancy wardrobe.

Anyway, I sit with a nappy in one hand, and a black marker pen in the other, awaiting instructions from Charlotte, who is so manic her whole face is essentially one diluted pupil.

'Right, ladies and gent,' she says, nodding her head towards Nicki's mate, George. He waves a jazz-hands hello and his glittery nail polish catches the sun. 'Here's a little icebreaker game so we can all get to know each other.'

Is there any collection of words worse than 'ice breaker game'? Other than 'rail replacement bus service'? Or 'destination hen do'?

'I want you to write a piece of advice for Nicki on the nappy. Then we wrap them up, and pass them along until we lose track, then open them up again and take it in turns to introduce ourselves and read out the advice.'

Am I just exhausted or does this game make literally no sense?

'This way, Nicki has lovely keepsakes from her closest friends that she can read through when the baby is playing up. Go on, write whatever advice you like! It's anonymous.'

I glance around at everyone else and wonder what the hell they could be writing. Nicki's mum is still bouncing Woody over in the kitchen. If she's anything like my mum, she's already given Nicki all the unsolicited advice she's ever going to need anyway. But everyone else seems suitably inspired to inscribe a Pampers with guidance. To my left, I look at what Steffi's written. She's half-heartedly scrawled '*ENJOY EVERY MOMENT* ' and is now checking her phone for the nineteenth time. To my right, I catch the eyes of this skinny woman covered in freckles. We both shrug at the same time and she rolls her eyes at the circle around us.

'I don't want to be a bitch,' she leans in, whispering. 'But, I can't imagine it's the most practical way to give a mother advice, is it? What's Nicki supposed to do? The baby starts crying, and she what? Has to unravel a pile of Pampers fortune cookies until she finds one that tells her how to burp it properly?'

I giggle, then feel disloyal to Charlotte for giggling, leaning closer. She smells delicious, like grown-up Ribena.

'What are you going to write?' she whispers.

'I don't know. What are you going to write?'

'I'll make a joke about gin, I guess.' She scrunches up her nose. 'Isn't that how women plaster over their ruined marriage, pelvic floor, and vanished place in society . . . *LOL but mummy loves gin?*'

I splutter with laughter and a few people look up so I cough as a cover. 'I take it you're not a mother?'

'Hell no.' She tilts her head and smiles. 'And I take it you're not a mother either?'

I point out Woody. 'Actually, my baby's over there.'

'Shit. Sorry. I'm sure your pelvic floor and marriage are fine.'

I keep laughing and she seems relieved. 'Both are fucked,' I admit. 'And I don't like the taste of gin. So, I guess I'm fucked from all directions.'

'Maybe that's what you should write then?' She points her pen at my blank nappy. '*You're fucked?*'

My loyalty to Nicki arrives a moment too late, and I don't let myself laugh at this one. Though, that's the sort of thing I wish I could write on this nappy.

You're fucked.

Yes, it's much harder than you ever could've imagined. Sorry.

Try screaming into a pillow rather than the baby's face.

Yes, you should've done your Kegels.

Apparently, it gets easier. I don't know when.

'Smile!' Charlotte's in front of us brandishing her phone. I blink like a blinded deer, noticing she's taken the photo from the angle where my postpartum jowls are most prominent.

Jowls. Another thing nobody tells you about.

'You must be Phoebe,' Charlotte says to the freckled lady, lowering her phone for a second. 'I recognise you from your profile picture. Thanks so much for coming.'

'Thanks for inviting me.'

'Smile again.' She takes another casual shot. 'Are you guys using the hashtag when you post?' She asks, gripping my hand.

'Just say yes,' I whisper through the sides of my teeth, and Phoebe smirks and nods.

'Fab. Brilliant. Perfect. Are you done with your nappies?' she reaches out, and I scribble 'Have gin in the cupboard' before handing it over. 'Great. We'll now swap nappies with people to get to know each other and mix them up before Nicki gets to open them.'

Nicki, sitting in the comfiest chair in front of the air con, is looking over at us. Her face looks physically pained at what Charlotte's organised, but she's cradling her stomach and going along with it. And, judging by the fizz of feminine excitement around us, most of the guests have drunk as much baby shower Kool-Aid as Charlotte – metaphorically and literally.

Woody starts wailing from the kitchen, and I get up, excused from making any more small talk. 'That's mine ringing,' I tell Phoebe, who grins. 'Oh, by the way,' I point to Steffi, lost in her phone next to me. 'This is Steffi. Steffi, Phoebe. And vice versa.'

Steffi looks up with a 'huh' while Phoebe gives a weirdly knowing smile. 'Oh, Steffi,' she says. 'I've heard a lot about you.'

But Woody's wailing prevents me from hearing any further.

Woody's starting to tire after Round Two of the games. I've known school sports days with less organisation, and, judging by how 'hook the dummies in the roll top bath' went, known them to be less competitive. An elbow fully went into someone's face during the grand finale, though George held his hands up and said, 'It wasn't me.' I momentarily feel I've staggered into some terrible cult while we all chant Nicki's name as she's challenged to change as many nappies on teddies as she can in one minute. There's been too much noise, and small talk, and cheering, and planned fun for my baby *(and me, to be honest)* and not enough baseline nap to see him through. He starts hitting my back, whinging, and rubbing his eyes constantly. We're all taking a time out and 'refreshment break' as Charlotte ferries baked goods from clump to clump. I end up sitting on a sofa next to Nicki, bookended by the two other mums there with their babies, trying to get Woody to latch. He's torn between wanting milk and wanting to hang backwards, exposing my nipple to everyone, craning about to see what he's missing. Then he wails, remembers he's hungry and tired, and starts sucking again before anyone makes any sound, and off he pops.

The mum next to me makes a sympathetic face. I think she's called Cara, from Nicki's work. 'They get so distracted as they get older, don't they?' Cara says. Though, I notice, her own baby's breastfeeding like she's just stepped out of a painting at the national gallery. She turns to Nicki, who's watching us intently. 'Do you know if you're going to breast-feed?'

Nicki shrugs. 'I don't want to put pressure on myself. Like, if it happens, it happens. If not, fed is best, yeah?'

Cara nods and her baby bobs on her breast, unbothered by the movement. 'Yes, of course. No pressure at all. It is lovely though. And so good for them.'

Nicki and I share a look. 'We'll see.'

I can't not look at Nicki's stomach. Woody must sense the adrenaline flow through me and bops off my breast again. 'Shh. Back on, Woody. Come on. You need to eat to nap.'

'Do you enjoy breastfeeding?' Nicki asks me, once I manage to get Woody back on again. 'You're still doing it, at what? Nine months? That's amazing.'

I have to stay perfectly still otherwise Woody will unlatch again. 'It's . . .' I start.

. . . It's impossible to explain, even to myself, what my relationship with breastfeeding is like. For the first few months, it was probably the biggest contributor towards my full-on mental breakdown. It was painful. It was terrible. Woody was totally shit at it. I used to call him Mr Crap Latch. '*Oh, there you have it, Mr Crap Latch strikes again,*' I'd think. Absolutely furious at him, as it meant he never drank enough and therefore he'd be hungry again in ninety minutes time, meaning I'd get no decent sleep. Back then I was still stupid enough to believe that decent sleep was a possibility. That it was just around the corner if only Woody would latch properly. If I'd told Past Me then that I *still* wasn't getting any sleep after nine months, I think I would've thrown myself off a bridge. I was so close anyway that I actively avoided walking across any. Tristan begged me to stop. 'Please, stop. I can feed him. We can try bottles. Why are you doing this to yourself?' That look in his eye again. The *my-wife-is-malfunctioning* look. The slight disgust. The *this-isn't-who-I-married.*

'He had a C-section so he needs breastmilk because he wasn't exposed to all the good bacteria in my vaginal canal.' I kept repeating it, wondering why he didn't listen, wouldn't believe me. Instead, he clenched his fists in frustration and didn't unfurl them for months.

'Lauren, we've gone through this. Those two things aren't related to breastfeeding.' He attempted a smile. 'Plus, Woody was stuck in your vaginal canal for quite some time if I remember. Plenty of time to lick some germs and have a good immune system.'

'You think this is funny? It's not fucking funny.'

Plus, the midwives acted like bottles didn't exist. '*Keep going,*' they said. '*Try this rugby position,*' they said. '*No no no, not like that, you're doing it wrong. It's not supposed to hurt but definitely keep doing it even if it's agony. What's formula? There isn't any in the hospital so if you don't get this right your baby will starve. You can't go home until you've figured out the latch. Let me check it again. No, position is all wrong. Unlatch him. I know he's screaming but unlatch him. Try again. No. Wrong again. He can't breathe. He'll get wind. No wonder he's up all night with that latch. Does he have tongue tie? We don't bother checking for it but he's likely got it. If you want to get it checked you'll have to pay a private lactation consultation £280 to tell you he has it, and then another £280 to cut it, and, oh, the NHS waiting list is three weeks long and your baby will die before then, but don't you dare use formula. Nipple confusion! You need to establish your milk supply first! Your post-natal depression will get worse if you stop! Keep going, keep going. Don't try using a bottle until it's way too late for the baby to accept the bottle. Oh dear, yes, now you can't leave your baby for more than three hours for about a year. Didn't anyone tell you that? Why didn't you introduce a bottle sooner? You're giving your child the best start in life though. Your entire life might've shrunk to a mile's radius from your front door, but at least the baby will never get sick, apart from all the times they get sick, and they'll have a higher IQ, even though, actually, it appears that evidence is overstated. Here's all the advice ever about how to start breastfeeding and how to keep breastfeeding as your life falls around you in tatters. Here's absolutely no advice on how to stop. Don't worry, they won't still be doing it when they're five years old. We don't think . . .'*

Nicki's watching me, noticing the long pause in my answer. I open my mouth again. So torn, always so torn, between telling the truth but also wanting to protect her from it. She'll find out soon enough. Or maybe it will all go well for her. Maybe she'll love breastfeeding and find it easy and introduce the bottle at the right time and manage to combi feed without fucking up her supply – therefore getting to leave her baby, and go on nights out, or to an art gallery, or for a long walk, or any other thing that makes you feel sane. Maybe it's just me that's rubbish, as per usual.

'Breastfeeding is . . . such an experience,' I manage to get out. 'There's . . . erm . . . it makes you . . .' *Mental. Resentful. Permanently hungry.* '. . . it's kind of cool, seeing your body make milk.'

Nicki smiles, relieved, then I feel an urgent sense of protection. 'However,' I add, just as Woody pulls off, rubbing his eyes, and nestles into my shoulder. My eyes check my watch. He's getting sleepy right on time. Maybe putting him down for his nap won't be hell on earth in this noisy greenhouse? Maybe today will be the day he just . . . sleeps. 'I really would try to get them to take a bottle early – to help you get some sleep. If you exclusively breastfeed, then you basically have to exclusively do the night wakes too. I wish somebody had told me that.'

Nicki nods, noted. But Cara shakes her head. 'Oh, I do all the wakes anyway,' she interjects, taking her delicate child off one nipple and switching it to the other with no fuss.

'You do?' Nicki asks.

'I don't mind doing them,' she adds, stroking her baby's hair. 'It's for such a short time, isn't it? I enjoy the cuddles. Plus, my husband is useless anyway. I wouldn't trust him to get him back down. But, also, yes, I'm a nice wife.' And she laughs.

I fake a smile as a calm rage lands on me like falling rain.

Cool Mum serenely copes with all the night wakes and lets her husband sleep. It doesn't make sense for them both to be knackered.

Cool Mum is fine on four hours' broken sleep anyway. She admits she's a little tired, yes, but then changes the subject rather than harping on about how she's stuck in actual hell. Who needs to hear that?

Cool Mum doesn't feel stone cold dread from 5pm onwards, worrying what sort of ridiculous atrocity of a night she has coming up. Especially as she does all the wakes, because 'she's a nice wife'.

Would you like a blow job, honey? Before you go get eight hours sleep? I'm actually really up for sex too. I'm not too tired, or touched out, or traumatised by my horrific birth, or dry because of the breastfeeding, or petrified about the thought of sex because I could get pregnant and there's no way I'm putting myself through this again. Let's do it doggy style, to prove nothing has changed! Now, come on my tits. Well done. And off to sleep with you, darling husband. Don't worry. I'll do the night wakes. Let's not let your life change at all. I don't mind, I'm a Cool Mum.

'Wow,' I say, and I can't quite help but deadpan. 'Your husband is a lucky man.'

Poor Tristan. I feel such guilt for all the times I've made him stay up with me, even though he can't help. 'Don't go to sleep,' I'd begged him, three weeks in, when he was practically drooling he was so exhausted on our seventh wake of the night due to cluster feeding.

'I'm no good to you awake,' he'd pleaded. His exhaustion matching mine. Both of us broken in the name of equality.

'No, you can't leave me. Don't close your eyes,' I'd shouted. 'Don't you dare close your eyes.'

Cara blushes. 'Well, I do often have to remind him. Men, eh?'

'Men,' I agree, shifting Woody from one shoulder to another so he doesn't fall asleep on me.

'Are you OK, Nicki?' I ask.

She starts shifting herself up, having to twist into at least three different yoga positions to get herself out of the comfy chair.

'Yes. Sorry. I'm just getting stiff. I need to keep moving. It hurts to sit for too long. I might go load the dishwasher.'

'I'll come with you,' I add, standing up, keen to escape this triggering nightmare. 'I need to keep Woody up another twenty minutes before nap time, and he has this weird obsession with watching me do domestic chores.' I turn back to Cara. 'It was lovely to meet you.'

I escort a waddling Nicki into the kitchen, jiggling Woody to keep him awake. We pass clumps of her guests who all turn like she's famous and throw out generic comments about how glowing she is, and what a lovely bump she has, and *oh I can't believe how soon it's coming.* The house is open plan, but the kitchen around the corner offers a tiny appearance of privacy. My phone vibrates against my leg as I wrangle Woody into the high chair Charlotte's provided and give him a breadstick from the nappy bag to keep him entertained. I start collecting discarded glasses up with my fingers, and, as predicted, Woody falls quiet and watches me, like I'm doing the world's most elaborate interpretative dance.

'Sorry about Cara,' Nicki half whispers. She's put two glasses into the dishwasher and is now attempting to get herself onto a stool. My phone vibrates again. 'She's really nice but she missed the memo on fourth wave feminism.'

'She was lovely,' I lie.

'She's our engagement ring marketing person. As you can imagine, she's perfect for it. She literally cries with happiness whenever any customer sends us a proposal story.'

I plop some more glasses down and scan the kitchen, seeing there's no more in here. There are loads scattered around the living space, but I don't have the strength to re-enter that performance of femininity yet. Plus, now Nicki's chatting about Cara, I figure cleaning up was an excuse to exit anyway. 'Matt better do some of the night wakes, anyway,' she adds. 'I want us to be totally equal.'

I nod as my phone judders on my leg for a third time.

'God, it's so stuffy in here,' she says, distracted and fanning her face. 'Will it break the air-con entirely if I crack a window? Do you mind? I'm too big.'

'Yeah, of course.' I lean over the sink and shove open a giant square of glass. The hot air streams in like a current but at least it's fresh. I lean towards it, not realising how stuffy I was until this alternative is offered. Nicki sighs behind me. 'That's better. Phew. How long do you think we can hide in here?'

'I say ten minutes before Charlotte brings you in to accept the animal sacrifice.'

We laugh together and say, 'Bless her,' and then Woody randomly joins in, clapping from his high chair. My love for him gallops back in, almost drowning me. I rush over to pluck him from his high chair so I can burrow myself into his scent. He laughs again and snuggles me back, and Nicki looks relieved for the first time in twenty minutes.

'Oh he's glorious,' she tells me. 'He's making me get impatient. Can I have another cuddle?'

'Of course.'

I tip Woody over and he spills into her arms happily – shoving his fingers into Nicki's mouth. I take the moment to check my phone, fishing my device out from my sack dress. I lean against the counter as I check my notifications.

Two replies from the account I messaged earlier.

Please leave me alone.
I've reported you. Please. Get some help.

The final notification was from Instagram, telling me I've breached their community guidelines and I'll have my account deleted if I continue my behaviour of harassment and intimidation.

The rain of my rage turns into a downpour, soaking me through. 'Are you OK with Woody for a second?' I ask Nicki, who is singing him a song. 'I just need a wee.'

I run past her before she even agrees, past the hubbub. Charlotte tries calling after me, telling me the food's served in twenty minutes. There's no queue for the bathroom and I fall to the toilet – shaking my hands to try and dislodge all this energy. Then I put my head between my legs, and I howl into the flesh of my flabby postpartum thighs.

Transcript: Inspector Simmons interviewing Steffani Fox

Steffani: I was having the best day of my life that day. Literally. All my dreams were coming true. Why would I randomly decide to commit *arson*?

Simmons: That's not strictly true, is it?

Steffani: What do you mean?

Simmons: Work might've been going well, but your friendship circle was strained – wouldn't you say?

Steffani: Was it? I was too busy negotiating multi-million pound deals to feel any strain with anyone.

Simmons: And Nicki didn't mind, you doing this at her party?

Steffani: Not at all. She was happy for me. They all were.

STEFFI

You see, this is the problem with posh glass houses – there's nowhere to hide. I desperately need to call Rosa but the downstairs bathroom's engaged, the upstairs one is off-limits, and I don't know which bedrooms contain napping infants. I end up sneaking out of the glass doors, muttering 'holy fuck' as I step into the heat. I crouch run across the decking, basically ninja roll down the steps, and end up whispering my very important conversation at the back of the garden, behind a half-dead tree.

'I know it's a huge decision so I wanted to give you as much time as I can,' I tell Rosa, sucking both my stomach and arse in so the tree will disguise me. If I move my head even slightly, the party can see me through the glass wall.

'I really want to say yes to Nina,' Rosa repeats. 'I love her.'

'I know. I love her too. But what Mountain Scape Studio are offering is huge. Even bigger than her. We're talking a Hollywood blockbuster, Rosa, with associated budget. Nina is amazing but her studio is still on the smaller side. She won't put up this much money.'

'But . . . I trust her with this.'

I smile to myself. It's crazy how my job can change a person in only a few short hours. When I called Rosa on the train platform, she still couldn't believe she was going to get published at all. Fast forward two hours and she's now not even considering a multi-million-pound film deal with one of the biggest studios in the world.

'Nina is amazing and her offer is an amazing thing,' I tell her. 'In another universe, one where you weren't the most talented human being I've ever shared oxygen with, we'd be face-down in a bath full of champagne right now.' Rosa giggles softly down the phone. Good. I need her back down to earth, so she can think properly. 'But I've never seen a film pre-empt like this in my whole career,' I continue, 'And, not to be weird, I'm really good at my job. Mountain Scape are aggressive though. It will only be on the table until the end of Monday. It's huge, Rosa. I just want you to really think it through.'

We talk a while longer until my stomach hurts from holding it in so tightly. We weigh up the things most authors want to weigh up – who will treat the book the most authentically during the adaptation? Who might let them co-write? Who is likely to play the main character? Who understood the book the most? I get all that, I do. I'm in the arts. I love books. But still, I'm an agent. And it's my job to only really care about, a) how much money, and b) who is most likely to get it green lit? Because getting the TV show or film *actually made* is what brings in more money.

'I'll think about it, I promise,' she reassures me. 'I . . . it's a lot. I still can't believe my book is going to be in a book shop.'

'Your book is going to be on a billboard in Times Square.'

She shriek laughs. 'Stop it. A book shop is enough for today. I'm going to go for a walk around Brockwell Park. Calm myself down and have a think.'

'Get an ice-cream.'

'Are you kidding? It's £4.50 for a 99 cone these days.'

'Rosa, you're about to turn down one actual million pounds. You can buy the ice cream.'

'Today doesn't seem real. OK. A ridiculously overpriced cone and a think, I promise.'

'I'm here.' I remind her. 'I'm at this party thing, but I can sneak out again and chat to you if need be.'

'Thank you.'

When she rings off, I collapse onto the dried grass, allowing myself my own moment to ride the adrenaline wave. I have to be calm for Rosa, but my body feels like a human party popper. I look out over the sprawling vista to try and stop my brain flailing about from strategy to strategy. I need to hire a real PA, and a film agent, and a foreign rights agent already. Could I poach Anna from JK? No. Stop it, Steffi. STOP IT. Don't rush ahead. Focus on the view. This view would be amazing if our country wasn't everything David Attenborough has been trying to warn us about. There's not an inch of green left in these rolling fields, just parched yellow rectangles, sewn together by browning hedgerows. Even Nicki's parents' lawn has fallen. They're the sort of law-abiding people who keep to a hosepipe ban, even though there's no one out here to see them cheating. That glass house must be heavily soundproofed because I can't hear a thing from the seven circles of hell inside. Dante's Inferno but with fertilised cupcakes. And that's just the first circle. We've not got to the vagina piñata yet, but I saw it flapping in the tiny breeze on the decking. I find baby showers trying at the best of times, but today's really does feel beyond satire.

It's not that I'm against celebrating pregnancy, or weddings, or hen dos, or all the other parties I've dutifully attended – but not particularly enjoyed – since I turned twenty-seven when suddenly these things started demanding most of my weekends. They are beautiful things. Huge, wonderful life moments in my treasured friends' lives. They were just so generic. So . . . gendered. So utterly lacking in any uniqueness, despite everyone's best efforts to make theirs different. Hive mind, groupthink, spoon-fed desires. And so, I've ended up attending precisely the same wedding multiple times. I could attend a wedding in my sleep, and a baby shower in my nap – they are so paint by numbers. Admittedly, today incudes every single paint colour and every number up until infinity but still none of it feels new. I turn my face up to the glaring sunshine, trying to time it so I get a good vitamin D hit but not too much to cause wrinkles, and I let myself feel hurt. Hurt that a party like this has never been thrown for me because I've not yet achieved any paint-by-number life achievement. Mum always warned me not to fall for the trap of these paths. 'The things people think make them happy, often don't,' she always said. 'Make sure you want things because you want them, Steffi, not because everyone tells you to want them.' She'd always been so honest about the hardships of being a single mum. 'Even married women are single mothers,' she told me. 'You just wait and see when you get older. See how your mother friends will end up basically doing it all themselves, just with the veneer of a husband and therefore society's blessing.' Mum always reassured me that I'm the best thing she ever did, but she was brutally open about the sacrifices. 'I never want you to make any sacrifices,' she'd whispered, over and over, year after year, as she got more frail until it was my time, finally, to look after her. 'I never want you to be held back, Steffi. Wings clipped. Stuck in a house, using feathers to make a nest rather than using them to fly.' And how I've flown, darling Mum – making you proud wherever you are now. I'm soaring so high but my career achievements have never warranted today's level of command performance. At my agency launch party last month, Charlotte didn't do all of this for me. And, even though I'd maxed out my credit card to pay for it as I had to pretend I was already successful, not all the Little Women even bothered to come. Lauren used Woody as an excuse – some shit about he wasn't weaned yet so she couldn't miss the bedtime routine. I have sympathy for that, I really do. However, I know that if it was my *wedding* or my *baby shower,* then she'd have pushed through whatever torture required to make sure she attended, like she's done for today. I wouldn't *want* her to do that, but the fact she didn't even think about *trying* showed that me setting up Foxxy Books wasn't in the same league as getting married or pregnant. And, yeah, Charlotte came and was so excited and manic that several publishing people came up to me afterwards to tell me they were '*obsessed*' with her, but she only brought a bouquet of flowers with her. God, I know I sound like a bitch, and they were lovely flowers, but they were what? Forty quid? Picked up from Victoria Station on the way. No homemade fertilised cupcakes for me. Throughout our friendship, I've paid to attend all their hen dos, which were multiple hundreds of pounds, even the low-key ones. I've attended all their weddings . . . again, multiple hundreds of pounds. Lauren had her wedding in frickin' Cornwall to get a 'beach vibe' so Tristan felt more at home and booked it for a Saturday in July. Do you know how much it costs to stay in a hotel, in Cornwall, at the weekend, in July? Then there was her spa baby shower too. All the money. *My* money. And I don't care. I'm happy for them, I really am. But a bouquet of flowers? When I'm achieving things so beyond possible for most people? When I'm being so brave rather than so *generic*? Nicki turned up to my party two hours late. *Late!* Can you imagine turning up hours late to a wedding? Friendship over. All I'd asked from them was to attend a party, in a bar, centrally located, from 6.30pm until 10pm, to support the hugest thing I could ever do in my life . . . and I get some flowers, a late arrival, and a flake out.

But it's too hot to stay out here getting angry. I love these women, I remind myself. I do. We just need to survive our thirties, when all our lives are so different, and come through the other side.

The tiny breeze has died down, stopping the gentle thwacking sound of the paper maché vulva hitting the glass. The air's so still I can now hear the party through the glass. I check my phone once more and feel both elated and disappointed I'm on Inbox Zero. No new offers in yet. God, I'm just as bad as Rosa. Yesterday I was desperate just to get this book published with enough commission to pay myself at the end of the month. Now I'm pissed off I've not been offered a million pounds in the last fifteen minutes.

I use the tree to yank myself up, the bark rough under my hands, and I climb the steps back onto the decking. Just as I'm taking a deep breath to prepare for re-entry, Lauren and Nicki's voices float through the open kitchen window, carrying on the still air.

'Thanks for taking him while I went to the loo,' Lauren says. 'Has he been OK?'

I hear the chuckle of a Woody being passed back to his mother.

'He's been a delight. You're so lucky.'

'Ha. Well, yes. He's lovely sometimes. Are you enjoying your baby shower?'

Nicki pauses before replying. You can build that woman a vulva (*including a clitoris*) out of tissue paper, and she still won't be fully satisfied. 'Yeah,' she says, before pausing. 'It's, Charlotte . . . you know. But bless her.'

I'm not sure why I'm staying here, lurking and listening. I dust off my legs to stand up and let myself in, when.

'. . . at least Charlotte gives a shit,' Nicki continues. 'Unlike *someone* . . . Tell me Lauren, where the hell is Steffi?'

I lower myself down at the mention of my name and put my back against the wall, my heart surging.

A babble from Woody. 'Shh, shh. Steffi?' Lauren asks. 'What do you mean?'

'I've hardly seen her since she arrived. Is she ill or some-thing? She's spent most of the time in the toilet.'

I roll my eyes. Nicki acts like she hardy registers me but I know I'm always being carefully monitored.

'. . . and when she's not hiding in the toilet, she's on her phone. Are we boring her or something?'

It's so jarring to hear Nicki discuss me in this bitchy, straight-forward way. It's so different from her usual fake politeness. This voice is natural and unguarded, revealing she's spoken about me using this tone before. I await Lauren's response, my heart racing.

'She's got this big work thing going on,' Lauren replies diplomatically, and I let go of my tight breath as she defends me. 'She feels terrible about the timing but it's all blown up today.'

'Blown up? Wow. Are things going badly with her agency or something?'

Does Nicki sound excited at the thought of my failure? I pull my knees up and keep listening – weirdly intrigued to hear more of this authentic Nicki, even if she's being a dick about me.

'The opposite. She's got some really exciting emails about the book she's launching Foxxy with.'

'If it's good news, surely it can wait til Monday?' Nicki says. 'I mean, God forbid she celebrates someone choosing to get pregnant and have a child. Did you see that article she posted a link to the other day?'

I wait for Lauren to defend me again. In fact, I'm almost looking forward to it. Instead, there's a pause. 'You saw it too?' She gulps.

'Fucking outrageous. Posting that when she knows I'm pregnant. It's a dig, surely it is?'

My mouth drops open and I clutch my knees closer, waiting for Lauren to defend me again.

Instead, I get, 'It did really upset me,' Lauren admits. 'When I read it, I basically went down a rage spiral.'

I almost gasp and give myself away. A red butterfly flutters past and lands on the hot decking for a moment, and I stare at it to try and steady myself.

'It upset you too?' There's excitement in Nicki's voice at this chink in friendship armour. 'I was so pissed off. I tried to talk to Charlotte about it earlier but she was determined we all play happy families today.'

'I just . . . don't understand why she felt the need to post that,' Lauren says – her voice reluctant but saying it anyway. 'Like, OK, read it, secretly agree with it. But to share it online, as such a public endorsement of such a hateful, selfish, way of seeing mothers? Like . . . I dunno . . . shh, Woody. Yes, we're going to sleep soon. I guess Steffi wants us to know how it feels to be on her side maybe?'

Nicki scoffs. 'Nobody *care*s about her side, that's the thing. It's a made-up fucking problem from someone who has nothing better to do but make up problems. Nobody *cares* that you've chosen not to have kids, Steffi. Sorry to burst your bubble, but nobody is thinking about you that much.'

I wait for Lauren's defence. I pray for Lauren's defence. My entire sanity depends on her defence. 'Exactly,' she replies, and my stomach hurts instantly and I blink at the butterfly.

'I've got bigger things to ponder on than, *"Ooh, I wonder why Steff doesn't want to have kids?"* It's like, fucking veganism, isn't it?' Nicki lets out a sharp laugh. 'How can you tell if someone's a vegan? You don't have to, they'll tell you themselves. It's the same with all these child-free people. Getting all wound up because a few people ask them about having kids during small talk out of politeness. I mean, have *you* ever judged someone for not having kids? No. Me neither. It's not a thing. We're all too busy doing the important job of fucking making the next generation to be thinking about them, judging them . . .'

I mean, Nicki, that is *exactly* what you're doing, you actual hypocrite. I hear her take breath to no-doubt launch into another well-rehearsed rant, but a piercing shriek cuts her off, and Woody starts howling so loudly I'm wincing with a wall between us.

'Sorry. Shh, shh Woody,' Lauren says. 'It's OK buddy. Sorry Nicki, he's just overtired. He didn't nap in the car. I had to pick up Steffi and she took ages coming out of the station and the parking woke him.'

'But, you know, *we're* the selfish ones.'

Lauren makes a non-committal grunt but the rest of their conversation is blunted by Woody. I can just about make out, 'Sorry, he'll calm down soon, I promise. I should maybe try and put him down, though I'm not allowed to for another four minutes.'

'Don't worry, he's a baby. I . . .' I lose them again behind Woody's cries, until, ' . . . we should probably close the window, for the air-con.'

I duck as I hear someone clatter closer. A flash of Lauren's hand pulling the glass wall shut and I hold my breath. Then it's just me, in the heat, with the birds too hot to sing and everything I've just heard.

I can't.

I rest my chin on my knees and the last five minutes seeps into my skin.

I honestly don't know what to make of it. I ping from self-righteous rage to paranoia at how much Lauren misunderstood me, to crippling hurt at what I overhead. To think I've come here, on the most important weekend of my life, smiling, polite, with a hundred quid's worth of gifts for Nicki in my bag, only for her to bitch, and goad, and ridicule me.

Fuck her.

Fuck her fuck her.

My phone almost explodes in my palm I'm squeezing it so hard. My breathing is ragged. My head full of a million comebacks and counter-arguments, defences and dramatic monologues.

I can't be here.

I'm going to leave. I'm just going to take my stuff and go.

Shit. I can't. I got a lift here.

With Lauren . . . Traitor.

Oh God, Lauren. Did she really think I agreed with THOSE parts of the article? Surely, she knows me better than that? I only posted it because of the dating part. Oh, how was I so dumb? No wonder she's upset. Part of that article was weird as hell, but the bit about dating was so good.

My heart bursts with guilt, but then righteous anger replaces it. Doesn't over a decade of friendship mean anything to her? Doesn't she know me better than that?

I don't know what to do. The drama of the day clasps its fingers around my neck – the opposing magnets of fate scrambling my brain. The publishing deals, but the being dumped. The thrill of my career cartwheeling into success, as a friendship cracks open like quaked earth. The butterfly's flown away so I've got nothing to focus on and centre myself. I start counting planks of the deck instead. One, two, three, four. The wood's been freshly varnished this summer. It gleams under the harsh light as my eyes skim and count . . . sixteen, seventeen, eighteen . . .

. . . hang on, what's that?

Stuck between two planks is a strange cylinder object, reflecting light off the alien metal. I lean over to take it in. It looks like an oversized can of coke. Weird. I twist it around and read the label.

What Will Baby Be? **Gender reveal smoke cannon.**

The top has been peeled back and the ring pull is standing up. Suddenly all the pink and blue food makes sense. There's more to today than showering. Christ – can I be pushed any further over the edge? I roll my eyes and twist the cannon around to see it's apparently filled with pink smoke.

Wow – today's gone so beyond basic, it's now fully complicated.

Transcript: Inspector Simmons interviewing Charlotte Roth

Charlotte: It was the perfect day. The perfect baby shower. Everything was perfect.

Simmons: Until somebody committed a terrible act of arson.

Charlotte: I still can't imagine that's what happened.

Simmons: Why not, Charlotte? Why is it so hard to imagine?

Charlotte: Because I used the best icebreaker games. Nobody could've felt alienated after those. Did you know, when meeting people in groups, you have to speak within the first ten minutes otherwise you disengage from the social situation? So, I ensured everyone at that baby shower had a chance to be noticed and listened to within the first ten minutes so the group would feel cohesive. Did you know, there was this research done at Harvard University, about the best way to 'break ice' in social groups, and it involved—

Simmons: —We're going off track here. Can you go back to your movements on the day in question?

Charlotte: That's what I've been doing. How am I supposed to know you don't want the exact details of the icebreaker games? It might be relevant, you know? Maybe I accidentally missed someone out and they didn't get a chance to speak within the first ten minutes, and they . . . started a fire in protest?

CHARLOTTE

Everything is melting. Everything is fucking melting.

It's fine. It's great. I'll make it work. It's fun! Fun, fun, melting baby shower. Who likes set icing on a cupcake anyway? It's much better when it's dripping down your fingers and ruining someone's nice sofa. I made the mistake of leaving the ice cube bag on the counter to try and take more photos, and it's now a bag of water. But who needs ice? Ice isn't important! Nobody really wants ice! I mean, many guests have asked if there's any ice left but they don't really want it. They want watermelon! I have watermelon. That's so naturally refreshing. I'll cut up more, serve it about, distract them from the ice. Watermelon doesn't melt. Hooray for watermelon!

Oh God, I do wish everyone would hurry up and eat the food before it melts. Eat. Eat! Come on everybody, eat it all, before it becomes soup. I check the time on my phone. We're running about seventeen minutes behind schedule, but that should be OK. We've cancelled the egg and spoon race and can always discard another one of my games. Though it would be a shame to waste the celebrity baby billboard I've made. I scurry about, asking people to say cheese while I take as many photos as possible, though people are more reluctant to pose while eating. Everyone *loves* the peony wall. I knew they would. When the devil tried to tempt Christ in the desert, they really should have used a peony wall. People seem to be mingling. That's good! The icebreakers must really have worked – they're now ice *melters*. Cry laughing face! Whoops.

I'm thinking in emojis again. I need to calm down. I saw Lauren chatting to that cool girl from Nicki's work – Phoebe. I don't know anything about her but there were loads of photos of her on Nicki's account of them on nights out, so I got in touch to invite her. Steffi's a seasoned mingler and needs no icebreakers but she's been distracted by this business deal. Hot air hits the back of my legs and I turn to see her sneaking through the sliding door, her phone in her hand. She has a weird, glazed look in her eyes until she senses me watching her, and grins sheepishly.

'Sorry, last duck out, I promise,' she says, putting her phone in her pocket.

'Watermelon?'

'I'm alright thanks.' Steffi never eats. No wonder she works in publishing, where she seems to live off bad white wine and canapés. She wouldn't last a day in my primary school where the only lunch option is baked potato and beans. 'It's going really well. You've done a great job, Charlotte.'

'Everything's melting and we're seventeen minutes behind schedule.'

She squeezes both my shoulders. 'And yet the day is still perfect.'

I pull her into a hug.

'Are you alright?' I ask her. I make eyes at her bulging pocket, 'All going well?'

'Yes. It's great. I'll be up all night. So much to do. But it's for good reasons.'

I let go and examine her again. She won't really make eye contact and looks on the verge of crying. 'Then why are you sad?' I ask her.

Her hand goes to her throat.' I'm not, I'm . . .'

'What's happened?'

'I . . . I . . . never mind.' She forces a grin. 'I'm great. Just stressed. And bowled over by your party throwing abilities. You're amazing, Charlotte. You know that, right?'

It's an unexpected compliment and it's just what I need to hear. I forget the melting stuff for five seconds. 'Thank you.'

'What can I do to help?'

'Take pictures,' I instruct her. 'Take lots and lots of pictures while I work out what to do about the melting . . . Do you know the hashtag? Do you mind trying to get one with Nicki and everyone? At least one of her with each guest? She's in the kitchen I think . . .'

Steffi pushes her hair back off her neck where it's starting to curl from the heat. 'You know what? Let's swap jobs. You know peoples' angles much better than I do. Why don't you round up Nicki, and I'll see which foods need rescuing and put in the fridge?'

I'm torn. She's right. I do know how to best frame a shot. It drives me crazy how bad people are at taking pictures. No rule of thirds! Cutting off people's legs. Leaving loads of weird head room at the top. It's not hard to frame things, people. You can easily watch a few YouTube videos about 'How to Take the Perfect Photo'. I even made Seth watch them because I was sick to death of him taking bad pictures of me on all our holidays. However, I also don't know if Steffi understands the urgency of the cupcake icing situation.

'I promise nothing turns to liquid under my watch,' she says, reading my mind. 'And it gives me an excuse to check my phone a bit more away from everyone.'

'If you're sure?'

'I'm sure.'

I pluck Nicki from the kitchen where she's been chatting to Lauren. 'Come on. Photos,' I tell her. She groans and struggles to get off her stool, while Lauren wrestles Woody like he's a wet fish.

'You say the bedroom is upstairs, second on the right?' she asks and we both nod. 'I'll try and put him down now. He's not had any solids yet, but he's too tired.'

I watch her carry him off on her hip and watch Nicki's swollen stomach dislodge itself from the chair. It strikes me then that our babies are all going to be basically the same age. How magical is that? Despite all the various odds, we've all ended up conceiving roughly around the same time. Maybe that's just a 32 thing, but I still think it's a good omen.

'I think we've got enough photos,' Nicki says as I drag her back into the main room where she's greeted like a celebrity.

'Just a few shots with each guest. Come on. You never regret taking photos. Especially when you're pregnant.' That's what I've been told after reading online. *Take loads of photos*, the articles advise me. *Document this profound change in your body. You will regret it if you don't. Mark yourself in history. It's a feminist statement*, even. Apparently, historically, mothers always take the family photos because it's emotional labour, so you have to make sure you're in the photo too so you're not erased. I explain this to Nicki as I round up various clusters, and, once I explain the feminism angle, she's more willing to pose. I do a group shot with her 'home friends', and then a family shot with her mother and aunty. I get a group of her work people, which is tricky as there's two babies in that cluster, and none of them look at the camera.

That cool lady, Phoebe, wanders back from the toilet just as I'm finished.

'Phoebe!' I call over. 'We almost missed you. Come have your photo taken with Nicki.'

She raises both eyebrows as she comes over. She really does have the most remarkable freckles. 'Here, here, by the balloons. That makes a nice backdrop.'

I gesture for them to move together but they stand almost a metre apart. 'No. Closer. Closer.' They are really messing with the rule of thirds here. 'Phoebe? Maybe if you put your hand on her stomach and, like, make a big open mouthed shocked gesture.'

'Not a chance,' Phoebe replies. 'Sorry. But that's not my thing.

I lower my phone. 'Oh, OK. It was just an idea.'

I expect Nicki to defend me but she's giggling. 'Charlotte, just a normal shot will do,' she says.

There's nothing abnormal about what I suggested . . .

'OK then. Just smile. One, two, three.' I don't even frame it properly. This Phoebe doesn't deserve the rule of thirds quite frankly. My phone starts ringing. Seth's number. 'I actually need to take this,' I tell Nicki but she doesn't hear me. Her and Phoebe are taking a seat, in deep conversation, acting like I left a long time ago. I pick up. 'Hang on, let me just run outside, stay on the line,' I whisper to him.

I patter past guests finishing up their pavlovas – everyone leaving the eco-disposal bowls on every available surface like they think some fucking servant is coming to collect them.

Woah. Where did that come from? The stress of today must be getting to me. Or maybe this is pregnancy hormones? What a delightfully bitchy thought. I slide open the front door which burns my palms, the glass is so hot. I step down onto the decking, almost hitting my head on the piñata.

'Right, I'm outside. Is everything OK?'

'The important thing is to not to panic,' Seth replies.

'Oh God. What's happened? Are you hurt? Are you dead!?'

He laughs. 'Yes, Charlotte. Totally dead. I'm calling from heaven. It has surprisingly good reception.'

'What's happened? Are you on your way? How are the doughnuts? What's gone wrong? Why are you calling?'

'Charlotte. It's fine.' Seth's using his best calming voice – the one I find slightly irksome as it's up to me whether something is fine or not. I'm the one with the schedule. 'The car is stuck, but it's all going to be OK.'

'Stuck? Stuck?! Where? Is Matt with you?' I knew this wasn't fine. I'll have to talk to him again about the appropriate time to use his calming voice.

'He's with me now. We have a plan. I've told you, it's going to be fine. You're never going to believe it but the car is stuck in tar. It's so hot one of these country roads has actually melted a bit.'

'The road has *melted?*'

This is what happens. You plan and organise and spreadsheet and account for all possible outcomes and everyone tells you to just *CHILL* but you can't ever chill because you'll never have accounted for everything. My brain didn't know, up until this precise moment in my life, that a road is capable of melting, especially in Britain! We're already 22 minutes behind now. I'm running out of slack time.

'Yes, it's just turned to tarry mush. It's crazy. I'm going to have to wait for the rescue people to come tow me. Matt and I have tried pushing, but the car has sunk surprisingly deep.'

'But you're supposed to be coming here. For the gender reveal! The big surprise! You have the wall of doughnuts!'

'Babe, I know. I have a plan. I wouldn't call you before I'd made a plan.'

Oh, I love him, this man with a plan. My husband.

'A taxi is on its way to pick up Matt. He's the star guest, so he's the only one that really needs to be there. I'll wait here and sort the car out. I've rung the taxi company twice and they've promised they're almost here. He won't even be late. We've kept the engine running so the air-con can protect the icing on the doughnuts. I'll probably go to hell for ruining the planet, but I knew you'd kill me if they melted.'

'OK, OK,' I nod. I'm still panicking. So much could go wrong. Taxi companies are notoriously unreliable in the countryside, everyone knows that. Oh, why is this happening to me? What did I do in a past life to deserve this? If Matt turns up too late, guests will start leaving before they realise the Main Event hasn't actually happened. They all think opening the presents is the Main Event, but they've been beautifully manipulated by me for the ultimate surprise factor.

'Are you OK though?' Seth asks. 'Really? I know you're not a fan of change of plans.'

'I just . . . he needs to get here in time.'

'He will, I promise. He's going to have plenty of time to surprise Nicki and whack out the gender reveal firework and the day is going to be perfect. How's it going over there anyway?'

He's trying to distract me by asking questions. He knows I'm spiralling. I cross my legs and bend over. The stress of all this has made me need a wee. I always need to wee when I'm stressed because I drink eight glasses of water a day using a special pink motivational bottle that gives me set measurements to drink each hour. Then, whenever I do a wee, I check what colour it is on the urine scale to ensure I'm not dehydrated. I used to have to hold my phone up to the toilet to check the colour, but now I know the WHO urine scale, and can tell if my wee is a two or a seven by sight.

'It's alright. Everything melting, of course, but Steffi is helping refrigerate the important bits. The games were fun. Presents to come. And the surprise if you get here on time.' I glance over at the firework which is still wedged where I left it. I get this sudden urge to pull it. All it would take is one small yank . . . My fingers twitch with this weird urge to sabotage everything.

'He'll get there in time. He's psyched. Can't wait to surprise Nicki. How are you doing anyway? I hope you're resting some, looking after yourself. Any sickness or anything yet?'

I shake my head. 'No, just a few cramps, but the internet has told me it's nothing to worry about.'

'And you're doing OK? It being a baby shower and all?'

I smile down the phone at Seth's emotional intelligence. Lots of women complain men are terrible – Steffi mostly – but they pick such awful men and value such random stuff. I've trained myself to only fancy good men with emotional intelligence. I read an article on the School of Life that your choice of romantic partner is probably the biggest decision you'll make concerning your odds of long-term happiness. Training oneself away from fuck boys is therefore essential.

'It's nice to be attending one and not feeling like sobbing every five minutes, yes,' I say.

'I'm so excited, I love you babe. I better go check in with the taxi company. Matt's on his way, I promise. Save me some melted cupcakes. A fertilised one please.'

'Okay, I love you too.'

I hold my stomach after he rings off, feeling so full of love for him – so delighted a combination of our DNA now resides inside me. All our fertility issues only brought us together, not apart, which I know is rare. And now we've somehow got pregnant, I feel so connected to him it's insane.

I notice the air con on re-entry, though it's still way too stifling in here. The food seems to have been successfully eaten and Nicki's mum is dutifully collecting up the scattered plates. There's a general air of stuffiness, and I see condensation growing in the corners of the window wall, but everyone's having too good a time to mind. Perked up by lunch, the peony wall now has a queue of people wanting their photo in front of it. And Nicki is reigning supreme, as she should, sitting on a yoga ball, glowing, and chatting to everyone. She laughs with that freckled Phoebe and I feel pride bloom at what I've curated today, what I've managed to give a friend through my own hardship.

As I pause, a toddler, not Woody, totters towards me and starts using my leg as a climbing frame.

'Hello there,' I say, bending down to help them up. It's a little girl, judging from the darling hair bow elasticated to their head.

Their mum scurries over, apologising. 'Sorry, she's obsessed with legs at the moment.'

She takes the child from me, and I wish I could say, 'No, don't,' as I was enjoying it.

'She's gorgeous,' I tell her, as she's scooped up into Mummy's arms and leans into her neck. I get a pang of broodiness so strong I have to bite my lip.

'You won't think that at 2am,' she replies. 'Then she's the devil.'

I make a sympathetic smile, though I do find it hard when mothers complain about sleeplessness. When they complain about their babies at all. It's not like anyone has ever proclaimed it's easy, so why is everyone so shocked? I want to shake them and scream, '*You don't know how lucky you are to be woken nightly by this gorgeous creature I crave so desperately.*'

She puts her down and holds her daughters arms. 'Sorry. It was nice to meet you . . .' she follows her daughter's lead without saying goodbye.

I watch them tiptoe away and feel the broodiness swallow me like Pacman. I allow myself 30 seconds of contemplative thought before realising I really do need the toilet. I've overdone the water drinking to keep my urine on the right gradient in this heat. I'm back in schedule mode as I close the bathroom door and pad past the roll-top tub. Right, time for one more game. Twenty minutes of celebrity babies . . . then presents . . . more drinks to serve as the presents are unwrapped? People will be thirsty. I start peeing and run through the logistics of the gender reveal as I wipe. Get everyone outside, pretending we're going to smash the piñata. Then, boom, off goes the smoke grenade, in comes Matt. 'Surprise!' I must make sure I'm standing at the best angle for photos.

I stand and get ready to pull up my cotton knickers.

I'm not sure what gets me to glance down, otherwise I could've easily missed it. But there, in my white knickers, is a speck of blood.

Transcript: Inspector Simmons interviewing Nicole Davies

Nicole:	So, I'm supposed to have, what is it I'm accused of? Deliberately burned my whole parents' house down, with a firework I didn't even know was there? A firework buried into the decking, when I'm so pregnant I can't even get off the floor without some kind of crane. I'll get on the floor now, if you'd like? See if I can get myself up? No?
Simmons:	We don't think you started the fire.
Nicole:	Brilliant. Also, duh. Of course I didn't. So why am I here?
Simmons:	Because we think you could be covering for someone.
Nicole:	Excuse me?
Simmons:	You didn't know the firework was planted there, but several other people did. [Silence] Who are you protecting, Nicole?
Nicole:	No one.
Simmons:	Who knew about the firework, Nicole? And why would you cover for them?
Nicole:	Why would I cover for someone who burned down my family home and almost killed me in the process?
Simmons:	I don't know, Nicole, that's why I'm asking you. [Silence] We received a phone call yesterday from an eyewitness. A cyclist said he saw the figure of a woman standing on top of the valley, watching the fire burn. Do you know who that was, Nicole?
Nicole:	It could have been anyone.
Simmons:	Or it could've been the person you're protecting, watching their handiwork.

NICKI

Phoebe's a riptide and I'm in her pull again. No matter how distracted I am by everyone telling me how much I'm glowing, and better get some sleep while you still can, and when are you due again, I'm only focused on her. My eyes are scanning the glass house for her, needing to know her exact location. I view myself through her gaze, imagining what she sees and how she interprets it. My tasteful maternity dungarees bought new from the tasteful maternity dress store. My swollen stomach bulging with my heteronormative decisions made at the stereotypical age. This Instagram clusterfuck of a baby shower we're attending. Honestly, Charlotte's just put us into 'teams' again, and I'm pretending to care what Keanu Reeves looked like as a baby when all I want to do is make eye-contact with her, share a moment, get back to who we were again.

It's been well over a year since I've seen her. She seems exactly the same. And yet, here I am, everything changed and about to change even more. She's on a team across from me on the other sofas, caught in the middle of a huddle of women, all being passive aggressive about who gets to hold the pen, pointing at their sheet and whispering loudly, '*I think that one is Taylor Swift.*' I watch Phoebe glaze over, drumming her slim fingers on the coffee table, not even looking at the sheet but, instead, around at the cornucopia of baby shower paraphernalia strewn about the place. The balloons, the stork decorations, that damn peony wall that's releasing such a sweet stench I'm almost choking with my supersonic pregnancy sense of smell. Then, what I've wanted, her eyes find mine. Immediately I wish they hadn't as she's so penetrating, so unafraid of holding eye contact. The room fades to muted tones, as she raises one perfect eyebrow and asks me, without saying anything:

What happened to you, Nicki?

What happened to us?

The room dissolves further and I'm back there, waiting with her for the night bus. It was another Tuesday Is The New Friday. Another night of clicking at the bartender for more shots, of complaining about our colleagues, the new Meta algorithm, the state of my marriage, how the last tube is always too early because fucking hell I've missed it again. Our weekly ritual. I could already taste the halloumi kebab we'd order at the place around the corner from hers on the walk home. My shoes were hurting so I was leant on the bus stop bench, dangling them off my feet, laughing at one of her jokes, when Phoebe leant over and kissed me.

'Phoebe, no,' I'd said, pushing her away.

Phoebe hadn't moved her face though. She held it so close her freckles blurred.

'Nicki.' She'd whispered my name, her breath hot on my face, smelling sweet from the cocktails we'd been sipping at a cool place I'd never known existed without her. Yet another night of her patiently listening as I endlessly complained about how I worried I'd settled down too soon, how I was too young to feel so bored, how I loved Matt but I worried I wasn't in love with him anymore. Then her cutting me off. ' *Why are you whinging when you could be dancing?*' Dragging me from our booth, and spinning me onto the tiny dance floor, where I could actually feel the shackles of my life drop onto the sticky floorboards. Phoebe's breath smelt delicious. When Matt drank, the sweetness of his breath repelled me. We never had drunk sex as I couldn't stand the reek of him – the beer sweating out of his pores, the bleary red eyes, the stink of hops on his tongue. We didn't have much sex anyway, and everyone says to get drunk to help things along, but don't they realise what drunk men smell like? And how shit and selfish men get in bed after a few too many? Matt could semi-regularly make me come but only if he dutifully followed the gentle foreplay and exact paint-by-numbers positioning I needed to get off. But, after three pints, he'd ignore all this knowledge and try to have porn sex with me. Always pushing me into doggy, always slamming into me, muttering filth, like '*I know you like it like this,*' when he knows I don't. When men are drunk, they have the sex they want. That's what Matt smells like after three pints – bad sex. Phoebe smelt like peonies, cradling my face as she knelt on the filthy East London pavement in front of me – eyes uncertain and full of lust. It took a moment to comprehend what had just happened. I could still taste her on my lips and it was like Parma Violets. I should've been shocked and disgusted. Annoyed at her, for taking a punt when I'm so clearly not interested. I should've felt deceived, even, that maybe our friendship was something she was using to try and 'turn' me or whatever, but, in the seconds after the shock wore off, I didn't feel any of those things at all.

All I felt was, *OK, wow, I need to kiss you back.*

Three night buses had stopped and lurched away again before we broke apart, panting, and then laughing in that delicious delirium you share after kissing someone for the first time. It had been over a decade since I'd had a first kiss. I'd forgotten how heady and frothy it was, to break that barrier with someone, knowing there was no coming back from it. For a moment or two, I floated on the euphoria of the sensation, and on the surprise turn this night had taken. Then, as Phoebe raised her eyebrow and leant in towards me, reality struck like a gavel in a courtroom, and I pushed her away.

'Hang on, what just happened?'

She laughed. 'We kissed, Nicki. Finally.' Phoebe leant in again, her sweet lips brushing mine and I responded again, pulling her into me, my hand skimming her back. Wow, it felt good. Amazing. Natural. And, yes, long overdue. Phoebe let out a moan and I joined her and went to stroke her chest, like how I do when I kiss Matt, though, of course, she had breasts, and, as I touched them – their softness, their not-maleness – something soured in my throat. I pulled back again, shaking my head.

'No no no.'

Phoebe, not getting it, laughed against and leaned in again. 'Yes yes yes,' she said.

'What the fuck? Stop it. How dare you?' My voice slurred, while my drunk brain tried to catch up. Phoebe was my friend. Friend. A lesbian friend, yes, but I wasn't gay. I was straight. Hadn't ever thought of women that way. Hadn't even kissed a girl as a dare, or to get boys off when I was younger so they could watch. Rage charged in, joining the mess. And, umm, I was fucking married! I'd just cheated on my husband. It was easier to be angry at Phoebe than disgusted at myself. 'What the hell is wrong with you?' I'd shouted, pushing her again, this time so hard she fell back onto the pavement. A group of drunk men outside the chicken shop cheered as she fell. She looked up at me, baffled and humiliated, and I couldn't take it. I'd stood up and started striding off in some random direction, letting the unknown streets of the city swallow me and what I'd done, while Phoebe scrabbled to run after me.

'Nicki? Nicki! Come on. Where are you going?'

'Away from you,' I called back, arms crossed, walking as fast as I could in my stupid work heels, past neon doorways to thudding music. 'How dare you kiss me!'

'You kissed me too. Please, we need to talk about this.'

I dodged a group of younger women, shivering outside a club in the smoking area, singing an Adele song to distract them from the cold. Phoebe continued to chase me through Shoreditch. 'Stop walking away. Please. Come on, Nicki. Be a grown-up.'

I halted and let her catch me up. Mainly, I was drunk and lost – I only ever ventured into East London with Phoebe to guide me through the graffiti and pop-ups and groups of youths inhaling laughing gas. I slowly turned around and her outline was neon against the glow of a nightclub sign.

'You've been lying to me,' I told her. 'You've been pretending to be my friend.'

'Nicki, come on, that's not true.'

'You've been making me vulnerable, getting me to open up about my life and marriage so you can . . . seduce me.'

Phoebe, to my surprise, burst out laughing. 'Seduce you? Nicki. Come on.' She took a delicate step forward. 'You know that's not it. You know we've been falling in love with each other.'

'What?'

'It's been as much as a surprise to me as it has been for you. But, please. Think about it. We've not been friends in ages. We've been so much more than friends.'

'Stop it.'

'We've been sharing a bed at least one night a week. We talk all the time. Go out alone all the time. Tell each other our secrets. Nicki, I think about you literally all the time. You feel the same, I know it.'

'No.'

'I love you, Nicki.' She looked so beautiful, stencilled by the city lights.

'Stop. I'm married.'

'And you're unhappy.'

'I'm not. And I'm not . . . g—'

'Gay? Is that why you're freaking out?' She tilted her head to one side, her eyes wet and wide with empathy.

Was it that? I held my head to stem the spinning. The thump of the nearby club matched my raging heartbeat. Everything I thought I knew about myself was spilling up onto the pavement. I'd just kissed a woman and I'd enjoyed it. A woman had just told me she loved me and I wanted to say it back. A woman! With a vagina! What do you even do together? I had no idea really. Did I want to do things to Phoebe's body? I felt vomit bubble up my throat as I thought through the reality of it, and within seconds, I couldn't acknowledge this evening. I put my hand up to hail a passing black cab and walked off.

'You can't honestly be leaving right now,' she called after me.

'Leave me the fuck alone,' I shouted back. The cabbie juddered to a halt and I jumped in while Phoebe patted the window. 'Clapham North please,' I told him. 'Ignore her.'

Nobody but millionaires get black cabs in London. Everyone knows it's about ten grand a mile, and the journey from north to south takes as long as a transatlantic flight. But it was my only escape route so I slumped against the seat, wiping tears away, and listening to the driver's low, bored whistle as he steered me through the smeared lights of the city. She kept calling but I turned off my phone, willing the driver to go faster. When I eventually got back to our flat, parting with £72, I ran to the bedroom and climbed into bed with Matt, spooning him from behind, sodden with guilt.

'Nicki?' he murmured, waking in the darkness, sleep heavy in his voice. 'What are you doing back? I thought you were staying at Phoebe's?'

'I missed you,' I told him, wrapping my arms around him, stroking his body. It was so dark I couldn't really see him and had to trace his outline with my shaking hands. The bulk of his muscles, the thickness of his thighs. I was instantly horny, and started stroking up his thigh, skimming over his groin through his pyjama bottoms.

'You're drunk,' he announced, catching my hand and stopping me. I leant in to kiss him. 'Definitely drunk,' he declared at the taste of my mouth but I felt him smile in the blackness.

'Not that drunk,' I told him, giving him permission.

I thought he would push me off. It was 2.30am. Work tomorrow. We'd not had sex under such circumstances in years. Obligation overruled any stirrings. We would save our sex for a more appropriate time with fewer consequences the following day, and then, of course, never get around to it. But maybe Matt could sense me slipping away. The end of us hovering in a mist over our bed. Because, when I reached for him again, he was hard. Hard with a thing I understood what to do with. When we'd finished, he fell asleep almost instantly, like maybe it was a dream he'll forget. Now accustomed to the darkness, I watched his face – innocent and unknowing in its unconsciousness.

As a woman, I had no such luxury to drift off to sleep beside him. I got up, bending over to keep as much of his cum inside me as I could, before running to our en-suite and cleaning myself up on the toilet, peeing to ensure I didn't get a UTI. I spent many moments with my head between my legs, sobering up, replaying the night, the kiss, the argument, the sex – scarcely able to believe this dramatic mess had found itself in my dull and orderly life. Impossible questions swarming around as I blinked at the bathmat hanging over the side of the shower.

Was I gay?

Bisexual?

These words. These labels. So definite. With such a storyline.

I always knew from when I was very young . . .

I didn't know.

I didn't want to have sex with women.

I'd never fancied one.

I didn't fancy Phoebe, did I?

Fancy.

What a strange word.

Childish. Simple.

The walls of the en-suite squeezed in. Sleep fell heavy on my eyelids, whispering, '*If you pass out, Nicki, all of this will go away.*' I wiped myself for a final time, stood up, brushed my teeth to rid the taste of Phoebe and Matt from my tongue, stared at my reflection for a while just because that's what I'd seen people do in films whenever they did something dramatic.

I had never done anything dramatic with my life, so I had only a script of clichés to follow.

I needed to turn my phone back on to set my alarm and a barrage of messages erupted. I didn't read any of them as I punched the alarm in – my phone telling me it would go off in only three hours and seven minutes' time.

Sleep.

Escape this.

I climbed into bed next to the warmth of my familiar husband and stared at the ceiling for three hours and seven minutes until my alarm went off—

Someone to my side shrieks with laughter and I'm jolted back. We all eww at a blown-up photo of Voldemort as a baby. Here I am again. At my baby shower. Sitting on a sofa, surrounded by everyone celebrating Matt's baby growing inside my stomach. From the outside, everything is how it should be. Conventional old Nicki, doing the conventional thing at the conventional time, with the conventional guy. Picture perfect.

Except Phoebe's eyes find me again, that questioning arch of her eyebrow, asking me the silent question. And me, trying to figure out how to communicate my silent answer.

Yes, I love you too.

The same words I'd typed out and sent to her the next morning. Imploding my life.

Transcript: Inspector Simmons interviewing Lauren Powell

Simmons:	Character witnesses for you have unanimously stated that you're a considerate and caring person. The phrase 'not a bad bone in her body' has been used many times.
Lauren:	That's very nice of you to pass on, thank you.
Simmons:	Do you think that's a fair assessment of you?
Lauren:	I try to be nice to people. Doesn't everyone?
Simmons:	Tell me, Lauren, is it 'nice' to send threatening and abusive messages to people on Instagram? [Silence] Phone records show that, on the day in question, you were blocked, after sending many unpleasant messages to a hypnobirthing Instagram account. [Silence] And, in fact, that's not just a one off. Our records show you've created multiple burner accounts for the sole purpose of targeting and abusing this person. What do you think your friends would say about that? [Silence] You look angry, Lauren.
Lauren:	I am.
Simmons:	For being found out?
Lauren:	No. For you saying it's 'abuse' to simply tell the truth to someone.
Simmons:	They weren't very nice messages, Lauren.
Lauren:	I'll tell you what's not very nice. Telling women to hold a fucking *comb* to help with the pain of contractions during labour.

Lauren

I breastfeed Woody to sleep in the pitch black of Nicki's parents' bedroom. True to Charlotte's promise, the blackout curtains work absolute wonders, and he drops off easier than usual. His breathing deepens, signalling that it's hopefully safe enough to replace my nipple with my little finger and progress to Stage Two. To be honest, it's nice to have a break from the party and the fairytale lie of what motherhood involves. It's basically deranged how baby products are all in such light pastel colours when they'll soon be covered in shit stains and piss stains and vomit stains and food stains once they start weaning. Why is baby stuff all cutesy animals and soft light fabrics when motherhood is blood and gore and chaos? I look at Woody's face, sleeping in the gloom, and remember receiving a pale, yellow duck towel from Charlotte at my baby shower spa day and simpering at how cute it was. I couldn't wait for the moment I'd wrap up Woody after his bubble bath, hair wet, pudgy skin slippery. How I'd cradle him on my shoulder and say 'quack quack' and we'd laugh together at our reflection in the bathroom mirror. Instead, I was still bleeding giant lemon clots into my knickers when we gave Woody his first bath. He shat in it, pissed in it, screamed every moment he was in there, frantically wiping the stinky green poo further into his body. I hadn't had a chance to change my giant postpartum sanitary towel for two hours because he'd been cluster feeding, so, as I scrambled to put him in the towel, my own bodily outputs overspilled with his, and the duck looked like it had been hit by a car and shat itself with fear as it was dying. The stains might've come out if we'd had the strength and time to try Vanish on it, which we didn't. We just threw the baby duck towel right into the bin, alongside our hopes and expectations of what we thought this life might be like.

I wait another two minutes with Woody's mouth clamped around my finger, before lowering him into the travel cot like a bomb disposal expert. Miraculously, he survives the transfer and I switch on the baby monitor and get ready to creep out. The king-sized bed calls to me and I fantasise about flopping down and sleeping while Woody sleeps. Being blissfully unconscious while I miss the presents and games, celebrating the horror that awaits poor Nicki.

Or maybe Nicki will find motherhood easy? Easy and fulfilling and life-enhancing.

Maybe I'm the only one who finds it boring, and lonely, and stressful, and hardly survivable?

Cool Mum can't believe how much love she's capable of feeling since her baby was born. It's like being upgraded, she says. Yes, sometimes it's tough, but just one cuddle and it's all worth it, isn't it?

Cope better. Cope better, I remind myself, leaving the sanctuary of the bedroom.

The hubbub greets me as I push through the door. I check the monitor four times but Woody's still out. Can I relax? Will this nap last more than twenty-seven minutes exactly? Dare I hope? Might I be able to have a good time today rather than merely endure it?

A frenzied Charlotte greets me without blinking when I arrive back.

'Oh, hi Lauren. Has Woody gone down? Is the travel cot OK? Good. Perfect. It's all going well, don't you think? Who won the celebrity baby game? I had to go to the bathroom. Everything's fine though, isn't it? Shall we do the presents now, what do you think?'

She gives me no time to answer and swerves back into the guests like a malfunctioning robot. The plates of food have been cleared away and Nicki's mum is bringing over the mountain of presents and arranging them around her daughter like they're part of a ritual sacrifice. Nicki's trying very hard to pretend the big pile isn't generating behind her and is chatting to the other two mothers here. One of them that terrible Cara again. She waves me over and I join them with tense muscles.

'Lauren, hi! Did Woody go down OK? Come join us.' She pats the sofa next to her and asks the mums to move down for me. 'We're talking about childbirth,' she adds when I hesitate. I want to turn and run, but Nicki gives me frantic eyebrows, and I realise she's hoping I'll rescue her from the conversation when it really needs to be the other way around. Cara's baby is asleep on her chest despite the hubbub around. The other mum – Jeanie – who has brought her wayward toddler girl, is in the midst of a full-on monologue, not even acknowledging me as I sit down.

'Seventy-two hours,' she's saying, leaning over to ensure Nicki can't ignore her. The toddler's shaking all the presents behind her, delighted to be unmonitored. 'You'll want an epidural. I promise you. Just so you can sleep. I was so sure I'd never have one, but you'll change your mind.'

Nicki glances down at her stomach in horror. I remember that late-stage pregnancy fear I had, when you can't quite conceive how huge your baby is and how it somehow has to leave your body in due course. 'I have to admit,' Nicki says. 'I really don't like the idea of an epi. A needle in your spine and, if they get it the slightest bit wrong, you're paralysed for life.' She joke-shudders.

Cara pipes up to the side of me, stroking her baby's back. 'Are you doing hypnobirthing?' she asks.

My blood turns to lead in my veins. The veil drops down and the celebrations around me turn to muted grey. Nicki's voice sounds underwater.

'Just started it this week. Did you do it? I love it.'

'Yes, yes. It's amazing, isn't it? I loved it too.' Cara's baby is smiling in its sleep. 'People love to tell you their birth horror stories,' she looks pointedly at Jeanie '. . . But I think it's so important to tell the positive birth stories too. Like mine. Honestly, I had three hours of labour, and I breathed all the way through it. No stitches. It was the most beautiful experience. I felt so strong. So empowered. I just trusted the hypnobirthing, I trusted my own body. And out she came!'

Nicki's jaw softens. 'You had a water birth, didn't you? I remember the pictures you put up.'

'Yes. We lit candles. I was sloshing about in the tub. I even bought myself a new bikini as a treat. Everything to keep that oxytocin going. It was so spiritual. Like going to a spa.'

I crane around the room, looking for an ally to anchor myself out of this conversation. But Charlotte's ferrying presents into a pyramid and Steffi's sat in the corner, her legs curled up, not even trying to engage anymore.

'. . . It's so important not to let the fear win. To keep those happy hormones flowing. Have you made a birthing playlist?'

Cara asks. 'I've got an oil diffuser I can lend you? Make up a special birthing blend and have it burning throughout to centre you when you're playing your favourite song.'

Cool Mum does hypnobirthing. Of course, she fucking does. Birth is such a breeze for Cool Mum. She just blew out that golden thread and got into her pool. Maybe she had a tiny bit of gas and air, but that just made her dizzy. To be honest, her birth was too quick for any painkillers. She sneezed delicately and the baby fell out. No prolapse, no stitches. She was just so full of fucking oxytocin that she accidentally donated £100 to charity while the baby was in the canal.

Cara's waving a finger at Nicki now. 'And, whatever you do, don't let them induce you,' she warns. 'It mucks up all the hormones. Trust your body. Trust your baby will arrive in the right time for them.'

Jeanie finally finds agreement with her. 'Oh, yes, inductions are *terrible*. They're pushing women into them deliberately these days, due to maternity cuts. It means they can stagger the amount of women coming into maternity wards so they're not overwhelmed.'

Nicki nods while her palm still caresses her stomach. 'Yes, I definitely don't want to get induced. I'd rather go right to a caesarean. Lauren?'

Her voice calls to me through the fog. The rage is spreading up my arms, making me want to slap these stupid fucking women and their stupid fucking opinions.

'Yeah?' I hear my voice say, staring at the pile of presents next to Nicki.

I had a baby shower spa day. I was given presents. I was so excited that day. So happy.

I did hypnobirthing . . .

'. . . You got induced, didn't you?' Nicki asks. 'I remember you sending me a message just before they did it.'

All their eyes are on me and I don't have the shield of Woody to use as an excuse to flee. This monster who got induced. No doubt I deserved everything that happened next. I should've just done what the BreatheItOut Instagram account told me to do, and let my baby die inside me, and then bleed out on the hospital bed, while refusing all medical intervention.

'I'm trusting my dying body,' I should've told the medical professionals. 'Don't induce me. My dead baby will come out in its own natural time.'

'Umm. Yes, I had an induction.'

'Oh . . .' Cara looks mildly panicked at my admission. 'Well, every birth story is as unique as a fingerprint.'

'Woody had stopped growing. They said there was a risk he might die if I wasn't induced. But, you know, I probably should've refused.'

Cara's eyes widen. 'Oh, wow, that's totally different then, isn't it? You poor thing.'

But Jeanie is having no such sympathy. 'They say anything though, don't they?' she says, her pointy finger carving a trail through the air. 'To pressure you into induction. It's impossible to tell how well a baby is growing in a womb, isn't it? You could've probably left it and Woody would've come out just fine, at a perfectly normal size.'

I nod slowly, glancing at him in the monitor. I try not to associate Woody with the process of getting him out of my body otherwise I worry I'll hate him irrevocably. 'Or he could've come out dead,' I reply.

I didn't want an induction either. Of course I didn't. I was going to have a water birth. I was going to do my breathing. I had done the classes and educated and empowered myself about birth. I was going to be calm and confident with the doctors. I followed the BreatheItOut hypnobirthing account and read all her posts religiously. I knew my birthing rights. I'd use the BRAIN acronym before making any major decision and not be bullied into distrusting my body.

But – when faced with a baby that hasn't grown in two weeks, your absolute terror of still-birth kind of makes the acronym go out the window when consenting to an induction.

B – Benefits. *My baby won't be fucking dead.*

R – Risks. *If I'm not induced, my baby might fucking die.*

A – Alternatives. *Refuse the medical advice and maybe my baby will fucking die.*

I – Intuition. *It's weird how being told your baby might die activates this intuition to agree to fucking anything that will help it not fucking die.*

N – *Nothing. I could just do nothing and hope my baby doesn't fucking die.*

'Was Woody OK?' Cara asks. 'His weight and stuff, when he was born?'

It's strange how she can jump from the induction, to Woody being outside my body in one sentence. Whereas the reality took five days and ripped me apart in every way possible.

'His birth weight was fine,' I admit.

'See!' Jeanie points her finger right into my face and I imagine snapping it off and the screams she'd let out. 'You didn't even need an induction. I told you!' She shakes her head. 'How was your birth after having one? Awful, I bet?' she asks it almost gleefully.

'Yes, how was the birth?' Nicki asks, softening it, making it sound more caring. 'You were OK, weren't you, Lauren?'

It's far too hot in here. Nicki's stomach is so swollen. There's no going back for her. She doesn't really want to know the truth of it. We can't handle the brutal truth about how most of us came into this world. What unimaginable trauma a woman so often puts herself through. I'll never think of the word 'birthday' the same ever again. I'm still hardly able to think about my birth without sweat erupting all over my body. The memory is an incoherent mess of a narrative, with just snatches of vivid trauma blasting through my brain like a Hollywood trailer whenever I walk past a pregnant woman on the street.

The shaky drive home from the hospital triage after I went in five days overdue. We were in the new car we'd bought because we were having a baby. The stink of pine from the dangling tree thingy on the rearview mirror. The doctor's words whirling around my head like poisoned vapour.

Baby hasn't grown for two weeks . . . Recommend we induce first thing tomorrow . . . You're five days overdue anyway . . . If we don't, something could go wrong . . . placenta . . . growth chart . . . risk assessment.

That night, the decision to induce made, Tristan and I triple-packed our hospital bags, ensuring ludicrous things were in there that we'd never use. A USB fan. A collection of puzzle books and magazines, like labour was a long-haul flight. A comb, hilariously, because the BreatheItOut account told me gripping it through contractions would help with the pain.

Sorry, not pain, *surges*. BreatheItOut said we should call the pain of contractions 'surges' to trick our brain into feeling them less.

I refolded our selection of babygrows and pushed them into the suitcase. I said to Tristan. '*Just think. This time tomorrow, we could be holding our baby.*'

Of course, we knew induction labours usually took longer. Of course, we knew they came with a higher chance of further interventions. Of course, we knew first births are often worse. But maybe we'll be one of those lucky ones you don't hear about much because so many women want to freak you out with their horror stories – these selfish, failed mothers who can't help but try and bring you down, it's not fair to share these things with new mums and scare the shit out of them, until it happens to them and they gasp 'why did nobody fucking tell me' . . .

'I'm scared,' I told Tristan. He hugged me as hard as he could with our baby between us. Back when we were still us, when Tristan still had the time and inclination to hug his wife. 'What if I die?'

'Shh. Shh,' he'd said, stroking my hair. 'Just remember your hypnobirthing.'

My hypnobirthing.

It wasn't just like bringing a knife to a gun fight, but a handful of fucking rose petals. Breathing out a golden thread was like bringing a dustpan and brush to clean up a natural disaster.

The pain. Nothing like it. I thought my body would rip in two. Screaming. Agony. Make it stop. How was this possible? I must be dying. Nothing can hurt this much and not be dying.

A stern midwife, pushing me back into the bed. 'Please, you're upsetting others on the ward. You're only one centimetre anyway. Your labour hasn't even really started.'

How can it not have even started when I was nearly dead and had been screaming in agony, on and off, for over two days? Pain I couldn't sleep through.

I watch Cara stroking the back of her sleeping baby. Cara with her three-hour labour and breathing techniques. Cara could trust her body, and so her body rewarded her. Unlike me and my body . . .

What day was it? So much pain. Tristan's face white, his eyes wide. What is happening to his wife?

Established labour.

I was wrong about the other pain being too much. Please give me back that pain. This is . . . can't remember. I remember thinking, *who let a cow in the hospital? Oh, it's me.* That noise is me. The comb was snapped in half a long time ago. They couldn't give me any gas and air because they had run out. They had run out of birthing pools too.

'Sorry, it's always busy in September.'

I knew I was dying. I was sure I was dying. I also knew that this fear was making my childbirth worse. *It's my fault it hurts this much because I'm letting the fear win.* The adrenaline from my stupid, weak fear at the fact I'm clearly dying was pushing away all the oxytocin. All of this was my fault. Just breathe out some golden breath.

Ask myself, 'Would I be able to do a poo like this?' That's what BreatheItOut told me to ask myself on her Instagram captions.

I don't think I'm going to die whenever I do a poo.

I don't sound like I've escaped from a barn yard whenever I do a poo.

I couldn't breathe through this agony.

Never. Known.

Anything like it.

Swearing at Tristan. Telling him I fucking hate him. Fuck him, for getting me pregnant. Fuck him, for not having this pain. Fuck him, for trying to comfort me.

Almost broke his hand squeezing it. *Don't you dare go to the toilet, you can't leave me.*

Blacked out from pain. Not literally, but no memories. Only of it hurting so much that 'pain' wasn't an adequate word.

Something was wrong.

Worried doctors. More monitors. People rushing in.

Woody was stuck in the canal.

Woody's cord was around his neck too.

Woody's vitals were crashing.

Rush rush rush, pushed through double doors, someone running alongside me, telling me the risks of an emergency cae-sarean section I had to agree to. I groaned in agony. My body felt ripped apart. My baby was dying and I was dying. I was going to be one of those women who dies in childbirth, or who loses a child. I am the statistic. I was sobbing. Tristan was still holding my hand, telling me it's OK, it's all going to be OK, Woody is going to be OK, it will all be fine in just a few moments.

'*The position the baby is stuck in means the caesarean is more complicated. Lower down. Higher risk.*'

Was I supposed to use my BRAIN before I agreed to com-plicated surgery, fucking BreatheItOut Bitch? Ask about the benefits as my baby strangled himself?

'You need to stay very still as we put the needle in . . . very delicate . . . risk of paralysis . . . do you understand? Lauren? Are you with us?

A nod. I think I nodded.

Just as they injected me, a contraction hit. Piercing, searing, agony, but I couldn't move otherwise I'd never walk again.

Cara didn't have a C-section. Cara had a water birth. Cara doesn't know what it's like to be fully conscious while your body is sliced open like you're on a butcher's bench. Lucky Cara. I stare at her with narrowed eyes, jealousy littering my blood with hot, toxic bubbles.

So many people were in the operating theatre. Tristan was in scrubs. When did that happen? I hadn't slept in so long. They were urgently shouting their names for some recording of the operation, one they'd use to defend themselves legally if me or the baby died.

I was no longer in my body. I watched my body as it was vigorously sliced into like a slab of dead pig. They'd used my surgical gown to create the screen between my head and the violence of what was happening to my body. I remember thinking, *'huh'* and *'what a useless bit of information to learn just before you die.'*

'Stay with me,' a woman's voice said. An anaesthetist. 'Stay with me, Lauren.' She started shouting about my heart rate. It was dropping . . .

Here it was. The crash. The attack. The dying.

Instead, there was the sound of crying. A baby crying. My baby crying.

I was back in my body and Woody's body was being lifted out of me, spread-eagled like he was Jesus on the cross. Covered in blood and gunk and screaming.

I wanted him. I wanted my baby. But they took him away. *He's slightly blue,* someone said. *Need to check he can breathe.*

The BreatheItOut account told me how essential skin to skin contact was the second a baby was born. It's called magical hour. It needs to happen immediately otherwise the baby is so fucked up it's likely to become the next Hitler. '*You are legally entitled to get skin to skin straight away. Know your right. Use your BRAIN.*'

But it's hard to advocate for yourself when the baby is blue, your insides are still exposed to a hospital ceiling, and you hear the surgeon say they're worried about how much blood you've already lost.

Tristan was right with me. He was weeping. He wouldn't look at the baby. He refused to cut the cord.

I remember that. The stern wobbling of my husband's bottom lip, his arms crossed like a child, as they tried to beckon him over to Woody, wielding a pair of surgical scissors.

'No,' he told the midwife. 'I don't want to. You do it.'

We've not once talked about that moment, about why he didn't want to cut the cord.

Not once.

I can't remember much more. I try to pick up a glass of punch from the side table, but my hands wobble too much to grasp it so I give up, and lean further back in the sticky sofa, praying the flashbacks will end soon.

Tristan was taken aside to hold the baby while they worked on me. Sew me up before I bleed out.

'Am I going to die?' I asked the lady holding my hand. Who was she? What was her name? I'll never see her again. I'm not even sure what her job was.

'You're fine,' she told me. 'The baby is fine. Congratulations Lauren.'

Congratulations.

Then the baby was plopped on my chest, wrapped in a blanket and hat. It was an ugly disgusting alien and it stared up at me with big black eyes and we were told to all smile for a picture. The nameless lady had Tristan's phone and we both grinned obligingly. In days to come, we would send this photo to our friends and family, and they would send back heart-eye emojis and congratulations like this photo was taken of a good thing, rather than the worst moment of my life. The first few seconds of this New Me that was forged that day – in blood and sweat and agony and fear.

I remember Nicki sent back ten rows of heart-eyed emojis. I remember laughing as it was such a Charlotte thing to do. She followed it up by '*OMG, this is perfect. It's making me so BROODY.*' And here she is, not very much later, body bulging with impending horror, thinking she has a chance in hell of an easy water birth, tilting her head at me, waiting for me to reassure her that it's all going to be OK.

'My birth . . .' What words to share. How can any of it fit into any words? '. . . it . . . it . . . it wasn't the easiest few days of my life,' I manage. It's the most I can sugarcoat it. The most I can lie.

'Of course not,' she says, rubbing her stomach. Nicki looks visibly relieved that I've not said worse. 'I have to remember birth is only a day or two, tops.' Her attention is then directed towards the pile of gifts behind her. Someone comes over and offers her a drink, and, without the glare of her and Cara and Jeanie, I'm able to pick up my punch with shaking hands without them noticing. I gulp it down, trying to steady my breath.

It may only be a day or two. Or five, in my case. But you're never the same, I think. Never. And it's not like I got a chance to recover from the horror. I went straight from that horror into the horror of having a newborn baby.

Maybe it could've been different. I think, often, at 2am, when I'm sending private messages to BreatheItOut with my burner account. Maybe if my birth had been different, my experience of motherhood would be different? Maybe if I'd trusted my body more. Maybe if I'd breathed harder . . . ?

Except it's bullshit and lies, bullshit and lies.

Because I've *since* learned that women have four different types of pelvises and some are basically incapable of giving birth naturally.

'*Can't breathe my way through that, can I?*' I type, sending them the link to the research before they block me again. '*How am I supposed to trust my body if my pelvis is literally not able to give birth and I would've died in the medieval times?*'

'*IT WASN'T JUST A SURGE, IT WAS FUCK-ING AGONY YOU LYING CUNT,*' I type out again. '*A*

CONTRACTION ISN'T A SURGE, IT'S A CONTRAC-TION. HOW ARE YOU ALLOWED?'

She blocks me so I start new accounts. I post publicly, to try and warn other women, and then I send DMs too, to make sure they really read them.

And, you know what? She has never replied until today. And she deletes my comments as quick as she can so others can't read my warnings. I once typed out my whole horrific birth story in fourteen long messages. I sobbed as I tip tapped out the entire mess on the toilet at 3am, during the two hours Woody would sleep. I felt this huge release as I hit send. Surely, she'd read and respond to this? At least say sorry I had such an unlucky experience. But she just deleted it and blocked.

Fuckers.

Lying fuckers.

Nicki gives her drink order and her eyes find mine again. She smiles. I try to return it. Her hand is massaging her bump without realising. I used to do that all the time too. Back before. Like Nicki, when I was so blissfully unaware of everything heading my way – imagining me pushing it out beautifully in a birthing pool, letting my body unfurl like petals on a flower in the morning sun.

Now Woody is clasped in my hand. A collection of pixels that shoot me with adrenaline whenever the screen grunts or squeals or turns over.

Nicki looks at the screen and beckons out for it. 'Can I?'

I hand him over. 'Oh look at him sleep. He's perfect, Lauren. Truly.'

'Thank you.'

I must be grateful. I must cope better and be grateful. I am so lucky to have gone through such a horrendous experience because look at this cute miniature person in my arms.

'Whatever happens, it's all worth it, isn't it?' she asks us.

All three of us nod. Though I take the longest to make my head do it.

Fuckers.

Lying fuckers.

Transcript: Inspector Simmons interviewing Steffani Fox

Simmons:	You've claimed throughout this interview that you and the other suspects are the best of friends?
Steffani:	That's correct. Yes.
Simmons:	You say you didn't have 'beef with anyone' there?
Steffani:	Not enough beef to set anything on fire.
Simmons:	Is sleeping with Nicole's husband not beef then? Seems odd.
Steffani:	That . . . How do you know about that?
Simmons:	We had an anonymous tip-off, someone who told us the truth about your *friendships* with these women.
Steffani:	What the hell?
Simmons:	We have a different word for 'beef' in the police force, Steffani Fox. In here, we like to call it 'motive'.
Steffani:	It's not what it sounds like . . .
Simmons:	Really? Because it sounds like you have very good reason to cause Nicki harm.
Steffani:	OK, so occasionally I want her to break a nail, but torching a house is quite different.
Simmons:	So you keep saying. But let's go through your exact movements on the day in question, shall we? Did you know that Matt was coming?

STEFFI

Fuck Nicki.

Seriously, fuck her.

Oh, how I've wanted to think that freely, for so long.

FUCK YOU FUCK YOU FUCK YOU FUCK YOU FUCK YOU FUCK YOU FUCK YOU.

It feels amazing to think it now without guilt. I only wish I could say it out loud. To her face. But I will have to make do with just leaving this hell site of a party without feeling any guilt about it. I'm almost tempted to take my presents back off the pile and rub all the Neal's Yard Bump Juice over myself, just out of spite.

However, the universe isn't going to allow me to flounce off just yet, unfortunately.

I peel back the sliding door and crouch on the decking under the piñata, staring at the top of the mysterious firework while I argue with the local taxi company.

'We're sorry, but we only have one driver and he's busy at the moment,' an elderly woman tells me, very slowly, down my crappy line.

'When will he stop being busy?'

'He's got this one emergency pick-up. Then he has to go straight from there to do his weekly hospital run. I'm afraid we can't fit you in.'

'Do you have the numbers of any other companies?'

'We're the only ones covering this area.'

'What if there's an emergency? What if I need to go to hospital?'

'You said you needed to go to the train station?' She's not getting it. 'Honey, if you need to go to hospital, it's better to book a week in advance. Or call an ambulance if it's an emergency.'

'Thanks for nothing,' I say, like a child. I hang up and feel guilty for being rude. This poor lady isn't Nicki. I should save my wrath for her.

If it wasn't an actual sauna out here, I would just go on a long walk around this tinderbox of a countryside until Lauren drives me back. Yeah, it would be awkward, as I'd have to tell her what I overheard, and it is quite acutely painful that she didn't defend me. In fact, she almost agreed with Nicki! Does Lauren honestly believe I think that about her since she had a baby? OK, so I feel stupid for posting that article now. I felt so seen by the dating part that I didn't consider how the rest of it came across. I can see how she misinterpreted it, but, then again, why was she so quick to believe the utter worst in me? At least it's outed what we all already knew anyway. Nicki hates me and wants me out of the group. Because Nicki's a petty, insecure bitch who can't get over something that happened *years* ago. Something where I feel, actually, *I* was the victim, not Nicki. I was the one who got hurt. I shake my head and feel sweat beads drip down my forehead. I'm going to have to go back inside and hold my tongue as she unwraps all the plastic shit people are going to give her that won't biodegrade until the dinosaurs come back. I refuse to participate though, after hearing that, and I won't feel guilty about sending important work emails. I'm just going to sit in silence, until I'm allowed to go home and make myself a millionaire, while she farts, and complains about her backache, and acts like having a baby is a divine experience rather than the most fucking obvious thing in the world to do in your thirties.

I sigh once more and go back in where the cooler air engulfs me. A circle's gathering around Nicki, who's sat in the nicest chair, bulbous like a buddha, wearing a novelty bird hat with 'Mother Goose' written across it. A mountain of perfectly wrapped presents circles her like chalk around a dead body, while she makes polite small talk. I find a chair in the corner and pull my legs up onto it, checking my emails.

'Has everyone got drinks before we start?' Charlotte asks. 'I can make more mocktails? No. Are you sure? I think we're ready to go, Nicki!'

'I don't even know where to begin,' Nicki laughs, finally pretending to notice what surrounds her. 'Guys, I said no presents!'

The circle laughs while I silently scoff. Anyone who actually turned up without anything would have a black mark against their name forever. It was like a little test – like when couples ask you to donate money to their honeymoon as a wedding present, and you're in this weird silent auction with all the other guests, figuring out a suitable amount without bankrupting yourself.

As I watch Nicki struggle to reach for her first gift, everyone laughing at her inability to move past her stomach, I see that smug smile I remember so well.

Cat with the cream.

A hateful smile.

Hateful.

Unlike the smile of her husband, who was my undoing twelve years ago . . .

'. . . Here, let me help you,' Matt said, as I struggled to pull a keg across the wooden floor of the Sheffield community hall. I left a stripe through the dust which came to an abrupt halt as I ran out of strength.

'It's OK, I've got it.' I've tried and failed to push it further. 'Hang on, no I really don't . . . thank you.'

He laughed and bent down to grip the bottom, and, together, we heaved the barrel over to the catering tables I'd set up earlier. We thumped it on top, and I theatrically pretended to faint over it. Matt laughed again.

'Thanks again,' I said, rightening myself and acknowledging him properly for the first time. 'I'm Steffi,' I added. 'I don't think we've been on a Nightline shift before?'

Matt held out his hand to shake, which I remember finding delightfully formal for a 20-year-old student. 'Matt,' he said. 'No, we haven't. But I recognise you from the training induction, I think.'

A part of me tingled. I also recognised him from the training induction. He had the best jawline I'd ever seen. In fact, I'd told the Little Women about him when I'd got home that evening, and we'd referred to him as 'Jawline Guy' ever since.

'*Maybe jawline guy dropped out of Nightline?*' I despaired to them when I hadn't seen him in any of my training sessions. '*Maybe he got kidnapped by a biscuit factory and they're using his perfect jawline to design cookies?*'

'Oh, yeah, maybe.' I dusted off my hands – pretending he didn't already have a nickname in my household. I subtly took in the rest of him. Alongside his ridiculous jaw, he had ridiculous green eyes too. He was the sort of tall and skinny that meant most girls would overlook his attractiveness. Plus, he dressed in that mismatched awkwardness of a boy who'd never had a serious girlfriend before to tell him what suited him. He wore a white long-sleeved top under a bright green t-shirt, making him look younger than a second year. Sixth form even. 'How have you been finding Nightline so far?' I asked him.

'Yeah, good. Intense, isn't it?' He rubbed his messy hair and looked a million per cent more adorable. Nightline was the university's equivalent of a Samaritan's helpline – open from eight til eight overnight, giving any struggling students a service they could use that was peer-run, and, therefore, hopefully more appealing than calling a random Sheffield helpline. 'But good. It's going to be crazy when we're let loose on the phone lines for real.'

'Yes.' I nodded. 'And sleeping in those little beds next to the phones? So surreal . . . if we can make them enough money tonight, I guess.' I pointed to the other two kegs by the door where they'd been dumped by the brewery. 'Do you mind helping me with the others? I am precisely as strong as I look, i.e. not very.'

He'd laughed for a third time. 'Of course.'

We spent the next hour making small talk as we set up the hall for the fundraiser. I'd given myself my Freshers' year off to just enjoy the student experience, but now that we were in second year, I'd decided to maximise everything on offer and started volunteering. I still had a month's training to go before I was allowed to do my first Nightline shift, but we'd all been drafted in to help with tonight's fundraising event. It was a Scottish ceilidh, in a random hall buried in the middle of the city. It was very much for the civilians of Sheffield rather than for students.

'Students are too broke to hit up for cash,' Ben, Nightline's manager had told us when we were drafted in. 'We have to fundraise using locals.'

Apparently, the Nightline ceilidh sold out every year and was a guaranteed hit for the 'civvies' of the city. It did feel strange, being out of the union bubble for the day, in a part of the city not heaving with students wearing Uni of Sheffield hoodies. Matt and I set up the rest of the bar – him tapping the keg, while I wrote the drink prices on multiple white boards. Ben directed others around us to mop the floor, stock the toilets with paper and put chairs on stage for the band, while he did the soundcheck, saying, 'one two one two,' down a microphone.

'So, what made you sign up for Nightline?' I asked Matt, while enjoying my attempt at artsy gastro-pub handwriting.

Matt squirted some beer into a plastic cup and tasted some. 'Got to check it doesn't taste of gas,' he explained with a wink, before squirting out some more and offering it to me. 'It's part of making sure it's been tapped correctly.'

I raised both eyebrows and downed it. 'Tastes good to me.'

'Me too. Anyway, I'm doing a psychology degree,' he explained, 'which I thought would be really deep and inter-esting, but it's mostly about the reliability of different research methods. I thought Nightline would be a good way to get experience in, like, actually listening to people. Plus, it'll keep me away from my Xbox.'

'Cool. So you want to be a therapist, or something?'

'Yeah. Maybe. After watching *The Sopranos*.'

I laughed. 'It didn't inspire you to be a gangster?'

He shook his head, squirted more beer, and necked it. 'Nah, too skinny to be a gangster, aren't I?'

I raised my eyebrows again. I have always, and continue to, find it vastly attractive when men are aware of their physical flaws and accept them with a shrug and a smile. Giant noses, male pattern baldness, skinny legs . . . I'm a quivering wreck if a man can make a gentle joke about them.

Matt made a dorky gun gesture with his beer tap and mimed shooting me. I threw my arms up and faked a death and he laughed appreciatively. 'Hmm, I really think we need to check this hasn't got any gas in again. Want some?' He squeezed out more beer and I drank from the red cup in his hands. 'Anyway, how about you? Why did you sign up?'

I wiped my mouth as delicately as I could. 'I do English so we only have two hours of lectures a week. I'm someone who always needs to be doing something, you know? There's only so much time I can spend at the gym, so I thought I'd try volunteering.'

'I mean, the gym is a terrible, terrible place,' he said. 'They've banned me actually. Not enough muscle mass. I was heartbroken, obviously. Do all the rugby lads go there and huff loudly when they lift weights?'

'I can confirm that happens. They "spot" each other too. Then there's lots of high fives.'

Matt mock shuddered and I laughed again. I couldn't believe I was sparking with Jawline Guy. He was as sharp as his cheekbones and our vibe already felt delicious.

'So, Nightline is something to keep me busy,' I continued. 'Plus, my mum was a single mum and she said she used to ring Samaritans when I was little as she got lonely during the day. We've always done charity runs for them and stuff growing up. I looked into training to be a Samaritan but it takes two years and we'll have graduated by the time I've finished and I have no idea where I'll end up getting a job. Probably nowhere with an English degree.'

He laughed, then I laughed, and we both laughed and that set the pattern for the rest of the night.

Hours later, drenched with sweat from the packed hall of dancing, Matt and I were doing our hour's shift at the bar.

'I need to check there's no gas in the beer again,' Matt said, belching quietly in his throat he was so drunk. I was so into him that I found this attractive. He poured us another pint and we shared it between us, watching the dance floor throb and flow to the jolly vibrations of the fiddle band. It was midway through some dance about stripping the willow or something so the bar was empty. People do not sit out at ceilidhs, I was learning. Everyone dances every single dance, even when soaked through with sweat and panting from the effort. It felt strange to be surrounded by people of all different ages. A good different – away from the student angst. I loved my course, and I loved the Little Women, but I did already feel a bit bored by the clichéd parts of the university experience. The Little Women watched *Neighbours* twice a day, unironically. I only scraped through one episode so I could join in their chats about who might die in the advertised upcoming plane crash, but the inertia of most students drove me crazy. The laziness of students. Charlotte and I bonded over this during our gym sessions. The needing seven weeks to write a 2000-word essay, and acting like you were more overworked than a Victorian chimney sweep. 'I never got to go to university,' Mum had said, driving me up on my first day in a rented car. 'Make the most of the opportunity. It's such an opportunity, Steffi. Squeeze the juice.'

There was so much juice to be drained from this night. I felt the fizz of anticipation – the buzz of something new starting. I downed the rest of my pint and let out a hiccup. 'We're drinking all the profits,' I told Matt, wiping under my eyes to keep my melting eyeliner off my cheeks. 'We're sabotaging our own fundraiser.' I had to yell to be heard above the six-piece band on stage who seemed to be having a moustache-growing competition.

Matt was doing that glorious thing boys did when they liked you on nights out – where they stand too close to pretend they need to be heard over the music. 'It's OK. I've chucked twenty quid into the cash box to cover us.' His sweaty chest touched my stomach and we blearily stared at each other with a knowingness.

We were going home together. It was so obvious. So brilliantly obvious. And the best part of that process lay before us – spending the evening pretending to each other we didn't know it yet.

It was just as well some other students came to relieve us of our duties, because, by the time they did, we were significantly past the twenty quid-mark contribution to the bar.

'Shall we dance?' Matt asked, holding out a sweaty palm and nodding towards the heaving dance floor. The band had just reached the end of a song and the couples were wilting, laughing, turning to chat to one another, wiping sweat from their brow.

'I've never been to a ceilidh before. I have no idea what to do.'

'That's why they have a caller.'

Just then, the said caller spoke into the mic. 'Ladies and gentlemen, I need you in groups of eight, please. Groups of eight. We start in five minutes.'

A circle of incredibly red-faced older men, all proudly in kilts, saw us loitering and beckoned us over. 'Come here young bloods,' one yelled in a thick Aberdeen accent. 'Are either of you medical students? Gus here is about to have a heart attack from the exertion.'

'Nonsense,' Gus replied. 'Hey, yous get yourselves over here. You need an initiation sup to join our group.' He produced a large hipflask of whisky and handed it to us. Matt and I made excited eyes – students will never tire of the joy of free alcohol – and each took a swig. 'No need to be shy, there's plenty more where that came from,' Gus added, eyeing our measures, nodding at us to take more.

Some violins started limbering up and the crowd around us quietened. There was sweat on my lip, sweat in my hair, sweat almost raining from the ceiling, and we hadn't even started dancing yet. Matt held out his hand, and I curtseyed and took it, while he laughed again. And oh, how we laughed when the dancing started.

The rest of the night took on a heady, dreamlike, quality with Gus's regular top-ups of whisky cloaking me in a coat of warmth amongst the jolly chaos. It was the most fun I'd ever had going out as a student. There was no ego in dancing to a ceilidh, no way you could look sexy. It was the total opposite to how students danced at the club nights – girls touching themselves, slut-dropping, looking faux-coyly over their shoulder while licking their lips – all with the hope that some acne-ridden rugby player in a shiny shirt would come and rub their dick through the back of their mini skirt. Some of the dance moves that night involved hops. *Hops!* The least sexy thing ever.

'I've broken both ankles,' Matt declared, stumbling into me, as drunk as I was.

'I'm so dizzy I might need to lie down.'

'There's no more willow to strip, surely?'

All I can remember is laughing. Laughing as we totally failed to strip the willow properly, Gus having to push us about, yelling at us for ruining the formation, punishing us by making us down more shots. Laughing as we were instructed to hold hands and gallop through a long arch of held arms. Laughing as we turned wrong ways; bumped into other drunk people as useless as we were. Laughing at the sweat; wiping our hands on one another to prove how sweaty we were and as an excuse to touch. Because we'd helped set up, we weren't on clean-up duty, and Matt and I kept laughing as the crowd spilled out into the sharp northern air. It was hilarious to order a Subway together. It was hilarious to wait for the bus back to mine. It was hilarious to point out other students, all only starting their nights out, when we were so drunk and finished at not even midnight. It was hilarious eating the Subway on my kitchen floor, the house empty, the rest of the Little Women out at the union's Saturday cheese night. It was hilarious when Matt started kissing me – first gently, then with serious urgency. It was hilarious having sex on top of our standing freezer. I giggled into his shoulder and pretended to come, wrapping my legs around his back, laughing and laughing. I found a bottle of gin and we took it up to my room, taking swigs, kissing more, giggling, taking it in turns to choose a song off my laptop. Hazy and too drunk, but both happy. We tried to have sex again but Matt couldn't get it up he was too hammered. That was hilarious too, even though he said, '*Stop laughing, it isn't funny,*' but then laughed himself, good-naturedly. Erectile dysfunction . . . another thing I apparently find attractive as long as you can make a joke about it.

We passed out, half naked, sprawled in my sheets, limbs floppy. I still remember us both stirring when the Little Women came home from their own night out. The smell of their take-away sneaking under the gaps of my door, the sounds of their drunken laughter and getting ready for bed noises. Matt pulled me closer to him, brought the duvet over our bodies as we were sobering up enough to get cold. We slept again in a drunken fog, until . . . sometime nearing dawn, I was woken by his fierce erection poking into my back.

'Sorry,' he said, noticing me stir. 'I can't help it. It won't go down . . .'

'I know something that will help.'

The second time we had sex wasn't funny at all. It was sleepy and cute, but sexy as hell. We whispered into one another's ears. He told me how glad he was I'd joined Nightline, how he'd noticed me on that first induction day. He kissed me how men kiss you when they're falling in love – searching, gentle. He kissed my lips, neck, chest, went down further.

'No . . .' I tried to push him off. 'I'm all gross from dancing and . . .'

'I don't mind,' he said, his tongue teasing me through my underwear. 'You smell amazing.'

I really did come that night, turning my face into a pillow as to not wake my housemates. I unravelled and writhed – in total awe that my body was capable of doing this under the touch of a boy, when it was something I'd only ever achieved myself before.

'Wow . . . fuck . . .' I mumbled.

'I want you so much.'

We had sex how I imagined Sting has it – breathing in one another's breath, taking it slow, eyes locked on each other's. I can't think of a less cringe way to say it than a *'soul connection'*.

Or so I thought . . .

We collapsed in a sticky naked pretzel as the sun rose behind my shitty student curtains – the light of dawn steaming through them. The last thing I remember is him gently stroking my back and kissing my neck one more time before his breath hit a rhythmic pattern. I fell into the heavy sleep of a satisfied body, a heart drumming with hope, opportunity tingling in my limbs. I'd slept with a few people since starting uni, sort of because I felt I had to.

'Go and have experiences,' Mum had begged me. 'I never got to. You never regret experiences – the good, or the bad.'

All three times had felt disappointing and a bit sad. All three times the sex had been bordering on terrible, but I managed to grind these nights down into diamonds of funny stories. 'Smegma Guy,' had become urban legend in our house. We squealed and ran away whenever we saw him on nights out. 'Washing Machine Mouth,' was in one of our seminars, and we all giggled silently whenever he spoke. I was, by far, the most 'experienced' out of the Little Women. Nicki had only just broken up with her first steady boyfriend. She'd since kissed a guy on a night out and spun it into the giantest drama of all time when he didn't ask for her number afterwards. Lauren was still messaging a boy from home things had never properly taken off with, so she said she couldn't fancy anyone new until she'd got over the 'wasted potential'. And Charlotte was unashamedly following the 'Good Girl Rule' where you don't sleep with anyone until after Date Seven because she 'knew her worth' – not realising, in saying that, she was implying I didn't. As a result, the whole house dined out on my own mild promiscuity. I admit I played the part a bit. It felt nice to feel worldly, and to have confidence in a part of my life where they all appeared to be lacking. They all came from solid homes and money in the bank. Charlotte and Nicki didn't even have student loans! Well, they did, but their parents had only made them take one out to get interest on it in a savings account, as an investment. My bad sex stories were almost my only status in our group – a way of transforming me from the poor, single parent one who couldn't have them stay in the holidays because there wasn't enough room at my mum's flat, into one they could almost be jealous of. But, after that night with Matt, I felt I'd had an experience they could be genuinely envious of. When we woke up at ten, I was already working out how to tell them the story to get the most whoops. How a drunken charity fundraiser turned into a Disney-level fairytale.

'Hello you,' I told his fluttering eyelids.

'Hey yourself,' Matt replied, smiling, before leaning over to kiss my forehead.

'Ouch,' I said, clasping my hands over where he'd just kissed. 'It hurts.'

The hangover was starting to kick in. Dry mouth, thudding skull, queasy belly.

'Gus was lethal,' he agreed. 'Shall I go make us toast and bring it up?'

'Only if you don't mind me proposing.'

He laughed again, stroked my side, making goosebumps dance on my naked skin.

'Have a doze. I'll collect the carbs. What bread is yours? Or do you all share a loaf?'

'Mine's the Hovis granary.'

'Of course it is, gym bunny. Right, coming up.'

I turned the pillow onto its fresh side, smiling at the soft thud of his feet going down our carpeted steps. Screw the toast. Maybe we'd have sex again when he came back up? Maybe he'd go down on me again? I never thought I'd enjoy that but I'd never had Matt do it to me. I smiled myself into light slumber, horny, imagining all the sex yet to come as the weekend continued. Hopefully continuing into the next week, or month even? I could see Matt being my boyfriend. Not just an average one, but a meaningful one.

He'd be ten minutes. Fifteen tops.

But, when I woke at the sounds of laughter from downstairs, with no Matt and no toast by my side, it felt much later. I checked the time and saw it was almost eleven. A whole hour has passed. More laughter and the deep sound of Matt's voice through our squeaky floorboards. A siren rumbled through my skin and I scrambled to get myself ready. I stepped into my sexiest pyjamas and quickly dashed to the toilet to pee and brush my teeth. I told myself stories to override the alert. He was just being friendly to my housemates. It would be great if they got to know each other – helped make it more 'boyfriendy'. He was probably just letting me sleep. So caring of him. Again, so not one-night-standy. If he was only in this for sex, surely he'd have come up and tried it on by now?

I ruffled my hair, smiled at my reflection, and banished the insecurity from my face. I heard laughter again, and padded downstairs, barefoot, in my tiny pyjamas, arranging a smile on my face as I pushed through the kitchen door.

Matt was sat with Nicki at our tiny, dilapidated table, two cold bits of uneaten toast on a plate before him, presumably for me. They both had mugs of her special frothy coffee in their hands, and they both froze when I said, 'hi.'

Matt looked momentarily stunned to see me, and then alarmed, my inner siren loudened, my ears buzzing. 'Steff. Oh my God! Sorry, I've been ages. Here. Here's your toast.'

He pushed the plate towards me, going red, while Nicki giggled.

'I . . . thought I heard voices.' I meant it to come out breezy but it sounded suspicious, *needy*. I winced internally and crossed my arms over myself. 'You've met each other, great.'

I watched their eyes lock. *Theirs* – not mine and his. Nicki giggled again.

'It's my fault, sorry,' she told me. 'We started talking about Pokémon. I got excited there was a fellow geek here and we went off on one.'

Matt pointed over with gun hands, like he had with the beer tap at me. 'She didn't just talk about Pokémon. She actually *fancies* some of them.'

Nicki shrugged, non-embarrassed. 'What can I say? Growlithe is weirdly hot.'

They laughed together and Nicki sipped more from her coffee mug. She was showing no sign of leaving the kitchen, even though her breakfast bowl was empty. She looked the total opposite of me in the wintery morning light. I was shivering in my skimpy silky short pjs, last night's makeup smudged around my eyes, my bob wild and bed-headed. While she wore almost comedically-cliched *pyjamas* – blue and white stripes with buttons down the front. Her face was fresh and clean, her hair plaited neatly into two cute braids.

I bit into my toast, and wondered how to invite Matt back up to my room without it being obvious I was up for round three.

'How was your night?' Nicki asked me. She literally leant back in her chair and put her slippered feet on the table – the ultimate sign of settling in. 'The barn dance thingy? Did you raise enough money?'

Matt winked at me and I practically swooned in relief at having his attention again. 'It was fun,' he said. 'Totally mad. Really nice to not be just out with students for the night. We got so drunk though, didn't we? I can't remember much.'

I bit my lip. Was that true? Did he not remember my heels digging into his bare arse, only hours ago, right here in this kitchen? Did he not remember the taste of me in his mouth? The groan he let out that I had to cover with my hand?

'Steffi?' Nicki asked, while I slowly and deliberately perched on top of the storage freezer to jog his memory. 'Was it good?'

I winked back. 'It was great. Loads of money raised for Nightline. The most important thing, really.'

Matt raised his mug to cheers me and I relaxed a millimetre.

'Anyway, what have you guys been chatting about all this time?' I asked. 'Other than the shagability of Pokémon?'

'Oh, everything and nothing. You know?' Nicki said.

No, I thought. *I don't know.*

Just as I was trying to figure out my next move, the door swung open again, Lauren in the threshold, cradling her head like it was falling off.

'Just so you're all aware, I'm literally dead,' she announced, plopping onto a chair and putting her forehead on the table. 'I've blocked the toilet with my sick and, I'm sorry but I feel too rough to clean it up right now. Please, take mercy. I just need a pop tart and I'll . . .' She looked up and her mouth fell at Matt's presence. 'You don't live here,' she told him.

Matt blushed into his frothy coffee. He looked beyond adorable. 'This is my friend, Matt, from Nightline,' I explained. The air hung awkwardly as we all filled in the blanks as to why he was here, in last night's clothes, so early in the morning.

'Oh . . . Matt's your name is it, then?' Lauren said, giving him a hello hug and then pointing behind his shoulders and mouthing '*Jawline Guy!*' to me. 'Sorry if I stink. Last night was a journey for all of us, mostly my stomach lining.'

'I told you not to get an Indian AND a fish-and-chips takeaway,' Nicki laughed.

'You were also correct that I shouldn't have tried mixing them all together in the same giant bowl to see if it created the best takeaway of all time.' She nodded at Matt. 'It quite closely resembled what our toilet currently looks like. Sorry,' she said, just as I objected. 'I think I'm still drunk. Nicki, will you come into my room and stroke my hair until I go back to sleep?'

Nicki heaved herself up with a good-natured sigh and went to escort Lauren out. She looked undeniably cute in her pyjamas. 'It was nice meeting you,' she told Matt. 'If you get a Nightline call at 2am from someone with a Pokémon bestiality issue, you're going to know it's me.'

He laughed and he looked so, so, hot when he did. 'Indeed I will. Good luck with the, er . . . hair stroking?'

Lauren winked as they left, all like, *look I've given you shagging opportunity time*, and I mouthed *thanks* back. It felt awkward, when we were left alone in the kitchen, the freezer underneath me haunting me with how un-awkward it had been in the early hours of this morning.

'I'm so jealous of girls,' Matt announced, stretching up and reaching over to eat my toast crusts. 'When I'm hungover, my housemates ruthlessly take the piss out of me, or force me to compete in eating challenges. I'd love it if we just lay about in our pyjamas and stroked each other's hair.'

'I'm not sure if all girls do the hair stroking,' I said, grateful we were bantering again. 'Lauren got blind drunk the first time we all went out together. We had to take her back to her halls, where she spectacularly vommed everywhere, and then started crying. She wouldn't go to sleep, and kept screaming, '*STROKE MY HAIR.*' All three of us ended up doing it, like she was a Roman emperor. It's become . . . a thing.'

'They're great,' Matt said. 'Your housemates seem great.'

'Thanks. I agree.'

I agree? Why was I talking like a fake grown-up? How did I get our energy back? How did I lure him back to my room where I'm sure we could restore things after Nicki's interruption?

'I . . . umm . . . you've left your jumper in my room,' I said, leaning against the wall as alluringly as I could.

'Of course, yeah. Thanks, I'd have forgotten it otherwise. I'll just head up and get it now.'

'I can help?'

He was already at the door though, rushing up the stairs. 'No worries, it'll only take a sec.' I crossed my arms further over myself. It was way too cold for these pyjamas and my nipples were sticking out. The sound of Matt running downstairs again, and he appeared in the doorway, wearing his jumper, looking very much like a boy ready to leave the house.

'Cheers,' he said. 'Right . . .'

'Umm . . . you can stay, if you'd like?'

'Oh, thank you. Sorry, but, I really need er . . . the . . . toilet, and it sounds like yours is blocked.'

I opened my mouth. I was about to say, '*I'll unblock it for you,*' then stopped myself. If he wanted to stay, he would stay. He'd hold it in, or suggest we go out for brunch or something. I couldn't understand how he'd become such a stranger so quickly. Last night was a popped bubble, leaving me blinking in surprise.

'Last night was fun,' he added, finding his trainers by the door and putting them on.

'Fun, yeah.'

Not amazing, or special, or magical, or even great. *Fun.*

'I'm sure I'll see you soon. Doing a night shift or whatever? It's going to be crazy when they let us loose on the phones.'

'Hmm, yeah.'

'God, I'm so hungover. Are you?'

'Yep.'

'Well, I better go. Dying for a piss actually.'

And the last thing I said to him, to try and convince him to fall in love with me, was, '*You can pee in our garden before you leave, if you'd like? I don't mind.*'

I was stupid enough to hope after that. Lauren came running down after he'd left and screamed, 'JAWLINE GUY!! Oh my God, you're right. He's like Robert Pattinson's and a protractor's love child. Where has he gone? No! Don't say I ruined it all by blocking the toilet. It's unblocked now! Ring him and tell him to come back. I'm so sorry!'

Nicki lurked behind her, a tight smile on her face. One I couldn't decipher. A strange distance fell between us like light snow.

'I . . .' It's only then I realised it with a cold dread. 'I don't have his number. We didn't swap numbers.'

We'd swapped bodily fluids. I knew what his face looked like while he slept. His sweat was all over my sheets. And yet he hadn't even left his fucking number.

'Oh . . .' Lauren looked as shocked as I felt. 'He'll just have forgotten and be kicking himself. I'm sure you'll run into him at your phone line thingy, won't you?'

'Yeah, maybe.'

'What happened last night anyway?' Nicki asked, still looking beyond cute in her giant pyjamas. 'Like, was it a one-night-stand vibe, or what?'

'I . . . we . . .' I hated the way they both looked at me. All, like, *look how being slutty backfires*. I was about to tell them the whole thing. How we'd clicked, how we'd chatted, and laughed, and danced all night, how it had felt special right up until the moment he went to make me toast. I was about to tell them how different it had felt with Matt. But pride closed my mouth. I was too thrown. Maybe I'd open up later, once he'd hopefully hunted me down for my number? '. . . yeah, just a one-night stand,' I confirmed, turning to go back upstairs.

It certainly became that. Especially as Matt never appeared at Nightline again. He wasn't in our final training, and therefore not on any of the overnight shifts. For the final term, every night I spent in the tiny helpline office, I stared at the little trundle beds, imagining what could've happened if Matt hadn't vanished. The Sheffield campus was big enough to not bump into anyone, and, as the Little Women preferred cheese nights to the indie rock Matt had told me he liked, there was a minuscule chance of bumping into him on a night out. I had no choice but to acknowledge it was a one-night stand after all – one where I'd maybe been blinded by the sex actually being good for once. It hurt for a while. I had a fling with some random Masters student, who actually took me out to Las Iguanas first, and paid, which felt remarkably grown up. But it was all rather empty and I thought of Matt the whole time. After a few months though, I stopped looking for him on packed dance floors, or floating through the union's forecourt. I wasn't going to forget him, I knew that. The night was too cinematic and the ending so abrupt and unexplained. But I was managing to feel less pained and preoccupied by it, until one day, Nicki finally, unexpectedly, filled in my blanks.

'Shall we go out for coffee today?' she asked me one morning in our kitchen. 'Just us two?'

'I mean, we're having one right now,' I said, holding up one of our matching JUSTICE FOR BETH mugs.

'Yes, but it would be nice to go out for a proper one, wouldn't it?' Nicki said. 'Have a chat?'

I think I knew it then. I pushed away my drink – unwilling to stay on her script. 'What's going on?'

Nicki pulled the sleeves of her cardigan down over her hands and picked up her mug again. 'What do you mean?'

'Something's happened. Tell me.'

'Steffi, stop being weird.'

'Me? You're the one who's been weird and offy for weeks. You keep being mysteriously busy. Until now, I feel like you've been avoiding me.'

'Well, I have, as a matter of fact. Sorry.'

'What?'

She blew on the top of her drink and raised an eyebrow as she looked up at me. Her face was set in this stony determination. 'I'd hoped to make this nicer, but if you want to do it now.'

'Do what now? Stop being weird. You're the one being strange, not me.'

She bristled. 'If you must know, I've been weird because I have a new boyfriend.'

My heart dropped into my guts and I hated her then, for the scene I was about to play. 'Oh wow,' I said in my fake voice. 'That's exciting.'

'It's been two months now so I'm ready to tell you.'

'It's not my dad, is it?' I joked, wanting to prolong this moment of not knowing for certain. 'You've tracked him down and now you're marrying him.'

'Steffi . . .' She took my hand with such patronising pity that my palm almost blistered. 'I'm together with Matt. Jawline Guy. It's serious. We're in love.'

'Right . . . oh . . .'

She rushed to explain the details, and the relief at having my curiosity satisfied was quickly replaced by sickening anguish. They'd just really 'clicked' that morning over break-fast. It was love at first sight, she was very keen to tell me, three times. Thunderbolt. He'd said he'd thought he was on a date with her. Strange as that sounds. He'd asked for her number. And, when it became clear that our thing was only a *'bit of drunken fun'*, they'd gone on a date. Then another. Now they were properly together.

I could tell when she spoke how much she'd rehearsed this, and how excited she was. By Matt. By her being chosen over me. Though that was all in the subtext. Considering she'd clearly rehearsed it, you would've thought she could've edited out some of the nastier inclusions. *'He said he was so drunk he hardly remembered that night with you.'* *'He said it was clear by the way you were with each other that it wasn't a relationship thing.'* *'He said he was so blown away by me that he honestly forgot you were upstairs.'* I chewed on my lip and tried not to show the blows landing, trying to give my friend the benefit of the doubt. She was so obviously in love with Matt, and, by the sounds of things, Matt with her. Everyone newly in love is an obnoxious prick. She was telling me as soon as she practi-cally could, 'I wanted to know for sure it was really something before jeopardising our friendship.' Plus, also, there was the obvious get-out clause for everyone involved. 'It was only a one-night stand, wasn't it?' Nicki asked, eyeing me over the steam of her mug as she backed me into a corner, knowing the only appropriate response was an affirmative. I nodded, telling myself I could get upset later, when my bedroom door was closed. I could cry with my head under my pillow then, obsess over what Nicki had and I didn't, endlessly doubt my instincts about men and how they feel about me.

'Of course,' I replied. 'Thanks for being so sweet in trying to protect me. But that night meant nothing. Nothing.'

And, in time, that became the truth. Nicki and Matt were so obviously supposed to end up together that it was almost absurd for me to think there was a chance between us. He basically moved in for the rest of uni. I'd often walk in on them in the living room, playing video games together. They were both into the same dorky stuff. Then, of course, I fell madly in love with *Terrible Malcolm* in third year and saved all my heartache for the many, many, times he cheated on me on nights out. Matt evolved into this sort of eunuch-esque, non-sexual, Blue Peter man in my life. I found his puppy-doggying of Nicki almost revolting, especially how she bossed him about while he quivered and apologised. I moved on. They'd obviously moved on. We graduated. They stayed together and made it work long distance between London and Leeds, where he got his first job. Everything was fine, all in the past, the Little Women were at peace, all very mature thank you very much, let's get on with our lives.

Until, randomly, five years ago, the day they got engaged, when it became apparent that Nicki wasn't over it at all. The day Matt 'surprised' her with the ring she'd designed for him a year previously, was the day Nicki decided she had a problem with me. Her insecurity was like fucking . . . dormant tuberculosis or something, and her diamond ring triggered its onset. It made no sense. It still makes no sense. Their marriage should've been the ultimate proof that I was nobody to worry about, and yet their engagement became the day I got declared the enemy. Nicki got uptight if I ever spoke to Matt, finding an excuse to come and tug him away, eyeing me like I was acting inappropriately by making small talk about the state of the publishing industry. She started trying to out me from the group. I discovered at least two Little Women meet-ups she'd organised where I'd been '*forgotten*' to get invited – much to Lauren and Charlotte's horror, but too late, they were already there. I wasn't included on any chats about wedding admin. Nothing about Nicki's wedding dresses or location options, which seemed strange until I discovered they'd been syphoned off to a separate chat. 'Nicki says it's cause you're not into all that wedding stuff,' Lauren told me. 'But I dunno. It's weird.'

The final insult was the wedding itself where I wasn't sat with the Little Women at dinner, and instead shoved onto some random table for single outcasts.

Maybe she'll calm down now she's married, I told myself, glugging wine and staring like a depressed Bassett Hound over at my friends on their table.

But the safer Nicki and Matt got, the more unsafe she seemed to find my general existence. Like she was worried I'd have delayed-onset-revenge-sex with him or something. The thing is, at this point, any revenge sex wouldn't be because she'd 'won' Matt, but for trying to push me out of the most important friendship group I'd ever had the delight of being in. Nicki could have her beige husband, but I'd rather die than give up Charlotte and Lauren. I feel like I'm holding onto my friends with greased fingertips, even though I never did anything wrong. And you could argue I should be the one angry at Nicki, not vice-versa. I still feel I handled the thing entirely graciously, all things considered. Especially as she didn't even let up when my mum was dying and got all funny when I uttered one sentence to Matt at the wake about where the kitchen was. And, here I am, still gracious, at her fucking baby shower, with a hundred quid's worth of presents celebrating her predictable life choices, and she's still bitchy and bored enough to start a pile-on.

Honestly, fuck her.

She's unwrapping the first gift now. All coos and *ahh* and *you shouldn't haves*. She clasps her hand in delight at some twee, oversized muslin squares – because it's motherhood and we have to make the souring puke of a reflux-ridden baby into a collectible retro print. I'm still surprised they haven't started tying pastel ribbons around the handles of forceps to be honest. That you can't get an Etta print *ventouse*. Her smile is exactly the same as the one I saw all those years ago, above the steaming cup of coffee. The plump smugness of a smile. The cat who got the cream smile.

Seriously, fuck fucking Nicki.

Transcript: Inspector Simmons interviewing Charlotte Roth

Simmons:	It must've been a hard day for you, Charlotte. The day of the baby shower.
Charlotte:	Well, the heat was far from ideal, yes, but I worked out ways around it. The air conditioning unit was a godsend, and we managed without ice. The food melted but everything tasted OK. The peony wall didn't wilt, which is another miracle. Hard, yes, but worth it.
Simmons:	I don't mean the heat, Charlotte. I mean the nature of the event.
Charlotte:	Excuse me?
Simmons:	A baby shower must've been a painful thing to arrange considering your own issues conceiving a baby . . . something you've spoken about extensively on social media.
Charlotte:	What's . . . how . . . what's that got to do with anything?
Simmons:	Some guests commented that it seemed to be more your baby shower, than Nicole's.
Charlotte:	I gifted her all my manifestation board ideas, yes.
Simmons:	That's very big of you.
Charlotte:	Thank you, but not really. You've got to let regrets go with light and love in your heart.
Simmons:	Or you can set fire to your regrets?
Charlotte:	Arson's not in *The Secret*, Inspector Simmons. I can lend you my copy if you don't believe me. I have two. One annotated, and one ornamental for my display bookshelf.

CHARLOTTE

It's OK. It's nothing. It's going to be fine.

Oh God, I'm having a miscarriage fuck fuck fuck fuck no no no no fuck fuck fuck.

But I'm not. It's alright. It has to be. It must.

I've been locked in the toilet for quite some time, reading every single article I can after googling a number of key phrases.

Bleeding six weeks pregnant.

Implantation bleeding or miscarriage?

Signs of chemical pregnancy

Why won't the world let me have a fucking baby fuck fuck fuck this fuck my fucking life

The last search term, admittedly, didn't yield the most helpful of results, though I did find a lot of 'emotional support' articles. But I don't need emotional support because this isn't a miscarriage. It isn't. I refuse it to be one. Plus, there's only a 21.3 per cent chance it is one. If I was given a 79.7 per cent chance of surviving cancer or something, I'd be delighted. Not worried in the slightest. OK, maybe I'd be slightly concerned and want the dodgy mole to be removed or whatever, but I wouldn't think I would die. So, this baby won't die. It's fine. It's just nestling in and dislodging some bleedy cells in the process. That scientific description hasn't come up in my frantic toilet research, but I'm sure that's what's happening.

I should probably call the doctor though, just to check. Google tells me I need to go and get a scan to see if there's a heartbeat, and if there is a heartbeat, that means there's a 90 per cent chance of the pregnancy being viable. That would be amazing, wouldn't it? Usually, you have to wait twelve weeks before the first scan. I've already booked a 'reassurance scan' for seven weeks through Seth's BUPA, but, with this happening, I can be reassured even quicker. By the end of today, even. Wow, I'm going to hear my baby's heartbeat today. That's so magical. How lucky is that? It's actually *good* this bleeding is happening. Not ideal timing, obviously, but it's *clearly* a test from the universe. I need to continue making this the best baby shower ever, to show the world I'm at peace with my endless fucking totally unjustified and inexplicable fucking infertility fucking universe, and then I'll be rewarded by hearing my baby's heartbeat.

That's science. I'm certain of it. I'm calm. I'm serene. I'm at peace with the world and everyone in it.

I want to stay in the bathroom and repeat my affirmations in the mirror, but some idiot keeps fucking knocking. I stuff my knickers with quilted toilet paper and look at myself in the mirror. My hair's wilting quite spectacularly in this heat and I'm glad I've got some good photos in.

'You're not having a miscarriage,' I tell myself and my wilting hair. 'You are pregnant. This is just the universe testing you, but you have never had a test you didn't get an A in.'

There's more knocking. 'Sorry but I really am desperate,' some fucking impatient cunt bitch calls through the door.

'It's OK. Just coming.'

Honestly, I TOLD Nicki's mum we should let people use the upstairs bathroom, but did she listen? No. Too worried it wasn't clean enough, but 25 women sipping mocktails and only one toilet is just a disaster waiting to happen.

I breeze out, apologising to the knocking woman – that girl from Nicki's job with the freckles and strange haircut – and return to making the present opening run smoothly. I feel blood drip into the toilet roll, but it's alright, it's quilted, it will hold until I've logged the gifts. I retrieve the printed-out spreadsheet I folded into my handbag alongside my special fluffy pen I bought especially for today. Nicki won't be able to keep tabs on who gave her what, not with baby brain, so I'm jotting it all down for her. Part of my gift is a big pile of thank-you cards with envelopes already addressed and stamped, to cut down Nicki's post-baby-shower admin. I read this idea online. Total genius. Honestly, how did anyone *cope* before Pinterest?

I take in Nicki's aura as we all settle around her and she's truly glowing. Her body is swollen with baby and blessing – her face almost distorted with the bloat of everything coming her way. I wonder if my own face will swell when this not-miscarriage turns into my most longed-for baby? I almost want to reach over and touch her, to get her essence on me to give me luck. She's unwrapping some home-knitted booties, squealing and exclaiming she can't believe how tiny they are. She holds them up to the bulge of her stomach and it's so perfect it hurts my teeth when I smile. I want this. I want this for myself so badly. It can't go wrong and it won't go wrong, even as I feel the loo roll dampen in my knickers.

I start asking the universe for signs as to when it wants me to leave. After the presents? If I wait til then will I pass this test? Then I remember the gender reveal. I've still got at least another hour. I can't duck out before then, I'm the only one who knows how to coordinate the surprise. A cool panic settles on my skin but this spreadsheet isn't going to fill itself, so I concentrate on inputting Nicki's presents with my best handwriting.

Present number two. Home-knitted booties from Nicki's mum's friend, Jill. I must get her address before she leaves. A lovely sentiment, but rather neglects the obvious which is we're living through the worst heatwave on record and this baby is likely going to be naked until September if the long-term weather reports are anything to go by. Still, I'm sure Nicki will keep them for sentimental value. She'll need to get a photo of the baby in them to send onto Jill as a thank you. I put a tick in the relevant column of the spreadsheet for presents that require a photo of the baby wearing an item. The giver gets pissed off otherwise.

'I can't believe their tiny feet will fit into these tiny things,' Nicki says, holding them at arm's length. She's taking longer to open this present than I thought she would. I budgeted one minute per present, and this has already strayed into two. If she takes this long with each, it's really going to throw off Matt's arrival. Usually, he could just wait outside in the air-conned car, but he's arriving in a taxi now because of the other universe test I've been set.

Thankfully she moves onto the next gift-wrapped box and dives inside the baby duck wrapping paper. My hope is, as the novelty of the present unwrapping wears off, she'll go faster and we can make up time. Nicki must think of her guests too. It's rude to make people watch you receive presents for too long. You need to balance the time of thank yous and exclamations so each gift-giver feels appreciated so you don't need to rush the end, leaving the last gift-givers feeling under-appreciated. I wonder how many seconds precisely . . . *I'm miscarrying, aren't I?* No, shh. There must be a golden ratio of maximising appreciation demonstrated by a gift by time saved opening it and—

'Oh, these little dungarees! I love them! Thank you. They're so cute.'

Who sent these? Oh, Jeanie, her school friend with the toddler. She's chatting Nicki through her choices. 'I hope you don't mind but I've gone a size up or two,' she explains, 'as I thought you'd be getting loads of newborn stuff and bigger sizes might be more useful.'

'That's genius!' Nicki squeaks, holding up a onesie. She's now taken one minute twenty seconds with this gift. 'Isn't that genius, everybody?'

They nod and coo and I pretend to nod and coo, but I'm actually really frustrated at Jeanie's huge mistake. She's right – giving baby clothes in larger sizes *is* very helpful to expecting parents. In fact, if she read the same article that I did online, it's *six to nine months* and *nine to twelve months* that are the most useful. That's when the presents dry up, and, also when the baby starts weaning so you need more outfit changes from all the mess. However, Jeanie has fallen at the final hurdle and not accounted for the change in seasons. These dungarees and sleep suit are both summery and lightweight. They'll be useless, sadly, in December, when the baby fits them. Poor Nicki. Two weather inappropriate choices in a row. What a waste. People always talk about what a drain babies are on natural resources, but then they go and buy a pair of yellow dungaree shorts in July in size *six to nine months!* What's wrong with everyone? Why are they all so fucking stupid? I almost write *fucking stupid* in the spreadsheet with my fluffy pen but I stop myself and realise I might, in fact, not be coping very well with this definitely-not-a-miscarriage.

Next present is a Sophie the Giraffe. Standard. Of course, there's no way they would've bought one if they'd watched the videos I have, of mums cutting into them with scissors and finding all the black mould inside. I make a note in the column marked '*Need to warn Nicki about this present*', just so she's aware of the mould risk. It should be fine if she dab-washes it with a damp cloth, rather than immersing it in water. However, my writing's coming out all wobbly on the paper, the letters slipping out of their allocated boxes. Now I come to think about it, I'm not breathing very . . . efficiently. It's so hot in here, isn't it? I feel more blood leave my body. It feels like a period, only it can't be a period because I've had a positive pregnancy test. If this blood becomes a period it will be a miscarriage after a 'chemical pregnancy' which is essentially just a Google term for people who are so desperate to know if they're pregnant they take tests too early and get a positive result which becomes a miscarriage that most women wouldn't even notice because their cycle isn't regular, *or* they're so smug they don't take a test right away because their fertility hasn't been the most painful agonising part of their entire lives . . . and I should really ground myself in this room, shouldn't I? I'm spiralling.

I look around at all the women straining in Nicki's direction. Lauren's chatting quietly to someone on her left, her baby monitor in her lap. She laughs and finally seems to be having a good time. Steffi, however, is curled up on a chair in the corner, face lost in her phone screen, scowling. Anger gnaws my stomach. Oh, lucky Steffi, who never wants kids. Her biggest worry in life is people judging her for that, when I wish she'd realise being child-free isn't this glorious feminist whateverthefuck *choice* for every woman. Some of us have it forced upon us. I stare back at Nicki's stomach, at how it strains through the fabric of her dungarees. The only time I've come close to my stomach looking that bulbous and fertile was on the day of my egg retrieval. Day after day, Seth had injected me with hormones that made me even more manic than usual. My skin got so bruised that Seth ran out of sites to puncture that weren't already marbled with purple. And, not long after, as my follicles bloated me like proving dough, it got even harder to pierce through my skin with our delusional hope.

'I almost look pregnant,' I'd said, taking multiple selfies in my hospital gown just before they put me under. I'd documented every inch of my IVF journey to merge into a multimedia set-piece to upload when I'm finally pregnant. It's part of my manifestation. I've even edited all the footage up until now.

Seth had stood behind me in the private hospital room, and gently lifted my gown to show off my bloated abdomen. He kissed the top of my head.

'And soon you will be pregnant,' he'd said. 'This is going to work, Charlotte. It is.'

But he must not have *actually* believed it because the first round of IVF didn't work, and Seth's lack of genuine manifestation was something we argued about when we didn't yield anything. Like nothing yields in my inexplicably barren body.

That's my official diagnosis, by the way.

Unexplained infertility.

A uterus that just shrugs.

A question mark where my Sophie the Giraffe mould should be.

It breaks my brain. Everything in life can be explained, surely? That's why Google exists. And I've been manifesting my family since I was a child myself. There was no present I'd want for Hanukkah that wasn't a doll. I even picked my degree, and career choices, around what suits being a mother. I didn't even sleep around before I met Seth as I was so scared I'd catch chlamydia and it would damage my fertility. Even then, when I slept with boyfriends, they'd have to do two STD tests, at two different sites, before I'd sleep with them, and even then they'd have to still use condoms. Honestly, it's amazing what boys are willing to put themselves through in order to get laid. Steffi always asked if I worried I asked for 'too much' from my boyfriends when I was blue-ballsing them before the results came in. But, if anything, she asks for too little. I know she thinks it's her child-free stuff that stops men committing to her, but it's not. She doesn't truly value herself and they smell it. Steffi acts like she values herself, with her amazing body and amazing career and life and friends and *have you seen this thing at the theatre that is impossible to get tickets for.* She's so seemingly happily independent, but the smell is there. Even through my phone screen. She doesn't doesn't know her True Worth. She doesn't believe in it. And men sense it and therefore treat her like shit. I'm only five-foot tall, very 'high maintenance' and make men do multiple STI tests before they sleep with me. Do they mind? Never. Because I know my worth and that makes you magnetic. Not that finding a glorious husband has helped me become a parent.

It's still amazing to me how *cocky* I was about becoming a mother. When Seth and I first started trying, I was even deluded enough to make us wait until December to conceive so our baby would be born in September. I had to balance the lifelong benefit of them being the eldest in their school year against the fact maternity wards are their busiest then, and I would therefore more likely have a negative birth experience, which impacts maternal mental health and therefore the long-term outlook for a baby. Also, I factored in the additional year of childcare to our costings but still found, ultimately, the benefits of a September birth were worth it.

'This baby is so lucky,' Seth said, after I'd shown him my spreadsheet and costings. 'What an amazing mother you already are.'

I was in my element initially. Fertility tracking was like *crack* to me. So much to read up on! Fertile windows and predicting ovulation and taking my basal temperature and monitoring my cervical mucus. It seemed insane that some couples just stopped using contraception and assumed they'd get pregnant. When you're only fertile for five days each cycle. And then the egg you release has to be good enough quality. And then the sperm has to meet that egg, and that sperm needs to be good enough quality too. Seth and I went teetotal for three months before trying. I set up a chemistry lab in our en-suite, peeing on ovulation sticks the day my period started, sometimes three times a day. When the first strip confirmed I was ovulating, I was almost too excited to have sex. I kept dancing around in my knickers, waving the strip about, telling Seth about how great my mucus was. 'It has an egg-white consistency,' I told him. 'It's perfect! And look how dark this line was.'

In two weeks' time, I just *knew* I'd be seeing another two dark lines, this time signalling my pregnancy. Manifestation was such an important part of the conception process. I'd read that your body and mind needs to be *ready* to conceive. If you're in too much of a fight-or-flight state then your body senses the stress hormones and doesn't fertilise you.

We did everything right. We had sex at the right time, multiple times, over the important days. I ensured Seth used my bullet vibrator on me afterwards so I could orgasm, because the shockwaves actively draw sperm further into your vagina. I was already taking folic acid – of course – and following a diet rich in fertility foods.

'We just made a baby,' I whispered, the first time Seth and I had unprotected sex. 'I just know we've made a baby. I just know it.'

Seth kissed my fingertips. 'I feel it too.'

He tried to kiss me on the mouth but I shimmied around to put my legs up against the wall. This isn't a clinically proven method to help conception, but sometimes you need to use common sense, and gravity is as powerful as manifestation. I lay upside-down for half an hour, eyes closed, not letting Seth talk to me while I did my visualisations. But Isaac Newton and *The Secret* failed me, two weeks later.

'This is clearly an error,' I said, when the test told me I wasn't pregnant. It was written in actual words because we still used Clear Blue tests back then. Seth's a hedge fund manager, but soon, I was taking two pregnancy tests a day, for at least seven days, every cycle, and the cost quickly added up. As things got more desperate, we downgraded from Clear Blue with word results, to Clear Blue with a two-line display. Then we slid down to Boots own-brand tests, until, eventually, I was bulk-buying pregnancy tests in the pound shop. I researched it online and discovered they're just as effective.

You don't worry for at least a year of trying, I knew this. I'd read this a million times. It could take a couple of cycles. Totally normal. Nothing to panic about.

'Our baby is going to born around Christmas if we get pregnant now,' I'd told Seth, on our fourth attempt. 'Nobody likes to have their birthday around Christmas. It will be a headache for buying presents, and party date clashes. Shall we hold off a month?'

And, stupidly, Seth agreed, and we wasted a precious month not trying.

A year later, with not one positive test, and not one late period, I couldn't believe my previous arrogance. I'd take a baby born on August 31 and just hire it a tutor. Sex was no longer something enjoyable we shared because we love each other – but a desperate chore. Doing it every day, for five days in a row, every month, because we knew we had to, really lost something for us. Seth is very well trained in sexual emotional aftercare, but he'd started getting up to shower afterwards while I used my vibrator to come, rather than trying to share the experience with him. I wouldn't even mind, I was trying so hard to orgasm. Sometimes I'd be there for fifteen minutes, my bullet on its highest setting, but unable to climax because I knew how important it was and I was already picturing another blank pregnancy test. I initially resisted getting us fertility tested as I wanted to trust the process. I couldn't comprehend that something might be wrong. Not when I was supposed to be a mother more than I was supposed to be literally anything else.

'Now, Charlotte,' Seth had told me, the day I finally agreed to go to Harley Street, his large hands wrapped around mine like scarves. 'These aren't tests like in school. They're just exploratory things about our biology, things we can't change about ourselves – that aren't our fault. They're not something to pass or fail or get a good mark on.'

I'd laughed. I was excited by the tests now. They would find a simple issue with a simple solution. By the end of this day, I'd know why we couldn't conceive and what would definitely solve it. I had my fingers crossed for a non-cancerous ovarian cyst. A simple operation would flick it out and there you'd have it. 'You don't know me at all,' I'd joked.

'I saw you cry after an eye test once.'

'That was only out of frustration. They ask you to read all these letters and then they won't tell you if you're right or wrong. It's maddening.'

He kissed my forehead. Seth kissed my forehead a lot those days rather than on the lips. Anything remotely sexual felt like a chore. 'Come on my lovely little Type A. Let's scan the shit out of ourselves.'

Blood tests. For everything. The nurse just kept swapping vials as it poured out of me. A full sexual health debrief with the expert doctor, who nodded approvingly at my strict condom use. A pelvic ultrasound which was basically like a dildo with a camera on the end.

'Any cysts?' I'd asked the technician, even though they weren't supposed to tell you the answers in the room.

'Nothing yet.'

'A polyp? Is that thing a polyp?' I pointed at the screen, heart racing with excitement when I saw a dark patch.

'No, that's your ovary.'

'And, does it have a cyst on it?'

'Doesn't seem to . . .'

'Well, let's check the other one. Fingers crossed.'

He gave me a weird look and proceeded to find nothing wrong with my other ovary either.

It's strange, the things you get jealous over when you can't conceive. Ovarian cysts, polyps . . . things that would usually be a painful cause of concern are covetable because at least they're an explanation. A week later, our results were read out to us. The results were that there were no results. There were no obvious reasons why we couldn't conceive. When I cried about it to Lauren down the phone one night, she said I was 'lucky' at least that we had Seth's private health insurance to run these tests. That it was a '*privilege*' to afford to know there was nothing clinically wrong with either of us. A '*privilege*' we were able to go down the IVF route privately rather than wait on the NHS list.

I guess I was so *lucky* that we could afford three rounds of IVF before giving up. Three times I was *lucky* enough to ride the insane hormonal rollercoaster that it made my previous PMS look like I was frolicking in a field of wheat. I was *blessed* to do an £8000 wee on a pregnancy test following each implantation only for only one line to show up. What I've learned since this infertility nightmare is that luck and privilege are such a messy scrawl of concerns, with no logic to them. In my darkest moments, I'd believed women who had miscarriages were *lucky* because at least they knew they could get pregnant. Women who had fertility issues that could be explained by science were *lucky* because at least science could likely mend them. And yet,

I was *lucky,* because I could afford to pay for tests that told me nothing was seemingly wrong. I was *lucky,* some might argue, that there's nothing wrong, and therefore I can hope my barrenness is just a statistical quirk – sperm and egg just missing each other in my uterus, like the two leads in a rom-com, that you just know will find one another by the end of the movie. I'm *lucky* I'm straight. At least I got to try the traditional way. I'm *lucky* I'm not a gay man, where the only uterus available is via surrogate, and, only then, usually the *lucky* gay men who can afford to pay for a surrogate abroad. Some women on the infertility chat rooms were devastated they couldn't get pregnant with their second child, but I consider them lucky they're able to have one at all. After Lauren fell pregnant, bless her, we all went out for dinner, and, when I came back from the toilet, I overheard her telling Nicki and Steffi that she hadn't expected to fall pregnant straight away. I loitered behind a pillar as she bit her lip and confided that she felt shocked and a little bit freaked out at how quickly they'd conceived.

'*We were told it would take months,*' she'd complained, not eating her food because the lucky cow had pregnancy nausea. '*You're told your whole late twenties that your eggs are combusting into cobwebs after the age of thirty.*' She'd sighed. '*I know I should feel lucky, especially with what poor Charlotte is going through, but I feel blindsided. Of course I can't share any of this with her . . .*' She'd then spotted me and I'd pretended to have only just arrived. Chirpy and saying we should definitely get a selfie in the toilets because the mirrors are really cool. When, inside, I sort of wanted to scream.

Nicki rips into another present. As predicted, she's speeding up a bit as she realises how many she needs to get through.

I've stopped taking pictures. I really should start taking more. She won't want anything missed. But, as I feel more blood trickle into my makeshift pad, dread freezes me to my chair.

How could I ever have been jealous of this? This panic? This insurmountable loss if the worst really is happening?

I was awful to think that about miscarriage. I know this now. I knew it at the time too, as I was thinking it, but that experience of seeing those two lines, of knowing there's a baby inside me, knowing its due date . . . the *realness* of it. The thought I might lose it now . . . No. It can't be happening. No. Please. I'm sorry. I take it all back.

Nicki holds out a light-yellow duck towel with a beak hood and everyone coos appropriately. I need to strategise. If I start bleeding more heavily, I'll need to leave early. If I start to bleed heavily, making today perfect clearly hasn't worked on the universe anyway. I bite my lip and weigh up whether to call Seth and panic him by telling him. Not yet. No. I can hold on. It's nothing. It's going to be nothing. It's going to be alright. But I need a backup plan, just in case.

To my left, I see that Lauren and that Phoebe woman who knocked on the bathroom door have got up together and made their way over to the punch bowl. I jot down the duck towel and make a bolt for it.

I catch them as they're sipping their drinks. Lauren's thrown her head back laughing and seems transformed from before Woody's nap.

'Hey lovely ladies,' I say, wondering why I sound like a caricature of myself. 'Can I have a seccy?'

Intrigued, they lower their punch glasses and I steer them further into the kitchen, away from Nicki's eye-line.

'Is everything OK?' Lauren asks.

'The peonies aren't wilting, are they?' Phoebe says. 'That would be a disaster!'

I know she's taking the piss out of me but it really would be a disaster, actually, as we have another load of photos to take in front of them when this baby shower turns into the gender reveal. The fact they've not died is a) a miracle, and b) because I've been spritzing them with a water bottle whenever I have the chance.

I ignore what she's said and launch into it. 'It's not a big deal. But I may have to dash off as something's come up. I've got this surprise planned and I need someone to step in to help with it if I do have to go.'

Lauren puts a hand on my shoulder and tilts her head. 'Is everything alright?' She knows something's significantly off if I'm bailing on today. I feel a deep twinge of love that she knows me so well.

'It's fine, it's just something with my grandma,' I lie, now worrying I'm accidentally manifesting my nana's untimely death. 'I'm waiting to hear. She's not going to die,' I added, just to let the universe know I'm not willing to throw Nana under the bus of fate for the sake of a small lie. 'But . . . there's a bit more to today than meets the eye.'

'A stripper! I knew it!' Phoebe says, clapping, and I resist this strong urge to stamp on this rude woman's toe.

'Actually, Matt is turning up as a surprise,' I inform her. Phoebe's smirk vanishes but I don't have time to analyse this now.

'Wow, OK . . .'

I give them the details as quickly as I can. 'You know how Nicki says she didn't want to know the gender of the baby?'

'The sex of the baby,' Phoebe interrupts. 'We don't know what gender it will be yet. The child gets to decide that.'

'Yes, whatever.' I shake my head. 'Anyway, it turns out Nicki was just trying to be cool. She's desperate to know. So, Matt and I rang the hospital for the results from the twenty-week scan. We'll go outside for the piñata and then Matt will appear, all ta-da! And then I've got the gender reveal firework thing lodged in the decking to go off. Isn't that great?'

I quickly run through the timings. I explain he's on his way in a taxi and we're currently running over schedule. I point out the window. 'All I need one of you to do is . . . when he comes . . . the firework is there. I've taken the top off the smoke grenade and wedged it into the decking, with the ring pull poking up. Literally all you need to do is yank it and it will go off and the smoke will come out. There's a bucket of water right next to it. When it stops burning, please put it in there because it's obviously a million degrees outside.' I take a breath. 'But you probably don't need to know *any* of this because my nana is going to be fine. *Fine.*' I add. I give them a giant smile as they digest their new roles. Roles they totally won't need to fulfil because it's all going to be alright.

Evidence recovered from Vista Cottage

Evidence item no. 24

A thoroughly charred 'Windee' was recovered from the ashes of Vista Cottage. The device, which we're assuming was a gift, acts like a reverse accordion to remove gas from an infant's anal cavity.

Evidence item no. 27

Burned wire sculpture of what appears to be a human vagina. Witnesses say it was hanging above the smoke grenade which caused the fire.

Evidence item no. 32

A burned extendable 'selfie stick', likely used to take the group photo of the main suspects.

NICKI

I'm officially overwhelmed. Way beyond whelmed. There is so much whelm in me and I am so over it. All this stuff, all this endless stuff. The pile of presents won't go down. It's like the magic bowl of porridge, except it's spewing out endless babygrows and muslins and wipes, and everything in the world with either a duck or an elephant on it. My baby is going to be *in* these things, *using* these things. The baby in my belly that's going to come out, and be real, and I'm going to have to look after it forever, in its fucking elephant everything, and not kill it, and I'm going to die in childbirth anyway, and it's too much. It's too much, and too hot, and I'm too pregnant, and I just want everyone to leave, and to get into a cold bath and sob and cry because I've given up so much for this baby. I've given up Phoebe for this baby. And now I'm scared and I don't want it anymore.

I just wasn't expecting Phoebe to be here. She's a living, breathing, stunning, magnetic, heart-beating person who I loved, and who I'll never know in the ways I want to because of the baby in my stomach. She's a life I could've led. It was easier when Phoebe was a memory. An idea to mourn. I forgot how my eyes can't leave hers. I forgot how she makes me laugh. I forgot how, just by her being in a room, shadow parts of me unlock – fun parts, untraditional parts. I'm not just Nicki, the girl who looks like she was incubated next door, who only has sensible boyfriends, and works sensible jobs, and hasn't ever tried a 69, or even watched porn, and doesn't like drinking because the hangover isn't worth it the next day. With Phoebe, I'm someone subversive . . . flirty . . . unpredictable . . . fun . . .

. . . Until I threw it all away to do the most predictable thing ever.

'Oh, wow, thank you. What is it?' I ask, holding up what can only be described as a 'thingy'. In my hands, they somehow multiply. They are now two thingies. Two little silverly thingies. They sort of look like metal rolled condoms.

'They're silver nipple shields,' Jenny from work explains, laughing at my obliviousness. 'They're amazing apparently. All the mumfluencers are using them. You pop them in your bra between feeds and the silver apparently releases microbes that stop you developing mastitis.'

'Oh . . . huh.' I slip one onto my tender breast in my maternity bra. They make me look like I have robot nipples. 'I never knew.'

Charlotte is about to combust next to me. 'What a good present,' she practically shouts. 'I've read about them. Amazing. Well done.'

She's dutifully writing down everything I've received, and by who, which is lovely, but also somewhat ruining the mood as she's also getting them to write down their address for her and the whole thing is feeling like homework. I slip the other nipple shield in, horrified to realise they only just fit over them. I knew my breasts would get bigger and saggier in pregnancy, but nobody tells you your nipples engorge and turn into giant thumbs sticking out of burgers. Just as I do, Phoebe wafts in from the kitchen with Lauren, holding a large glass of punch. She eyes my giant nipples sticking through my top and winks while making a clicky sound. I blush and rip them out again, asking, 'OK, what next?' Trying to stay here, in this sweltering box rather than tumbling down another rabbit hole of unhelpful memory.

Matt was surprisingly furious when I'd told him about Phoebe. I'd made us mugs of tea and explained what happened and why our marriage was over. Things had been so lacklustre for so long I assumed he'd be relieved but, instead, he was an unpinned grenade.

'You kissed her? You've cheated on me? All these nights at hers? You were getting with her?' He paced up and down our living room, palms pressed against his face, shaking the walls of our new-build flat.

'I didn't realise you'd be so upset,' I got out, through sheets of tears. The second I'd told him, I'd started to cry at this unexpected end to our marriage. It was over between us. It had to be. The feelings I had for Phoebe, there's no way I could have them if things were right between us. That's what she'd told me. Sending me message after message, explaining it all, helping it make sense. '*The light can only get through the cracks,*' she'd said. '*Don't feel guilty, Nicki. You wouldn't be feeling like this if you guys were meant to be together.*'

'Why the hell wouldn't I be upset? My wife has been cheating on me and is now a lesbian. I'd say that's quite upsetting. Oh, am I supposed to fucking congratulate you for coming out or something?' He bowed down with a flourish. 'Well done on your personal growth, Nicki. So brave.'

'You're being a dick.'

'You've cheated on me and I'm the one being a dick?'

'It was only a kiss.'

'You told me you're in love with her!'

'Yeah, but I'm talking to you about it before I do anything.'

'Wow. Lucky me. So grateful.' Matt turned and paced again, the walls wobbling around us, his face blooming red with rage. I'd never seen him so animated, so full of fire. It turned me on a bit. In fact, it was the first time I'd fancied him in years. Now I was losing him, all his features were as alluring as they'd been initially. That incredible jaw, the moles decorating the left side of his face like a trail to follow, the crack of skin threading between one of his eyebrows, the deep stark green of his eyes against his dark lashes. I started crying harder, which I knew was unfair on him. I just couldn't believe I was blowing our lives up. Matt and I didn't know how to be adults without each other. Our lives had been so gorgeously entwined for so long. Our parents had even been on holiday together. This separation was going to be such an atrocious, humiliating, confusing mess, and suddenly I really wanted to have sex with my husband. Though, with such anger thrumming through him, I was too scared to go near him.

'I still can't believe this,' he said, almost verging on spitting. 'After all the shit you've put me through over the years about sleeping with fucking Steffi . . . when I didn't even know you existed! And, all these months, you've been cheating on me . . .'

'Those are hardly the same things.'

Why was I defending myself? Why was he bringing Steffi up now? Why was he thinking about Steffi right now? What the hell did she have to do with anything? One of my biggest fears was that Matt would've ended up with Steffi if he hadn't met me. I worried there was something more between them . . . lingering . . . every time they saw one another. I hated that she also knew the noises he made when he came. I hated that she knew what a good kisser he was. How big his dick was *(surprisingly so, actually, considering he's so scrawny)*. I hated that, technically, from an HPV point of view, I'd now slept with everyone Steffi had slept with, which, let's face it, is a lot more than most.

'Of course they're not the same things,' he said. 'I did nothing wrong when I slept with Steffi. Whereas what you've done is pure adultery.'

'I didn't realise it was.' I cried harder, hugging a sofa cushion to stop myself trying to hug him.

'Oh, yes, I forgot. Your lesbian seductress.'

'Don't speak that way about her.'

'You do realise how unfair this is? If I'd cheated . . . if I met some girl from work and stayed all these nights in her fucking bed, and then kissed her, and told you I was in love with her . . . it would be so black and white. *I'm the arsehole. She's a bitch.* But no . . . not with this. Somehow perfect fucking Nicki stays the perfect one . . . fuck this. Fuck you, Nicki. Honestly. Fuck you.' I flinched. It was the first time he'd ever sworn at me, and it left a bullet hole.

Then he'd left. He left before I could even tell him the whole story which would help him understand. Which would help him know that I wasn't to blame. This wasn't my fault. I still wanted him to like me, to love me. To listen to me. To hear me out. To comfort me. Like he'd comforted me and protected us all these years. Even, yes, when I made unreasonable demands, like him not being allowed to talk to Steffi at social occasions . . . Matt had *always* listened and taken my side and protected us. But the Matt-shield was smashed and in our bedroom, shoving shirts into a duffel bag, pushing past me to get to the bathroom to take his toothbrush and shower gel, muttering something about staying at Seth's.

'You can't stay there,' I yelled. 'Charlotte will find out.'

'You don't get to tell me what to do anymore,' his spit landed on my face even though he was at least three feet away. I collapsed to the carpet then, to try and stop him. Surely, he wouldn't leave if he saw me this upset? He'd drop to his knees and kiss it better. I wanted him still, even though I also wanted Phoebe. Nothing about how I felt made any sense and I'd only had 24 hours to be allowed to feel it. I'd told Phoebe nothing could happen between us before I'd spoken to Matt.

Phoebe:
Of course, hon. Of course you want to do things right, that's one of the things I love about you. We didn't ask for this to happen. I'll wait for as long as it takes. I know it's a lot. I'll never stop waiting for you xxxx

But Matt did leave. In fact, he left so roughly that a painting fell off the wall as he slammed the front door. I waited on the floor for him to come back, arranged as daintily as I could for when he returned from walking around the block to calm down. I kept myself crying, even when I was running low on tears, as I wanted him to see fresh tear stains on his return and feel guilty for waiting so long to talk it through. Matt couldn't leave me like this. He was my husband. He loved me. He never left me. Part of what was so annoying about him was how utterly invested he was in me. How I never had to wonder how he felt about me. The only thrill I got was when we had to hang out with Steffi, and I'd get intrusive thoughts of them fucking, and I'd want to be sick, but also want to have sex with him the second we got home.

But that night he left me. He left me and didn't come back for two weeks.

And that, somehow, changed everything.

I glance over at Phoebe again, the magnet pull just as strong as always. For the first time in the third trimester, I almost forget about the baby twisting in my stomach and let myself fall into the fantasy of what life would've been like if I'd chosen differently. Life with Phoebe. Living in East London, going out most nights, figuring out my sexuality, exploring, touching, tasting, panting. Who am I with the brakes off? With my hair untied? Travel. Spontaneity. Being cool . . . A life like Steffi's . . . adventurous. Phoebe's eyes meet mine. She winks again and I know with that wink that she's here to cause trouble. She must be. Why else would she come? Is she going to tell everyone about us? Or is she just here to fuck with me? To remind me of what I've missed? Does she know her being here is fucking with me enough? Phoebe never took revenge, even though she had every right to. I treated her as appallingly as I treated Matt – marinating for two weeks in my total selfishness. What do *I* want? What's best for *me*? Is there any way I can have both?

I was so unfair to her.

I feigned a horrific flu at work and took a fortnight's leave – messaging her to say I needed space. I also messaged Matt, to tell him I wouldn't see Phoebe. I wouldn't take my betrayal any further forward while I figured things out.

He replied with only this.

Matt:
Take your time but also know I'm not here forever. I know I'm worth more than someone having to ago-nise over wanting to be with me. You're not just fuck-ing your life up, Nicki, you're fucking mine up too. Ours. The life we've been building, brick by brick, for over ten years now. But I'm not going to beg you to stay. You've already taken the piss. So much. I know you want me to beg, but I won't.

Matt was right. He knew me so well. How my selfish brain works. I was distraught he wasn't at the door, on his knees, crying and pleading for me to choose him. He knew the worst of me but he'd always loved me anyway. He then added:

Matt:
Really think about the life you want, and whether this woman can give it to you, Nicki. In the long-term, not the short. I see you as the mother to my children. My family I'll have forever. But I can find that with other women . . . can you find that with Phoebe?

I read and re-read that last message maybe a thousand times, marvelling again at just how well Matt knew me. Before Phoebe started working at my company, we had started talking about kids. For the first time since meeting her, I remembered those conver-sations and how . . . exciting they'd been. Honestly, what had I done? What was I doing? What was I going to do? The worst part of my agony was that I was completely alone in it. Matt hadn't stayed at Charlotte's after all, but gone to bunk with David, his bachelor mate who lived in Canary Wharf. Nobody in my life knew about Phoebe and I was too ashamed to confide in anyone, so I just shuffled around my flat in a dirty pair of pyjamas, festering with shame. What was I ashamed of? The emotional affair? Though I kept reassuring myself I didn't know I was having one. Potentially being gay? Though I still wasn't sure if I was. I didn't want girls, I just wanted Phoebe, and how being around Phoebe made me feel. I wanted to tell the Little Women, but then Steffi would know, and I couldn't bare her knowing there were chinks in mine and Matt's marital armour. The smug satisfaction she'd take in our downfall. In those wretched nights of sleeplessness, twisting in my empty bed, literally holding my head from the buzzing of the decision making, I'd add to my anguish by picturing Steffi and Matt getting together if I left him for Phoebe. Maybe they'd end up married and she'd have Matt's children – not me.

That word.

Children.

That thought.

I was 30 years old. I'd always seen Matt as the father of my children.

Alone to figure this out, I spent my days essentially feral, in bed, my Google search history a meandering list of increasingly desperate despair.

Can you be gay and not realise it?

Am I lesbian?

How do lesbians have sex?

Can you love two people at the same time?

Am I bisexual?

Should I leave my husband?

What counts as cheating?

Lesbian porn

Lesbian porn for lesbians not men

I had an emotional affair

How to choose between two people?

Nando's Deliveroo menu

How do lesbians have children?

How do sperm donors work?

Success rates of sperm donation

Success rates of IVF

How much does IVF cost?

I read loads about IVF, and how many rounds you have to finance privately if you're a lesbian couple, before getting help on the NHS. I also started to truly understand what Charlotte had been going through the past two years. At 2am, I scrolled through video diaries of the egg retrieval process, shuddering at photographs of swollen bellies riddled with injection bruises and wondered how Charlotte had been able to keep up her almost toxic levels of positivity throughout three rounds of this. Whenever I'd asked her how it was going, she'd always crack into her manic grin, and told me she had a really good feeling about this upcoming round, or that *the destination was worth the journey*, and all her other typical Live Laugh Love soundbites. But I now realised just how devastating it must've been for her, just how expensive, and invasive, and disheartening, and holy fuck, I never realised how shit egg freezing was. The statistics were terrible! All through my twenties, all I'd ever heard was, '*Freeze your eggs! Everything will be OK if you freeze your eggs! If you get a job at Meta they let you freeze your eggs! You can wait until you're 82 to have kids as long as you freeze your eggs.'* It sounded almost like a luxury spa treatment. Something you could slip in between appointments for a laser regeneration on your sunspots and a back, neck, and shoulder massage. But actually, it seemed to be a hugely medical procedure, including general anaesthetic, and injections and hormone nightmares, and even then . . . only about a 30 per cent chance of it even turning into a baby? Plus, it cost £350 a year to keep the little critters frozen.

I snapped my laptop shut. 'You don't even know if you want children,' I'd whispered to myself. 'And there's nothing worse than having them with the wrong person.'

I wasn't totally alone. Phoebe practically suffocated me with messages every day.

Phoebe:
How are you? Thinking of you.
I'm so sorry. I know how hard this must be.
Here's an article about internalised homophobia that
I think you'll find helpful
I love you.
I miss you at work.
I wish you'd call.
I know you want space but I'm going out of my mind
here, Nicki. Sorry. It's just . . . never mind.

One night, she was obviously drunk and she got nasty and threatening.

Phoebe:
Look, I get that you're scared but aren't you more
scared of being bored fuckless your entire life?
Is it the sex stuff? We can take it slow.

Fuck u Nicki, not even replying. It's not fair. Why do
u get all the power? Fuck this. A woman is hitting on
me so hard in this bar right now. Give me one reason
why I shouldn't go home with her.
I'm going home with her. Fuck you.
I didn't. I couldn't. Sorry. Please just hurry up and decide.
I'm going to leave the company if you back out on us.
I can't see you every day. It will hurt too much.

I ignored them all. I didn't even write replies and then delete
them. Each message from Phoebe would make everything so
real that my brain would short-circuit and I'd just turn my
phone off, wishing I could bury it in a sandpit.

In contrast, Matt only messaged every few days, checking I
was OK, but mainly checking I was watering the houseplants,
and asking if a package had arrived for him. The coolness froze
the blood in my veins. Matt had always been the warmest man
ever. I tortured myself with how it had felt when we'd first met.
That bashful, scrawny, guy, scratching his ear in our kitchen,
laughing at a joke I'd made about Jigglypuff looking like an
angry ovary. The way he held eye contact the whole time after
Steffi came down in those tacky tiny pjs – not realising she
was too obvious and too late. It had only taken an hour for us
to fall in love, for him to know I was The One, he'd told me.
Over and over. Year after year. As we delighted at ourselves,
and our happiness, and how much suffering we'd both dodged
by being lucky enough to find one another so early. Where had
that Matt gone? Had I lost him forever? After months of complaining about how boring and comfortable my life was with
Matt, I'd disintegrated it in one evening. Undone it, maybe

forever. And I didn't find this unknowingness as exciting as I thought I would now it was a reality.

I would never have enough time to make this decision, but life hurried me up. Work emailed to check how I was doing, and to politely remind me that if I needed any further time off I'd require a doctor's note. The email arrived on Friday, I'd be expected back in on Monday. 72 hours to decide the rest of my life and still no idea what decision to make. That night I had dinner pencilled in with the Little Women. I thought I'd cancel, but I realised I'd come no closer to certainty by being a mad hermit for a fortnight, so, I dragged myself into the shower, into a jumpsuit, and onto the tube – blinking into the lights of the South Bank as I steered my way to Wahaca. We'd always met there in our early twenties, thinking drinking margaritas by the Thames was the height of London sophistication and living our best Carrie Bradshaw fantasies. It took half a decade to realise we were surrounded by tourists, and there were probably literally a million unique places to eat in the capital, but it had become our place by then. We revelled in the tacky sameness, and how Lauren flat-out refused to ever share her bowl of guacamole.

'I need a drink,' I announced, when I arrived, taking my seat between Lauren and Charlotte. 'Don't ask,' I added.

But only Steffi and I ordered the classic margarita. Charlotte was on her last round of IVF and didn't want to have any sugar since that makes implantation more difficult. And Lauren . . . well . . . after Steffi said, '*Shit, you're not pregnant, are you?*' after Lauren ordered a mocktail, had shrugged, and said, '*Well, I was going to wait until after the drinks had arrived, cheers Steffi. But, yes, yes I am.*' We'd all started screaming in shocked happiness. I was stunned. I didn't even know Lauren had started trying. I couldn't believe someone was going through an even bigger life change than me right now. While Steffi and I squealed, Charlotte seemed less shocked.

'We got coffee yesterday and she told me,' Charlotte explained, sipping from her sparking mineral water. Her smile was wide and real. Strained, but there. 'I've almost exploded keeping it to myself.'

I squeezed her hand and rubbed it. Reached out and took Lauren's too. They were the best of us – these two. Lauren carefully telling Charlotte privately, to give her the time she needed to digest it. Charlotte, genuinely happy for her friend, despite the pain the news no doubt caused.

'Shit, Lauren, I'm so sorry,' Steffi said, hand over her mouth. 'I didn't mean to ruin your big moment. It was just a thoughtless joke.'

I tried not to roll my eyes.

'No, don't worry. You weren't to know,' Lauren replied. 'I was only going to tell you tonight that we'd started trying, but it's happened really fast. Like, straight away ... sorry Charlotte,' she added awkwardly.

'I'm so happy for you,' she squeaked, leaning forward, her face a Cheshire Cat. 'Honestly. No apology. My time will come soon.'

As the lights blinked on the water outside, and waves of tables arrived and left around us, we chatted until late, celebrating this seminal moment in our friendship group. One of us was pregnant. One of us was having a baby. That was so grown-up and huge. We'd all been playing at adults for years, me especially. Even on my own wedding day, I'd felt slightly like Matt and I were playing mums and dads in the playground. Like I was slipping around in a pair of grown-up heels I'd stolen from my mum's cupboard, that my veil was fashioned by Andrex toilet tissue. When Lauren and Charlotte got married it was still hugely surreal, that these big adult days were our days now. These things we'd grown up wondering about were an actual occurrence. Marriage seemed so huge at the time, but now, downing another cocktail and licking the crunchy salt flakes off my lips, those wedding days felt nothing like Lauren's news. She was pregnant. That meant she was going to become a parent. *A mother!* One of those tired-looking people sighing into a disposable coffee cup, pushing a kid on a playground swing as I jog past them at 6.30am. It was so grown-up. So unimaginably adult. And, as I tossed the lime liquid to the back of my gullet, I had my first clear thought in over two weeks.

'*It should be me.*'

I should be the pregnant one. I should be the one who goes first. I'm the most mature. I'm the one who's been with their partner the longest. I'm the one it's expected from.

It was such a selfish and self-indulgent thought, and luckily nobody could hear it, but it had diamond clarity and was slicing me up as I leant in and listened to Lauren's story.

' . . . Tristan basically passed out when he saw the test. I thought he'd be happy, but he went white and said he needed to go play tennis. I've been so sick since . . . sorry if I've been such a shit friend but, honestly, I've hardly been able to get out of bed . . . I can't stop sleeping . . . I'm sick whenever I brush my teeth . . . got bruised ribs from all the retching . . . I'm due in October . . . still can't believe it . . . excited now, obviously . . . I can't wait for you all to become aunties.'

Lauren kept stroking her stomach without realising. Her eyes were dewy, her skin looked insanely good. She was quite clipped in her responses, out of respect for Charlotte, and kept trying to move the conversation on, but we wouldn't let her – Charlotte especially. She was asking questions I'd never even thought to ask. '*What will the baby's star sign be? You haven't been taking standard folic acid, have you? You need to get the tablets that are made from ground-up food otherwise it doesn't absorb properly. Are you going to do hypnobirthing? It's supposed to be amazing. Are you going to have a doula? Let me get you one – my present . . .*'

Her manic determination to show how totally OK she was allowed me to sit back in my seat and let the crashing waves of realisation pull me into the tide. I wanted what Lauren had. I wanted a baby. I wanted a baby. I wanted a baby. I needed a baby. I needed a baby now. Yesterday. I needed to become a mother. To know what it feels like to have life grow inside me. To birth it, and raise it, and probably fuck it up but try really hard not to. To teach it how to ride a bike, to get a splodgy paint-ing of a shit daffodil on Mother's Day, to zip it up into one of those squidgy snowsuits when it's cold with only their red chubby cheeks peeking out. I wanted this traditional, boring, obvious, clichéd path. Desperately. Hurriedly. Now. And, I real-ised, crumbling a tortilla chip to dust over my side plate, I want to have a baby in a traditional, boring, obvious, and clichéd way.

With a man.

With Matt.

Who I knew would be an incredible dad, which had always been one of the reasons I loved him. I always found it weird when women fancied men who were so obviously going to be shit dads. Steffi seemed to find them attractive, but I guess she has that freedom as she never wants kids herself.

By the time the bill was paid, I'd squashed my feelings for Phoebe like the tortilla chip I'd crumbled to dust earlier. Matt was no longer boring and predictable – he was safe – the best thing you want in a co-parent. Our 'dull' life was actually just a sign from the universe it was time for this next step. Phoebe tried to ruin something so important – tried to twist what it was into something that served her – and I was angry. I closed the gates, I pulled back my shoulders, I got my fucking shit together.

What the hell was I doing? I wasn't a *lesbian*! How ridiculous was that?

I walked miles home, through the dark, letting my love for Phoebe alchemise into rage. How dare she kiss me? How dare she try and use our friendship to get close to me and then make a move. Matt was right. If a woman had done that to him, we'd have thought she was a home-wrecking whore. Does Phoebe really get a free pass because she's gay? It was underhand. It was deceitful. She took advantage of me. Of my innocence. Of my vulnerability – using our friendship and trying to use it to get me to fucking have sex with her. I didn't even think of her in that way until she'd kissed me. And she made a move when I was drunk! Again, if she wasn't a lesbian . . . And, not only was I the *complete victim* of this situation, so was poor Matt. We were both victims of this . . . predator . . . yes, that's what Phoebe was . . . a predator.

I rummaged for my phone in my coat pocket as I marched along the Thames, anger keeping my toes warm in my slightly holey boots. She picked up on the third ring.

'Oh my God, she finally answers my calls.'

'Fuck you,' I shouted with the conviction of a woman who'd drunk four margaritas.

277

'Excuse me?'

'Fuck you. How dare you? How dare you try and fuck up my life. How dare you try and stop me having a baby.' I could hear a heavy bass in the background. She was out again. Drinking too much. Probably preying on someone.

'A baby? What? Nicki? Are you drunk? Are you OK? Are you alone? You're not walking home alone, are you? It's gone midnight. Where are you?'

'Shut up. I'm not telling you where I am so you can come and pretend you care when really you're trying to sabotage my life.'

'*What?*'

'I want a baby and I can't have one with you!' My shouts bounced out over the dark water of the Thames.

She sighed. 'I can't hear you properly over the music. Hang on, let me step out.'

But I wouldn't let her have a second to get her story straight. As I staggered along the river, swerving in all sorts of directions, vaguely aware I should probably give up and order an Uber soon, I let Phoebe know all the conclusions I'd come to. How she'd tricked me. Used me. Deceived me. When the music died in the background, so had the care in her voice.

'. . . and, yeah, so, I just want you to leave me alone, Phoebe. Get out of my life. I love Matt. We're going to start a family.'

'OK.'

'Is that all you're going to say?'

'OK. I'll leave you alone, like you've asked.' Her voice was crisper than the night air seeping through my Zara coat.

'Well . . . er . . . good.'

'Is that all?'

'Umm. Yes.'

'Thanks Nicki. I appreciate the call. I wish you every happiness in your totally beige life filled with utter self-denial.'

She hung up and left me in a rare silence of the capital city, staring at my phone. A grief started tickling the back of my throat. An urge to cry. I was shaking, but only because of the cold, I told myself. I fell to a nearby bench and shivered as I replayed every memory of Phoebe that I had. The lunches, the laughter, the late nights, the thrill, the sweet taste of her mouth, and I let one tear fall down my frozen cheek. 'Stop it, Nicki,' I whispered, and instead I pictured Matt's hand in mine on a maternity ward. His face bleary with tears as he held our baby before leaning over and kissing my forehead. 'Yes,' I said, into the dark. I stood up and swallowed the feeling that part of me was dying, an important part. In the following months, before Phoebe took a giant promotion at a mainstream kooky jewellery company, we only traded formalities. I didn't even go to her leaving do. I had dinner with the Little Women and their partners instead. I cooked them a strange meal of the only things Lauren could stand eating during her pregnancy. It was part of Matt and I's plan to return to ourselves – surround ourselves with people who support our way of life, our path. People who think it's lovely, not weird, that we've been together for a decade.

Steffi was replaced as the albatross in Matt and mine's marriage. We were now victims of Phoebe. Just as well we never had to see her again. It was all a strange blip. But we told ourselves it was a necessary blip because it made it clear to us how much we loved each other, how much we wanted to move forward as a couple. Start a family. Go to the next step. Phoebe's interference actually moved us forward and our happiness was our revenge on her.

When we had our first scan, and our baby's heartbeat echoed through the darkened hospital room, I wept at what we'd created. At how worth it everything was. Afterwards, I stared at the pixilated scan several times an hour, tracing the blob that was our baby with my finger, clutching it to my chest, and felt sheer relief and gratitude.

My baby.

I'd made the right decision.

I'd made the best decision.

And I still feel that way. I do. At this ridiculous baby shower, with everyone I love around me, and a mounting pile of tiny clothes to my side that will soon have a warm and wriggling creature in it, it feels so right.

But, as my eyes are dragged back towards Phoebe's, something else feels right too. So utterly, wonderfully, complicatedly, right. My eyes moisten, and I pretend it's at the sheer joy of receiving an ugly plastic teething necklace. The delusion I've cloaked myself in drops away to the ground, and the extent of my sacrifice pummels into my chest.

Phoebe tilts her head at me, knowing. She knows the tears aren't for the atrocious necklace.

They're for her. For *us*. For the life – and love – I had to throw away to get here. Not just throw away – torch to the ground and act so atrociously she could never forgive me and try and tempt me again.

But Phoebe's here, despite my horrific behaviour, she's here. Does that mean she has forgiven me?

Or is she here to mess with me? As one final act of revenge?

LAUREN

Nicki's practically blended into the mountain of opened presents around her. Only her face sticks out from the pyramid of pastels and duck-adorned thingymajigs. She's been very polite about the fact she's unwrapped four hand-knitted blankets and artfully reacted to each like she's never seen one before. I'm not sure why anyone gives you baby blankets. I counted seven by the time Woody was one week old, and they were mostly used to mop up milky reflux or stuffed around myself to try and concoct a comfortable breastfeeding position. (Note: Comfortable breastfeeding positions do not exist – embrace the inevitable calcifying into a Quasimodo-esque hunchback).

It's hard not to remember my own shower of presents – sitting here, watching her coo over a tiny sunhat that will make her baby have a sunflower head. Since that awful birth conversation, I feel like I'm only half here. The other half of me is trapped in the memories of everything that came next and I can't press pause . . . No Lauren, think of the good times. Think of that lovely spa day you had with the Little Women. Little did I know – blobbing around a hydrotherapy pool – that it was more a goodbye to my friends before I was wiped from the face of my own life, like chalk being blown off an eraser. A goodbye to the person I was before the bad things happened . . . the birth . . . so awful . . . then . . .

The movie is determined to play. I'm yanked, once more, from this party and into the hell pit of those days. My hands grip on the baby monitor in a failed attempt to combat the PTSD, but I'm lost again.

Lost.

Again.

I was so lost.

I thought the birth was the end of the nightmare. Woody didn't even need to go to NICU in the end. We had our delayed 'golden hour' as I came to in the recovery room, machines gently pumping my legs, Tristan taking off his top and gazing down at his son. Modern man. Skin to skin. I watched it with this detached peculiarity I felt towards the baby. Did I love this squirming thing? Were they sure it was mine? Sun streamed in through the window as a midwife came in and plopped Woody onto my breast, latching him without asking permission first. My baby glubbed down his colostrum greedily.

'He's a natural,' she told me, smiling, like everything she'd just done was OK. 'Well done.'

I hadn't planned to breastfeed. But now, I guess I was breast-feeding. It was my sixth morning in hospital. They brought me marmalade on toast. I hoovered it up, was allowed more. Maybe the worst was over. Maybe I would be OK. Maybe, with some rest, I could recover, and . . . .

'Right, come on Lauren.' The midwife took the last piece of toast away. 'We need to get you walking.'

'What?'

'We need the room. You're to join the ward.'

They heaved me up roughly. The epidural was wearing off and sharp pain sliced through my torso. 'No,' I whimpered. 'Ow . . . OWW.'

'Into the wheelchair.'

Two of them manhandled me as I screamed out. 'Come on. You need to take a few steps before we can move you.'

My feet stumbled all over the place. The pain. The pain. 'One step, two step.' The midwives hoisted me across the lino with my feet half dragging. 'There you go. Right, let's take you to the ward. I'm sorry, but visiting hours are over so your husband needs to leave.'

'Excuse me?' Tristan and I both said.

'He can come back later. And then tomorrow morning. You'll probably need to stay two nights, so we can keep an eye on you.'

I was wheeled away, Woody wheeled in a Perspex cot next to me, waving in shock as my husband, my life raft, was left behind. I was heaved onto a hard thin bed and left alone.

The ward was worse than the birth . . .

I can't.

I don't want to remember. I can't remember most of it.

There's the sound of ripping wrapping paper. Women all around me gasp. Jeanie's kid, bored, starts yelling to the right of me. Nicki's holding up a present. Everyone coos. The air is too thick in this room – it's all mass-recycled breath. I've not been around this many women since those days and nights on the ward.

So many babies crying. All the time. My baby crying in his plastic thingymajiggy. I knew I needed to get to Woody, feed him, comfort him, but the thing is, I was sort of paralysed. You know, from the major fucking operation, and all.

I needed Tristan.

I needed painkillers.

I needed the medication they'd promised would stop my skin itching from the epidural.

I needed someone to help me feed this creature that wouldn't stop crying. He wouldn't latch well again. I couldn't lift him. I needed someone to help me change him as black oil-like shit spouted from him, getting all over me, all over him. I tried to bend over to clean him but I cried in agony. I'd been sawn open only hours ago and now I had to look after this thing, all alone? In chaos? In agony?

Pushing the red button for painkillers. Button down. Wait for help. Help will come . . .

Too understaffed. Help not coming.

Ringing Tristan, begging him to bring ibuprofen when he came. 'They keep forgetting to give me my pain medication.'

Ringing him again, telling him to come and get me. I can't do it. Can't stay here. Everything hurts. So much. Why does nobody care about how much it hurts?

No sleep. I hadn't slept for six days now. I was in agony. Baby kept clamping onto my nipple. That hurt too.

The BreatheItOut account said breastfeeding doesn't hurt if you do it properly.

Nighttime.

No sleep. Babies crying. Sometimes it was mine, sometimes others.

The sting of them taking the catheter out.

The laugh of a woman when I pissed myself getting out of bed.

That laugh.

I've never known shame like it.

If I had the chance to stab her to death – whoever laughed at me on that dark first night – I would stab her until she was mush. I imagine doing it often. Finding her. Killing her.

They came to clear up my urine from the floor, but they wouldn't give me a painkiller. They weren't allowed to do that. Some other midwife had the authority and she'd come when she could but they were very busy because it's September, and a full moon, and the NHS maternity crisis and, can you please tend to your baby, his crying is keeping the other mothers awake.

Should I have used my BRAIN then, fucking hypnobirthing lady? Does BRAIN work against a staffing crisis? Yes, feminism! And advocate for yourself! But how does that work when you're begging for painkillers, and they won't come, and someone has laughed at you for pissing yourself, and you think you almost died, and your baby almost died, and now it's alive and won't stop shitting itself, or attacking your nipple with gums as hard as cement, and your husband isn't allowed to be here and advocate on your behalf, and how is this legal? To do this to women? To leave them alone, behind a flimsy curtain, with a creature that needs 24-hour care, when the woman hasn't slept in six days, and just had seven layers of fat and tissue and muscle ripped into, and her bladder is fucked, and she's scratched her skin off, and she has no idea how to look after a newborn baby. None. Because fucking hypnobirthing lady never told you about looking after your baby. They only lied and said that you can sneeze your baby out as long as you use your BRAIN and secrete enough oxytocin.

Tristan rescued me before the second night.

'She can't be discharged without her papers.'

'Yes, she can. This isn't prison. In prison, they give them medication.'

He told them he'd complain to PALS. He cried when I told him about the woman who laughed. On the drive home, he gripped the steering wheel so hard that I thought it would snap off. Woody, so tiny in his car seat. I thought every slight jolt in the road might cause him brain damage. Every jolt had me gasp in further pain.

Then we were back in our house with this tiny thing to keep alive. Even though I couldn't walk. I couldn't get out of bed without wincing and holding my stomach so my guts wouldn't spill out. And Woody wouldn't sleep. At all. He screamed and screamed and wouldn't sleep. Tristan and I watched him in incompetent horror – clueless, useless, broken beyond repair.

I was hollowed out. I wanted to rest. I wanted to sleep. I wanted to run away. I wanted to scream. I wanted to sue. I wanted to kill myself.

What had happened to me?

I needed to go to some kind of Priory-like facility, with a spa, and have two weeks, at least, to recover and process from whatever the fuck had just happened to me. Someone to cook me food, and change my dressing, and hoist me out of bed, and let me sleep, and have intensive EMDR to stop the horrors of my past week dancing behind my eyelids in the rare moments Woody allowed us to sleep for more than 40 minutes.

People kept sending cards, and presents, like something good had happened to our lives.

I didn't want to see anyone, but people came anyway. Pretending they cared about me, but only really caring about holding my baby, and getting their picture taken with it, and telling me '*oh, but it's worth it*' if I dared mention the hell I'd just endured.

Tristan and I almost divorced about his parents coming to visit us.

'They can't come,' I told him, sobbing on the bathroom floor for the fortieth time that day, while the other NCT mums made jokes about my tears on the group chat. '*Sounds like your milk has come in.*' 'They can't come,' I repeated. 'Nobody can come. You've got to stop guests coming around. I need to be alone. I don't have the strength. No. *No.*'

'Lauren, they've flown from *Australia*. These flights have been booked for months. You *wanted* them to come. You told them to book those tickets.'

'That was before.'

'Lauren, they're coming. They're even staying in a hotel, please.'

'No. Everyone needs to leave us the fuck alone.'

'Lauren?'

'Nobody. No visitors. I mean it, Tristan. I can't . . .'

Except, of course, I could and I did, because I didn't matter anymore. That's what the last week had taught me. I am a mother now and mothers don't matter. I'm no longer a human because I created a human. Rather than reward for this, there is only punishment.

I haven't mattered for nine months now.

Woody is what matters. Woody is what people care about. I am just the inconvenient, fat, frumpy, mess with a greasy bun lugging the precious thing about.

Tristan's parents came and didn't even bring me anything. Only presents for Woody, who could still only see in fucking black and white. He, of course, needed the presents. Treat the baby. Give the baby special things. Not me. Not that inconvenient mother. And I was bleeding and bleeding, and my scar hurt, and my womb was contracting back in on itself, and I was dripping milk through my clothes, and I couldn't stop sobbing, but still, somehow, I was making cups of tea for guests, and, *oh are you hungry? I guess I could make you some sandwiches, yes you must be jet-lagged, how very awful.*

Shut the fuck up, that's all I realise people want me to do.

Be a mother and shut the fuck up.

You chose to do this to yourself so shut the fuck up.

You're lucky you were able to have children so shut the fuck up.

And, if your baby is crying, make sure it shuts the fuck up too.

Cope better, cope better, cope better.

Nicki's almost come to the end of her giant pile of stuff. She's practically dwarfed by the ocean of pastel presents surrounding her chair, despite Charlotte doing her best to organise them into piles at her feet. What was it Charlotte told me and Phoebe? Earlier in the kitchen? Today is a gender reveal, as well as a baby shower? I vaguely remember that I'm supposed to be in charge of some kind of firework but I'm so tired. I hope Phoebe listened more earnestly . . . I can't stop looking at all the piles of all the stuff. The endless, endless, stuff.　　Like Nicki, I'd also received an overwhelming amount of well-meaning crap. After I discharged myself and took Woody home, staggering through the door, bleeding into my adult nappy, crying with relief I was finally out of that horrific building, the doorbell wouldn't stop buzzing from parcel deliveries. Flowers, more flowers – all of which withered to death, still wrapped in cellophane, on the counter, while we tried to cope with Woody screaming and never sleeping. More knitted blankets. Countless numbers of soft toys – all made from that achingly soft material, but, nevertheless, likely to cot death the fuck out of him, so we had to find room for it all. I hardly had time to shower daily to keep the stitches that were holding my insides together clean, and I remember feeling actual rage as the door buzzed and more crap accumulated. Where does one put six blankets? Two Sophie the Giraffes? Where should I store all the baby clothes my baby does not yet fit into because people were thoughtful enough to size up?

None of it was what I really needed. Which was a night nurse, an emergency pelvic floor examination, months of intensive trauma therapy with childcare so I could attend the sessions, or advice about baby sleep that actually worked. Wrapped in none of those hand-knitted blankets was a hand on my shoulder, and a caring, *'Are you really OK, Lauren? Your birth sounded awful and you've not slept since. I'm so sorry you've gone through this. What can I do to help you feel human again? I don't care about Woody right now, I care about you.'* But, you know, baths toys are great too.

Cool Mum's so grateful for the beautiful baby gifts she receives. She takes a professional quality shot of her perfect newborn wearing each outfit and gets it printed onto postcards. She handwrites thank yous on the back and posts them all within two weeks of her baby being born. Even though she can't walk as far as the post box after her C-section, she still manages this, around a puking, screaming, insomniac newborn, when you have no idea what the time is, or day, or sometimes even year . . . Oh, hang on, I forgot. Cool Mum would never need a C-section – she did hypnobirthing – plus her baby slept through from three days old. Even when the baby wakes, Cool Mum doesn't mind. She loves the cuddles, she knows it will go so quickly. She swaddles the baby up in six home-knitted blankets and makes artwork out of all the useless soft toys . . .

I was so sleep-deprived that I hardly have any memories of those first few months. Only a trauma deep in my guts of this desperate, relentless helplessness and trying not to scream with each painful latch, panic about jaundice, projectile vomits and poonamis splattered across our wall, begging for more painkillers, worrying about how much I was still bleeding. Hardly able to blink with the shock of what had happened to me. My pulse throbs in my neck as I remind myself of what Nicki has coming her way. Of what she needs to get through and survive. I finish my second glass of punch and allow myself to feel a sliver of smugness that my newborn hell is in the past while hers still awaits. Nothing can be worse than the last nine months of my life, surely? It can only improve from here. It must do. It already has. I'm here, at a party, drinking my second glass of punch. God, it's great, Woody being asleep, I think, letting my shoulders unhitch as I glance down at him in the monitor. It's so nice to be around people and to be me – rather than stopping him crawling into every available danger, or ripping down my top to try and breast-feed, or grabbing everything off the table to chuck onto the floor. Nicki's friend, Phoebe, is really funny, too. We had a chat in the kitchen and she had me in stitches talking about gender roles in childcare.

'How terrible is your husband then, on a scale of one to ten?' she'd asked, outright. Her blatancy made me blatant in response.

'He's the least worst,' I replied, that second glass of punch making itself known. 'But the bar is basically so low it's under-ground.'

Wow, I really have missed alcohol. How it softens the edges, gives life a glow, blunts reality. I'm two cups down, probably over the limit to drive, which I'm sure is the worst parenting ever. I won't have a third, and I'll have to stay a bit later to sober up, but, for now, it's worth it. I'm smiling. I'm relaxed. I'm back in the present, nestling into this ludi-crously plush sofa. Woody twitches on the monitor but I shh him through the screen. Maybe he'll nap for two hours, like other babies seem to, and I'll get to enjoy the whole party? Miracles happen every day and I'm tipsy enough to believe in them right now.

Nicki's shaking a large box, hastily wrapped in leftover Christmas paper.

'Oh, that's mine,' I call over from my chair. 'Sorry. I forgot to write a tag.'

Charlotte's eyeballing the Santa paper like I've wrapped the present in my own shit. She writes something on her spreadsheet and I wonder if she's grading people. Have I just lost points for not crafting my own wrapping paper using a potato print of my baby's arse or something?

'Love the paper,' Cara says, and everyone laughed. 'Spot the mother!'

'Yeah, err, sorry. I . . . Woody . . .' I blush in the heat as the circle laughs again.

'Don't worry at all,' Nicki says, holding the gift up. 'I think you and I have been giving each other wine in the same recycled gift bag for ten years now.' She pushes a pudgy pregnant finger under a seam of my shoddily-wrapped gift.

'The rose gold metallic one?'

She smiles at me from across the room. 'That's exactly the one.'

She rips off the offensive paper to find an Amazon box inside, because, yes, I got all her presents off Prime. Taking Woody shopping is currently impossible because he cries whenever I put him in his buggy. Nicki tactfully ignores the box, and reaches inside, pulling out a baby thermometer, two bottles of baby Calpol, two bottles of baby Nurofen, a snot sucker, a Windi and the intensive nappy rash cream that's basically neon yellow Chernobyl in paste form.

'Oh, wow, it's . . . er . . . medicine.'

Bemusement etches itself on her features as she peers at the digital thermometer. I rush to explain, aware that nobody is cooing at this offering like they did whenever an elephant appeared in various forms.

'Honestly, you never have any of this stuff in, and you only realise you desperately need it at, like, 2am, when all the shops are shut.'

'Right, of course.' She holds up the yellow tube and reads the back of the box. Polite til the end.

'That stuff is amazing,' I add. 'Honestly, when they start teething they get such bad nappy rash. This is the only stuff that works. And, that thing that looks like an accordion?' I lean over. 'It's really gross but you kind of put a tube up their arse and suck out their farts when they've got trapped wind.' The entire table goes 'Eww', a proper eww way, not an amused eww way.

'That's disgusting,' someone mutters and my blush deepens.

I thought so too, I thought. But I've been amazed at the level of grossness I'm willing to endure to bring peace to my baby. I've sucked out Woody's snot with my own mouth to try and get him to sleep *(before I bought the snot sucker)*. I've sat covered in vomit that's slowly cooking in the heat from the radiators, making me stink of mouldy cheese, because Woody was sick but then fell asleep on my chest and I knew the sleep would help him get better. I've carefully wiped liquid shit from every crevice of his body, multiple times a day. I've wiped it off the wall, from the sides of his baby bath when he injected the bubbles with his diarrhoea meaning I can't look at Molton Brown bath products in the same way ever again.

'You'll need the Calpol for before the baby's jabs too,' I add. I feel everyone's judgement and try and get them to understand what a good gift I've given. 'It stops them getting a fever. But honestly, the digital thermometer is so useful. They always get their first fever at some godawful hour, and 111 always want to know their temperature, and you're going spare for not having one, or for trying to use an adult one on a squirming, sick, baby. If it's over 38, you need to go straight to hospital, but, without a thermometer, you don't know, and you just panic, and end up in A&E without needing to, which is no fun with a baby, I promise you.'

'Right,' Nicki nods slowly, holding up the thermometer with the tips of her fingers, almost in horror. 'That's, er, a bit fucking dark, but I'm sure will be quite useful. Thanks, Lauren.'

A bit fucking dark.

I wilt back into my seat, the leather attaching itself to my hot bare dimpled skin, as Nicki reaches out for a present wrapped in paper with scented strawberry eco-glitter.

Fuck you, I think. You think you're going to be grateful for an elephant onesie at 2am, when you're convinced your baby is dying? Will your sensory Moomin mobile help then? No, it fucking won't. One of the worst things about having a baby is the love. Yes, it's the best thing too, but that love is the most terrifying and overwhelming feeling any human can feel. You will worry about your child dying, daily, multiple times. You will picture all the obscene ways it could happen. Meningitis. Kidnapping. The pram being hit by a car while you wait at a pedestrian crossing. When your baby cries, it peels you back to the bone because you love them so much and want to stop the pain for them. Your whole life will become an endless, failing mission to prevent them from ever crying because it hurts you so much. So, Nicki, yes. When your baby gets sick for the first time, which it inevitably will, because babies are like fucking lemmings, obsessed with danger and shoving everything into their dribbling gob, especially things that other germ-ridden babies have shoved into their gob . . . you will fucking *LOVE* me for getting you this *DARK* thermometer. For not having to frantically google which pharmacy might be open while your baby screams red in your arms, and you weep with desperate hopelessness. This thermometer will give you relief and comfort deep in your very soul, unlike a fucking Jellycat platypus. But, hey, yeah, *a bit dark,* go actually fuck yourself. This is the best present you're going to get today, even in the Santa paper, you fucking fuck.

Phoebe sits next to me and holds up her drink to cheers me. She seems slightly drunk, her eyes not quite focusing. 'Your gift is the best gift,' she whispers, the smell of punch sweet on her breath.

I sag into her with relief. 'Thank you. Everyone else seems to think I'm crazy.'

'I'll tell you who will be going crazy.' She points over at Nicki. 'This one, if her baby has a temperature in the middle of the night, and no Calpol.'

'Exactly!'

'Honestly, best gift here. Well done.'

I grin, liking this woman more and more. She's so different to the rest of Nicki's friends. Spiky – so not Nicki. I can't imagine them getting on but she's here, so they must. 'I mean, it's so clearly a competition. And the Santa paper really finished the look.'

She shrugs and waves the comment off with her hand, revealing some kind of tribal tattoo up the side of her wrist.

'You've got a baby too, right?' I nod. 'The fact you're here. Dressed. Not crying. You were on time, right?' I nod again. 'That's amazing. That should be present enough, to be honest. My big sister has three kids and, I swear, it takes her so long to leave the house she often doesn't bother. Forget the Santa paper. You're a marvel for being here.'

'I like you,' I tell her, reaching out and swigging a swallow of her punch while she nods in approval. 'You are officially allowed to be friends with Nicki. I grant you permission.'

Phoebe's eyes travel to where Nicki's unwrapping the last gift, with much less enthusiasm than she unwrapped the first. 'Aww thank you. But I'm sure today will be the last day I see her.' I tilt my head, confused, and she corrects herself. 'I mean, everyone vanishes off the face of the earth when they have a baby, don't they?'

'What's earth?' I joke. 'Where's that? I miss that place.'

She reaches over and squeezes my shoulder. 'You'll come back. I promise.'

I almost well up, at her saying that. 'Thank you. I hope so.'

'Umm, is that thing yours?' She points at the baby monitor in my sweaty hands, and Woody is awake. Of course he's freakin' awake. I've turned the sound off but I can see him crawling about, his mouth open, probably crying. He's always crying. I check my phone. Yep, he's been asleep for precisely 27 minutes. There's no way he's had enough nap. I look at the screen, and my pixelated baby going berserk in the travel cot. It's easier to emotionally detach with the sound off. I know I should go to him and comfort him – sacrifice myself, and my day, and this nice conversation, and go be a caring mother. If Tristan was here, he'd already be in the room, being the

Perfect Dad and never losing his temper because he's not had to sacrifice as much as I have. Normally, despite my irritation, I'd already be in the room, self-sacrificing as Woody refuses to self-soothe. But today, a part of me has hardened or maybe just plain broken. Instead, I find myself turning the screen over and burying the device in the lap of my ugly dress. The expensive sleep consultant said we should be giving Woody a '*chance*' to '*get himself back to sleep*'. Maybe now is the time to try? She promises his cries weren't cries of distress, but merely '*frustration*' that he's awake. Tristan doesn't agree, however, and hasn't let us implement her plan. 'How the hell does she know why he's crying?' he'd said, refusing to let us leave Woody crying for more than twenty seconds, condemning us to potentially unlimited sleep deprivation. But Tristan's not here, and I'm having a nice time, and maybe this is what needs to happen to fix Woody's sleep right now? Something *has* to change. It must. I can't be this mentally deranged anymore. So broken that I limp through each day like it's a time-loop of a car crash. *I'll give him ten minutes,* I decide. He can't get permanently damaged from ten minutes crying, and, who knows? It might actually *work*. I dare myself to imagine an alternate reality where Woody slept through. Maybe I'd get myself back? My sanity, my figure, my marriage, my hope. Maybe I'd *enjoy* Woody more if I could scrape some sleep?

I push the camera further down into my skirt – decision uneasily made. The party's so loud nobody will hear him upstairs, and it's only for a few minutes. I am here. I'm going to have a nice time. My baby will learn to sleep.

I turn to Phoebe. 'You've got to tell me all about working at Roar Girls Jewellery,' I say, just as Nicki applauds herself for finally getting through all the presents. Everyone joins in while Charlotte pushes the wrapping into a recycling bag and runs off somewhere. Probably spraying the peony wall with glitter juice or something? 'I'm obsessed with their jewellery. Do you get a discount?'

I think I hear a yelp through the ceiling, but I tune it out.

STEFFI

My phone starts ringing the second Nicki finishes unwrapping her pointless future landfills. I'd already withdrawn my present from the pile before she started opening them and hid it under the sofa to take home later because, yes, I am nine years old. So what if I don't have a bump for the Neal's Yard Bump Juice? I'm going to smother myself in the whole tub when I get home from this godawful greenhouse of hell. Spite smells of organic lavender and ylang-ylang – who knew?

I see that it's Rosa again and run to the bathroom to take it. But the door's locked and a queue's already forming outside it. I message her, saying I'll call in five, and stalk about trying to find somewhere quiet. Downstairs is all crepe paper, cranes, and crowds, so I duck under the makeshift rope on the staircase and sneak up. Four master bedrooms branch off from a glass corridor that overlooks the entire countryside. Two of the doors have signs in Charlotte's cursive writing that say, 'Baby Sleeping – *Do Not Disturb*'. But, past them, there's an empty bathroom. I duck in, locking the door behind me, and put the loo seat down to use as a chair.

'Rosa, what's up?' I ask, taking in the monolith bathroom. The toiletries don't match the bathroom itself. An own-brand Sainsbury's hand soap nestles between the two sinks, and a neon bottle of lime Original Source swims in a puddle on the floor of the rainforest shower.

'I want you to withdraw the book,' Rosa tells me breathlessly. 'Sorry, but I can't do it. I don't want to be published.'

'Ahh.'

'. . . I'm sorry for wasting everyone's time, but I think this book was just meant for me, you know?' She rushes on. 'Just a nice thing for me. I don't want other people to read it and judge it. I don't want my life to change. Honestly, Steffi, sorry, but is it too late to back out?'

I take a breath. Rosa's following the debut author algorithm perfectly. I have no doubt that, by the time we hang up, everything will be fine again. She's just having the freak-out all major debuts do when they can't trust their wildest dreams are coming true. All the smartest authors freak out. They know nothing is ever going to be the same again. And they're right, it won't. But it will be better, so much better, especially as my author care is second-to-none. It's so important to monitor and support an author's mental health in their debut year. Everyone goes a bit loopy. It's a mixture of things. Often, it's hard for them to adjust to the actual realities of their dream being realised. The publishing industry is brutal. And when they imagined getting a book deal, they didn't imagine tax forms, bad reviews, bookshelf placement (or lack therefore . . .), being snubbed for awards, and needing to write a second novel within a year. I'm happy to guide them through the adjustments, overwhelms and disappointments until they're out the other side – slightly embittered but mentally healthier.

'It's not too late to back out, no,' I tell Rosa calmly. 'I'll support you whatever you decide.'

God, it feels so good to be on the phone, being good at my job, after overhearing that awful conversation earlier.

'It's just all too much. All of it. Nina Baldwin . . . the Hollywood stuff. I . . . I . . . I never even thought I'd get an agent, let alone you. And then I never thought I'd get published, and now this . . .'

'It's because you're talented and you've worked your arse off,' I say.

'But I'm not. Writing is just a silly hobby.'

'Rosa, you're a star. I know that's overwhelming to hear, but you're a star and you were always supposed to be a star. The world needs your book. The world needs your perspective.'

'But—'

'—I've told you before how *Blood Moon* completely changed my opinion on about five key things. It opened my mind, it opened my heart. I learned so much, and, what's so amazing about your writing, is that I *loved* every single moment of that learning experience. It would break my heart to deny the world of that.'

'But Steffi . . . I'm . . .'

I swap my phone to my other ear and apply my very best soothing voice. 'I know all of this is overwhelming. I know it feels surreal. I can't tell you nothing will change, because it will. But don't you want it to change? Isn't that why you sent me this glorious manuscript? Because you want people to read your work, to get that perspective? Part of you, a part that might be a bit buried and overwhelmed right now, knows that, it believes in you. It believed in you enough to get you to write this book. Listen to that voice, Rosa. It believes in you, and I believe in you.' I smile so she can hear it in my voice. 'Yes, the next two years of your life are going to be insane, but I'll be holding your hand every single step of the way. I won't let go.'

'I don't know.' Rosa's breathing starts to match mine. She's speaking from her chest now, not her throat.

'Holding your hand every step of the way.'

'But . . . the money. What will I even do with it?'

'You'll move out of the flat share that you hate.'

She laughs. 'Then what?'

'You'll hire the amazing accountant I recommend to sort your taxes out, and you'll realise you're not as rich as you think because you're going to lose half of it to tax. You will suddenly get about 30 per cent more right-wing the second you calculate your tax bill.'

She splutters with laughter then falls quiet again.

'This book . . . it's my soul, Steffi. It's who I am . . . If I get a big deal, a film . . . everyone's going to hate on it.'

I nod. 'It's going to utterly transform some people's lives in the best way. There will be millions of people out there, myself included, who will divide their lives into 'before' and 'after' the time they read *Blood Moon*. Your work is going to inspire and save people.' I pick up a tube of toothpaste on the side, squeezing it around to give my hands something to do. 'But, I won't lie to you. Lots of people will hate it and will tell everyone they can how much it sucks. That's the nature of writing books. Honestly, go onto Goodreads and see what idiots say about your favourite books. *To Kill A Mockingbird?* One star. Not enough birds in it.'

She laughs down the line and I leave a long silence, hearing my heart thump through my thin dress. I'm confident I've got this, but, if she does back out, I'm so utterly fucked. I blink away thoughts of emailing the most powerful people in the business and withdrawing the manuscript . . . I'll be blacklisted . . . I'll go bankrupt. Rosa cannot know how important she is to my future. 'I'm just . . . a bit freaked out.'

'Of course you are. But my hand. It's here. Holding yours.' I leave another lengthy silence. 'Have you considered this might be the best thing that's ever happened to you? You never need to worry about money ever again. You can write every day for the rest of your life. What you love the most. No more squeezing it in around your day job.'

'Hmm . . .'

'Whatever you want to do, I'll support you.'

'I . . . I . . . You're right. It's all good. I just feel a bit freaked out.'

'Are you alone?'

'Yeah.'

'Ring your friends. Go out. Tell them the news. Make this real. Don't just stew in this alone. No wonder you're going a bit mad.'

'I can't tell my friends yet! What if it doesn't happen?'

I smile and replace the toothpaste, knowing we're safe, as she's worried it will be taken away. This is just a wobble. 'Rosa, I promise you now, this book will be published in a major deal with a major publisher. That is definitely going to happen – in the UK, and the US and Germany, and judging by my emails so far, probably at least another twenty countries too. That is all definitely going to happen. The film stuff? That I can't promise you. I mean, we're definitely going to get a major option deal, but that doesn't mean anything will get made because Hollywood is crazy and nothing ever gets made. But this much is real and you can trust it. You can trust me.'

There's a deep sigh down the line and I cross my fingers and wait. '. . . OK . . . you're right . . . sorry. I'm thrilled, I really am. It's just a lot.'

'It is, but I've got you. Now, go ring some people. Do you want me to come to Brixton? I'm stuck in Surrey but I can hop on a train and be with you by late afternoon?'

'I'm actually meeting friends for lunch. I wasn't going to tell them, but I might.'

'Tell them. This is real, I promise.'

We chat for a few further moments and I admit I drag it out a bit as I really don't want to go back downstairs. When we hang up, I wilt on the toilet in relief, my head hanging between my legs, my hair drooping to the ground. Now the crisis is over, I can allow myself a second to let it panic me. I cannot imagine what a disaster it would've been if I hadn't been able to talk Rosa around.

But I did. I did.

I wash my hands even though I didn't pee and look at my reflection in the mirror. It's speckled with toothpaste, and between the flecks, I see my face melting off, my hair frizzing, and there's an undeniable pain coming off me like a literal sweat. I was grateful for this work distraction, but back outside is a world where I overheard my best friend openly bitch about me. It hurts so much I don't even know how I'm going to drive home with her. I stare out the one-way glass at the dusty mess of countryside and let the view calm me. I allow myself one more deep sigh and, I'm just about to descend back into the party, when I hear a baby cry.

Through the doors, a symphony of women's voices float up the staircase. The punch must be getting everyone loose and there's a collective hum punctuated with the occasional shriek of laughter. There it is again. A baby crying out from down the glass corridor. I turn back, listening out, trying to locate which door it's coming from. There's a scream and I grasp the doorknob, ready to go in and help. But I hesitate. What if the mum's already in there, comforting the baby? They'll hate me if I barge in. I lean against the wood and listen out for a hushed lullaby, but I just get another shrill scream.

It's unbearable.

This one is so awful, my bodily response so visceral, that, without even making the decision, I push into the dark bedroom.

'Is everything OK?' I call out.

It's midnight black inside. I blink to acclimatise and the light from the hall streams in, revealing a distraught Woody. He's standing up in the cot, holding the bars like a caged pirate, face streaming with tears, his whole body shaking.

'Woody, baby. Shh, it's OK, it's OK.'

I glance around for Lauren, expecting her to run through the door any second to comfort him. But now Woody's aware someone's in the room with him, he screams even louder. He drops to the bottom of the cot, thrashing around like he's having some kind of fit.

'Hey Woody, it's OK. It's OK.' I run over and sort of hover next to him, figuring out what to do. The baby monitor must be broken. I could dash downstairs to tell Lauren, but I don't think I can leave him for even one minute.

He screams so loud my stomach hurts.

'Yes, I know. Baby showers are awful. I want to go home too.'

He reaches out his pudgy arms, speaking this weird language, begging me to lift him. Actual real tears spill endlessly down his face.

'Shh, it's OK,' I bend down and heave him out of the cot. 'We'll go get Mummy, I promise. Shh, shh.'

Woody buries himself into my shoulder, howling, and I bounce him up and down as he wets my dress with his tears.

CHARLOTTE

I dash to the toilet the second Nicki unwraps her last gift. I don't even fill in the final slot of the spreadsheet. I've bled through my makeshift sanitary towel and I gasp with actual horror. I've bled through my knickers and some of it has dried to either side of my thighs in this heat. I wipe and blood comes off the toilet tissue. I'm going to have to get to hospital immediately. This blood cannot be argued with – I can't manifest away this much biology. I bite my wrist until it leaves a mark and then try to mop myself up. When I shakily open the bathroom door, there's a line of women waiting, and I apologise sheepishly before running to locate my phone. Nicki isn't on her throne. Most people have dispersed to the kitchen to top up their drinks. Lauren's still sat down, red-faced and laughing with that terrible Phoebe and her terrible undercut. I should be helping with drinks, but the blood . . .

The blood . . .

The heat's still a surprise as I run outside and down the long gravel driveway. I only have one bar of reception but it's enough to get through.

'Charlotte, are you OK, babe?' Seth asks. 'Matt got picked up by the taxi just fine, I promise. He should be arriving any moment. It's all going to be per—'

'I'm bleeding,' I tell him. I fold over, holding my stomach, sweat dripping across my back as the sun throbs down on me.

'What?'

'From my vagina.' My wobbling lip vibrates through my voice. 'There's a 20 per cent chance it's a miscarriage. We

307

won't know for sure until I get to hospital. If they hear a heart-beat, the odds improve drastically.'

'Charlotte. *What?* Are you OK? Where are you? Fuck. You're bleeding? For how long?'

'Just an hour.'

'An hour? Why aren't you in hospital?'

'The baby shower. I have to—'

'Fuck the baby shower. Why didn't you call? Oh shit. OK. So, the car's still being pulled out, but it's alright. Matt's taxi is arriv-ing any time now. Wait outside for it and get in it once he's out. Tell the driver to come back and get me and we can go together . . . but that will take a while . . . no. Can you drive? You could get him to pick me up but drive yourself there. Do it, Charlotte. Now.'

'But . . .'

'But nothing. It's going to be alright. I'm sure. But we need to go to hospital.'

'I don't think I can drive.' I stare at my hand in detached wonder, watching it shake against the gravel. I glance over at my car parked by the balloon arch. 'And my car's blocked in.'

'OK. So, wait for the taxi, and come get me. I'll google the nearest hospital.'

'What if the driver doesn't take us?'

'Then get someone at the party to come.'

'I can't . . . Seth, it will ruin Nicki's shower.'

'So?'

'The surprise is about to happen. I can't ruin it. I can't make today all about me.'

'Charlotte, you're bleeding. That's not being selfish. You can't help it.'

'I'll wait for Matt and the surprise. It's only a few extra min-utes. It will be alright.' I look up at the clear sky and it strikes me just how blue it is. As blue as the two lines on my pregnancy test. *I get why they call it Clear Blue now,* I find myself thinking. *Because the lines on the test are the same colour as a sunny sky . . .*

'Honey? Are you with me?'

'I won't ruin the baby shower,' I tell him. This is a test from the universe. The shower is going perfectly and soon my reward will come. If I cope without ruining Nicki's day, then I'll hear a heartbeat at the hospital. If I make this about me then I'll be punished.

'Charlotte . . .' Seth's trying to use his calm voice but it's shaking. 'You know whatever is happening to you right now medically can't be changed by magical thinking?'

'Don't be ridiculous. I'm not—'

'This baby shower has nothing to do with the bleeding. Leaving early won't change what's happening to you biologically.'

'We don't know what's going on with me biologically,' I scream as two birds fly out of a nearby tree. 'It's unexplained infertility. Nobody knows why we can't have a baby.' I start crying then. Oh no. Please. It will ruin my make-up and then everyone will ask why I'm crying and that will ruin Nicki's baby shower and then I won't hear a heartbeat. 'If the world can't explain it – if it doesn't make sense – then surely the only way to fix it is by something else that doesn't make sense! If today is perfect—'

Seth yells back. 'Charlotte, stop. Come on. Please. Don't make any further sacrifices. This is my baby too. Promise me you're going to be on your way to hospital in less than fifteen minutes. Either in Matt's cab or get someone to drive you.'

I nod but I might be lying. I'm not sure yet. My stomach cramps and I drop to the gravel. 'I'll keep you updated,' I say. 'I love you.'

'It's all going to be OK, Charlotte.' Seth doesn't know that for sure. He can't make that promise. I ring off, I sit fully down, behind a big rose bush. I decide to allow myself one strategic cry. I hug my knees to my chest and let myself get out all my emotion in one effective burst. I must stay focused, and I can't concentrate with a wayward bottom lip. I cry more than I thought I would, making high-pitched guinea-pig noises that hurt my throat. Then I smooth down my dress and get ready to stand up. I'll say I popped out to get something from the car and that I got really sweaty, and that's why I'm all red and blotchy. Then, I'll lurk by the door waiting for Matt. I might even be able to get the taxi driver to wait five minutes while we do the firework surprise, so I can ensure it goes completely to plan, before I go to hospital to be told I'm miscarrying and all hope is gone and I'll never get to hold my own baby in my arms, even though it's all I've ever wanted in life and . . . I start crying again, much harder. These big shaking silent sobs that reverberate through my whole body, like I'm shedding my skin. I tell myself only two minutes more – I need to stop falling apart. It's hugely unhelpful. Then the front door opens and voices travel across the humid air.

'Oh Christ it's hot out here.' Shit. Nicki's voice. I duck further behind the rose bush. 'It should be illegal to be pregnant and this hot.'

I peek out through the branches to check I'm not in eye-line. She's settling herself down onto the front step, her giant stomach making her sit with her legs wide open. She's with Phoebe who laughs at Nicki's deep squat. As she sits next to her, she reaches out and strokes Nicki's hand as she takes it, squeezing it to her chest. The sheer weirdness of it yanks me from my distress.

'So, you did it. You're having a baby.'

Nicki puts their entwined hands to her face and kisses them. 'I am. I hope it's OK. My friend, Lauren, is freaking me out a bit today.'

'She's great. I was just chatting to her.'

'She's not. Well, she's great, but today, if you knew her, she's not herself.' Nicki lets go and leans up to bake her face in the sun. 'This is the first time I've seen her in months and she's . . . different. She's so . . . frumpy, for one thing. I'm not judging, but if you'd known her before, you'd be shocked.'

'It will all be worth it, I'm sure. That's what mothers tell everyone anyway. That's what you'll tell yourself.'

Nicki lets out a small snort. 'You can't even reign it in on my baby shower, can you? Of all days?'

Phoebe does this bitchy cackle. 'Nothing's been reigned in about this baby shower, Nicki. I mean, I get that you've chosen the heteronormative path of least resistance, but I just saw a vagina piñata outside.'

Nicki snorts again. 'It's a vulva actually.'

'Seriously, what even *is* today?' Phoebe asks. 'I feel like I'm living in a fever dream, and this heat isn't helping.'

My arms prickle as I wait for Nicki's response. I wait for her to tell this total bitch of a woman how perfect today is, and how hard I've worked and how grateful she is. There's nothing I haven't thought of. No extra details I didn't add. As a gift for my best friend. I hope she tells Phoebe to leave; quite frankly, she's been messing with the energy all day.

But Nicki says none of that.

'I know. Today is my worst nightmare realised. I promise you, I've had nothing to do with any of this.'

I gasp but they're both laughing too hard to hear me.

'Can you say that in calligraphy for me?' Phoebe cackles again. 'Nothing can be said today in normal handwriting.'

'Poor Charlotte probably took an online evening course to learn calligraphy for today.'

'Well, so she should. Personally, I can't piss unless signs for the toilet are spelled out in calligraphy.'

'I'm surprised you saw them through the wall of peonies.'

'Don't. I've developed hay fever. Whatever today is, I'm allergic to it.'

As tears mix with sweat on my face, as my knickers fill with blood, as I squat in the gravel, I can only listen, stunned, as one of my best friends shamelessly rips the piss out of me. Ridiculing the day I've spent weeks planning for her. I'm frozen with shame and humiliation. Nicki hates today? She hates all this? Everything I've done? As I peer out again, her face is crumpled with laughter. She's not only ridiculing me, she's enjoying it. Then, somehow, as the universe has obviously decided to enter me into some super-advanced test today, it gets worse.

'Is your friend Charlotte on Ritalin or something?' Phoebe asks. 'Does she chase her pill down each morning with a bottle of butter icing?'

Nicki snorts for a third time. 'Charlotte's always been a lot.' Then she stops laughing and her voice quietens and I strain to hear her properly. 'She means well, she does. But today is a bit *selfish* of her . . .' I gasp again. 'It's awful, but she's not been able to get pregnant, even though she's tried everything. Three rounds of IVF that didn't work. It's been so painful to watch. All she's ever wanted is to become a mum. And it's come so easily for Lauren and me . . .'

'So easily,' the Undercut Bitch interrupts. 'Nicki decides she wants a baby and nothing could stop her. You've never looked back.'

'That's not true. You know that.' Nicki reaches out and takes her hand again, interlocking their fingers. They lean into each other, their faces almost touching, but Phoebe pushes Nicki away.

'I think you love everything about today. I think you're more like your friend Charlotte than you realise.'

'What? I'm not.'

'You're basic, Nicki. Admit it. Today is basic, and you've pretended to be above it, but secretly you love this.'

'What? I don't love this. Today has been something to *endure*! The cupcakes! The games! It's not fair. Charlotte's been using me to have the baby shower *she's* always wanted. And I've just had to go along with it otherwise I'm a bitch. This isn't me. You must know that!'

My insides line with lead. I can't quite compute what I'm hearing. I've spent hundreds on today – thousands possibly. I've been up late for weeks, making all the craft, ensuring every last detail was perfect. I've . . . I've . . . I can't believe she thinks—

'—Charlotte might be basic but I'm not basic. When you sent me a picture of that invite this morning I felt sick, wondering what you must think of me. The *glitter* . . .'

My legs are standing up when I really haven't told them to. And my hands are at it too, curling into fists against my will. Slowly, I rise from the gravel.

'. . . You know I think baby showers are weird, gendered, archaic, wasteful ego-fests. My baby doesn't need any of this shit and neither do I. I'm blessed enough, you know? Do I really need all this . . . capitalism . . . but come on, Phoebe. Let's get to it, shall we? Why are you here? What do you want? Are you just here to . . . oh my God, Charlotte.'

One hand goes to Nicki's mouth and the other to her bump as I stand before her, shaking my head.

Transcript: Inspector Simmons interviewing Nicole Davies, Lauren Powell, Steffani Fox, Charlotte Roth

Simmons:	We've been going through the photos taken on the day in question, and there's quite a few, Nicole.
Nicole:	It's a baby shower. People take photos.
Simmons:	In total, going through the phones of everyone who was in attendance, over a thousand images were taken that day.
Nicole:	It was the peony wall. It just brings something out in people.

***

Simmons:	You took no photographs on the day in question, Lauren. There's not one on your phone.
Lauren:	I didn't have a spare hand all day.
Simmons:	Is it not strange? For a mother to not take a photo of her baby at an event like that?
Lauren:	Charlotte was there. I knew she'd send on all the semi-professional shots she took.

***

Simmons:	Can you tell me a bit about this fight that broke out?
Steffani:	Which one?

***

Simmons:	Charlotte, your phone has over 400 shots on it from the day in question.
Charlotte:	It was a day for memories to be made. I wanted Nicki to have photos she could cherish forever.
Simmons:	In fact, you've forensically documented the entire day, from Nicki's family shots at 9am, the group shot of you and your friends in front of the balloon arch at around 10am, through the games, the meal, and the presents. There's also photos of every attending guest in front of the wall of peonies.
Charlotte:	I pay Google £5 every month for extra cloud storage.
Simmons:	However, your phone records state that you stopped taking photographs right around 2pm, when these documented fights broke out.
Charlotte:	Well, who wants photos of a silly falling out? That's not one for the baby book.
Simmons:	True, but, if what you're saying is true, if you and your friends reconciled and then decided to have a miniature gender reveal, just the four of you, well, where are the photos of that? [Silence] Surely the gender reveal firework is the pièce de résistance? The ultimate content? Surely the main reason you brought the smoke grenade was to take photos of it going off?
Charlotte:	I . . . we must've got carried away in the moment and forgot.
Simmons:	Forgot? The woman with over 400 photos on her phone already?

Charlotte: I . . . we . . . it was A Moment. Everyone knows you don't take photos when you're having A Moment as it ruins it and pulls you all out of it.

Simmons: Well, it certainly was A Moment.

NICKI

Charlotte's just emerged from a rose bush like some kind of horror villain and she runs towards me, her eyes wild.

'Fuck you,' she shouts at me, before I even have a second to compute the situation. 'Fuck you, Nicki. Fuck you, fuck you, fuck you.'

The situation starts explaining itself in my shocked baby brain. Charlotte is outside. Charlotte has been listening to everything I just said about her. Charlotte's heard me take the piss out of this huge day she's organised for me. The baby kicks hard through my dungarees, complaining about the huge rush of adrenaline I've injected into their placenta.

'Charlotte . . . I . . . I didn't know you were out here.' She's storming up the gravel, almost like she's about to attack me. Phoebe, sensing it, stands up to act as a breaker, putting her hand up.

'Hey, come on. Calm down.'

'Get out of my way.'

Charlotte's ducking around Phoebe to try and find my face, her own tear-splashed and snotty. I never see Charlotte sob. She just makes squeak noises when she watches *The Notebook* (which is every six months) that we've always taken the piss out of. '*If a guinea pig could cry, they would cry like Charlotte,*' Lauren once said.

Yes, she's a character, but she's one of my best friends and, with dread, I replay what I've just said about her in a stupid attempt to impress Phoebe.

'Charlotte, I'm so sorry. Obviously, you weren't supposed to hear any of that.'

'Oh, you think so, you two-faced bitch?'

'Come on,' Phoebe puts her hands up again while I jerk back in shock. 'That's no way to speak to a pregnant person.'

'Oh, you and your subversive haircut can piss off, too. Thinking you're above all of this.' She turns her tiny wrath to Phoebe. 'You're not above it. You're here. You're drinking the punch I made, eating the food I paid for. Fuck you. You're elated I've thrown a baby shower so . . . *basic*, was it? You get just as excited about them as I do. Only you find them exciting because you can take the piss on social media to show how above it all you are. Making snide little jokes about them.' Charlotte's hardly breathing she's talking so fast. 'That's still using social media and baby showers to . . . what the hell . . . I don't know . . . to further your fucking *personal brand identity*, or whatever? You're doing exactly the same thing, you hypocrite. Just as some judgmental twat with a stupid haircut.'

Phoebe leans back and raises one impressed eyebrow while I scramble to mend things. 'Charlotte. Please. Sorry. I'm so sorry.'

She spins back to me, eyes wide and wet with hurt. 'Do you honestly think . . . Have you really been cringing all day?' She asks. 'I . . . I wanted it to be perfect, I . . .' She starts crying again, proper body-shaking sobbing. I go to her but she slaps me off. 'You've ruined everything,' she half-whispers to me. 'You did this. *YOU DID THIS.*'

'Did what, Charlotte?'

She laughs, almost manically, then starts crying harder. 'I have to go to the bathroom. I . . .'

'Charlotte, please. Let's talk this through.'

'I have to go to the bathroom. I'm not very well, I . . .'

I stand to the side as she swooshes past me, shooting us both a look I didn't realise she was capable of. The cooler air from the air-con hits me as she opens the front door, then I'm left with Phoebe, in this heat and guilt.

'Shit,' I say.

'She'll be OK. Let her calm down.'

'She heard everything. Shit!'

'Don't get too upset. You're pregnant. The baby.'

My mind's whirring up now, processing it all, figuring out how bad things are. The guilt is huge. Awful. The baby protests at it, the fabric of my overalls twitching as they complain in my body. What did I say about her? About today? That she was *using me*. I wince and the baby complains again. I used the word 'basic' – multiple times. About my friend. My friend struggling with infertility, who probably spent months organising this. For a moment, there's only acute horror at this, an open-mouthed gasp that I've hurt someone so much. But another emotion is pushing its way through . . . *Relief*. Charlotte hadn't overheard Phoebe and I talk about our affair, which was so obviously why we'd come out here. I'd pretended I needed a bit of air and Phoebe, catching my eye, said she'd come sit with me. On these steps, we have delicious alone time. A chance to talk after a whole year. To explain. To rewrite our story a little. And, though I'm desperate to run after Charlotte and make everything OK, Phoebe's looking at me with such . . . hunger in her face. I want to speak stupid and dangerous truths to her. I want to burn down my life, just so maybe I can hear Phoebe tell me she loved me, and still does.

I start crying. With the guilt and confusion and shock of everything. Not just today, but my life. My choices. Lauren got pregnant and I just fell down this indescribable hole where the only clear thing was that I wanted a baby. And I threw everything away that would come between that happening. It was this biological, powerful, almost hot urge that top-trumped every other urge, and, it's here, in my stomach, almost ready to meet me and hopefully make it worth it. 'Everything's such a mess,' I stutter out. Seeing Phoebe today has forced me to confront the sacrifice I made to have this life, to have this baby shower. I've been blocking it out because I knew it would be too huge and confusing to confront, but she's here, and she looks so beautiful, and she's made parts of me dance that didn't know the steps without her. 'I'm . . . I don't know what I'm doing. Today is so surreal. I didn't expect you to come, and now you're here, and I feel so terrible for how I treated you but I wanted this . . . this . . .' I clutch at my stomach and cry harder. 'I couldn't have both. It's all been such a rush. And now you're here and I still . . . your eyes . . . and I've made Charlotte cry . . . I don't . . . can't . . .' I can't talk anymore, I'm crying too hard. Phoebe tries to hug me but I shrug her off as I don't deserve it.

'Shh, it's alright,' she whispers. 'It's going to be OK.'

'Look, if you're here for revenge, fine. Do it. Tell everyone. I deserve it. I'm a terrible person. And I'm going to be a terrible mother because I'm a terrible selfish person.'

I sob and sob as I voice my darkest thoughts. I am selfish. I've always quietly known this about myself. Maybe it's because I'm an only child or something but I've always prioritised myself and my own happiness. On my better days, I believe it's a healthy sense of esteem, but now, seeing Charlotte's hurt face, Phoebe's hurt face . . . the things I do and say . . . I'm going to be such a bad mother, the thought closes my throat and I can't stop crying.

Phoebe hugs me close and I surrender to her warmth, wrap my arms around her neck, try to get as close as I can with my giant stomach in the way. 'Shh. Oh my God, I'm not here for *revenge*. I just wanted to see you. Shh. You're going to be a great mother,' she tells me. 'You're already learning the most important thing you can learn for that role . . . that mother-hood requires huge personal sacrifice. There are so many things you're going to have to give up.'

'I didn't want to give you up. You must believe . . .'

'I get it. I get it. Hey, hey, it's going to be alright. Nicki? Nicki. Listen to me. You've made the right choice.'

I go still in her arms. 'I did?'

'Yes, you did. Because I don't want children. I've never wanted children. Which is very useful as it's obviously much harder for a lesbian to have a child.'

'I . . . You never said.'

'You never let us get that far. I didn't even know you wanted kids so badly until you ended it.'

'I didn't know I wanted them until I thought about not being able to have them.'

She strokes my puffy face. 'But you do want them. And you're about to have one. It's a good thing. A beautiful thing.'

I snuffle into her shoulder and bury my nose into her neck. If I move my head even slightly, I could kiss her. 'And not just because of the peony wall?'

She laughs and her breath is added heat on my bare skin. 'It's going to be alright.'

We hug too tight and for too long, especially as Charlotte is off crying somewhere. I hear the crunch of a car on some gravel but stay hugging Phoebe. This is the goodbye we didn't get to have. These are the feelings I didn't allow myself to feel. They're not going to change anything. I'm so all-in with Matt now. We've created flesh and blood and bone together.

I bury my nose into her skin, inhaling deep breaths of her to commit into memory.

'Thank you,' I whisper. 'For coming today. For being here for me.'

'There's no way I'm turning down an invite with bio-degradable glitter,' she replies and we laugh into one another's necks, still holding on. The moment has stretched out way beyond appropriateness, but I tell myself it's alright because it's a goodbye. An honest, well-intentioned, wave backwards to a curious path I've chosen never to walk. I hold her and hold her, until a car door slams and we jump.

'What the actual hell is she doing here?'

I turn and there's Matt, his face painted with rage.

LAUREN

Woody's been crying for ten minutes now. Ten whole minutes. I've got the monitor sound off so I can't hear it, but I can see his increasing distress. Nobody can hear him above the party. Phoebe hopped up a short while ago – offering to take Nicki out for some air, so I'm alone to stare at the monitor and feel like the worst mother since Norman Bates. Seeing Woody cry, even in silence, is like having the whole world's fingernails scrape along my nerves. It feels abhorrent and unnatural. I want to rush up and cradle him, and yet the sleep lady told me he needs to learn how to 'self-settle'.

'*Don't be too quick to go in there and interfere,*' she'd said, each word she uttered costing about one precious maternity-leave pound. '*You've got to give him a chance to get himself back down.*'

It seems highly unlikely that Woody's going to go 'back down' considering he's literally standing up in the travel cot now, howling like a wolf at the moon. I try to remember how long you're supposed to leave them to cry if you're doing the Ferber method. Was it thirteen minutes, or three? I'll wait five more minutes, I decide. That will hopefully not be so long that Woody turns into a psychopath when he's older, kills women and wears their skin, and tells everyone on the stand it's my fault. I sit back in the sofa and look around the bustle of the party to try to enjoy this 'me time'. If I'm permanently damaging my child, I may as well have fun, right? But the rest of the Little Women have vanished and everyone seems to be clumping together in their relative friendship groups. I want another glass of punch. I want five. I want to drink until I'm floppy, and uninhibited, and I think going dancing until 4am is a brilliant idea. I want to move my body to music I don't like, feel the smears of sweat from strangers against my skin as I queue at a four-person-deep bar. I want to squat over a gross toilet with no seat so I don't catch HPV from the rim, and later stagger into a 24-hour McDonald's, blinking into the neon screen, ordering fries I'll sick up within half an hour. Then I want to fall onto an unmade bed and lose consciousness immediately – waking thirsty and sick, with vomit on the carpet next to me, and then spend the next day tucked up in bed, watching shit TV on my laptop and messaging people to ask how embarrassing I'd been. I had no idea how free I was before having a child. And I'd wasted it. I was lonely even, *lonely*. I used to dread Sunday nights before I met Tristan, when I was living in that crap house-share with a bunch of junior doctors who were never in. I'd make desperate plans to have dinner with people I didn't like just to avoid a few hours before bed of my own company. I would sell a kidney to be alone now. Properly alone. Not just *paying-for-childcare* alone. Because that won't be the same, I know it already. Even those times Tristan takes Woody for a few hours between feeds, I'm not alone because all I think about is Woody. Is he OK? Safe? Having a good time? Missing me? Following his schedule? How much has he eaten? The alone time will now always come with a cost. Either – literally – when he starts nursery. Or, as part of a bargain with Tristan. Both of us in a back-and-forth trade of who gets to do something nice while the other one is stuck solo parenting. Forever in a tit-for-tat land grab for freedom. *Nothing will ever be the same again.* Everyone always tells you that going in, but you can't understand the heavy significance of that, until it's too late to go back and change your mind, or at the very least enjoy how fucking free you were.

I push tears back into my eyes and stand up. I'm not having enough fun to do this to Woody. I can try again tomorrow. I can pay the sleep consultant for another consultation, and then google everything she's told me to do, and read how it will damage my baby's attachment, and then not follow any of her instructions, and wonder why nothing is getting better. It's a plan at least, if a suitably doomed one. I step past a group of women returning from the kitchen with fresh glasses of punch and glance down at the monitor again.

Just in time to see a pair of hands, that aren't mine, appear on screen and take my baby out of his cot.

STEFFI

'Shh, shh, it's OK, it's OK.' Woody buries into my armpit and lets out another wail. 'Mummy's coming, Mummy's coming.' I'm not sure if she is. I'm quite stunned she isn't here yet when he's clearly been upset for so long. His hysteria is almost unbearable. I bounce him, shh him, walk around the dark, whispering babyish sweet nothings into his hot, tear-soaked ears.

'Don't be sad, Woody. Hey, Woody, you're so cute, but you can't be cute when you're sad, can you?'

I can't help it. Judgement is seeping out of me at Lauren. His sadness is so acute, his desperation for his mother so strong, and he's so tiny and helpless. *Something must've gone wrong with the monitor,* I tell myself. There's no way Lauren would leave him to cry like this. She never leaves anyone to cry. I remember, one night at uni, shortly after all the Matt stuff had happened, I'd got paralytically drunk and had such a dreadful one-night stand, I'd left straight afterwards and walked home barefoot because my shoes were on his side of the bed and I didn't want to wake him. Lauren heard me weeping in the bathroom at 4am, and sat outside, comforting me through the door, until I eventually let her in. There's no way that woman would leave Woody on purpose. He screams right into my ear and I scrunch my face as a thousand hearing hairs shrivel and drop out of my ear. He clearly isn't going to be consoled by me, so I give up and scramble around for the door handle, blinking as I step out into the fuggy brightness of the landing.

Lauren comes running up the stairs towards me, her eyes almost red.

'Lauren, I. . .'

'What's going on?'

Woody's already out of my arms and curling himself around her like a baby snake. His crying amplifies at having found his mother, and he shrieks as she pushes his hair back, turning to me, her face still poison.

'He was crying and . . .'

'You just went in and picked him up? Without asking?'

'I didn't know what to do. I just heard him screaming and you didn't come . . .'

'Oh, you're accusing me of neglect are you?'

'*What?* I . . . Did you know he was crying? Couldn't you hear him?'

'I . . . he was fine. It was all in hand.'

I can't help it again. 'So, you left him that upset . . . on purpose?' I can't quite believe it.

'Fuck you. Like you know anything about being a mother, Steffi. Fuck you.'

My mouth drops open and I'm truly and utterly speechless. With her shots fired, Lauren turns her attention to soothing Woody who's absorbing up the energy and crying even harder. 'Baby. Baby. I'm here. I'm here. I'm sorry this strange woman came and bothered you.'

I shake my head. '*Strange woman?* Lauren, you asked me to be his godmother.'

She ignores me. 'Silly woman. You were just trying to sleep and she comes and pokes you and makes you cry.'

'Lauren, are you being serious? He was crying long before I went in there.'

Her head snaps back. 'What are you saying?'

I throw my arms up. 'I'm saying, I just went to the toilet and I could hear him crying and nobody came and it was too much, so I went in and—'

'Are you saying I'm a shit mother?'

'What? No. I assumed your baby monitor's playing up. I was trying to be nice! Helpful! Next time shall I leave your baby screaming alone in the dark for two hours?'

'How dare you? You don't know anything.' Woody's quietening now. He leans his cheek on Lauren's shoulder and sucks him thumb, also looking at me accusingly, with a tear-streaked face.

Don't judge mothers. The rule I live by. Especially mothers that are your friends. I gain nothing but napalm in response. I cannot, literally, say anything about anyone raising any child, in any way, without everyone wanting to rip my head off and swallow it. *I don't understand. Couldn't possibly. How dare I weigh in on this conversation. Why don't I wait outside until the selfless martyrs who understand just how much love humans are capable of feeling have finished moaning about their perfect babies they also complain about constantly.* Lauren, more than anyone, is someone I'd never judge. She's one of my oldest and dearest friends – we have each other's backs. Or that's what I've always assumed. Except, today, earlier, out on the decking, Lauren didn't have my back at all. She happily bitched about me and now she's hurling abuse when I was only trying to help. Our Geneva Convention has been dissolved, and, already too pissed off at today, I take off my gloves.

'I may not be a mother,' I snap. 'But I know what it feels like to hear a desperate baby scream alone in the dark. I'm sorry, Lauren, but I couldn't let that continue. It's cruel.'

'He's *supposed* to be left to cry.'

'What?'

'The woman said—'

'What woman? Hitler's wife?'

'No, the sleep expert.'

'That's not a sleep expert, that's an abuse expert, asking you to do that. Look at the state of him.'

The word is a cluster bomb that detonates the second it's out of my mouth. I actually smack my hand over it, like I can catch it before she hears it, but it's too late. Lauren jerks back so sharply that Woody starts crying again.

'Are you saying I'm . . . *abusing* my child?'

'No. That's not what I said.'

'*You?* Who knows literally nothing about being a mother, apart from that you don't want to be one . . . Can't stop banging on about that can you?'

I put my hand out but stop myself retaliating. Woody's still screaming and, over it, I can just about hear another commotion downstairs. A man's voice, the sound of dozens of people getting up.

'I wasn't saying that about you, but this woman who said you should leave a baby to cry . . . I mean, Lauren, he was *screaming*.'

'Shut up.'

'Excuse me?'

'Shut up. You have no idea what you're talking about. Don't you dare touch my baby again, do you hear me?'

'Lauren?'

'You're so selfish. *Blah blah blah, I don't want kids.* Who fucking cares? If you're not interested, fine. But don't you dare come and touch my child and judge me.'

'I didn't *touch* your kid, I picked up a screaming baby!'

There's a thumping on the stairs. Woody's burrowing into Lauren's dress, yanking it down, trying to feed even though she's standing up.

'Well you shouldn't have.'

I stand back. 'Oh? I'm so evil and selfish, aren't I? And yet I'm not the one who left a baby to cry.'

A voice jolts us from our fight.

'Who's left their baby to cry?' Charlotte asks, appearing at the end of the landing, her face wild, with all of its makeup cried off.

CHARLOTTE

I have to get out of here. This hell of my own creation. It's heaving with ungrateful bitches, stuffing their faces with the food I made, plonking their plates down and leaving them without thinking who's going to be clearing them up. I run back inside, past the peony wall, and, without even thinking about it, I push it over so it lands face-down, the petals squelching onto the wooden floor. Some people notice and gasp, but I don't give a shit. I just need to check myself in the toilet, get my belongings, and get out of here. Let Nicki clear up the fucking mess. Let her wash all the glasses and take down the decorations. Let her sort all the wrapping paper into the recycling. I'm taking my spreadsheet with me. Ha. Let her see what 'cringe' really means when she can't remember who got her what and it fucks up her thank-you cards. *Oh, Charlotte's so embarrassing,* is she? You know what's embarrassing? Having a friend pick out a lovely gift for your unborn child and being such a selfish and ungrateful blob that you can't even remember who gave you what?

It's not fair. Why does she get to have a baby and I don't? Why is my baby haemorrhaging out of me while hers swims around in her self-obsessed amniotic fluid? I dash to the bathroom but there's a long line, and the thought of queuing is unbearable. I remember the spare upstairs that Nicki's mum asked us not to use. I turn back only to find Matt storming in and clapping his hands.

'Hey guys, I'm sorry but something has come up, and the baby shower has to end early,' he booms. His voice is so low and masculine in this glasshouse of oestrogen that everyone startles. He claps his hands again. 'I'm not kidding. Nicki needs you all to leave. Now.'

There's confusion. Nicki's mother heads over to him, asking what's going on, but he dodges her and flings open the front door where Nicki is still standing with that undercut bitch, crying. He starts herding the guests like sheep.

There's confusion and chaos as everyone struggles to digest what's happening.

'What's wrong?' 'Is everything OK?' 'Is Nicki OK?'

'Yes, yes,' Matt says. 'It will be OK. It's the heat, it's too much. Nicki needs to be alone right now.' He says it with such authority that they all start leaving while throwing each other confused glances. 'Thank you for coming. Nicki is very grateful. Very sorry but there's been an emergency and you all need to leave. Thank you, thank you.'

My thank-you bags are next to the door, and, somehow, Matt manages to pick them up and lob them at each person as they leave, clutching them to their stomachs and turning around as they exit, like they're checking if this is really happening. I should probably care he's not giving people the right ones. I've handwritten everyone's name on the sides in calligraphy but *Calligraphy Charlotte* is done. Fuck calligraphy. Fuck making an effort and trying to make things nice for people. Especially your friends. Nobody is grateful. In fact, you're ridiculed for it. *Stupid Charlotte with her stupid*

*parties and her stupid Instagram posts and her stupid mal-
functioning mystery womb.*

I weave through the leaving crowd, trying to locate my
handbag which has my car keys in it. I can't find it amongst
the mess of plates and presents and ungrateful carnage,
and, by the time I've scouted the bottom floor, the room's
empty apart from Matt and Nicki arguing by the front door.
I remember that I stashed it in the bedroom after erecting the
travel cots.

The baby shower's ruined. The surprise is ruined. And
so, my baby is dead. I know I need to fall apart but not here.
I won't give Nicki the satisfaction of seeing that. I'll go to
the bathroom, sort myself out, maybe fall apart for ten minutes while everyone is forcibly exiting, and then figure out
how to get to hospital. If Matt's here then I've missed the
taxi, but if everyone's leaving then my car will be free. I race
upstairs, leaving the chaos beneath me, only to find more of
it on the landing.

'I'm supposed to leave a baby to cry?' Steffi's shouting at
Lauren. They're in the middle of an argument too – apparently oblivious to downstairs.

I lock eyes with the Woody in Lauren's arms and pain rips
through me. His chubby cheruby cheeks, his pudgy hands, the
hair curling at the back of his neck, clasped lovingly to his
mother like a baby monkey. I want this so much. I want a baby
so much. It aches.

'Who's left a baby to cry?' I ask, trying to figure out what
I've just walked into.

Steffi throws her hands towards Lauren. 'Woody was screaming in his cot and Lauren's having a go at me for picking him up.'

'Because you had no damn right.'

'Hang on, hang on. Why was Woody crying? Is he OK?'

Lauren wipes a stray piece of hair behind her ear and bounces Woody on her hip. 'He's fine. He just needs to learn how to fucking stay asleep, that's all.'

Both Steffi and I flinch.

'You . . . left him to cry?' I ask.

'He was alright,' she insists, bounce bounce bouncing him. 'He's not hungry, or wet. All his needs have been met. He just needs to learn how to self-soothe, that's all. We've hired someone to get him to sleep better, and she said we should—'

'Cry it out?'

'No! Just help teach him how to sleep. And he would've if Steffi hadn't . . .'

Steffi shakes her head. 'I'm not going to apologise for tending to a screaming baby. I know you guys don't think it, but I am actually human! Just 'cos I don't want babies myself doesn't mean I'm some uncaring bitch. Do you not remember my mum? Have you forgotten how fucking caring I am – literally? I'm sorry Lauren, but he was inconsolable. I couldn't leave him. I don't know how you could.'

They're blocking my way. I don't understand how anything extra can be happening now when already too much is happening. My womb aches and I lean over. I can't stop staring at Woody. At this beautiful miracle being rocked in Lauren's arms. Does she have any idea how lucky she is? How vulnerable and tender he is?

'I can't believe you can let your baby cry,' I tell her. 'How? I don't understand.'

'Oh don't you go judging me too.'

'You? Of all people? Doing controlled crying?'

'Charlotte, stop it. Please. You can't possibly understand—'

'The research about controlled crying is mixed,' I interrupt her. I need Lauren to understand how precious Woody is. How lucky she is. He should be treated like the miracle he is. If I ever . . . If the world ever gives me a baby . . . I will hug it every second of the day. I'll co-sleep. I'll do all the wakes. I'll enjoy all the wakes because it's time with my baby. Oh, why won't the world let me have a baby and then lets Lauren have one, when she's happy to let them scream themselves to sleep? It's not fair. 'Lauren, you can't trust these sleep consultants.' I start parroting what I've read online, because of course I've googled it to death, alongside best breastfeeding positions, and the Montessori method, and baby first aid videos, and Wonder Weeks – all preparing to be the best mother ever except today is ruined and now I'm never going to get a chance 'You need to be careful,' I say. She needs to understand what a risk she's taking. One I'd never take, no matter how exhausted I was. 'It could really impact Woody's attachment. It's not learning how to self-soothe, it's learned *helplessness.* The baby only goes quiet after controlled crying because they give up hope of being rescued and wants to

337

preserve their energy because they feel abandoned and that they're about to die and—'

'Shut up,' Lauren screams at me. 'Shut up, shut up, shut up.'

Woody starts wailing again, and I hear footsteps on the stairs behind me.

NICKI

My waters almost break. What's Matt doing here? He's watching Wimbledon all day at the pub. He's not here at my parents' house – 'The Museum of Unhappiness' as he calls it. I physically push Phoebe back the second I see him, so much that she stumbles, but it's too late. 'Matt,' I say, guilt lining my throat. 'It's not what it . . . I didn't. What are you doing here?' Is he going to explode? Or cry? Or what? For a moment or two, he seems as confused about his expected behaviour as I am. He keeps shaking his head, looking at me, our bump, at Phoebe . . .

'Today's not just a baby shower,' he informs me. Going for the facts first, before the emotion, maybe while he decides what emotion he's feeling. 'Charlotte and I have been planning a special surprise.' His eyes land on Phoebe again and they narrow. When we decided to mend things, he insisted we go on my social media and unfriend her, out of respect. Now he's seeing her without pixels for the first time. 'And yet I'm the surprised one.' He points between us. 'What's going on here?'

Phoebe stands in front of me protectively and I get a flash of the tattoo on her neck.

'Nothing. We were just talking. Is that not allowed?'

'No,' Matt says simply. 'Not with you, it's not. Not after you two had an affair.'

She scoffs. 'Hardly an affair.'

'I think I'm the one who gets to decide what counts. Me and my wife. Who chose me by the way,' he adds. 'Despite your underhand efforts to undermine our marriage . . . her sexuality.'

Phoebe scoffs again. 'What do you know about her sexuality?'

Matt laughs and shakes his head with his hands either side of it. When he looks up at me, I see such intense hurt and anger, that I know he's saving a lot of face in front of Phoebe. 'There's a baby in her stomach,' he replies. 'My baby. Guess how it got in there.'

'Matt?' I yelp, stroking my stomach to try and calm the baby down. 'I'm sorry. I know what it looks like. But we really have just been talking. Charlotte invited her. She obviously doesn't know.'

'And you decided to come, did you? Thought that would be appropriate?'

Phoebe crosses her arms, revealing another tattoo – the one of the Deathly Hallows on her wrist that she now regrets. 'She chose you,' she sounds almost bored. 'As you say, look at her stomach. If you guys were as strong as you say, this shouldn't bother you.'

'Oh, for fuck's sake. You know it's not about that. It's about respect.' Matt's temper spills a drop or two on the steps. 'You're showing no respect for me by showing up here. And none for Nicki either. Who you claim to love still, I bet? Is that why you came? To tell her that? When she's heavily pregnant and emotional and quite far into this decision to not be with you? Have you even thought about what this means for Nicki? How it might feel for her? Ahh, no. Of course. 'Cos you're only interested in yourself.' Sweat's beading on his forehead and he wipes it with the back of his hand. I can't believe he's defending me. Love rises in me like soufflé. He's right. Phoebe coming today isn't good for me. It feels good, like it always does with her, but, I am heavily pregnant. She knows this is a headfuck.

'Can you please leave now?' He asks, award-winningly calm, standing aside and gesturing out. 'I need to talk to my wife.'

'You can't just ask me to leave.' She twists around. 'Nicki?'

She's asking me to what? Fight for her? Here? At my baby shower? With my guests inside? Why did she come here? What did she expect from me?

'Phoebe I do think it's better you go,' I say, watching each word land on her face and make craters. Matt and I are one, a team, about to become parents together. He's here, defending me even when I've let him down. I made a choice. I have to stick to it, and I literally can't back-out anyway. I can feel the consequences of my decision literally kick me in the guts, reminding me of the path I chose and therefore the other paths I need to let go of.

'Fine, I'm going. If I stay here for one more second, I'll probably turn straight anyway.' She nods her head to the party inside. 'Enjoy your obvious life choices. Post the pictures online to convince yourself you're happy with them.'

Matt comes and stands by my side. 'She is happy with them. Now, if you excuse me, I need to talk to my wife, and I can't do that with all these people inside, playing pin the sperm on the egg.'

He clasps my shoulder as he passes me, heading inside, and I hear him tell everyone the party's over. That I'm too hot and need a rest. There are shocked murmurings, the collective sound of dozens of women packing up their stuff in a gossipy hurry. My mind hums while it struggles to metabolise everything that's just happened. I've upset Charlotte. I've upset Phoebe. I've upset my husband. I've just ruined my own baby shower. I can hear Matt reiterate that they all need to leave immediately. I get this huge urge to nap, but Phoebe still hasn't left. She's staring at me, jaw set, the sun behind her, lighting her silhouette with gold.

'I'm sorry,' I say, feeling tears itch my eyes. 'I . . . I . . . I don't know what's happened today.'

'I shouldn't have come.'

'No,' I say. 'You shouldn't.'

'You won't hear from me again.'

It's a childish move. One designed to break my heart, to give me a terrible choice. Incinerate my life, right now, sweating on this porch, or never see someone I love again. It's a mistake on her part as it shuts my heart and makes the following easier. I can't be around people who behave like children just as I'm about to have one.

'OK then. I guess I won't hear from you.'

She blinks away her own tears. 'Fine. Your funeral.' She turns away and shoots me a look I can't quite read. Is it hate? It looks terribly close to that.

I open my mouth to say one last thing. I'm not sure what, but something profound and caring, something suitable to give this an ending – whatever it is. She senses it, waits for it, and I'm about to talk, but the front door swings open again and a stream of guests pour out, clutching goody bags and rushing to hug me goodbye.

'Nicki, darling. Thank you so much, I've had the best time.'

'Nicki, I hope everything's OK. Are you sure you're alright? Thanks so much. Let me know when baby comes, yeah?'

'You're going to be such a good mother.'

'Go put your feet up and have a nap, mama. You got this.'

'Sorry it had to end early, but I've had the best time. Now go have a cold bath.'

I'm lost in an ocean of hugs, air kisses and people clutching my bump. I say thank you, thank you, act the part, trying to distract from the inevitable curiosity of this party's abrupt ending. The stream of people keeps on running as the glass house empties, and I'm told what a good mother I'll make, and what a lucky baby this is, and how exciting, and I bet I can't wait to meet them, and oh, if I get a moment, can I ask Charlotte to send over all the pictures she took. By the time the stream runs dry, I scan the driveway for Phoebe, wanting so much to have one last moment – one that does us justice – but she's gone. There's no time to mourn this, to mourn her, and us. I want to cry but I can't go into that house to sort things with Matt if I'm visibly upset that she's left. I can't *believe* he's forgiven me *again*. The forgiveness is a balm that I apply over the pain. I've made the right choice with Matt. He's an amazing man. He defended me. He's supported me. It's all going to be alright. I push inside, sighing in the lush blast of air conditioning, and find Matt leant against the kitchen counter, drinking a glass of the non-alcoholic punch. It's neon pink and filled with edible glitter that catches the light as he tips it down his throat. I point to it, smiling. 'Careful, that stuff is called emasculation potion. If you finish the glass, your penis shrivels up.'

I wait for a laugh to break the tension, but he gulps it to the bottom, and when he's done, the look he gives me over his stork cup makes my blood stop.

'I can't believe you, Nicki,' he says. 'What the actual hell is wrong with you?'

'I can explain. I thought . . .' He holds up his hand to stop me.

'Are you the most selfish person alive? Seriously? Who the hell have I married? Who the hell am I having a baby with?'

343

I realise then the show of solidarity outside was a façade. An exercise in saving face. I'm not forgiven. 'Matt!'

Mum rushes into the room with a pile full of empty cups in her arms. 'Nicki? Darling? Is everything OK? Are you too hot? Should I call 111, just in case? You look OK, but still . . .'

We stand, suspended, in our fight, both of us adjusting our posture like we're teenagers trying to hide we're drunk. 'Thanks Jane,' Matt says. 'But Nicki is fine. I'll look after her. We actually need to discuss something very important and private that's just come up. I know it's your house, but do you mind giving us some space?'

Her eyes go straight to me, wanting to protect her baby. 'Is everything alright Nicki?'

'We're fine,' I lie. 'But, Matt's right. We need to talk. Can you give us an hour?'

There's one good thing I can say about my mother and that is she's always been able to cartwheel with the punches. 'Of course,' she says, like it's a totally usual request to be evicted from your own home. 'I need a breather after all that. I'll go treat myself to an iced coffee before addressing the clean-up. Charlotte promised she'd do it, but she's gone all funny. I think.'

We're interrupted by shouting upstairs. 'You know what? I'm just going to head off. Leave the kids to it.'

She grabs her handbag and is out within seconds, checking in with her eyes one last time. There's more shouting upstairs. What the hell is going on? Why does the world keep ending? Why has everything gone berserk?

'What's that?' I ask, pointing upwards where the shouts are getting increasingly shrill.

'I don't care.'

'Matt, please . . . I didn't know she was coming.'

'Until when? Did it surprise you when she walked through the door?'

I wonder about whether to lie and, sensing it, he shakes his head. 'She messaged me early this morning saying Charlotte had invited her,' I admit.

'And, let me guess, you said, very clearly, "*it's not appropriate for you to come because you tried to ruin my marriage*"?'

'No . . .'

'Show me! Show me what you messaged her. Where's your phone?'

'I'm not showing you my phone!'

'If you wrote something innocent back, you wouldn't mind.'

'You can't go through my phone. That's, like . . . abuse.'

'Oh my God.' He crushes his stork cup with his fist, truly exasperated. 'Are you actually? Fucking hell, Nicki. Are you literally the victim of everything? I can't . . . I need . . . I can't talk to you right now. Fucking hell . . . Fucking actual hell.'

'Matt, come on. You have to trust me. I . . . I'm having your baby.'

'No, I have to *stay* with you because you're having my baby.'

The words slap me with their significance. 'What did you just say?'

He thumps the counter, runs his hands through his hair, and looks mildly deranged. I clutch my tummy and have to perch on a stool, such is the fear of what he's just said. It took a lot to get him to trust me and forgive me, to get us here. To where I so desperately wanted.

'I actually don't think I can talk right now after all,' he says, leaning over on the counter. 'I need to calm down. You know I came here as a surprise, right? I know the sex of our baby. I rang the hospital to talk me through the twenty-week scan. I know you want to know. Charlotte has this firework thing all set up . . . After everything you did, I'm still trying to be so nice to you, and . . . fuck . . . have you just used me as a sperm donor or something?'

'What! No. Matt, I love you.' I start crying again. He can't be saying these things. This moment can't be my life, surely? He knows the *sex of our baby*? Despite everything that's happening right now, I'm desperate to know. I've been gagging to know for so long. He knows me so well and I'm ruining it. Ruining it when I'm weeks away from giving birth and us having to look after this thing forever.

'If you did you wouldn't have let her come.'

'I . . . I just got confused . . .'

'No. Stop it. I'm going to get too angry if you try and Nicki this right now. I need to walk and sort my head out.'

'It's a million degrees outside.'

'I don't care. I need to just . . . not be here with you.'

He pushes outside before I can get myself off the stool, punching the balloon arch on his way out. I waddle after him desperately, but I'm only hit with a blast of heat that's rushed through the entrance as the door shuts behind him. My hand goes to my mouth, my heart hurting. What have I just done? It's too big. Too much. My brain physically hurts in my skull as it tries to comprehend the possible fall-out of all of this. I need the father of my baby. I need my husband, holding my hand as I give birth. I need us to be a family together. That's what I chose, and it wasn't without a cost. I can't lose it. I . . .

. . . but my spiral's interrupted by even more shouting upstairs.

LAUREN

I can't cope with how they're looking at me. My friends. My supposed *best* friends – who've had my back since I was nineteen, are now staring at me like I've openly smacked Woody around the face, rather than left him in his cot for a moment.

'What the hell is going on?'

Nicki appears at the top of the stairs – her puffy face tear-stained and red – and Charlotte explains like I'm not even here.

'Steffi picked up Woody after Lauren left him to cry.'

'I didn't leave him to cry!'

I rock him and bounce my baby like he's a newborn, but he won't stop crying. He's still, clearly, traumatised by what I've done to him and I feel so guilty I want to bite off my own tongue to punish myself.

'Lauren!' Nicki says. Her judgement is immediate and searing as she takes in Woody's distress.

I twist to her, pregnant and clueless. 'Oh, fuck off. You have no idea what it's like. You will soon though, then I'll just love to see what you do.'

'What? You can't tell me to fuck off.'

'I just did.'

I bounce Woody harder, his roars short-circuiting my brain, feeling my grip let go, finger by finger. Why won't he stop crying? Why is he *always* crying? I have given him literally everything and he still always cries. He's taken my body, my identity, my free time, my sleep, my sanity, my marriage, my sex life, my independence, my savings, my friendships . . .

everything that's good about my life, I've pulped it to blood on the altar of motherhood, and yet he still always cries. It's still never enough. Every day, I realise, it won't be enough. I'll forever fail him and let him down and fuck him up and hate myself for it, and he'll hate and resent me for not doing a better job. And now my friends think I'm doing a terrible job, when I literally couldn't try any harder than I'm trying . . . I have nothing left to give this and yet they're staring at me in utter disgust.

Steffi steps in between us. 'Hey, come on. This is all going a bit mad.'

'Oh you can fuck off too,' I say. 'You started this.'

'I started this? By trying to help you?'

'You're judging me,' I scream. 'And not just about Woody crying. You're judging how fat I am, and how boring I now am and how shit my clothes are. I saw your face in the car park when I picked you up . . . thanks for keeping me waiting for so long my fucking baby woke up.'

I can almost see Steffi's skin prickle. She takes a step forwards, 'Oh and you're not judging me? I heard you and Nicki earlier, outside on the decking. Saying I was, what? Selfish? You're allowed to openly judge me and bitch about me and I'm not allowed to, too?'

She heard us? There's a faint pang of guilt but very little room for it when I realise she does think I'm fat and frumpy and a shit, boring mother. I knew it. Why does everyone lie to my face? I've had a child, not become one.

Nicki steps forward. 'Steffi, I really don't think you're in a place to judge mothers. I'm just saying . . .'

348

Steffi turns on her, practically growling. 'Oh, what a surprise! Sweet, wonderful Nicki is jumping on any opportunity to shove a knife in my back. You're so boring.' She rolls her eyes. 'I'm sorry Nicki, you know. I'm sorry I shagged your husband before you met him. I did it deliberately actually. You see, I'm psychic, and I knew he was your future husband and I deliberately did it to spite you. *You're* the victim. Congratulations! Not me. Not the one who happily stood aside.'

'Stood aside?' Nicki laughs. 'Matt wasn't interested in you.'

'Oh thank you for pointing that out again. You've been so nice throughout this whole thing. You do realise I did nothing wrong? And you've been nothing but hateful to me since you got engaged. I've taken it and taken it and I'm even here. At your fucking baby shower, with a present, and you still bitch about me . . . But, yeah, *you're* the victim.' Steffi starts clapping. 'Poor, poor Nicki. Well done.'

STEFFI

I feel a bit hysterical. Maybe it's the heat, but my brain is just letting it all out, telling everyone how I really feel. I feel almost victorious as I look at Nicki, cradling her bump, her face more sneer than actual face as I finally get to say how I feel. I'm so done with their judgement. It means nothing about my personality, or my levels of caring, that I don't want to have children. Currently I'm more maternal than bloody Lauren, who is now crying as hard as her baby. I'd feel sorry for her if she hadn't been screaming abuse at me. I honestly don't know who this wreck of a woman is. If this is what having a baby does to you, I've definitely made the right choice.

Charlotte steps forward into our bullring and I stand straighter, preparing for further attack. I've ruined her perfect baby shower. I'm selfish and I'm awful . . . but, instead, she turns to Nicki.

'Nicki's got a lot to say today, hasn't she?' Charlotte's eyes are squinting into currants. It looks like she's been crying. In fact, all of us appear to have been crying. 'I overheard you too just now, bitching about me with Phoebe, calling me basic. You were taking the piss out of today.'

'Charlotte, I'm sorry. I said I'm sorry.'

'So, I'm extra? So what? You know that about me. I've always been like this. To ridicule me, when I've worked so hard to make today perfect. To give you this surprise.'

Nicki lets out a sigh. 'I said I'm sorry Charlotte, OK? But come on. Please. Let's all be honest here.

Today wasn't about me. It was never for me. It's all for you. Sorry to be the bitch who says it, but you've been using me today. To have the baby shower you can't—'

We all gasp. Charlotte actually takes a step back.

'Did you honestly just say that out loud?' I ask.

'Come on, Steffi. You think it too. We've all been thinking it.'

'Nicki, I think you've said enough today,' I warn her.

'Oh yeah, yeah. It's not like you'd listen to me anymore anyway, as I'm one of those bores who drone on about having a baby. It's obviously so *beneath you*, this hugely important thing people do. I mean, my children are going to be paying taxes so someone can wipe your arse in the care home, but you're upset because a baby might be noisy in your restaurant . . . then you wonder why men think you're selfish . . .'

'Oh, shut up,' Charlotte screams, so loudly even Woody's momentarily silenced. 'All of you just shut up.'

CHARLOTTE

They don't know how lucky they are. These women. These women I'm so stupid to have called friends.

'All of you just to shut up,' I hardly recognise my voice. I never knew I could be so loud and throaty. 'Lauren, yeah, having a baby is hard. But you know what's harder? *Not* being able to have a fucking baby. Do you know how much that hurts? You have the most precious thing in the whole world. I'd sell a kidney to have what you have, and then you let it cry in the dark because you're tired? You didn't even try . . .' I start crying. I need to go to the bathroom. I need to check how bad it is down there. I need to get to a hospital. It feels bad. Everything feels so bad.

'No!' Lauren shouts back. 'I'm sorry Charlotte, but no. I'm so fed up of being told how lucky I am, when my life's been actual hell for nine months. Hell.' She starts weeping again, getting her tears in her baby's hair. 'I'm sorry for what you're going through and I'm so careful, but I'm so fed up of not being allowed to say what it's like, what it's really like. How hard it is.'

'I'd kill for your hard life right now.'

'I get that, but I'm allowed to complain. Please!'

'No. You don't get to complain! You *chose* this . . . and babies don't sleep! What did you think would happen?'

Lauren shakes her head. 'You have no idea . . . no idea—'

'Well, I'd kill to be as tired as you. So shut up.'

'No, *you* shut up. I feel so gagged. Like I can't complain. When every day is so long and hard and . . .'

'SHUT UP.' I'm so angry I could combust.

Steffi steps into the middle. 'I really think we need to stop telling each other to shut up—'

'Oh, shut up,' Nicki hurls at her. 'Go and post a link to another article about how boring parents are. You don't think that's telling us to shut up?'

'You shut up,' she hits it back. 'You smug fucking—'

'You can't tell me to shut up, I'm pregnant!'

'Oh whoop de doo, you're pregnant,' I scream. 'Everyone's so fucking pregnant. You all get pregnant just by blinking and then you can't shut up about it.'

'Stop it, Charlotte.'

Woody's screams are a horrific background noise to this horrific argument. We're all crying now, all of our fists are clenched. I hate them. I hate this. I hate today. I hate my broken body. I hate how I have to be happy for everyone when I'm drowning in grief.

'Shut up.'

'You shut up.'

'No, you.'

The baby's howling. Lauren sobbing as she tries to console him. I don't even feel sad, just curdled with envy that she has a baby she gets to comfort.

'Shut up, shut up, shut *uuuuuuup*.' I scream so loud that they all stop for a second. Then, in the few seconds of silence, as we all stare at each other in shock, I realise I can't be here. Not with these women. These sad excuses for friends. Their energy is so toxic, no wonder my body is malfunctioning. I push past Lauren and run into the bathroom, locking the door, letting the rest of them scatter behind me.

Transcript: Inspector Simmons interviewing Nicole Davies, Lauren Powell, Steffani Fox, Charlotte Roth

Simmons: So, you say you were doing the gender reveal with your three best friends and that's how the fire started?

Nicole: Yes. I told you. We all went out onto the deck to set off the smoke grenade that Charlotte had bought. But it kind of exploded backwards, landing in the lawn. Charlotte had a bucket of water nearby, but it didn't put the whole thing out. By the time we got another bucket of water, the fire had already spread to the whole garden.

***

Simmons: And then what happened?

Lauren: We tried to put it out but the fire was moving so fast. We were running back and forth with cups of water but it was useless and so dangerous. We were all coughing. I had Woody with me and he was my priority. Our priority. We ran towards the house, calling 999 on our phones, but we quickly realised the house wasn't safe. The fire was everywhere.

***

Simmons: So you just left it to burn?

Steffani: No. We tried to put it out, but the water did nothing, and then the fire was all around us and we had to run. The heat was so intense, I honestly thought we were in hell. The 999 operator told us to get out. We ran to the front of the house and crammed into Lauren's car. It was a nightmare – we couldn't get Woody into his car seat. I had to clutch him on my lap. Nicki struggled to get into the front seat. She was coughing. I honestly worried we wouldn't get out in time.

***

Simmons: Is there anything you'd like to add to this statement?

Charlotte: Nothing further your honour.

Simmons: I'm not a judge.

Charlotte: Whoops.

Simmons: And what if I were to tell you that I don't think this adds up? The timings, the lack of photos taken of the reveal, the way I'm supposed to believe you were all suddenly best friends again after a big fight?

Charlotte: I'd want to know a bit more about your childhood to understand where your trust issues are coming from, to be honest. Because I don't lie. It's bad for my frequency.

NICKI

Charlotte screams and runs past Lauren, before locking herself in the upstairs bathroom. For a moment, we're united in our stunned silence, all desperately trying to metabolise what's happened.

I realise, in the course of only a few hours, I've managed to derail my entire life. I've ruined my marriage, and my most important friendships, only weeks before my baby's due. I clutch my bump in abject terror and try to figure out how to cope with the next five minutes.

'Fuck all of you,' Steffi announces, descending the stairs two at a time, her phone already out.

'Pleasant as always, Steff,' I call after her, before trying to make eyes at Lauren. We're the only two who haven't verbally attacked one another today and I could really do with having someone on side, but, as I take her in, I realise she's somewhere else entirely. She's blinking madly as she comforts Woody, but her eyes are unfocused, hovering in the mid-distance. She doesn't see me. She's just shhing him and bouncing him while tears pour down her face. She looks . . . I don't mean this in a cruel way, but she looks totally insane. Like, somebody needs to come and catch her with a butterfly net insane. I take a step forward, thinking I should help, but my brain's already racing back to its selfish default setting. Where's Matt gone? I need to catch up with him and fix everything. I can't deal with *this* right now. Lauren . . . the way she's been . . . I find it hard to be near her. It feels dark, contagious. I won't be like this when my baby is born, will I?

'Shh, shh, Woody. Don't cry. I'm here. Mummy won't go anywhere ever again. I give up. I won't try to have a life, I promise. Not when you hate me doing it so much. It's over. You won, baby. You won.'

'I just need to go find Matt,' I tell Lauren, who gives a tiny nod of her head. A snippet of a sane response. 'Then I'll be back and we have a cup of tea, I promise.' I don't think she's really heard me, but I make my way down the stairs as hurriedly as I can. When I reach the bottom, I hear her mutter to herself.

'Woody won't let us have a cup of tea anyway. Woody doesn't let me do anything.'

And, still, I leave her.

The heat is just as ridiculous as it's always been as I waddle outside, down the front steps, and onto the empty driveway, desperate to see Matt. But there's no supportive husband here to reassure me, just tyre marks in the gravel, and a message that comes through on my phone.

Matt:
I've taken the car for a drive. I need to clear my head.

I sink onto the gravel, my bump weighing me forward, and weep into my hands with my face pressed into the stones. He's going to leave me. I'm going to be a single mum. I can't be alone with this . . . this thing . . . this tidal wave in my life. I cry and cry, massaging my bump and panicking at the sheer irreversibility of it – apologising to it, telling it I don't know what to do, how I've let it down already.

My nostril wrinkles as I smell something off. I lean up, look around, and see smoke blowing across the driveway.

LAUREN

I'm a terrible mother. I'm a neglectful, resentful and awful mother. The horror in their faces. I will never be able to un-see their faces. I will never be able to un-see Woody's face – so confused and scared in Steffi's arms, wondering why I didn't come for him. Why didn't I come for him? I'm so selfish, and shit, and not cut out for this. Being a mother. A parent. Having a baby. It's broken me and keeps further breaking the shattered parts within me and I don't know what to do. I have to somehow keep going because I have a baby, and the only thing you can do is keep going, but I feel like I'm dead, and I don't know how. I'm sobbing so hard I can't stand. I try placing Woody down, but he crawls right to the edge of the stairs in an instant, so I scoop him up again, and carry him back down into the remnants of the party. There's wrapping paper everywhere, streamers, balloons, a wall full of flowers smashed to the floor. His face brightens at all the things to poke and shove into his mouth, and I figure he'll be OK here, for a second, while I fall head-first into the abyss. I plop him down and sink face-first into the sofa, sobbing in a way that shakes my entire body, as I contemplate the rest of my life and how fucked it is. There's no going back to before. To when I was happy, and free, and capable. When I could get a train and pick up a coffee and a croissant and a magazine at the station and look out as the landscape sped past the window, taking small, slow, sips. When I could work late, deliriously high on a deadline for a project I loved so much I felt it in my soul, messaging Tristan to say I'd sleep in the spare room, as the office cleaners sprayed desks around me, feeling so present, and wired, and complete. When Tristan and I would sleep late on the weekends, one

361

of us dashing out to get the good coffee and the croissants from the bougie deli, bringing them back to our sheets, sprinkling them with pastry dandruff, flicking through a newspaper supplement, before having slow, steady sex as the sun grew higher in the sky behind our thin curtains, our eyes locked on one another. When I would see at least one friend, at least once a week, gossiping over the syrup of cocktails, throwing my head back laughing, psycho-analysing every shred of their dating partner's childhood, getting into super niche discussions about super niche parts of a subcul-ture we were both into, while swirling delicious pasta around a silver fork, in total awe at how smart and brilliant my friend was, and how precious they were to me. When I could pull up a pair of jeans and do the button up. When I could set an alarm at nighttime on my phone and it would tell me, confidently, how much sleep I would get before I woke up. When I could read books. Go on walks. Go away for weekends, to see friends or new cities or cute cottages with a good pub next door. This life I had. This wonderful life that's a rotten carcass now because I've had Woody. I miss that life. I miss who I was. I hate this person – fat and sobbing on the sofa after giving her son his first traumatic core memory. I've been drowning every day since he was born, dead by the end of each of them though I lose track of the days – bloated with stress and worry and unpredictability, and yet, love too. Pulsing, powerful, *want-to-eat-him* love. The love is too much, very often. It hurts to love this much. To worry this much. To need to put him first this much. I almost don't want the love because it can only bring pain and worry and guilt. The guilt. I let my baby cry, alone in the dark, because I'm too weak and I never should've been allowed to have a baby and . . . and . . . I almost can't breathe I'm crying too hard. I bury my face further into the sofa and give into it entirely.

I don't notice anything other than my own misery until I hear a horrific shriek.

STEFFI

Well, I guess I'm back in this downstairs bathroom again. I should pay rent on it. It really does have a stunning view, looking out across the dried vista, as I push tears back into my eyes and get out my phone to comfort myself. The worst has happened now, I guess, and a calm settles – as I've learned it does when the worst happens. I was almost tranquil when Mum finally let go.

So, my friends do think my life is less than theirs because I don't want to have children. They *do* think I'm selfish and frivolous, and what was the last one, oh yeah, *unsafe* to look after them. I sniff again and go through my emails from today, re-reading all the amazing ones that have come in. I wouldn't get sent emails like this if I had a baby. The idea women can have it all is bullshit, Mum had always been honest and clear about that with me. She loved me and wouldn't change me for the world, but her life would be very different if she'd not had me. 'And it's not different in any better or worse way,' she'd once told me, one boring day in hospital. She was listing all the things she'd never be able to do now she'd been given a six-month time limit. *'Don't believe that lie my darling. Having a child isn't the better option that leads to the most happiness. In fact, it's a very limiting option that closes off a lot of paths. Be sure that path is worth it, that the others won't make you feel more whole.'*

Look at Lauren. Look what she used to be like. Amazing career. Lovely husband. And now look at the actual state of her.

The path does not seem worth it to me. I can see, now, why mothers judge me so harshly. It *has* to be worth it, in their heads, because their sacrifice has been so huge and it's so never-ending. They're jealous of my life and how they can't have it anymore. And they know – underneath their own propaganda – that my life is as good as theirs without such unrelenting sacrifice. I have all the things they claim their babies bring them and yet I have more.

A message dings in from Rosa and I read it with a half smile.

Rosa:
I will never have the words to thank you. You're my fairy godmother. You've changed my life, forever, in the best possible way. How can I ever make that up to you? I can't. But I can only ever be thankful.

I've let this bloody baby shower overshadow too much of today. A life-defining day. There's no party or presents for me, no punch or games or group activities. But today has been a magical achievement and I'm angry at myself for hiding from it all day. I start punching out emails, sending strategy voice notes to myself on my phone, I lose myself in the gorgeous warm bath of my career, the sanctuary of my inbox. I'm not sure what gets me to look up, but, after some minutes, I glance at the window and gasp.

The entire garden is on fire.

CHARLOTTE

I bend over on the toilet, and I howl and howl and howl. Everything I've kept in all these years. The envy, oh God, the envy. The resentment at how easy it is for everyone else. The endless complaining about how hard it is to have something I so desperately want. I can't do it anymore. I can't do more *I'm so happy for you*, and *don't worry about me my time will come*. If I have to like another baby announcement online, clicking 'like' on a black-and-white scan, writing '*congratulations*' and lying when I say, '*what amazing parents you're going to be*,' I will implode. So many people I know will make terrible parents and get to become them anyway. I'm not going to lie, I have my doubts about Nicki. She's always been quietly so selfish and used to getting her own way. There, I said it. You'll probably be a shit mum, Nicki, and yet there you go, out a baby pops. And Lauren. I thought she'd be amazing. She's so warm, and works with children's books, and was always there, crouched next to whoever was drunk and crying at the bus stop on a night out. But she just left her baby screaming . . . why? If I ever get pregnant, I promise I'll be the best mum. I promise I'll never leave it to cry. I promise I'll read every book, attend every class, be so responsive that I'm changing a nappy literally as the baby poos into it . . . please, God, I'll do it, I promise, if I just . . .

. . . but this magical thinking gets me nowhere. I have to accept it's the desperate nonsense of a pathetic woman who can't face reality. I thought if I threw the perfect day today,

I'd be rewarded, but there's just cramps in my stomach, and a trip to hospital to be told what I already know. I bend over and let myself feel sad, feel rage, feel shame, feel desperately sorry for myself. I know I need to call Seth, but I can't stand yet. I just can't. My entire soul is exhausted. There are no energy frequencies to tune into.

Then I hear the scream.

THE GENDER REVEAL

Woody crawls from exciting distraction to exciting distraction while Mama lies down. This is incredible. What a treat. He finds a mountain of wrapping paper and his hands crunch into it. He lets out a shriek of delight and crunches it beneath his palm, in awe at the force of himself. His eye catches the paper plate with cream on it, left on a side table. He crawls over and heaves himself up, pulls the plate down, where it lands with a splat against his chest. He giggles, then sits down and pushes his fingertip into the plate, noticing the feel of the cream against his hand, and how it leaves a trail of where he's touched it. A plastic cup draws him away. It must be held and sucked on. It's quite far away, near the big glass expanse of sky, but the journey is worth it. He will not rest until he's put the rim of that cup in his mouth. He crawls further away, lured by the cup, until he reaches it. The bliss of making it his. Of getting to crunch it as liquid dribbles through his vest. It tastes sweet like the milk. Mama doesn't usually let him do the grabbing he wants. She's always pulling him back and saying that '*no*' sound and, irritatingly, has a knack for taking something from him just before the delicious moment it reaches his mouth. But, as he looks behind to check on her, he sees she's still face down and making funny noises into the soft thing. Perfect.

This cup is just as amazing as he thought it would be. It feels great on his gums. A new sensation drifts against his skin, a warmth, coming from somewhere. The cup is dropped. This feeling must be investigated. He crawls towards the brightness where a breeze drags in more hot air. Someone has left open the sliding doors onto the decking. Woody giggles again, crawling faster until the texture beneath his hands changes from laminate floor to rougher wood. There's birdsong out here and gaps in between the planks to poke his fingers through. Something shines in his eyes and his gaze settles on a metal ring, poking out from a gap. He crawls over, checks once more on Mama, who, in the dark inside, is still here but not watching, and gets to the shiny hoop. It's hot in his hand. He tries to lift it to his mouth but it's stuck. This won't do. He must put it in his mouth, that's what needs to happen to everything. He tugs. It doesn't move, but the tugging is fun. He wraps all his fingers into the hoop and tugs some more, sitting upright in the sun with perfect posture. Is there a loosening? He senses it. One more big tug . . . almost . . . almost . . .

Too many things happen at once.

He falls backwards as the ring comes with him and knocks the back of his head on the decking. He lets out a scream, just as there's a clanking sound of metal landing on dry earth below, and pink smoke bellows out and up, rising up over the deck. Woody doesn't know whether to cry because he's knocked his head, or clap because this smoke is very pretty and exciting. He cries and claps at the same time. Then the smoke changes colour. It becomes grey and fuggy and it's too hot, too hot. Another scream comes from behind him.

NICKI

I clutch my bump and waddle back towards the house, too stunned to consider how dangerous it is for our lungs. The smoke streams over the glass walls in cascades while I try to figure out what's going on. Is there a barbecue in a neighbouring property? But they're fields away, it would have to be a big barbecue . . . I push through the front door and start coughing. Smoke's billowing into the house from the back garden through the open sliding doors, surrounding total chaos. Lauren's collapsed on her knees in the middle of the sitting room, clutching Woody and screaming hysterically while Steffi frantically rocks her.

'My baby, my baby, they're going to take my baby,' she's screaming. 'They're going to take him . . .'

'Lauren, we need to get out of here. Get up, get up, please.'

Charlotte's got a stork napkin held to her mouth and she's shouting down her mobile phone. 'Yes, there's a fire. It's an emergency. Come now. There's four of us here, and a baby.' She coughs. 'Quickly,' she shouts down the line. 'The whole garden has gone up already.'

'What's going on?' I shout, lifting my elbow to my mouth. I'm still in some dumbfounded state, not quite able to take it in. My parent's garden is on fire. My best friend's screaming on the floor. I'm pregnant yet inhaling heavy smoke. The heat feels like it's melting off my top layer of skin.

'My fault, my fault,' Lauren screams over the flicker of flames, rocking back and forth, pushing Steffi off her. Woody screams desperately in her arms.

Charlotte makes frantic arm motions to me. 'Nicki! Get out of here. You're pregnant. Go now. Drive.'

'Matt's taken the car.'

'Go to the driveway. Get far away, it's spreading quickly.'

There's a gentle hush of breeze, but in the inferno outside, it's like a dropped can of gasoline. We all scream as the fire seemingly jumps from the burning grass up onto the decking and sets that ablaze too.

'My parent's house . . .' I'm finally starting to comprehend the sheer disaster of the situation. 'It's burning . . . I have to . . .' What? Rescue what I can? Try and put it out?

'We need to go,' Steffi's yelling, trying to pull Lauren up but she's still lead on the floor. 'Lauren? Please.'

I can't let my parents' house burn down. I move forward to the kitchen. If I get some water, maybe I can . . .

'Step back,' Charlotte yells, stopping me. 'You're pregnant. You need to leave.'

'I can't let it burn, I—'

'The fire brigade is on its way. They've told us to get into a car and drive away. There's a wildfire risk. We have to get out of here. Lauren, you have to leave, now.' She bends down and fully smacks Lauren around the cheek. I gasp and it makes me start to choke. I feel distress kicking inside me. I start backing towards the door, my eye streaming from the smoke, the air in the room bubbling and warping under the heat.

'If you don't get up now, Woody is going to die,' Charlotte screeches at her, dragging her to her feet. 'Get the fuck up. Get the fucking fuck up now.' They carry Lauren towards me, Woody crying in her arms. I lead them out of the house, my back burning up from the temperature. The air's only slightly better out here. The fire's now spread to the trees on either side and they're dancing with angry flames, engulfing the whole house.

'Where are your keys?' Lauren sobs something about them being in her handbag. Steffi grabs the bag as we rush down the steps and holds them up. The driveway's empty now and as we rush to Lauren's car, I dimly think how, only half an hour ago, it was crammed full of guests for my baby shower. My baby shower which is now burning down inside my parents' home. A house I'm fleeing and allowing to incinerate. The flames feel like they're almost licking us from the burning foliage around the drive. We're all coughing now. Woody's stopped crying and is coughing too.

'I'll drive,' Charlotte pushes Lauren down into a backseat, who's still wailing, 'My baby, they're going to take him, I'm sorry, I'm so sorry, I . . . don't . . . please . . .' She points to me. 'Nicki, get in front. Steffi, take Woody.'

I fling open the door and try to get inside but my bump is so bulbous and huge that I feel like my face has melted off by the time I manage to get into the seat. Steffi's yelling behind me. 'I can't do up the car seat. The buckles . . . I don't know how.'

Charlotte's already turned on the engine. 'Just hold onto him and let's go,' she shouts back. 'Now.'

She slams the car door and we're flung back as she revs down the gravel and out onto the countryside lane. Lauren's wails are all I can hear as we leave the house in the rearview mirror, shimmering in the heat.

LAUREN

My baby. My baby. They're going to take my baby. I left him and he's started a fire and almost died and they're going to take him. I hate myself. I hate myself. Please, God, no, don't let them take my baby. Everything's burning down. I don't understand what happened. I left him for one minute. One. How can this happen in one minute? Charlotte's driving my car. Woody's screaming in Steffi's lap. I can't breathe. Going to take him away. All I've wanted is for someone to take him away, but now I'm ripping at the seams, every organ is screaming, they can't take him, they can't. But he could've died. A house is burning. I can't. I can't. No.

STEFFI

Charlotte's so tiny she can hardly see over Lauren's dash-board. The heat in here's so intense that we roll down the windows, but the burning horizon engulfs the car. The smoke is following us downwind. Woody's squirming on my lap, and, even though Charlotte can't be doing more than 40mph, I'm clutching him with every ounce of my being; I'm so scared he's going to fly out the windscreen. My lungs ache from the smoke. I still can't understand if this is real or not. I can't have read an email on the toilet while a house burnt down around me. Lauren is gurgling next to me, her eyes rolling about in her head. The state of her. My best friend – the one who's always there, always cheerful, always the glue of the group – is now a broken toy. I want to cry but the baby in my arms is already too upset. Thoughts surge through me as the smoky breeze blasts my hair. *I could've died. Any of us could've died. Woody could've died.* The fire's still burning, it's everywhere. *Is someone else going to die?* I pat Woody's hair, say *shh shh*, to both him and Lauren. I try to keep going through each breath.

Nicki's on the phone to her parents. 'Mum? Mum. There's been a fire . . . it's bad . . . where are you? Stay away . . . fire brigade coming . . . Yes, I'm safe. We're all safe . . . Where's dad? Are you sure he's still that far away? Call him and check . . . Yes . . . I know . . . I'll call again soon.' She hangs up. 'What the fuck just happened?' Nicki twists around, sees the state of Lauren, and faces forward again. 'What happened?'

'My baby,' Lauren just sobs and sobs, folding inward on herself. 'They're going to take him. Please, stop them, please.' Charlotte and I share a desperate look in the rear-view mirror.

'I'm not precisely sure,' Charlotte says, speeding along, her voice deeper and calmer than I've ever heard it. 'But I think, somehow, Woody went out onto the decking and managed to pull the top off the smoke grenade.'

'My fault, it's my fault,' Lauren says.

'Shh, honey. He's OK. Everyone got out OK.'

'It's my parents' house,' Nicki says, almost dumbly. 'We need to go back.'

'Yes, yes, in time,' Charlotte says. 'Let's just get out of the way of the smoke first.'

Her complete air of calm is jarring considering Char-lotte generally acts like every second of her life are the final ones of cramming before a major exam. She's almost *zen*. I've never seen her zen. Not even when she accidentally ate half a pot brownie at a third-year house party, insisted she would die, and made me take her to hospital for 'monitor-ing'. She dictated her funeral plans into her phone while eating the entire contents of the Sheffield hospital vending machine.

'I'm a terrible mother,' Lauren cries to my side. 'I'm awful. You all think it.'

'Shh, honey. It was an accident.'

'I left him. I left my baby and look what happened. Everything's on fire. He could've died. You're all going to tell. I'm going to lose him. I can't lose him.' She screams and Woody starts screaming too, fighting to go into his mother's arms, squirming against me as I struggle to hold him.

'Lauren, careful . . . careful . . . Woody, no, Woody.'

'I need to get out. I can't breathe. I need to get out. LET ME OUT.'

She lurches past me and makes a grab for the door handle. Woody attaches himself to her hair and we become enmeshed in a disastrous web of entangled limbs.

'Please,' Charlotte calls back. 'Please stop, Lauren, please.'

'LET ME OUT LET ME OUT LET ME OUT.'

'Hang on. I need to find somewhere.'

'I can't hold them both,' I yell. Nicki awkwardly tries to twist and help but she's blocked by her bulging stomach. The car tilts as we ascend a winding countryside hill and I close my eyes for a second to ground myself in whatever mad hell is occurring around me.

'LET ME OUT LET ME OUT LET ME OUT.'

'Lauren, please. I see a viewpoint. Hang on. Hang on.' Charlotte hard turns right and we're flung around the car, everyone yelping, until we screech to a halt on a tiny gravel parking bay with a long bench overlooking the view.

'Give me my son.'

I'm too startled to do anything other than let Woody hurl himself into her arms. Then Lauren's out of the car with him, running past the bench, into the horizon. She stands and watches the view for a moment before her knees cave in and they both drop to the dusty ground. She hangs her head and sobs into her baby's hair, while the rest of us stagger out towards her. Above their silhouette, the smoke billows across the vista and dancing patches of orange flicker as they eat their way through the parched field like termites. Below us, we hear the urgent wail of a fire engine.

CHARLOTTE

I've been preparing for a catastrophe like this my entire life and now it's here, like I always knew it would come. In emergency situations, only ten to 25 per cent of people behave reasonably and make life-saving decisions. Most people – around 80 per cent – will be generally stunned and bewildered. And the final ten per cent totally malfunction, often with associated screaming and hysteria. Seth's made fun of me our whole marriage that the first thing I do whenever we book into a hotel is to look at the fire evacuation posters and then inform him of our means of escape. I also go out into the corridor and count how many doors there are between our room and the fire exit, as you often have to do it in darkness or in a corridor filled with smoke. Right now, everything is playing out, statistically, pretty perfectly and yet I'm on the very edge of coping. I'm the only one holding us together and the one keeping us alive, but it's much harder in real life than the simulations I run in my head. *I got us out,* I tell myself, as Lauren cries and screams on the ground. Steffi's bending down to try and calm her and I allow myself a few moments to gather myself. *We're alive.* The biggest mistake people make in disasters is not getting out quick enough, and I managed it. The memories are already fireworking around my brain in technicolour, setting off further adrenaline shots. Catherine wheels of disjointed sequences . . . running downstairs and finding the garden ablaze. Woody sitting, unaccompanied on the decking,

almost eclipsed by smoke as Lauren screamed herself frozen
. . . seeing the bucket of water and chucking it over the fire as
soon as I could but knowing it was way beyond that . . . how
Lauren wouldn't move . . . she grabbed Woody and wouldn't
move . . . trying to help her and everyone evacuate, but also
trying to put out the fire . . . My hands are shaking against
the parched ground but they are allowed to shake now. We're
out. *We're alive.* But the entire horizon is burning and I still
can't believe Lauren would allow this to happen.

She's screaming into the sky like she's having some kind of
exorcism.

'They're going to take him away. They will. They will.'

'Shh, it's alright,' Steffi's rubbing her back while sending us
panicked eyebrows. Nicki's staring in horror down at them.
They are the stunned 80 per cent. Lauren's the malfunctioning one. It's up to me to pull this together. I must prioritise.
We escaped. We're alive. We're out. First priority sorted. The
fire. The engines are on their way, there's nothing more I can
do. Nicki's parents' house . . . I doubt it will be salvageable.
But the most pressing matter is my friend in front of me. My
friend who, for whatever reason, was lying down when her
baby went out onto the decking and pulled open a smoke
grenade. How is that even possible? How is it Woody's alive?
Seemingly unharmed. But Lauren's right . . . she left him . . .
he almost died. We all did. If social services find out . . . it's . . .
this, right now, this is the priority. Mending Lauren. Calming
her and Woody down. Then I need to check we're all OK
from smoke inhalation, and, yes, I really do need to get to
hospital about this potential miscarriage. But not yet. Not
quite yet.

We all gently crouch around Lauren who's still hyperventilating into her baby, wailing as he wails. I've never seen anyone so broken. She's stroking Woody's hair which is sodden with tears. Her eyes are wild and unfocused, her legs splayed at awkward angles. And, as I stare at her, everything that was said between us evaporates like vapour. Any jealousy or resentment or rage, it just goes.

I put my hand on her shoulder and she jolts. 'Lauren? What happened?'

Each word is uttered between sobs. 'You know what happened. I left my baby unattended and he's burnt down the whole country.'

Woody's clambering out of her arms, wanting to seek refuge from her smothering. I bend down and collect him and Lauren lets me, folding in on herself, crying harder while Woody burrows into my neck for comfort.

'I ask this without judgement,' I say, using a calm and steady voice as I pat her back. 'But what was happening when he crawled out?'

'I . . . I was upset . . . I was crying. I was crying so hard I couldn't . . . I thought he was safe in there, didn't realise the door was open . . . I . . . I'm so exhausted. I didn't check though. I'm so careful with him, I promise. But I'm so . . . today has been so much . . . the one time I don't check,' she says. She lowers her head to her knees and gives herself a moment to fall against rock bottom again. Woody's gone still, clutching the material of my dress in his tiny, chubby hands while we all watch his mother. After a second or two, she raises her head and talks again. 'I've fucked up my life. Everything is fucked up. I hate my life. *I hate it.* I'm so trapped and there's no . . . respite, ever again, and today, it just got too much and I only needed a minute, one to cry and get myself together, and this . . . this . . .' she throws her arms out to the smouldering vista '. . . this happens because I dared to give myself a moment. And now they're going to take him, take him, my darling baby . . .'

Lauren cries into the breeze carrying fire across faraway fields. We all share a look as our own personal dramas fade, our focus on this crumpled heap of our best friend. Steffi rubs her back. While Nicki lowers herself tenderly to the ground to join her.

'I thought everything was OK?' Steffi asks, her fingers running circles around her spine. 'With Woody? You seem—'

'I'm a fat disgusting miserable mess and a terrible mother,' Lauren interrupts. 'If I seem anything else then it's a lie. I'm so unhappy,' she starts crying harder, somehow, trails of phlegm landing in her hair. 'I'm so agonisingly unhappy. Having Woody has taken away everything that I loved about my life. I worked so hard to have all these good things in my life to make sure I was "ready" to try for a baby, and then, overnight, having a baby has robbed all those things from me. Honestly, each day I wake up and it's like being punched in the face. I haven't slept for more than three hours in almost a year. He just won't sleep. And he won't take a bottle so I can't get any rest.' She thumps the ground. 'And fucking Tristan keeps leaving me with him, even though I'm on the brink of drowning at any given moment, and I lose it with Woody all the time. I shout in his face. I tell him to shut up. I once threw him across the bed . . .' She gasps. '. . . you can hate me, I hate me. For what a shit mum I am. For how I'm getting so little joy from my baby when I know I should feel lucky. I get to the end of each day and all I can do is catch a breath, maybe take a shower, then I go to bed by 8.30 as I'm so exhausted, and another day is over, and all I've done is survive it. Then I'm woken three hours later, and it all starts again. I have no plans for my life anymore, apart from to just survive each day, and I honestly don't see how this will ever get better.' She smacks the grass again as she shakes her head and tries to wipe her tears away with sooty, dirty, hands. 'And, do you know what?' She asks, almost in a whisper. 'Now this has happened and they're going to take Woody away. They'll probably put me in prison, won't they? And you know what I thought, as we were driving away from the fire just now? I thought "*at least in prison I'll be able to get some sleep*". I may never see my baby but at least I'll get eight hours and be able to take a shit by myself, and maybe exercise and read a book in jail . . .' She has no words left, only sobs, ones that convulse her whole body. We clutch at her and she clutches back, while I sit Woody on the ground in front of me and he happily grasps at dandelion clocks. I admit I'm starting to waver at holding it together. The significance of the last half hour is smacking me full whack as we try to comfort our drowning friend. Prison . . . Lauren's right. She could go to jail for this . . . I stare out at the faraway blaze that's nowhere near finished burning. So much damage already . . . Even though it was an accident, so much has been destroyed, the police may have to prosecute someone . . . Will I get prosecuted too? I'm the one who took off the safety cap. Then Lauren lets out a gasp and fully hugs us, her smoky hair in my face, and I'm pulled back to now and filled with love. This moment. My friend who needs us right now.

'I had no idea,' Steffi murmurs. 'You've not said anything. Not at all since he was born.'

Lauren sniffles and pulls away. 'What can I say? I can't tell Nicki because she's about to go through it all herself and I can't be the bitch who scares her off. Anyway, maybe it will be fine for you, Nicki. I hope so much it is. Maybe you won't almost die in childbirth, and hypnobirthing will work for you, and you won't want to scream every second since your baby comes out because you're not a shit mother like me.' Nicki opens and closes her mouth uselessly. 'And I can't talk to you, Charlotte, sorry, because I know how much you desperately want this. And, Steffi, I love you, but I couldn't . . . I know part of you would be . . . well . . . thinking you're right about this *having a baby* stuff.' It's Steffi's turn to open her mouth and close it again. 'Not out loud,' Lauren adds. 'But you're thinking it . . . I've tried to get help. I called my doctor but all they can do is give me medication that will give me side effects for a few weeks before they help. I'm hanging on by such a thread that I can't even imagine things getting worse before they get better, so I've not filled out the prescription. There's a waiting list for counselling,' she said. 'Probably about *two years,* said the GP, if I'm not dead by then. I'm hoping things with Woody will get easier anyway. Everyone says it gets easier but then they also say it stays hard, but gets hard in different ways, so you can never get on top of it and never feel like you're doing a good job. I used to be so good at my job! At being a friend. At being a wife. A daughter. And now I'm failing at everything but most of all I'm failing at being a mother, I've never failed so much at something, and look at today, look at that . . .' She thrusts her arm out towards the blaze below us. Nicki takes my hand and I can't even imagine what it's like for her, being pregnant and hearing this, watching her parents' home disintegrate from afar. But, like me, we're currently focused on Lauren and the things she's saying, the pain she's bleeding. The pain I can't believe I've missed until now. All I saw were her occasional social media posts, with jokes about no sleep juxtaposed against a picture of a baby made almost entirely of pudgy cheeks that made me shiver with envy. I saw the picture but didn't listen to the words. I saw the baby but didn't see the mother. I didn't see my friend when she most needed me to see her.

'Tell us about it,' I say, stroking Woody's hair, who is still in my arms, sucking his thumb, oblivious to the chaos he's caused with his innocent, beautiful, existence. 'Tell us what's happened to you.'

Nicki takes her hand and holds it to her heart. 'Yes, tell us. I won't be scared. I'd rather know, Lauren.'

'And I won't secretly think I'm right,' Steffi promises. 'I'll just be here for you.'

'We're all here for you,' I say. 'Just tell us.'

The sirens can be heard in the distance, but they're background noise, undistracted by Lauren having a chance to say it and have someone listen. She talks us through her birth, in explicit detail, weeping as she details the agony and fear. She details the days left alone in hospital afterwards. The helplessness. The feeding issues. The sleeping issues. The tongue tie issues. The everything-but-nowhere-to-get-help issues. She tells us how she hurts herself sometimes so she doesn't hurt Woody when he wakes. All of it's a horror story and yet I've heard it all before from other mothers. I've just not wanted to listen because it wasn't happening to me, and I was too jealous. They've tried to tell me that birth is terrible, that services are broken, that husbands are useless, that babies don't sleep and society still expects you to function like they do. I know that breastfeeding is incredibly difficult. I know that everyone hates mothers – the space they take up, the way they sag, their prams in our way, their children ruining the nice dinner you're paying for. I know that childcare is cripplingly expensive and oversubscribed. I know post-natal depression is incredibly common. I know all this. They keep trying to tell us. But I haven't listened or tried to see it properly – for my own reasons. But, today, I stop wishing Lauren would shut up and be grateful. I stop secretly thinking 'well you chose this'. And I try to listen instead. I let her cry on me instead.

Lauren details every meltdown, breast infection, failed attempt to improve Woody's sleep, failed attempt to improve Woody's feeding so it might improve the sleep, every argument with Tristan, every person tutting at her in public for not controlling Woody or leaving the pram in the wrong place. Every strange physical symptom of severe sleep deprivation – the eye twitches, the hallucinations, the intense tempers, the endless tears. She details every call to the health visitors' centre that never gets returned, the blocked accounts on Instagram for accusing others of misinformation, the 'car crash' of her postpartum vagina and how she once dared look at it and vomited. She detailed every full-on minute of the never-ending process of growing a baby and birthing a baby and then keeping it alive and happy. Feed by feed, nap by nap, wonder week by wonder week, tooth by tooth, developmental leap by leap, health scare by health scare, play group by play group, nursery rhyme by nursery rhyme, tidy-up by tidy-up, bedtime routine by bedtime routine, night wake by night wake. The sheer, audacious, everyday relentless effort of motherhood – such an exhausting, all-encompassing 'gift'. One I'm still desperate for, but, for once, I'm looking at the mother and feeling something more than jealousy. I'm ready to try and understand.

'In that moment on the sofa, all I wanted was for someone to take it all away,' Lauren says. 'To just have it taken away so I could be me again, just for a second.' Her voice goes up. 'And now this has happened and they really will take him away . . . I can't . . . I love Woody so much, I promise.' The sobs explode out of her. 'I know that makes no sense with everything I've just said, but I love him . . . I can't bear . . .' She reaches towards me and pulls him into her lap and he nestles into her neck. I marvel at what a happy baby he is, the love so evident on his face. A safe baby. A secure baby. Lauren's somehow doing such a *brilliant job* through all this, if only she could see it, believe it, get some help, have a break, be seen, be heard, be listened to.

She rocks with him, presses her nose into him, and takes deep sniffs of his scent. 'I know what I've done . . . Just look at what I've done . . . Neglect . . . I . . . Social services. Prison. They can't take my baby, can they? Will they take my baby for this?

'No,' I shout. 'They won't take him. I won't let them.'

I know there's due process. I know there's law and order. I know a valley is burning to ash, but no. I love due process.

I love law and order. But no. It's not right, or fair, and I refuse for my friend to be punished.

'Me neither,' Steffi adds, hugging both Lauren and Woody at the same time, like she's throwing herself in front of them as a car heads right for them. 'We'll think of something,'

'We will,' Nicki adds, joining the hug as much as she can. 'We will.'

I push myself into their mass of bodies and we huddle together on the hill, breathing in each other's breath, painting each other with our sweat. I clutch tighter and they all copy, and, for a quiet, perfect moment, we are one organism – a fusing of womanhood and the love we have for each other. A new thing I know for certain arrives in my head. Today wasn't about making the baby shower perfect. It was about protecting Lauren. Rescuing Lauren. Loving Lauren. If I protect her as a mother, then I'm going to be OK. If I make Lauren alright, then my baby will be alright. If Lauren's alright, then I'll be alright. And Nicki will be alright. And Steffi will be alright. Woody starts laughing at being the centre of a human sandwich, clapping his hands. His laughter is the most precious sound I've ever heard, and it carries out over the vista.

Together, we're all going to be alright.

As the horizon burns, we make our plan. We will tell the same story. We will protect our own. None of us will break. None of us will give her up. They can't prosecute all of us. We are together in this, as it should be. I see that now.

'You can't do this,' she keeps saying. 'If you're caught lying . . .'

'We won't get caught lying,' Nicki says. 'We're in this together.'

She has her hand on her stomach, and Lauren reaches out and puts her own hand on top of it. Steffi follows and then I, until our fingers build a tower and Woody laughs again and reaches out to join in. Too much time has passed already and we break apart and make our way back to the car, our thighs sticky on the seats, the stench of smoke on our hair as it lifts on the breeze as we drive towards the hospital.

In hushed voices, we start to tell each other the truths we've been hiding. And, under the hum of the car engine, and the hum of our confessions, Woody finally falls asleep in his car seat.

Transcript: Inspector Simmons interviewing Nicole Davies, Lauren Powell, Steffani Fox, Charlotte Roth

Simmons: So, who was responsible for the fire?

Nicki: None of us. All of us. It was an accident.

***

Lauren: Nobody. It was awful, but none of us meant for it to happen.

***

Steffani: All of us, I guess? But it was just a terrible accident.

***

Charlotte: God?

NO CHARGES PRESSED FOR 'BLAZE-IC BITCH' BABY SHOWER FIRE

Police have dropped the arson investigation against the four women involved with a baby shower inferno, citing insufficient evidence.

The 'Blaze-ic bitches' – who started a giant wildfire with a 'malfunctioning gender reveal firework' – had been taken in for questioning, facing charges of arson for either starting the fire maliciously, or recklessly. But police say they are now satisfied the blaze was an unfortunate accident.

'We believe that the four women did everything they could to stop the fire spreading,' Inspector Simmons said. 'And, though it's clearly unwise to set off a pyrotechnic device during a heatwave, they did have water on hand to try and extinguish it and did everything they could to put it out.

'But obviously the huge devastation the fire caused will have a lasting impact on our community, and we're warning the public to use their heads when it comes to planning events that look good on social media.'

Transcript: Inspector Simmons interviewing Nicole Davies, Lauren Powell, Steffani Fox, Charlotte Roth

Nicole: Is that everything, Inspector? Because I really will have to pee in your helmet soon.

Simmons: That's everything. Your husband is waiting outside to pick you up.

Nicole: He is?

***

Lauren: Thank you, Inspector, sorry if we've not been more helpful.

Simmons: Are you sure there's nothing else you want to add to your statement, Lauren? There's nothing else you can think of?

Lauren: Yes, actually, the creche here is great. Can I only use it if I'm being accused of a crime, or, can I, like, just turn up sometimes with Woody?

***

Steffani: To be honest, I'm surprised you've not charged me just for not having a child. Surely that made me a key suspect?

***

Charlotte: And then we finally got to the hospital and I was rushed through, which is such a relief because the *germs* in hospital waiting rooms. Honestly. I had a head-to-toe film of antibacterial hand gel over my skin, which isn't ideal because of the alcohol content, it's very drying, you know? Plus, I was worried it would get absorbed through my skin and impact the baby even though Seth said that wasn't possible. Anyway, we were all rushed through, 'cos Nicki was pregnant, and Woody was so young, and I was pregnant, which was such a weird way to tell the girls . . . definitely not what I'd imagined. I was going to do this thing, after the 12-week scan where I officially invite them to be the godparents with special boxes of gifts . . . but . . . yes . . . thankfully none of us had any lasting damage from the smoke. They put Woody on oxygen just in case, but he was fine. Then I was rushed through to my scan, and guess what! A heartbeat! Can you believe it? I was crying and Seth was crying, and then I went out and told the girls and they were all crying. It was so magical to have something good happen that day after that awful fire. I can't believe I'm having a baby. Did you know that you need to tackle pregnancy nutrition from a three-point perspective? You need your daily nutrition needs met, which is really hard when you have nausea and only want to eat beige food—

Simmons:	Charlotte?
Charlotte:	—and, ideally, you should get those vita-mins made from ground-down food so you can absorb them properly. Then you need a high-quality fish oil to help the development of the nervous system—
Simmons:	Charlotte?
Charlotte:	—then a pro-biotic. Again, check it's good quality. You have to ensure the good bacteria is still alive by the time it hits your digestive tract and—
Simmons:	Charlotte!
Charlotte:	Yes?
Simmons:	You can go now. You're free to go. Go! Please!

Epilogue

The ice sculpture glistens in the middle of the nightclub, lit by neon purple, and surrounded by people attempting to take selfies with it.

'See,' Charlotte says, glancing over as she takes a delicate sip of her cocktail. 'Everyone was like, *"Charlotte, we don't need an ice-sculpture, stop being mental,"* and now the whole world wants their picture taken with the stone-cold fox.'

Steffi reaches over to hug her, almost spilling her drink in the process. 'I'm sorry. I was wrong. I was an ungrateful cow and I'm wrong. Please, always, immortalise me in ice.' Jasper's hand laces with hers and he tugs her back, kissing her cheek. 'Is it weird that I sort of fancy the ice-sculpture?'

Steffi hits him while the women at the table crack up. 'Not at all,' says Lauren, head tilted in the accepting, adoring way women tilt their head when they really *really* approve of a friend's boyfriend. 'I fancied Disney Robin Hood as a child, which is basically the same thing.'

'Didn't we all?' Nicki adds, pushing her drink into the table to get everyone to cheers. She is on her fourth and definitely on her way to having the most fun there.

Music thumps around them in the surrounding club, but it's almost drowned out by the clumps of industry people, dressed to the hilt, circling and networking, thirsty and grafting. The novelty of the A-list celebrities was sort of wearing off, although Steffi was still low-key concerned Charlotte was going to corner one in the toilets for a selfie. She gives herself a moment to stop and take it all in. This dream sequence of an evening. An afterparty to end all afterparties, following the movie premiere of all movie premieres. She thought she was legitimately going to combust with pride when she watched Rosa walk the red carpet – still as a deer in headlights as she'd been on that first hot day, all those years ago, when Steffi had told her the news down the phone. Now, she glances over at where she's huddled with Nina Baldwin near the ice sculpture, their arms around each other like best friends. Their eyes meet and Rosa mouths 'thank you' for what is likely to be the millionth time since they met. Steffi shrugs back, smiling, then returns to this table. The warmth of Jasper's hand in hers, and warmth of her three best friends falling as hard in love with him as she has.

He leans over and kisses her. 'I'm just going to the bar,' he whispers, his breath hot on her neck. 'Want anything?'

'Only for you to come back very quickly.'

'Done.' He leans in for one more kiss. 'By the way,' he adds. 'You're amazing. You know that, right?'

She manages to game-face – all the Little Women do – as he says 'ladies' and tips an imaginary cap before extracting himself from the table. But the moment he's absorbed by the crowd, the other three squeal and clap and wave their arms in the air.

'Oh my God, Steffi, I love him, LOVE HIM.'

'He's so obsessed with you. Honestly, the way he was looking at you when you made your speech. If you could bottle that look . . .'

'It's giving me hope,' Nicki says. 'Hope in men. At last! Hooray!'

Steffi isn't sure she'd be able to stop smiling even if someone paid her a million pounds, and not only because she doesn't need the money. 'He's great, isn't he? He's, like, such a cheeseball. But not a red flag cheeseball. Like, an actual one. He said "wowsers" when I got ready earlier. Out loud. In full sincerity. *Wowsers.*'

Lauren pats her head. 'He's not like anyone I've ever seen you with before and it's brilliant. I'm so *so* happy for you.'

'We all are,' Nicki says.

'Yes!' Charlotte adds, 'and not just because this has given us a reason to leave the house for the first time in months. '

Steffi finishes her cocktail and beams. 'Thank guys. And, yes, I really appreciate you all getting sitters.'

'Are you kidding?' Lauren asks, finishing her sparkling water. 'This is probably my last night of freedom in forever. I would leave Woody with Stalin to be honest as long as I can go out.' She rubs her giant stomach. 'Though I'm really hoping, this time around, it will take me less time to integrate into society.' She sighs. 'And I'm also, of course, really hoping I won't go stark raving mad again.'

'You won't,' Charlotte says. 'I'll send you a night nanny myself if needs must. Honestly, I don't know how I would've coped myself without Gillian. She even weaned me off my breastfeeding spreadsheet.'

Lauren rubs her hand. 'Thank you, but hopefully I won't need Gillian. Things will be different with this one. Tristan and I are in a much better place, plus we're going in with our eyes wide open . . . which is just as well as our eyes will be open a LOT next month, once they're here.'

'I promise you, if the sleep is bad again, Gillian is coming over.'

The women laugh and start chatting about the movie again, reiterating to Steffi how good it was. *Blood Moon* somehow did even better than anyone could've expected, and everyone expected a lot. The book was still on the New York Times bestseller list, almost two years later. And, if there were some people left in the world who hadn't bought a copy, they surely would after the movie came out, widely tipped to sweep the board at award season. Steffi still isn't sure this is all real – that tonight could get any more perfect. The premiere, Jasper, watching Rosa become a giant sensation, running the most successful boutique literary agency in London . . . but none of it was as important as the three women around her, there, supporting her, understanding just what it's taken for her to get here. Her family, really.

Nicki glances down at her phone and flinches. 'Eww.'

'What is it?' The others crane over to see.

'I thought dick pics were illegal,' Lauren says. 'Like, seriously? Men still do that?'

Nicki pushes her hair off her face and sighs as she hits the 'report' button. 'It's so strange to think that, until recently, I'd only ever seen two whole penises in my entire life.'

'No half penises?' Steffi quips and Nicki laughs.

'. . . then, I've been single now, what, a year? And I've seen dozens. Maybe even over a hundred. All unsolicited. It's . . . obscene.'

Charlotte grabs the phone. 'You should report them to the police,' she says. 'It really is illegal.'

'I've had enough to do with the police to last a lifetime. Honestly, it's fine.' She lays her head on Charlotte's shoulder. 'I'll adjust. Well, that's what I keep telling myself.'

'You will,' Charlotte pats her. 'And, in the meantime, I love having you in my granny annexe every other week.'

Steffi surveys Nicki with sympathy – something she never thought possible. Things between them had been much better since the fire, but it was only last year she felt she truly forgave her friend. Shortly after Matt and Nicki announced their divorce, she'd received a drunken voicemail from him at 1am. *'Do you ever think about what would've happened, that morning, if I hadn't gone down to get toast?'* Matt had slurred, so plastered she could hardly make him out. *'Because I do. I did. I've thought about it this whole time.'*

After she hung up on him, she'd not been able to get back to sleep, and turned on her light and stared at her walls for a very long time. Watching Matt and Nicki unravel had been one of the most painful things she'd ever witnessed. Poor Belle had been the total opposite of a 'band aid baby'. They fought constantly and relentlessly since she was born, and Nicki had finally accepted that Belle being a 'child of divorce' was better for her than a child of whatever the hell Matt and Nicki had become. They were now 'birdnesting' for a while. A term Nicki had used like Steffi was supposed to understand what it meant. Googling it afterwards, it seems to be an ill-fated attempt to minimise disruption to Belle's home life by taking it in turns to spend a week living in the family home with her, while the other parent stays elsewhere. Something only rich people could do, or, if you were Nicki, someone rich with even richer friends. Her and Charlotte had been seemingly having a blast in the granny annexe every other week – watching girly movies and wearing matching pyjamas. Steffi predicts the birdnesting will only last for as long as it takes for one of them to meet someone else, which if Matt's drunken call was anything to go by, won't be very long at all. She sighs into her drink, eyeing her friend, thinking how, maybe, at some point, she would've relished receiving that voicemail and the power it gave her. Now, she just felt sad and pissed off. And, she realised, with it, she'd totally understood Nicki's previous paranoia about her. It hadn't stemmed from nowhere. It had just been aimed at the wrong person. Not that Matt had ever behaved inappropriately with her their entire marriage, but still. An instinct is an instinct, and it turns out Nicki's was spot on. Steffi's own personal instinct is that Nicki was making a huge mistake by dismissing the Phoebe situation as a 'one off' regarding her sexuality. But things were still so new and raw with the divorce, maybe, with time, she'll be able to open up that side of herself? She leans back in the red leather of the booth, and gives herself one more moment to drink this all in. You know what? Having her friends here, celebrating this with the credence she had celebrated all their more-typical achievements, felt just as bloody good as she thought it would. And, she's the only one who got an ice sculpture.

She puts out her hand to interrupt them. 'Can I just say something?' She asks, and the three of them turn to her, eyebrows raised.

'I bloody love you, guys, just so you're aware. I really bloody love you.'

Three smiles return to her, the warmth of them like a furnace. 'We love you too, Steffi.'

'So much I immortalised you in ice,' Charlotte points out.

'I don't think it's immortalisation unless you drag that thing home and keep it in the freezer.'

This will be the last big celebration for them before the fortieth birthdays begin. The last invite requiring a paper invite and an RSVP.

We made it, Steffi thinks. Smiling back at them. *Whatever the last ten years are, and how babies changed everything, we made it.*

The Moment is interrupted by a loud clanging coming from across the club. A gong being bashed. A crowd parting. The Little Women turn their head with the rest of the room towards the direction of the noise, to find Jasper, heading right for them, his face gleeful and lit by the flickering gold of a firework. They all jump until they realise what's happening. It is one of those clubs where you can order a magnum of champagne and the staff bring it over with an indoor firework and a hoo-hah. Steffi rubs her heart, her shock morphing to embarrassed endearment.

'Surprise,' Jasper shouts, nobody ever looking prouder of themselves. He places the flaming bucket on the table in the middle of them, not noticing the Mexican wave of flinches. 'I got us champagne,' he adds, unnecessarily.

Steffi leans over to kiss him thank you while the bar staff continue to bang the gong to the side of him, the room cheering Steffi on, lit up by the spluttering fire.

Her eyes meet those of her best friends, the flames dancing in all of their irises, and they all reach for each other's hands, and hold them until the firework goes out. Even then, when the crowd bursts into applause, they keep holding hands.

Acknowledgements

WARNING, CONTAINS SPOILERS!

I have next to no memory of writing this book as I was so sleep deprived. The only proof I have that I wrote it at all is the book itself and various photos I took of myself with a laptop precariously balanced at an odd angle, trying to type while a newborn baby slept on my chest. I will forever consider this fever dream of a novel as one of my greatest achievements – one I couldn't have pulled off without the help of some amazing people.

Firstly, and most importantly, this novel couldn't have existed without the support of my incredible husband, W. In a stroke of delusional feminist optimism, I took only two weeks maternity leave while he 'took the career hit' and stayed at home to look after us and support my writing. Caitlin Moran once wrote that women marry their own glass ceiling, and I thought of how lucky I was to have done the opposite – typing out this story in delirious bursts between feeds while you held our darling baby. Thank you, and thank you, and thank you. Thank you for never being like the men I write about. Thank you for not even wanting to be thanked for doing this, for saying it shouldn't even be remarkable, let alone rewarded. I'm thanking you and rewarding you anyway. I could have so easily been Lauren, and Lord I came close, but you were always there to pull me back from the brink.

I also need to thank the brilliant Kimberley Atkins for taking me seriously when I rang her to say I wanted to write a book about a baby committing arson. Thank you, my dear friend, for not thinking I was crazy, but for instead spending the best part of two hours figuring out with me how we could make it plausible. Thank you for letting me send you multiple links to gender reveal fireworks online saying, 'do you see the ring pull on this one?'. Friends and cat sisters forever, no matter what happens.

Thank you, as always, to my agent Madeline Milburn too. I will never forget telling you I was pregnant, and then panicking over lunch that I'd ruined my career. I'll never forget the way you took my hand and told me the opposite could be true – that this could very well be the making of it. Your unwavering belief in me is such a life-support and I will never, ever, take it for granted and always try my best to make you proud. Thank you, also, for encouraging me to throw 'Your Baby, Week by Week' onto a bonfire. You were right. (What is it with me and fire, postpartum?).

My publishing team at Hodder has shown such huge enthusiasm for this book and I am so grateful to them for their passion and commitment. Thank you especially to Phoebe, for your insightful edits and giving me the confidence to push this manuscript to its limit. And thank you to Becca, for your excitable WhatsApp messages and unwavering support of my stories. I know there are many people behind the scenes who work on my novels who I never-to-rarely get to meet, but I am so grateful to all of you. Truly.

As always, my friendships have pulled me through the rough times of this transformative period of my life. Thank you to all of you who have held me steady. To Becky and Rachel, we DID go to the spa, and having our safe space to chat all things motherhood has been such a lifeline. To those of you who are always there: Josh, Claire, Ruth, Lucy, Sara, Tanya, Christi, Lexi, Sophie. To my 'mum friends' (obvs so much more than that) forged and cemented through sleep-deprived voice notes and panicked yelps for advice – Gillian, Farley, Natasha, Maartje, Marlene, Alice, Louie, Rosie, Suzie . . . basically any women out there in my life who replied instantly, with empathy and tips and solidarity, I'd be so much less sane without you. Also, huge thanks as always to my writing and publishing besties – Katie, Krystal, Sam, Alywyn, Nina, Kat and everyone else in the UKYA/Women's Lit world – you are always so supportive and awesome.

I really must take a moment to thank the legendary Sarah Carpenter, the woman who helped my baby finally sleep. Your generosity and wisdom and tolerance of my endless panicked WhatsApp messages is so appreciated. This book couldn't have existed without you.

I'd be nowhere without the support of my family, especially during this part of my life. To my parents – thank you for coming over so I can nap, the endless pots of red beans and rice, for being the best grandparents ever. And to my sisters, Eryn and Willow, the best aunties too.

And thank you, finally, to all the women writers who have come before me and spoken uncomfortable truths about motherhood. It's such an act of compassion and bravery, and I couldn't have found Lauren (or myself) without you.

Reading Group Questions

1. Were you surprised by who started the fire? What point do you think the author was trying to make, if any?
2. How did the author use symbols, metaphors and imagery to set the atmosphere of the novel?
3. Steffi reflects on how much effort she's made to attend her friend's weddings and baby showers, and how they didn't make the same effort for her agency launch. Do you feel we are less likely to celebrate the choices of child-free women, and if so, why might that be?
4. Who did you suspect while you were reading? And who did you have the most empathy for?
5. Discuss how social media impacts the characters and their relationships, considering baby announcements, hypno-birthing accounts and all the 'content opportunities' of the baby shower itself.
6. Lauren often compares herself to the concept of a 'Cool Mum' as a way of shaming herself for not coping. Where do you think this pressure comes from? Do we have a real-istic blueprint of motherhood for today's mothers?
7. Discuss Nicki's trajectory towards motherhood. Why do you think she made the decisions she did? Can you under-stand why?
8. Reflect on the scene where all the Little Women are screaming at one another to shut up, and discuss the ways in which women are silenced when talking about the issues around motherhood.
9. Did the Little Women do the right thing at the end of the novel by covering up the truth?
10. Did anything surprise you about the epilogue?

Keep reading for an extract
of Holly Bourne's hilarious and
searingly honest novel

How Do You Like Me Now?

Olivia Jessen

Six month bump alert. The belly has popped people, the belly has popped. #BumpSelfie #Blessed

81 likes

*

Harry Spears

I liked it so . . . I put a ring on it.

Harry Spears and Claire Rodgers are engaged.

332 likes

*

Andrea Simmons

Poo explosion! But look at that cheeky face . . .

52 likes

> *Comments:*
> **Olivia Jessen:** Oh no, Andrea. I've got all that to look forward to.
> **Andrea Simmons:** I'll give you a nose peg at your baby shower!

*

Event invite: Olivia Jessen's super-secret baby shower.

16 attending

*

Tori's WhoTheF*ckAmI? Official Fan Page

Alright my f*ckers! Who's coming to the London show tonight? I can't believe it's sold out! I love and adore you all. See you at seven. I'll be the one on stage with the microphone, wondering how the hell I got so lucky in life.

2434 likes. 234 comments.

★

I look out at a sea of earnestness.

There are too many faces to make anyone out individually, but there is a collective look. A collective glow. Their eyes are dewy; their hands are clasped.

They hang on my every syllable.

I'm getting to the good bit. The bit I know they've been waiting for. The bit I've been building up to. I walk across the stage in my designer heels and smooth down my designer dress. I look exactly how a successful woman should look. Groomed, plucked, highlighted, contoured . . . but not in an obvious way. I look right out at them. At their anxious, eager faces. And I say:

'That's when I realised it.' I raise one threaded eyebrow. 'Sitting there, cross-legged in that fucking tent in Sedona. Chanting bollocks with a load of wankers, wearing a rosary necklace for God's sake. That's when it hit me . . .'

I pause.

The audience stills. You could float a boat on the expectation filling the air.

'I was trying to *find myself* how everyone else finds themselves,' I say. 'I was having a nervous breakdown exactly how everyone else has a nervous breakdown and I was healing myself how everyone else tries to heal themselves. And I said to myself *NO MORE*.' I hold out my hand like I'm signalling stop. I pause again, waiting for the beat. '"Just who the fuck *am* I?" I asked myself. "What do *I* want?" Because life isn't a paint-by-numbers. You cannot find yourself along an identikit path. And, actually, even after my quarter-life crisis, even after this whole year of self-discovery, I was still twenty-five and doing exactly what had got me into this mess in the first place. I was doing what I thought I *should* be doing rather than what I fucking *needed* to be doing.'

A stray whoop. The audience softens into gentle laughter. I laugh, too, and it echoes around the walls, bounces out of the various speakers.

I nod. 'Exactly.' I pause to let them settle. I clop back to the other side of the stage. There is a hush. I blink slowly, trying to remember that moment. Trying to invoke the triumph I felt. Six years ago. On that day, that incredible day. The day where everything started going right for me.

'So,' I tell them. 'I opened my eyes, I uncrossed my legs, and I walked out of that stupid meditation yurt and never looked back.'

The applause is overwhelming, like it always is. It takes about five minutes for them to calm down, like they always do. I make my own eyes go dewy to show my appreciation, like I always do. Then I get around to telling them the rest of my story. The story they all know already. Because all of them have my book clasped in their hands, waiting for me to sign it afterwards. Waiting to have their moment with me. To tell me about their own messy twenties, their own terrible boyfriends, their own shitty jobs, their own smacking disappointments. And to tell me how my book, my words, my story helped them through. *Still* helps them through.

It's crazy really. I sometimes forget how crazy it is.

We don't sell many books despite the queue that snakes around multiple corridors. They all already have their copies. Battered copies with crippled spines and Post-its to highlight their favourite parts. I sign for over three hours – my grin stapled on, trying to keep my energy up for all the women who've waited so long for this moment.

This moment with me.

Like I'm special or something.

So I smile and smile and I high-five them when they tell me of their own adventures. I hug them when they cry. I lean in and listen carefully as they whisper their secrets. My publicist hovers, twitchy, and asks if I'm OK. If I need a break. If I want some water. I smile at her and say no. I'm OK. I'm fine. I'm managing. But thank you.

Every single person asks the same questions:

'So, when is your new book coming out?'

'What are you working on now?'

'Do you have a new project coming out soon?'

'I'm so impatient. How long do I have to wait?'

My smile goes tight and I tap my nose and say, 'Wait and see' and 'Watch this space.'

Then, of course, they also want to know:

'So, are you still together?'

'The guy you met at the end of the book? Are you still with him?'

'Are you still in love?'

They ask the way a child asks their parents if Santa Claus is real – their eyes big, wide with a mixture of excitement and fear. I know why they're excited and I know why they're scared. They're excited because if I can find him, they can find him. If I can make it work, they can make it work. If magic is real for me, it is real for them. I am the reflection of everything they want in their own lives. I'm essentially the Mirror of Erised.

They're scared because I could also be their albatross. If I can't make it work, who can? If magic doesn't work for me, it most certainly won't work for them.

I nod and simper and coo and look all bashful. I repeat the phrase over and over. 'Yes, we're still together. We live together now.'

Oh, how that makes them happy. They gasp. They demand photographs. They swoon, they sigh. Their eyes grow bigger and wetter and they are so relieved. It makes my own eyes water and I blink like crazy to stop it. Because they make me remember Us. The Us we were. The Us that we were when the story they clutch finishes. I can remember it so clearly – maybe because I've been forced to talk about it non-stop for six years . . .

'Are you OK?'

'Huh?'

I blink and look up at the face of a woman standing over me. Her entire body jolts with nerves; her fingers tremble on her copy of my book, which has over one hundred Post-its glued in.

'Sorry.' I smile and take the book off her. 'Now, what's your name?'

'Rosie.'

'Oh, that's a lovely name,' I say. It's what I always say.

'Thank you.'

I sign her book with the message I always write:

Dear Rosie,
Live the life you fucking need to live.
Love,
Tori xx

She's crying.

'Oh wow, thank you,' she stutters through her sobs. 'Can I . . . can I take a photo?'

I hand her book back. 'Of course, of course. Are you OK?'

She laughs a little and says, 'I'm fine, it's just so amazing to meet you.'

I hold out both arms warmly. 'Come here for a hug and a photo.'

Rosie hands her phone over to my publicist and is so

overcome with emotion she forgets to even ask if it's OK for her to take the picture. Then she clatters around to my side of the table and quivers next to me. I pull her in, putting my arm around her. She's hot and sweaty. Her dampness sinks into the crisp fabric of my dress, but this moment is worth more than my dress.

'Smile!' my publicist says, holding up the phone.

I smile with my good side facing towards the camera – chin down to give me better jaw definition, eyebrows relaxed so my forehead wrinkles don't show. There's a flash and Rosie giggles and steps back to her side of the table, retrieving her phone and checking the photo.

'Thanks so much for coming.' I hand her book over.

'No, thank *you*. Thank you so much for writing it. You don't understand. When I was twenty-three, I was such a mess . . . then I found your book and . . . it changed my life . . . it really did.'

I am tired of smiling, but I need to smile at this because it's important to her. 'Wow, I'm so touched to hear that. How old are you now?'

'Twenty-five.'

She's only twenty-freaking-five. They just keep getting . . . younger.

'Well I'm so glad you enjoyed it.'

I'm looking past her now, to the next person. Because it's gone ten and I've got the wedding tomorrow. But, just as I reach out to take the book off the next shaking fan, Rosie discovers the courage to say one more thing.

'Hey, sorry. But, can I just ask? Rock man? The man from the book? You are still together, aren't you?'

Rock man.

The man who found me on the rock. Who found me on top of a vortex in Sedona screaming *'fuuuuuuuuuck'* and throwing my rosary beads off into the skyline, and somehow found that endearing.

Tom . . .

The man who could've been anywhere else in the world that day, but whom a thousand gusts of fate somehow blew to Arizona too. *Sedona* too. Climbing up to the vortex too.

My happily-ever-after.

The one you're always rewarded with in stories where a character decides to be brave.

'Yes,' I confirm, feeling like my smile might snap. 'We're still together.'

She lets out a little squeal and a yelp, arms flailing in the air. Then she blushes. 'Sorry. I'm fangirling.'

'That's fine.'

I'm looking past her again because, in the nicest possible way, she is taking too much time now. There are still at least fifty women waiting not-so patiently any more. Rosie doesn't read my vibe. My response has only given her more confidence. She is conducting the conversation that she needs. In her head, we are friends now. Already great friends.

'And you're still blissfully happy?'

I close my eyes for a second longer than I should. When I open them, my smile is still there. It has to stay on. For the next fifty people it has to stay on. I give Rosie my dimples and my charm and my glowing, golden happiness. My wisdom. My serenity. Everything she expects. Everything she has paid for in her ticket price.

'Of course,' I tell her. 'We're still blissfully happy.'

★

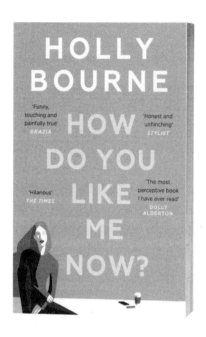

'Truly a f***ing good novel'
Evening Standard

'The most perceptive book I have ever read about the female interior'
Dolly Alderton

'Injected with such reality it can't help but be hilarious'
The Times

***How Do You Like Me Now?*
is available in paperback,
eBook and audio.**